The Radiance
of Ashes

Cyrus Mistry

The Radiance of Ashes

PICADOR

First published 2005 by Picador
an imprint of Pan Macmillan Ltd
Pan Macmillan, 20 New Wharf Road, London N1 9RR
Basingstoke and Oxford
Associated companies throughout the world
www.panmacmillan.com

ISBN 0 330 48250 5

9 8 7 6 5 4 3 2 1

A CIP catalogue record for this book is available from
the British Library.

Typeset by IntypeLibra, London
Printed and bound in Great Britain by
Mackays of Chatham plc, Chatham, Kent

To my mother

and Ikeda Sensei,

both of whom taught me never to give up

Let thy speech be better
than silence, or be silent

Dionysius of Halicarnassus

This is a fiction. Any resemblance to recent historical events is entirely deliberate.

Prologue

I have always lived with a strong sense of unreality.

(Lived . . . ? Not quite the word, surely. Endured? Survived? . . . One is flushed with a strong sense of reality, I suppose, when one truly lives.)

Events that were shaping my life, or deflecting it off the course I thought it was running, often passed me by unnoticed. I was undisturbed by this in earlier days. In later life, there were moments when I raged against the randomness of it all . . . But always, on the tattered fringes of experience, that powdery haze of insubstantiality. As though it was all happening to someone else, not me.

I dare not attempt this narration in the first person. Too many selves are involved, too many 'I's. And I'm not sure 'I' can tackle any of them with honesty or insight. My best chance is to tell it like a story. I have a secret hope, though – should I disclose it? – that in

*its telling at least a few of these selves will
make peace and merge.*

*Perhaps later generations will be better
placed to judge whether the story that follows
is an aberration of a life, peculiar only to its
author, or symptomatic of a post-colonial
turmoil that ravaged individual lives as much
as it did entire societies. The problem is, I'm
not sure I'll be able to carry it off. Or even
bring it to any sort of completion.*

*I have no choice but to try, though. My very
survival depends on it.*

*Over the years, a sporadic journal helped
bring the blurred edges of life into sharper
focus. Occasionally, I reproduce bits of this
journal alongside the main narrative with the
intention of making the fare more intelligible
to the reader. But then again, I'm not at all
certain whether such intervention will aid
perspicuity or further obfuscate it.*

I should begin at the beginning . . .

A muddy golden sun slunk out from a chink in the overcast sky. Heaps of great grey clouds parted momentously,
momentarily, flashing bright beams of yellow light that
refracted in the wet surfaces of tarred roads, on the hoods
of cars and buses hedged in and twisting in choked traffic,
on the bemused gargantuan faces of heroes, heroines and
bloodthirsty villains staring out of gaily coloured cinema
hoardings.

Clutching his bag against a damp shirt, Jingo shut
his umbrella. Then he referred to the slip of paper in
his pocket. The ink had smudged, but there was no

mistaking the address. He stared in dismay at the grimy dilapidated structure that loomed above him. A concrete carcass. A house on stilts.

Manoeuvring through a maze of wooden beams that supported the entrance to the crumbling edifice, Jingo came to a narrow staircase, soggy and steep. Some of the steps had splintered or given in. But when he had ascended the first flight and crossed the landing, he found he could climb no further. The stairway was barricaded by a plank of wood, and a crudely painted sign on the wall read: DO NOT USE – BY ORDER.

Staring dully at this peremptory placard, he became aware of two men conferring in low voices a short distance away. The older of the two, thin and grey-haired and stooped, suddenly raised his voice.

'Every day, every day she goes to him for injection?' he cried shrilly. 'Shows him her bum, and he pokes it for her! Taking a full course, it seems.'

'Easy, boss, easy . . .' his friend soothed him, caressing his back.

The two men saw Jingo approach and glowered at him with brazen inquisition. Jingo nodded vaguely at them and continued down the corridor.

When he had turned the bend, he found the passage suddenly bustling with people. Ignoring the curious glances, not slowing to glimpse into the gloomy interiors of people's homes, Jingo walked past a fat man in a rocking chair reading a newspaper, a thin woman cleaning rice on a plate, a young boy holding a puppy over the balcony by the scruff of its neck, the puppy yelping piteously. Several of the tenants seemed to have their radios tuned to the same station. Every time the rambunctious Hindi film song that was playing began to waft into diminuendo, it would suddenly blare up again from yet another of the tenements.

At last he came to another staircase, this one wider and brighter than the first, though just as rickety. Treading gingerly, he continued his ascent to the top floor. That was a rule with the agency. Always start at the top and work your way down.

At the next landing he was greeted by a small signboard that read LONDON HOTEL. The hotel's name was painted in red. Below it, a blue plastic arrow directed prospective clients, presumably to their rooms, or to the reception desk. But there was no one in sight and every door in the passageway was shut.

Suddenly it had grown dark again. Outside, a soft steady rain began to patter. Jingo continued to climb.

A little girl was playing hopscotch on the landing at the top of the stairs. The first door on his right was bolted and a forbiddingly large padlock hung from it. He consulted his call sheet, marked a cross on it and moved on to the next.

'Who do you want?' the little girl sang in a high-pitched voice. Her stringy hair was tied in bunches by two shreds of ribbon. Her frock was crumpled and buttonless.

The next door was ajar. A slight shove, and it yielded with a creak. He caught a glimpse of a darkened living room in obvious disuse. A chair with a missing leg and a broken back lay on its side in the middle of the floor. A spider scuttled out from under it and froze, mesmerized. He tasted dust in his throat.

'No one stays here! No one stays here!' shrieked the child, hopping ferociously from square to square, legs apart, on the chalk-drawn pattern. Jingo walked past the next two doors making a mental note that these, too, wore padlocks.

'And anyone stay *here*?' he asked the girl.

'No one, no one, no one stays here at all,' she cried, triumphantly making an about turn mid-hop and landing on the next set of squares with her back to Jingo.

Suddenly the door at the end of the corridor flew open and a strange, harried creature rushed out. It was an old woman, clothed in an astonishing number of woollens – socks, mittens, a flannel longshirt and pyjamas, a moth-eaten red coatee, a knitted scarf that covered her ears and was knotted under her chin – all ragged and sooty and patched. Her feet were swaddled in a tiny pair of checked canvas shoes. Her sharply hooked nose pinned down a pair of excruciatingly thin lips, above which the faint outline of a moustache could be seen.

'Deceitful heartless horrible horrible wench!' The muscles in her scrawny neck stood out, but she seemed able to produce no more than a hoarse fierce whisper. 'Who stays here then if no one stays here, if no one's here who am I? Who am I?' she demanded, using a mysterious, pained logic. 'Liar! O you horrible!'

The little girl danced away and down the stairs gurgling a shrill and merry laugh.

'And you?' The woman turned to Jingo. 'Who are you and what'll you want?'

But before Jingo could reply, the nastiness in her expression dissolved and in its place, in her beady bird-eyes, flashed a glimmer of hope, and something of sadness. She clutched his shirt with her small, mitten-clad fingers and drew his face closer to her own. Jingo gaped foolishly at a mole on her chin from which two long hairs grew. Oh no, he thought, limp in her grip, she's mistaken me for somebody else.

'You have news – you have some news of him? How is he? Where is he?'

'No, no! I'm sorry . . .' What have I got into now, wondered Jingo.

The woman's eyes darted from his face to the clipboard and papers in his hand, to the bag slung on his shoulder, and back to his face again. Now they were shrewd and hard. 'Oh, oh. From the tax-wallahs, are you? Come round to snoop a bit, ask a few questions? Don't deny it. I can see you're from the Tax!' She turned and flung open her door which she had left ajar. 'Look!' She gestured. 'See for yourself. Paupered, everything gone . . .' Now she was bawling in a gruff, frightened voice. 'Nothing left, I tell you. Everything gone!'

'I'm not! I'm not from the Tax!' Jingo shouted back, excitedly. 'I'm from market research.'

'Eh?'

'Yes. I'm doing a product survey for some advertisers.'

'Ah, market research!' She pronounced the words solemnly, as though weighing their import. 'That's different,' she said, having thought it over. 'Come in, then. Come in, boy. Why didn't you open your mouth and say so in the first place?'

Inside it was dark and unventilated. The air was damp and carried a faint smell of faeces in it, and that other sourly fetid odour, not easy to describe, that hangs about the habitats of the sick and the aged. The roof was leaking in two places. Two copper pots on the floor collected a steady drip of rainwater, but they were overflowing, and there were small puddles around both.

The room was cluttered with the unaccountable

accumulations of a long past. Six chairs were lined up in a row against the wall, their cane seats mostly ruptured. A large cupboard with an inset mirror leaned forward at a jaunty angle, one of its front legs broken. In a dark mahogany chest of drawers, a black rectangular slot nestled, where one drawer was missing. About a dozen empty and half-empty bottles of physician's mixture stood on the chest's flat top. A four-poster bed sprawled in the centre of the room, a thin mattress rolled to one side of it. On the bare planks of the other half, over a lining of old newspapers, stood a blackened wick stove, a cutting board, a large kitchen knife. Under the bed, the empty concave of a sewing machine lid. Beside it, a small table heaped with all sorts of odds and ends: a Petromax, a chipped porcelain cup, a screwdriver, a large screw, a set of dentures in a jar of water, a tattered prayer book, a big ball of thread, a baby's red shoe and something in a saucer that was green with fungus, probably a piece of cheese. On the wall, an ancient pendulum clock was ticking loudly. Jingo noted with some surprise that it showed the correct time. Next to it, slightly askew, hung an old calendar print of Nehru holding a lurid red rose to his nose.

On being invited to take a seat, Jingo chose an oddly ornate wooden stool; as soon as he had settled on it, a queasy suspicion awoke in him that he was occupying the shuttered top of an old-fashioned chamber pot. He wanted to move. But none of the other chairs in the room looked like they would hold his weight, and the old woman didn't seem to care about where he sat. Hastily, she had clambered onto her bed and was waiting with breathless anticipation for Jingo to begin.

Jilla Gorimar – for that was her name – appeared to

have considerable experience at answering market research questionnaires. No sooner had Jingo noted it down and her age, she began to volunteer a flood of information. After a while, Jingo gave up trying to control the interview and listened in silence. Swinging her canvas shoes energetically, which dangled a foot above the floor, now wheezing with pleasure to have someone to talk to, now inaudible, talking only to herself, Jilla Gorimar told Jingo the story of her life, as it came out, garbled in details of the electrical appliances she had used, the tea she drank, the health foods she abjured and her graded preferences from a list of washing powders soaps shampoos toothpastes and talcs.

'My Keko, my husband, he was no ordinary man. Nothing to his name, only his dreams and fancy tastes. Empty pockets, but so much huff and puff . . .

'Such chums he was with the British soldiers. Drank with them in their military bars where civilians were not allowed, rode with them in their military jeeps. He'd walk into the canteen stores and pick up whate'er foodstuffs we wanted. Such things you could get in those days. During the war who used to use Indian-made stuff? Foreign, everything foreign. No, we never used all these Indian things.' She handed Jingo back his list of products under survey without so much as glancing at it.

For a fleeting moment Jingo wondered if he should protest, insist on answers to the questions he was paid to pose. But the premonitory sweetness of a wet, wasted afternoon rendered him docilely polite, reluctantly engrossed.

'But he had looks, my Keko . . . What looks! Tall, handsome. You couldn't get your fill of looking at him.

He'd say–' and she quoted him with dramatic flourish – '"I am a soul misborn. I should have been a maharaja's son. Or an Errol Flynn. Or, for that matter, Errol could have been my understudy."' Jingo heard a curiously muted chuckle. 'That's the kind of man he was. He could have had any woman in the world he wanted. But he chose me . . .

'To tell you the truth, he was only a bank clerk. Much of the time, I supported him, paid off his gambling debts.' Was it annoyance at remembered profligacy that stuck in her throat? Her small frame was convulsed by a wheezing, but she continued to speak in a raspy whisper: 'When my father died, we got a little money. Wanted to quit his job. Imagine . . . I said no, absolutely not. Hated doing an honest day's work, my Keko! A dreamer with bushy eyebrows. And a moustache like Flynn's too. I don't denigrate. A man's wishes are a man's wings. He flies on them. Keko flew. But that was later. Much later. After he'd bought us the German toaster.

'It was a pop-up. Ting, a bell would ring, and out would pop the brown-brown toasts. You won't get to see the likes of it now. He wouldn't let anyone touch the toaster. Except his mother. She sat there at the breakfast table polishing its chrome flanks with a soft cloth while Keko ate his toast and tea and jam. She's dead now, the witch, toasting in hell, I hope.'

Jingo had begun to find the room's stuffiness oppressive, but the old woman suddenly began to shiver in her ragged woollens, her breathing audibly hard and strangulated. Jingo thought selfishly of his forty-five rupees. That's how much he had been promised for each of these interviews. He wouldn't be able to claim it if she went on like this. Unless he fudged the answers.

'Earth is my witness, I'm not lying – a real hellcat! She tried to set my hair on fire! I had hair that reached down to my hips. She couldn't bear to see it. One afternoon, I woke up to the smell of frizzling hair. When we got married at first she welcomed me with great pomp and kindness, as though I were a princess entering her husband's palace. A month later, everything changed. Ugly slut sat around all day, expecting me to cook her all kinds of goodies. Such a monstrous sweet tooth I've never seen. Fried bhakras. Chaapat! Malido. And if nothing was ready, she'd stuff her mouth with fistfuls of sugar. Huge she was, like that, and strong as a wrestler.

'Ate up everything with great relish, wiped the tureen clean. But nothing I made ever found favour with her. She'd pull me by my hair and slam me into the wall. "You no-good wife, you dared set foot in my house? I'll see how you last. My poor Keko deserves a thousand times better. I'll chop a fine mince of you, see if I don't," she'd scream, swishing the meat cleaver in my face. While she was alive, Keko would often side with her. But in the end even he saw who lasted out . . . One day her wicked head began to ache unbearably. She whined and roared with pain, for two days and nights. And then her head burst! Blood trickled out of her ears and nose and blackened her pillow. The neighbours heaved a sigh of relief that her screaming had ceased.'

The dry, stained skin around her lips and her small chin was convulsed by a violent twitching. For some time she muttered to herself, her words inaudible, her entire being stirred by the bitter disquiet of an ancient, un-finished battle. Presently, however, she resumed the tale of the toaster.

'Kept it safely wrapped up in an old blanket in this

cupboard. Thinking my Keko will come back when he starts missing his crisply golden-brown toast. I cried, I prayed. I lit a *deevo* every morning in his name for so many years. But after a time, I knew he wouldn't come . . .

'It was his one big chance – money, freedom! – what he'd always dreamed of. Just two months after his mother died he had three lakh rupees in his briefcase, carrying it from the Kalbadevi branch of his bank to the head office in Fountain. Suddenly – I still remember that first BOOM, my little Hoshi was in my stomach then – the dock exploded – BOOM, BOOM – what fireworks, what flames – and from a sky as black as smoke and red as amber it started to rain hot gold bricks! Yes, I'm not making this up. Huge, big-big bricks, like that. One fell right here on the street outside and killed a man in front of my eyes.

'Did Keko get blown sky high too, reduced to ash and smithereens along with those three lakh rupees? A security guard accompanying him fled in terror. He couldn't say what became of Keko. But an arm, a leg, a tooth – something should have been found of his? Nothing. Police, insurance-wallahs, for years afterwards they kept harassing me. They thought I knew where he's hiding. In those days, three lakhs was like three crores! Even today sometimes they come to check on me. But I gave up on him long ago. If he's gone, he's gone, I decided. There's no law on Earth can compel a man to love his wife.'

The dates evaded Jingo, but the events she had described took place at least ten years before he was born. A British ship with a full cargo of dynamite had exploded in the harbour. Among other sundry stock, like barrels of oil and bundles of cotton, the ship was also carrying a large quantity of bullion. Gold ingots had been flung far and high into the black smoke-filled air, though most of it, it was said, melted and was washed into the sea. Many firefighters and ordinary bystanders lost their lives or went missing in the great dock explosion. Dozens of bodies were never recovered. He'd read about it quite recently in a magazine article commemorating – what was it – the forty-fifth anniversary of the explosion?

'I stopped lighting the *deevo*, I stopped praying for him to come back. I didn't care if he was alive or dead. But because he went away, something more terrible happened, something much more terrible . . . and I blame him for that . . .'

Suddenly Jilla Gorimar narrowed her eyes and crept out of bed with a finger pressed to her lips, urging Jingo to be silent. 'Shhh. There . . . there he goes . . . do you see him? Here, take this.' She handed him the baby's red shoe from the table and whispered, 'Smash him!' She was pointing to a corpulent grey mouse that was casually ambling across the floor. As soon as Jingo moved to take the shoe, the mouse was away in a flash, disappearing behind the furniture.

'It's gone,' said Jingo, feigning disappointment, though actually quite relieved.

'Oh, never mind. There are hundreds like him. Even bigger ones. They come and go.'

He took advantage of this interruption to ask her a few questions from his cyclostyled proforma. She answered them precisely and tersely. Next, he handed her a plastic folder that contained cut-outs of frequently seen newspaper ads. He asked her to judge which ones she considered most effective. She pondered, knitted her eyebrows, chose judiciously; but on coming upon one of a plump baby licking its lips over a spoonful of infant gruel, she became transfixed. She stared at it for a few moments at first, it seemed to Jingo, longingly, then with an icy contempt. She shut the file with a loud slap and handed it back.

'Farex-barex is all utter nonsense! Worthless as sawdust! I fed my Hoshi only mother's milk till he was four. You should have seen him. My son is a bodybuilder. A giant! I would look at him and think: this – this once fitted in my belly . . .? Oh, if only I had a single photograph left to show you . . . Nothing! But nothing's left! Not even a single photo!' The old woman burst into a series of peculiar noises that sounded like hiccups. Only when the tears began to stream down her cheeks, did Jingo realize she was crying.

For a while, all was silent. Only her soft snivelling and the drip-drip-drip from the leaking roof. Outside a darker, heavier rain began to fall.

Jingo was moved, sickened. He wanted to say something to her, to console her. But her strange raggedness, her smallness, the smell from her unwashed body, her hoarse halting speech, everything about her made her remote, weird, a creature to be watched from a distance. Besides, he wasn't sure what she was crying about. Then, as abruptly as she had begun her sobbing, she stopped it and went on.

'I should have known. If the father could do the disappearing trick on me, so would the son one day . . . yes. But him, I miss . . .

'When Keko left us, I had to start working and Hoshidar suffered for it. He mixed with a bad lot. I couldn't control him. One day Tehmina, my next-door neighbour, she came to me and said, "Jilla, I cry for you, *mai*. You gave birth to a devil. Today I saw him swagger out of a wicked woman's *kothi*, buttoning up his pants in full view of everyone!" She was my good friend. But I yelled at her. Told her never to step into my home again if she was bent on spreading such scandal about my son . . . When she and her family moved out some years back, she didn't even come up to say goodbye. I don't know why I did all this. Aimai downstairs had told me the same thing before. And I knew from a pain in my heart that it was not a lie. A mother knows such things.

'On his sixteenth birthday, he too walked out on me. Stole my small savings, my two gold wedding bangles and, what do you know, he took the toaster as well.

'What did I do to him? Did I beat him, did I bite him, did I burn him with a red-hot skewer? Some mothers do that. I raised him on love . . . He was my best friend, my only one. But he's gone . . . I know he's here somewhere. Not far from here. I know it, I feel it in my bones. Why won't he write? Why won't he come to see me?

'Twenty years I worked in a post office selling stamps. You wouldn't think to look at me that I am an educated woman. I am a Matric pass. Only woman employee in my post office. The one at the Balaram Street junction? Just to be able to send him to a good school. When I retired, the office staff bought me an alarum clock. Would you believe it? Alarum clock! An old woman, tired to death, who stays up all night tossing and turning – they buy her an alarum. Make a note of this, I'm not just talking, this is relevant to your research! The clock was an HES. It stopped working within three months. Five rupees was all I could get for it . . .' She paused for breath. Then abruptly, 'Okay, I've talked enough for one day. Any more questions?'

There were several in fact. But as Jingo glanced

through his list, they swam before his dazed eyes in a murk of profound irrelevance.

'Oh whooo.' She shuddered. 'This damp makes my bones ache. On nights of heavy rain, the ladies in the hotel downstairs take pity on me – give me an old quilt, a corner to sleep in. Oh, they're no ladies, I can tell you that.' She lowered her voice to a whisper. 'And you're not a baby, you know about such things. Drunken men come to visit them at night. If I'm sleeping there, they make jokes at my expense. It's shameful. But I ignore them. What to do?

'To tell you the truth, I'm scared to be alone here at night. There are bandicoots about. They crawl up the drain or down from the roof, their bristly hides wet, their tiny eyes shining in the dark. Sometimes, if it's not the rats, then it's those two fat pigs . . . They come to question me, huffing and puffing in their ties and terylene shirts. They say they're from ITHO. Income Tax Head Office. Show us your returns, they say! *Marere mua*, when I don't even go out anywhere, how can I file any returns? If they had their way, they would take away my home and put me out in the street. I have no income, I have nothing hoarded up, I tell them. But they refuse to believe me. Sometimes I wake up in the morning and find everything unsettled, drawers emptied out, furniture all topsy-turvy . . . and I know they have been searching. No matter how firmly I bolt the doors and windows, somehow they always find a way to get in.'

Many times before, his work had led him to see places and meet people he would never have dreamed existed. The women at the desk in the market research agency he freelanced for picked out addresses at random from old electoral rolls. Sometimes the building in the address he had been given had been demolished long ago, or had perished in a fire. Sometimes he found it deteriorated into a slum – though his questionnaire was aimed at middle-class consumers.

But this was his strangest encounter yet. A beggarly, half-crazed woman crouching in moth-eaten woollens on her large twice-deserted bed, rodent-like herself from living in terror among rats, her home a dark, damp burrow. A picture flashed in Jingo's mind as he stared at Jilla Gorimar, somewhat dazed by her non-stop ranting. Perhaps it was just the idea of a picture. Or perhaps it was an illustration from a book he had once owned, a very long time ago. A colourful scene livening a snugly told tale in large print: a large-eyed blue mouse in a dressing gown and frilly apron, clean round ears sticking out from under a white bonnet, pink nose a-glow . . . Ten little mice sat down to spin. This was Grandmother Rat.

Before he left, Jingo offered to empty the two copper pots on the floor which were now overflowing with rainwater. Jilla Gorimar blessed him for his thoughtfulness.

He carried them to the rear of the room where, just outside a back door, there was a washroom with an open drainhole. Here, he emptied them; first one, then the other. Gorimar. Unusual name. He had heard it before . . . Slowly, the sound of the water swirling through the black orifice aroused something in Jingo's mind. In an instant, the son's name and the mother's name combined, sending up a flare from the deep sea of misplaced memories. Hoshidar Gorimar . . .

The name electrified him. He saw rows of brown desks and benches disfigured by puerile carvings. He saw a dozen red-faced boys in beige shorts, cream bush-shirts and the hated brown tie. He saw himself among them.

And one face, particularly pug-nosed, pugilistic, hirsute beyond its years, fitted with a set of grinning horse-teeth and a pair of small cunning eyes. He felt a wrench in his elbow and a hot breath bellowing in his ear.

'Motherfucker! Call me that? Call me that again? I'll break your arm. I'll squeeze your balls till you piss blue!'

'Aaieee . . . nooo! Le' go! Mercy, Hoshi, mercy . . .'

Then, darting out of reach and halfway across the quadrangle as soon as the vice-like grip released him (for he was a good sprinter himself and Hoshi too lazy to give chase), he screamed: 'You lousy Hip-pip-pip-ho!'

The picture cleared and other scenes came to him as well: Hippo G. heckling the language teacher. Hippo G. splashing half a bottle of Camel's Royal Blue ink on the rear of a priest's white cassock. Hippo G. dissolving an entire pack of Purgo-Lax in the art master's coffee. Hippo G. passing around pornographic picture cards during prayer assembly. Hippo G. with his pants down measuring the size of his engorged member with a footrule to settle a wager. Finally, the great Hippo, who had by now achieved the stature of a folk hero, expelled from school.

The final, precipitating offence had been shrouded in horror and secrecy. If there had been speculations about the nature of his ultimate crime, Jingo couldn't remember them now, except that they had been of the most dreadful. Afterwards, diverse fates had been attributed to him by his classmates. Some said he had become a pimp, others swore he was minting money as a bootlegger and smuggler, still others claimed they knew for sure – though few boys were willing to credit this story – that he had become a millionairess's paramour and was living in Nepal. For a couple of days after his expulsion, he was seen loitering outside the school gates during recess hours, a cigarette suspended from his lips in defiance of the Jesuits who had no jurisdiction over him now. Then he disappeared altogether. Life at school returned to its humdrum routine and the guys stopped discussing him.

Jingo held his breath as he asked Jilla Gorimar, 'Hoshidar. Was he at St Joseph's?'

Her face changed colour. Her eyes lit up and began to blink furiously.

Jingo's heart sank. It was a mistake to rekindle her hopes.

'You know him, then!'

'I remember him. We were in the same class for a while. But—'

'O God, I say a prayer of thanks!' She clasped her hands together and looked up at her leaking roof. Then her words tumbled out excitedly, tripping one over the other. 'You're a *farohar*, an angel sent to help. He has sent you to help me find him. From the moment I set eyes on you I knew you had a special purpose, a mission to help me . . . Find him for me. Go! Tell him his mother is still alive.'

'But where? How? I haven't seen him or heard of him in fifteen years!'

'He's your brother. Your lost brother. Go, son. Find him.'

Her voice had dropped to a tearful whisper. Now she was embracing him tightly, caressing his hair, peering up into his eyes. Jingo cursed his thoughtlessness. Whether he liked it or not, he was implicated now in the old woman's tragedy.

'It's a big city, Jillamai . . .' He touched her small shoulders and squeezed them gently. They were only skin and bone.

'I know,' she whispered, releasing him from her grip while nodding her head obediently, like a frightened child. 'It wasn't like this before. Today if I step out I feel I am in some wild jungle. Dangerous beasts are about. No one has time for the mad old lady. No one has any respect . . . I stumble back into my corner as quickly as I can. That's why I know He has sent you, and I thank Him. Without your help, my Hoshi would be lost to me forever.'

'I'll try. I'll ask around . . .'

'He's there.' She stretched her spindly arm in the direction of the half-open door. 'He's out there, somewhere. I know you'll find him.'

As if challenging her assurance, a cacophony of horns from the rain-jammed traffic in the streets below floated up. Wild discords tore at each other for a few minutes without break, a berserk fugue for wind which seemed to Jingo to pronounce: 'We are the city. We are a hundred million rats. We live in our holes. We are part of the greater galaxy of rats. Come, hunt out one of us if you will . . .'

Several promises and reassurances later, Jingo took his leave. Jilla Gorimar saw him to the stairs and called after him to come again soon.

No more interviews today. What Jingo needed was fresh air. He thundered down the creaky wooden stairs at a reckless clip. It was 3.45 p.m. and there was no one around.

On weekday afternoons, at that very hour, surging hordes of uniformed boys would hurl themselves savagely down the stairs of the old school building, spurred on by the bright peals of the electric gong which announced that like sudden manna from on high school was out. Why was he momentarily transported back to that sudden burst of freedom as he left the old woman's smelly habitat?

But he stopped short. A lean old man was cowering against one side of the first-floor landing, clutching an orthopaedic walker with both hands. He was staring at Jingo with open-mouthed terror.

Now walking quietly, Jingo passed the fat man, who had fallen asleep in his rocking chair. His newspaper was spread over his face and belly like a tent, and he was snoring. The thin woman and her children were not in sight, nor the two men who had been talking excitedly about a doctor and his willing patient. In the corridor lines of washed linen had been hung to dry.

Outside, he breathed more freely. It was still raining. The traffic was completely jammed. Horns bleated, but hopelessly. Here and there a car would try and squirm its way out but only succeed in complicating the knot. As he walked down the street, Jingo saw the obstruction that was responsible for this impasse.

A wizened grey man, nearly bald, naked except for a loincloth, was dancing in the middle of the street. His ribs stood out of his sparrow-chest, his eyeballs were inordinately large and protruding in a fixed, incredulous expression. But on his lips sang a mad, exultant grin. He was dancing in the rain. He would hop thrice, first on one leg, then on the other, throw his arms in the air and gyrate like a top. Then he would turn cartwheels, right there in the middle of the stalled traffic, produce a few timid cheers and yelps for his performance from his own throat and start hopping again. A crowd of urchins and loiterers and some office peons with portfolios had collected around him, some laughing, some snickering, some applauding.

No one saw the traffic policeman approach. Then he was there. He fastened one hand around the almost-naked man's neck and dragged him to the sidewalk. The dancing beggar began to squawk like an old rooster. The policeman punched him in the belly. The man doubled up and his face met the policeman's knee. In a moment he was down and gasping in the slush. Two kicks in the ribs. He seemed to lose consciousness. Then the policemen turned to the traffic and began to gesticulate.

The crowd dispersed. Cars and buses began to move again.

Part 1

Highrise

Twenty-five storeys below, the city looked different. Almost beautiful.

Clutching at the moist handrail, Jingo felt his stomach shrink. Did he have a touch of vertigo? The view was breathtaking, he couldn't turn away. A bay full of ships: large ones outlining the curve of the horizon with a festive Morse of illuminated dots and dashes, closer to shore small fishing boats whose hurricane lamps bobbed in the dark like a broken string of shiny beads.

The murky expanse of water heaved and ebbed like the powerful respiration of some submerged beast. Colonies of squat little buildings huddled in irregular clusters, spilling occasionally into viscous blotches of tin and thatch. A handful of concrete cuboids rose among their ranks: headless trunks that seemed somehow more stunted than their neighbours, pinioned against a vast windowless sky. It was late. Only a few flats remained lit in these towers. Little rectangles of yellow light encapsulating the unbreachably dull secrets of people's lives. Then, one by one, even these began to be snuffed out.

The two whiskies Jingo had knocked back on arrival lent his vision a penetrative insolence that seized on every piece of the massive jigsaw spread at his feet. Under tiny fluorescent street-lamps, the wet black roads glistened like reams of unravelled satin ribbon: magical pathways to an infernal playground. That's what it looked like from up here. An immense playground he could stomp and tear through, sweep up and topple, or rearrange. Heap like an anthill, or flatten like a dungcake. Or just let his fingers run through, and watch the pieces crumble. He remembered doing just that to the 1,000-bit puzzle Uncle Rusi had once given him after an European junket. How perversely satisfying it had been to wreck the labour of a whole month of diligent evenings (Dad not willing to extend the lease of his writing table any longer) and watch those random jags and chips of an idyllic English country scene revert to their original state of entropy.

So that's what gives the bourgeoisie their cool inscrutable composure, thought Jingo, their supreme indifference – this vision of the world from a tower. From up here, the city was a lavish speckled confection, draped with cobwebs and mouldy with fungus no doubt, but still very pretty. Some Miss Havisham's wedding feast. A celebration gone awry.

In the blue smoke-filled room behind him, another celebration was in progress. Dilber's birthday. Why on earth was he here? Why was he never able to say no to parties? Free drinks, for one thing. The opportunity to ogle and gloat and jabber. And at Dubby's, one was assured of a six-course spread. That had been a serious consideration, he admitted, feeling rather hungry already. Down to his last twenty, he'd had only a misal and two paos for lunch. Six-hundred-odd rupees were coming to him for all the interviews he'd completed in the last ten days. But would Bhangera, that red-eyed stoat in charge of Accounts, pay up tomorrow or procrastinate? He didn't want to ask his mother for yet another loan this month.

Two bearers in white weaved noiselessly through the crowded living room. One was fetching drinks for those too indolent or inebriated to walk to the bar; the other, distinctly more harassed-looking, was carrying in endless trays of barbecued hors d'oeuvres from the kitchen. Overhead, a large chandelier glittered, its crystalline pods catching curiously exaggerated glimpses of the proceedings. Dozens of people milling around, glasses in hand, creating a terrific din of blurred loquacity. The music was turned low – Dubby's parties were never of the dancing kind – but the tall quadrophonic speakers nevertheless created waves of throbbing rhythm on which conversation floated like driftwood.

People were discussing Californian wines, psychology, other people. A textile designer just back from attending the film appreciation course in Poona was talking about the pathos of *Hiroshima Mon Amour*. A social worker in a green backless dress was recounting the problems she encountered trying to teach English to a class of dyslexic slum kids. An advertising executive was making a case for the use of civic-oriented publicity techniques to bring about a gradual transformation of society.

'Jimmy Moos!' an astonished feminine voice trilled in his ear in the same moment that a plump forearm grabbed his neck from behind and a big slobbery kiss was planted on his cheek. Some of his drink spilled over.

'I like that, Jimmy. You sneak into my birthday party and lounge around without so much as wishing me!' Dubby was the only one who called him Jimmy, instead of Jingo, or Jahangir.

'Just walked in, Dubby,' protested Jingo, smiling.

'Sorry I'm so late.' He saw her eyeing the glass in his hand. 'That's my first drink, honest. I *was* looking out for you. Then I got involved with the view.'

'Great to see you, Jimmy,' said Dubby. 'Didn't honestly think you'd make it.'

Dilber was short and heavy-hipped, wearing long artificial eyelashes and bubbling with merriment. Her friends called her Dubby or Dabs. Jingo hugged her and kissed her cheek. 'Happy birthday, darling.'

'Where've you been hibernating, hunh, you big teddy bear?' She cuddled him. 'Come to think of it, you *have* lost a lot of weight. Haven't been eating or what?'

'And you're just as lovely as when I last saw you,' said Jingo expansively, feeling immediately insincere. Dubby's fleshy cheeks, already glowing with good health and expensive lotions, flushed pink. Her large moony eyes misted over and Jingo thought to himself, not without affection, she's still very fond of me.

Dubby pulled him towards a group of young men sitting on the carpet. 'You know most of these guys, don't you?'

A lean, bearded Bengali in a kurta called Shambhit was holding forth.

'So, I agree, I agree,' cried Shambhit, pretending exasperation. 'But aren't you forgetting something? *Form* . . .' He made mysterious scooping gestures in the air with his open palms, to signify his meaning, while also acknowledging Jingo, who had just walked up with Dilber. 'Hi!'

'Hey, Shambhit! There are ladies around, man,' said Jingo, lowering his voice to a stagey whisper. 'Should you be making those lewd gestures in public . . .?' Shambhit, an ad filmmaker who had just shot one half of his first feature film when both luck and financiers deserted him, was arguing patiently with a pugnacious George Paul. The latter, a stocky Malayalee with a droopy lower lip and days of stubble on his cheeks, was well known for the radical work he did with a civil-liberties group in the city.

'I am talking about the importance of form to any work of art,' said Shambhit, undeterred by George Paul's loud guffaws. Now looking directly at Paul, he said, 'I mean how can you make a comment about something and not make a comment on your own comment? That would be so one-dimensional. So fascistic!'

'All youer sof'sticated fo'm an'all is okay, but what about the massus?' shouted George Paul indignantly. Shambhit shied away from the rain of spittle that flew in his direction. 'How the massus will make sense of youer fillum?'

'In the end no one fully understands, I agree. Perhaps not even the director himself. I mean there has to be a dialectic, it's part of the filmmaking process. The whole crew is involved. In the end we don't know whether he has really killed her or it is just an aspect of his fantasy,' declared the director gravely. 'I want to make it realistic but also slightly grotesque. That way I can keep the line between illusion and reality thin, and also comment on my own comment.'

'You are working in a vacuum, my friend,' said George Paul with unconcealed disgust.

'I tend to agree with George actually,' put in Dubby, her finely tuned instinct for hospitality springing forth to soothe a bellicose southern temper she knew could get out of hand. 'After all, we *are* talking about a mass medium. I suppose such an approach – too much concern with form – could easily become so self-indulgent.'

'Masturbatory,' put in George.

'Especially when you consider the stark realities of the people who are to be your audience. What do you think, Jimmy?' asked Dubby, trying to draw him into the conversation.

Jingo shrugged. 'Well, I would let him complete his film first. Then the masses can judge it for themselves. No need to patronize them, what, Shambhit?' He winked at the filmmaker. 'If I were you I'd throw in a few good fucking scenes. That way, both masses and critics will enjoy. And none can accuse you of being a wanker – in your films, at least. What you do in your bathroom is another matter, of course.'

'We don't need your wisecracks, Jimmy,' said Dubby rather crossly. 'This is a serious issue which keeps coming up all the time. Anyway, do tell us, Shums, what's the score on the finance scene? Any luck?'

'Happening . . . it's happening,' said Shambhit holding up both hands with fingers crossed. 'I won't say any more just yet.'

Grinning foolishly, Jingo withdrew to get himself another whisky. His stomach was rumbling hungrily. Everywhere, people were talking, talking, and he was gulping down his drinks much too fast. What to do? He'd promised himself he would leave the party early, go home and read a bit, perhaps make some notes before turning in. Had he really meant it, even at the time? Or had he been merely creating another fib? To gag his conscience? Deflect the pointer of his priorities?

Jingo chuckled inwardly at the phrase. Stop writing in your head, you fool. The pointer of his priorities it was, in all probability, which had led him to this party . . . A strong inducement for attending Dilber's bashes had always been the bevy of slinky, dazzling women he'd be sure to find there. And here they were, in strength. Classy, tall women with a cultivated sang-froid that Jingo longed to puncture. Ice maidens in whom Jingo would have loved to activate a total thaw. Disarm, arouse to submission, then leave them clamouring, whining for more. Calm yourself, Jingo-boy, he made a mental note: your celibate days are turning you sadistic!

Take a look at that one, for instance. Dark beauty in shining silvery outfit, elegantly poised on arm of sofa. Legs tightly crossed. In one hand a gimlet, in the other a cigarette in a long holder. If Earth's gravity were turned off for a moment and she found herself suddenly floating away into the ether like those astronauts in outer space, she would scarcely have altered her expresssion. What was the reason for her inaccessibility? What deadly secrets was she guarding beneath her designer space suit? . . . He had met her once before – at the time she had been working for the same ad agency as Dubby – but now she maintained her distracted aloofness, pretending not to recognize him. And for all that glamorous panache, was he not correct in reading behind her whimsical hauteur – puckered lips, slightly raised eyebrows, betrayed by occasional bursts of rapid blinking – the efforts of a faintly timorous person quite ill at ease trying hard to appear detached and imperturbable?

There was much arrogant assumption in such face reading, he knew, but Jingo believed he had a powerful gift of empathy that allowed him to identify so totally with the mind of another that he was able to enter and explore it. The gift worked better, he had noticed, if the other was a woman. And if he had four or five drinks under his belt.

Dammit, wrong glass. He'd just taken a deep swig of a very sweet gin. Where had he left his own drink? It *was* vain of him to think like that, wasn't it? In any case, if he had really planned to leave early why had he arrived so late? Predictably, a pleasant numbness was creeping into his legs which had become insensible to the idea of leaving at all. Somehow, such evenings had a way of tumbling vertiginously – no matter how firm his determination to resist the slide – into comatose extinction. Most of tomorrow would be spent nursing smouldering regrets of rash statements made, caddish behaviour only vaguely recalled and probably a powerful hangover as well. Hey, hold on, you've got work to do tomorrow. Of course, I know that. But now I'm here, may as well enjoy myself. He took a glug from a fresh glass of whisky he'd just fixed himself and dug his teeth savagely into a succulent piece of tangdi kabab.

Dubby's pet dog, a golden retriever named Bonzo, ambled through the room offering his paw in turn to each of the seated guests. Everyone found him so charming, so 'well trained', especially the women, who cuddled him like a rug and nuzzled his fluff against their perfumed cheeks until he gently broke away to sniff at one more fragrant body, offer his paw to someone else for yet another squeeze and shake. Oooh, to be cuddled like that . . .

He didn't wait his turn for an audience with Bonzo, and wandered out once more onto the vast balcony. In a darkened alcove created by potted creepers entwined in a large wooden lattice, a couple was kissing passionately.

Most of Dilber's friends at the party remembered Jingo from their college days. Some had known him quite well, others might only just remember him as Cristina's boyfriend. He hadn't graduated with them. After a few weeks in the Commerce course he had shifted to Arts and, after another year and a half, dropped out altogether. Even that was a long time ago. Now, if they passed him in the street on a working day, many of them wouldn't notice him at all. He'd prefer to avoid running into them himself. By the glow of a roomful of well-to-do young people, he felt shabby and self-conscious. Every detail of his appearance betrayed fairly conclusively that he hadn't made much of himself. A dropout from college, he had remained one in life. And every one of these young people, besotted by success or dreams of achieving, had little time or interest in failure.

Somebody clapped a hand on his shoulder.

'Oi, Jingo! Long time no see!'

It was Juggy. The two had been quite friendly at college.

'In fact, believe it or not, I saw you just the other day,' said Juggy. 'When was it?' He knitted his brows in an exaggerated effort at remembering. 'Two days ago? Along Grant Road? It's impossible to find parking space on that stretch, or I would have stopped. I was on my way to the Excise Office. You were trudging along carrying a slingbag stuffed with some very important-looking papers. I thought, boyoboy, someone's really busy . . .' He cleared his throat and gave a sickly smile, which Jingo assumed was his way of implying that beneath the apparent insincerity was some well-meant concern for his college friend. Juggy had put on weight. The hairline on his high forehead had receded further, giving him a more learned and academic look than became the prosperous owner of a popular restaurant and bar. But his bulbous nose looked more misshapen than Jingo remembered it, as though it had been taking quite a few punches.

'So, what're you doing now? How's all the writing-shiteing stuff getting on? Are you going to put us in your works or not? Ha-ha! The whole blooming rogues' gallery of your old buddies?'

Juggy turned to the coolly attractive girl he was with. 'This guy's a writer, you know, Babli. Old friend, Jingo, only guy I know who's managed to stay out of the rat race. Stories and all that sort of thing. Real brainy sort of guy,' he said, tapping at his own temple with a crooked index finger. 'Careful what you say in front of him. Or next thing you'll be reading about it in some storybook!' He burst into loud peals of laughter, then patted Jingo on the back deprecatingly, as though begging to be excused for his frivolities.

Jingo had noticed Babli earlier that evening. The low-cut dress that barely managed to contain her breasts, that perpetually dreamy seductive expression, had caught Jingo's eye. Probably she had been offended by the brazen lechery of his gaze, for now she refused to acknowledge him with even so much as a smile.

'Have you eaten?' she asked Juggy in an unexpectedly stern and guttural voice with a strong Bengali intonation. 'Come on, hurry. I'm feeling so sleepy . . .' She yawned loudly.

'But we can't leave without trying the dessert,' he said to her. Then to Jingo, 'Don't miss it, man, looks abs super. Trust Dabs to do the imposs. And custard apples aren't even in season just now.' Before Jingo could say anything more to either of them, Juggy had moved on, whooping with delight at encountering another old chum, this one from his days at Doon's school.

Jingo shut his eyes and took several long deep breaths of the damp night air.

That afternoon, he had visited his parents. The phone at Gurdeep's had been dead for a whole week now. His mother had left a message at MIRA, the agency he freelanced for, asking him to come to lunch.

He arrived an hour late. His parents had given up on him and were only just sitting down to their midday meal.

'Sorry. I just got your message an hour ago,' said Jingo. The furrows of habitual resentment on their faces softened a bit. Actually they were delighted to see him.

Even before he could join them at the table, his father announced proudly, 'Do you know why your mother asked you to come to lunch today? And why she's cooked dhaun-daar and tareli machchi?'

Jingo had become aware of the aroma of frying fish and the murmur of sizzling oil when he entered the flat. Now he felt uneasy. Something was afoot.

'It's all been worked out, son. No time to lose. One passport-sized photograph and your signature on that form – where's it, Khorshed, where have you put the papers?'

'On the sideboard, under the Zarthost-Saheb frame,' Khorshed called out from the passage.

'Of course, if you already have a recent photo we can trim it to size—'

'No, no. Better to take out a new photo only,' said his mother, bustling into the living room with a pot of hot rice. 'Fresh beginnings call for a fresh picture,' she said. Then, interrupting herself – 'Oh, oh, one minute, one minute' – she scuttled away into the kitchen. Presently, she came back holding aloft a platter of three steaming full-fried pomfrets.

'Saved,' she said, 'in the nick of time.'

'Well? Aren't you pleased?' demanded his father, slightly offended by Jingo's unbroken silence.

'What, that the machchi didn't get charred?'

'*Arrey,* tell him properly, from the beginning,' his mother said, ladling out a helping of rice for his father. 'And you listen properly,' she said to Jingo. 'Let's start eating please, while the food is still hot.'

'Okay, let's start. I'll tell you—' he said, putting a morsel of plain rice into his mouth, then sucking his breath in loudly to cool his scorched tongue, 'I went across on Monday to meet Kersi Golwalla. By appointment . . . You know who that is? A very important man. He's even come to our place once. Had tea and khaari with us. For some time, I was very annoyed with him, of course.'

'You're always in a hurry to get annoyed with people,' said his mother, not unpleasantly.

'Some daar, please,' he said to her, holding out his plate. 'I'll admit I had misjudged the man. Not much up there,' he said, tapping his forehead, 'but thorough gentleman. What a reception he gave me. When I told him it was about you, he said, "Bomansah, what's there to ask about in this? In fact, just now we are on the lookout for promising Parsi youth like your son. And if it's a question of *your* son . . ."Oh no, he hasn't forgotten how I campaigned for him during last year's Panchayet elections. All my articles and letters in the *Jame* . . . He told me he's the only trustee in the entire history of the Parsi Panchayet who's ever won by such a thumping majority.

'Now you see what this means, son? It's going to be

quite simple after all, God willing, to wangle that loan for you. Kersi Golwalla is Chief Trustee of the Kooverji Choywalla Trust. And he's assured me, in confidence, of course: trust is flush with funds just now and he'll do the needful.'

Jingo said nothing to his father. 'I'll help myself,' he muttered to his mother who was asking for his plate to serve him.

'Today being Behram Roje, your mother thought we should offer thanks and give you the good news . . . Look, there's nothing to be anxious about, Jahangir. He knows all about you,' said his father, reassuringly. 'I told him you were a dropout from college, couldn't finish your graduation due to family problems. He remembers about my angina attack, too, which was around the same time – even visited me while I was at hospital. Just stick to that story. He'll see to it the committee doesn't ask too many awkward questions. They'll sanction the loan like that!' He snapped his fingers. 'Only two per cent interest, imagine! And ten years to pay it back in. After you've finished your studies and found a good job . . . Now first thing is, go through that heap of prospectuses you've been collecting and see which universities you want to apply to. Do it soon. Don't sit on it again.'

'You know how I feel about all this, Papa,' said Jingo, reluctantly. 'I'm not at all sure that I want to go anywhere.'

'Not sure?' His father paused dramatically before he spoke again. 'Do you hear him, Khorshed? And please, sir, when will you be sure?' He was trying sarcasm, but couldn't sustain it. 'A fine mess you've made of your life, as it is! I thought we'd agreed there was no scope here for you – a better university, where your talents can blossom . . . You said you'd be willing!'

'I said I'd consider. But I'm not ready to go anywhere just yet,' said Jingo, and remained sullenly silent. He'd been buying time. He hadn't expected his father to be able to arrange a loan so easily.

'Look,' fulminated Boman, 'they're doing this out of respect for me. For my grey hairs. Once I'm gone Golwalla won't even let you enter his office!'

'But I don't *want* to.'

'What?'

'Enter Golwalla's office. Take a loan for further studies. Go abroad. Any of those things which every Tom, Dick and Hormaz does straight after college.'

'Straight after college? It's six years since you dropped out! We gave you a chance to do what you wanted. Now better take my advice seriously. No trust is ever going to consider your loan application seriously after this.'

'But I like it here, in my own city. I don't feel the need to go anywhere.'

For a moment there was a stunned silence. From there on the argument tumbled along its predictably precipitous course.

'Okay, Mr Special, so what are you going to do with yourself here? Live off handouts from your aged parents? Even an office peon needs to be a graduate these days. Look at Porous and Rayomund.' His father appealed to him, trying once more to sound reasonable.

'Who?'

'Now you're forgetting your own neighbours, the boys you grew up with?'

'Oh, you mean the Karanjias of B-Block. I heard Rayomund had a nervous breakdown when he went to Syracuse. He still seems a little weird whenever I meet him.'

'Weird? You're weird if you ask me,' said his father, a pitch of desperation entering his already shrill voice. 'Staying in some hovel like a ragamuffin. Porous and Rayomund both have degrees in business management, they're earning five-figure salaries. They keep their parents in luxury. Porous has just bought a new Fiat!' He heaved a deep sigh, and masticated while mumbling. 'For years I worked myself to the bone, without complaining. Without stopping even for a holiday . . . and now when it's time for me to retire I must start worrying about my grown-up hulk of a son' – his voice grew steadily louder – 'who doesn't want to do anything in life? Who doesn't *know* what life's about? You're spitting on your own future, you fool . . . and after I've got it all ready for you on a platter!'

For an instant, Jingo imagined his future as a trio of full-fried pomfrets waiting to be consumed.

His mother remained resentfully silent. She had never forgiven her son's decision to move out of home and stay with a friend in Byculla.

'Well, I suppose you have nothing to say.' His father addressed her at last. 'Am I to go on braying alone?'

'What do you want me to say now?' she asked spitefully. 'None of this would have happened if you had put your foot down when you should have.'

'Aha, so it *is* my fault after all. I knew it would come to that, has to.'

'Of course, then who else's? Didn't I warn you right away when he was starting his *lafru* with that Christian girl? But what did you say? "He's young, let him have his fun." Fun?'

'*I* said! Now just a minute, I like that!'

'Never mind she's Christian or anything, does she have

no feelings? Is she not a human being? Poor girl lost her mother so early in life. Should we look away and allow this kind of immoral—'

'Oh God, Mama, don't start on that now please. It's all over, anyhow.'

'Net result – his mind switched off studies completely.'

'Now let's just get the record straight! *I* wasn't the one—'

'So long you've been holding the floor, now let me speak.'

'Okay, then speak your fill. Blame as much as you want—'

'She's not even here now, Mama. She's gone away . . .'

But they weren't listening to Jingo's pathetic interjections, both too engrossed in the parry and lunge of apportioning blame for Jingo's moral degradation. Unexpectedly, they closed ranks and turned on him.

'You said you wanted to become a writer,' his mother said. 'That's why you were leaving home to live alone. Well, what have you written? Why haven't you published anything?'

'Now all you do is go door-to-door like a lousy salesman prying into other people's affairs. Is that some way to earn a living? Snooping about the place? Having the door slammed in your face by strangers? Better to sell some tasty pickle or papad,' his father mocked, 'or even a good durable toilet brush. You'll earn more money that way, believe me. And at least you'll be making an honest living.'

'I *am* working,' protested Jingo, raising his voice intemperately, 'I *am* making an honest living. Doing what I enjoy!'

'Life is not all about enjoyment,' said his mother. Then,

a moment later, with surprise, 'Oh, so you mean you don't want to be a writer any more?'

'Ah, the fickleness of this boy . . .' His father indulged in a theatrical aside.

'I'm collecting material,' Jingo answered his mother sheepishly, 'making notes for a novel.'

'Novel!' Now they were both speaking at once again.

'What is your novel about?'

'Six years! By now I'd have completed an epic. A trilogy! And even if you do write one – *when* you write it – God knows in what era – who's going to want to publish it – or read it? Go abroad, get a diploma in journalism from a good university. It's the only way, if you want to write.'

'Just because you wrote one story that won a prize doesn't mean you should give up everything else. Write stories in your spare time!'

'He's on a full-time vacation, my dear.'

'Okay, if it's really only writing you want to do, then write, Jaungoo. But set yourself a deadline.'

'Novels aren't written in a day. They have to gestate, like babies.'

'Say anything, this is all because of that girl. And to think that you have given up everything, your career – your family, too – all for a girl as black as pitch!'

'Oh, stop it now, you're going too far!'

'Is she any match for you?'

'I told you, it's over with Cristina!'

'Well, now you listen to me, sonny,' said his father, 'you're not so young any more. By the time your baby is born, we might have to find you a bed in the Parsi General's geriatric ward!'

'*Ovaaryu!*' his mother hissed, backing down and

hastily snapping her fingers to avert any baleful effects of the unintended malediction. 'Your tongue is running away with you again, Boman.'

The auspicious dhaun-daar lunch was ruined.

'Now don't not eat just because of an argument,' said Khorshed to her husband, who had just pushed his plate away.

'My appetite is dead,' rumbled Boman with solemn finality, and stood up. Jingo pleaded that he had an appointment to keep and wasn't hungry anyway. His mother threw him a hurtful look, but didn't argue.

The Moos family had never been very good with greetings and goodbyes. Silently, Jingo went through their ritual gestures for departure. His mother held out a glass to him. 'Take a sip of water at least before you leave.' Then she put an arm around him and gave him that awkward sidelong cuddle which was the Moos' guarded version of an embrace.

His father had moved from the table to his favourite easy chair, where he reclined with legs outstretched. Jingo held out a contrite hand, and his father responded by joining his own to it in a clutch of unspoken truce. He grunted, but avoided meeting his son's eyes.

At the door, Jingo's mother nudged him to remind him to pay obeisance to the small oval-shaped photo-frame of Zarthost-Saheb that hung over the exit. Briefly, Jingo touched the hoary-white beard of the kindly sentinel who stared into space looking rather aggrieved himself, then touched his fingertips to his chest.

His mother believed in an old superstition that if you turned to look at a place you were leaving, you were sure to come back to it some day. For a long time, Jingo spitefully refused to turn. But in the end, knowing that she'd be craning to glimpse his last gesture of farewell, he stopped at the Colony gates, looked over his shoulder and waved.

As soon as he had descended the hill, Jingo went into the cheap Udipi restaurant across the road and ordered himself a misal and two paos. He remembered to ask for an extra sprinkling of chopped onion. The fragrance of his mother's cooking had made him quite ravenous.

Below, a large white sedan drove up to the gates of Dubby's building and honked. A watchman trotted up briskly and swung open one half of the tall, wrought-iron barricade. The car slipped in noiselessly, lighting up the driveway with its headlights.

It was Dubby, in fact, who had introduced Cris to Jingo; the girls had been at the same convent school together. He had noticed her before that, too, in the huge classroom of seventy or more freshers: a dark, snub-nosed girl with a shock of curls and sparkling eyes, sitting by herself. Most of the students in the class were girls, who tended to stick together, in cliques. She must have noticed him, too – there were so few guys around – and he had just made the shift from Commerce to Arts, a good six weeks after term began. But they had never spoken to each other.

In that moment of recognition, when they first said 'Hi!', something joyful happened. Both of them felt it, and both knew that the other had felt it too. It was as if a hundred veils of pretence and affectation that kept young people apart had evaporated in that instant. The feeling was new to both of them. But it was overwhelmingly real and they were willing to acknowledge it. Shyly at first and with a great deal of trepidation, both knew that they belonged.

Inside Dubby's drawing room, the babble had grown dizzyingly boisterous. A swarthy bearded man who looked like the model for Zodiac ties (could it be him, in fact?) was declaiming loudly, 'Oh, she's a great cook. Her prawn pulao is the best you'll ever taste, I can tell you that . . . Mmm. You should get her to make it for you some time.'

'Shernaz?' said a sharp-nosed woman with a clipped accent. 'I know Shernaz very well, in fact. Thin girl, face full of acne? I like her, mind you, don't get me wrong . . . Once I'd invited her to breakfast. Now it so happened there was a teeny-weeny bit of uncooked white floating on her fried egg. Just slightly uncooked, you know. The way she retched! We had to abandon breakfast, and only drank the orange juice. She admitted to me, later – in strict confidence, of course, now don't whisper this to a soul, Ravi – it seems floating egg white reminds her of semen. Yes, that's what she said. I mean, just think – such hang-ups! Poor thing.'

Nearby, a young stockbroker was plucking his lower lip with one finger in time to the music. 'Money has no value left . . .' he said dolefully. 'I bought that place for four and a half. Now prices are anywhere between eleven and twelve. For smaller places. In the same building, mind you!'

'If you look at it squarely, what she was trying to do made a lot of sense,' said his friend, a chubby well-groomed executive who was also a well-known amateur golfer. 'I mean, with land ceiling and all that . . . Now real estate has really hit the roof!'

'Mrs G.? A great lady. I still miss her.'

'She was doing a bloody good job, too,' said the creative director of a large ad agency. 'They called her a dictator, authoritarian, whatnot. But we *needed* someone like her. As a people we have no sense of discipline at all. None whatsoever. And now where are we, without her?'

'Those two bloody *namak haraam surdee*s!'

'Shh. Biswajit can hear us. His family in Delhi suffered.'

'The only party with any nationalistic feeling left in this country is the BJP,' said the stockbroker. 'At least they want a temple for Ram built in Ayodhya.'

'Aha, but even they can't afford to alienate the minorities,' said the bearded model who had joined in the conversation. 'In a country like ours, votes count.'

'Oh, I hope you-all are not going to start talking politics now,' said a woman with him who had remained silent all along.

'No, no, no politics today. Things are depressing enough as it is,' said another young woman, who was wearing a gorgeous brocade sari. 'Anil, did you know, I was reading somewhere: narrow ties are back in fashion.'

'So, who cares, ya?' said the ad man. But a moment later he knitted his eyebrows, as though puzzled by a thought that had just struck him. 'Narrow with a flat edge or a tapering edge?' he asked.

Go on, listen in. They're having their fun. How about you? Jingo wandered in the general direction of the bar. And what does it make you? A perpetual eavesdropper on the hollowness of other people's conversations?

Bonzo the golden retriever was still doing the rounds of the party guests, beseeching a handshake, raising his paw limply in the air. But now everyone ignored him, pretending the dog was non-existent. In the course of his earlier cuddling, Bonzo had developed a little pink erection that had since grown to quite astonishing proportions.

'I saw *Deer Hunter* on video. Al Pacino was marvellous,' said the social worker in the green backless gown.

'Actually, I preferred *Coming Home*,' said the textile designer seated next to her.

'Did you really? I found Jon Voight quite disappointing.'

A loud shriek rang through the room. The dog had mounted the lap of the girl in the silvery space suit and was making vigorous back and forth movements. She gave him a violent shove but the dog held tight with his forelegs and went right on. She pushed him again with greater force and he fell back, whimpering, squealing with hurt, then growling in his throat. People stopped talking and stared, the girl smoothed her dress with her handkerchief and dashed into the passage towards the bathroom. Dubby's sharp voice rang through the room:

'Shankar! Bonzo *ko bahar le jao*! Crazy dog!' Then she too followed after the girl, perhaps to assuage violated nerves or ascertain the extent of damage done to expensive party apparel.

Once again, Jingo found himself out on the balcony staring at the ships in the bay. It was true. Like two cogs, temporarily disjointed, Cris and he had slipped back easily into a familiar union whose gears had been exactly carved by the compulsions of some previous existence. Or so it had seemed. With fierce certainty, the feeling of possession had overwhelmed them both. Later on – five or six, seven years later – when they had succeeded in nearly destroying each other, yet never managing to sever the link that bound them, they had to pause, each for survival's sake. Now at least, thank God, she had taken a decision bravely, unilaterally, and freed them both.

So, he was alone once more. No Crissy here tonight to dampen his exuberance, his wayward attractions. Yet, he had to admit he couldn't bring himself to feel genuinely interested in any of the gorgeous women he saw lolling all around.

Jingo tossed his cigarette butt over the rail and watched the glowing end catapult into the dark. For what seemed like a very long time he could see the stub falling, its descent cradled by a gentle waft of breeze till it became a mere spark and vanished. The effort of watching it made his eyeballs ache. He felt small and crushed and dizzy. In the street below, not a soul was in sight. A light shone in the watchman's cabin at the compound gate. In the parking lot, six cars crouched, a family of snails.

Then he felt an arm nestle around his waist.

'What's the matter, Jimmy? Not having fun?' It was Dubby. 'You just don't know how to have a good time, do you?'

'I've had a lovely time, Dubby, thanks. No, really. I've stuffed myself on the excellent biryani, two scoops of custard apple ice cream—'

'Oh stop it, Jimmy Moos,' cried Dubby. 'Conceited swine. Below that silly grin of yours, I know, I can *see* you're miserable.'

'But you're wrong. I'm not,' said Jingo obstinately. Dubby remained silent. In the overcast sky two red lights glimmered faintly, and for a few seconds the rumble of jet engines lay over them like a shadow. Suddenly, Jingo felt terribly alone. He wondered again why he had come at all.

'How's Cris?' asked Dubby. 'Haven't seen her in a long while either.'

'Cristina's gone. To Baroda.' His reply came out steely and sharp, and Dubby was taken aback. He covered up his own surprise by adding more gently, 'She's joined the Baroda School of Art, you know.'

'Oh, I didn't . . . That's great news. She was always so good at art. By the way,' said Dubby, 'you don't have to go back home all the way at this time of night. Crash here, if you want. My folks are in Khandala.'

'Can't. I've got work tomorrow. Thanks anyway, Dubby . . . Look, I'd better start moving.'

Someone had turned off the music. In the drawing room behind them a chorus of voices was imploring a man in a saffron kurta to sing them one of his songs. The man was quite dark and plump with a medallion hanging round his neck on a long chain. He lived somewhere up in the hills, Jingo knew, and owned an apple orchard. He had a guru somewhere up there too, whose picture was on the medallion he wore. A visionary of sorts, thought Jingo, to have decided so early in life to get away from the city, but his compositions can be terribly dull. Must make tracks before he starts singing. He felt a tremendous urge to be out in the open. Descend in the elevator and quit this terrestrial space station, walk home through the night streets alone. Perhaps there'd be a drizzle. But a box guitar was quickly produced out of nowhere and handed to the reluctant balladeer. He struck up some chords on it and began singing in a thin reedy voice:

> O Seagull . . .
> Gliding gently through the sky,
> Is that a tear I see in your eye?
> Is it true what we have heard,
> Can this really be the end of the world?

A couple of verses followed in the same vein.

'How are you for money, Jimmy? I could . . .' Dubby whispered cautiously.

'I'm fine, Dabs. This market research racket gets me
by.'

'Still smoking that pot?'

'Hardly at all . . . And anyway, it's not such a deadly
poison, you know.'

When the song ended, there was clapping and calls for
an encore. Under cover of the applause, Jingo left the
party without bidding any of the other guests goodbye.

*

For a long while, he walked alone. It must have rained
without his noticing it, the streets were slightly wet. There
was a strong smell of earth in the air. Earth and a whiff of
sewage. He decided to walk rather than wait for the
hourly night bus. There was no way of knowing what time
the next was scheduled, or whether it would come at all.

Once he had left behind the skyscrapers and the old
bungalows with their Gurkha watchmen posted at each
brightly lit gate, he came to a dark stretch where the
streetlights were out. There were small shops on both
sides of the road with their shutters down. Occasionally
a car passed, with a family in it, or noisy revellers returning home from some party. Once a large lorry filled with
gunny sacks rumbled past, presumably headed for the
wholesale market near where he lived. The juddering of
its engine became a receding purr. Jingo felt a sudden
coldness creep into his bones which made him shiver. The
street in front of him was deserted, except for a clutch of
dark bodies asleep under the awning of a shuttered shop.
The rumble of the truck could still be heard from very far
away; then it faded.

A thought occurred to him: at the heart of the city
lurks a terrible silence that we can't bear to listen to. All

the tumult of its waking hours, the rattle and throb of its ceaseless shuttling, the insidious flashing of its neon lights, the wild cachinnation of its party animals were all no more than devious, neurotic attempts to smother that silent shriek.

In the beginning, Cristina and Jingo had been universally acknowledged as an inseparable couple. They were regulars at Dubby's parties, indeed at almost any party that was happening. Some said they were perfectly matched. They had probably meant that in physical terms, though she was shorter than he. Others, he was aware, wondered what he was doing with her. But hardly anyone knew of the problems they were having. Usually, it was only after midnight, once they had left the party, their most fierce quarrels began.

'So,' she smiled, snuggling closer to him in the local train rattling northwards to the suburb where she lived, 'won't you tell me her name at least?'

Cristina was being seductively friendly. The train was quite packed, mainly with millworkers returning home from the late night shift.

'Who're you talking about?'

'Why, that girl in the black tights and red boob tube. You were practically slobbering over her all evening. Don't remember?'

'Slobbering?' Jingo repeated the word with a quizzical frown to show that he deplored the exaggeration.

'Oh, you know what I mean. You did take a fancy to her, didn't you?'

Jingo stared dully out of the window of the moving train.

'You can tell me,' she said. 'We're friends, aren't we? We can speak frankly, surely? She's very attractive. I thought so myself.'

'Oh, come on,' said Jingo, refusing to be drawn in. In the dank yellow light of the compartment, his face looked flushed and tired.

'Well, didn't you think so? I thought she looked really sexy, no? And seemed willing, too.' She slipped her hand into Jingo's reassuringly. 'You don't need to be scared of me, you know. So tell. You were turned on by her, weren't you?'

'Well, okay . . . Maybe, just a bit.' He smiled involuntarily. 'She wasn't bad-looking.'

Suddenly he felt a sharp pain in the hand she was cradling. She'd dug her long nails into the tendon between his thumb and index finger. He turned to her sharply, just stopping himself from crying out aloud. She was still smiling, but her eyes had turned glassy. Nobody on the train noticed a thing as she whispered between clenched teeth, not easing the pressure of her nails, 'Not bad-looking? You think I didn't notice your fucking prick was up all evening for her? If I hadn't stopped you, you'd have raped her right there on the dining table!'

'You stopped me? I didn't notice. There *was* nothing— Hey, will you stop this shit! That hurts.' He raised his voice a bit. 'Or do you want to make a scene right here?'

The man sitting opposite them had been dozing with the whites of his eyes showing while his head wobbled to the movement of the train, but now he half opened one eye and regarded the couple before him. Cristina released his hand, but Jingo knew they hadn't exhausted the subject yet.

When they reached Cristina's house, she slipped off her heels and raised a finger to her lips. Quietly, they tiptoed up the wrought-iron stairway that lead to her attic room from behind the building. She slipped the bolt gently and they entered in darkness. 'Shh.'

She turned on the light, but wouldn't let him speak, listening for footsteps of her father who sometimes stayed awake waiting for her to return. Tonight, though, there was only the singing of crickets.

Once they were in bed together, he tried to explain. He tried to be kind, knowing that was what she longed for.

'Okay, so what's so terrible about a little flirtation? Why do people go to these silly parties anyway? To eat, drink and flirt.'

'Yes,' she said, thoughtfully. 'But, if I had not been there . . .'

'What?'

'You would have taken her into the bedroom and fucked her.' There was a great sadness in her voice when she said this.

'Well, supposing – now just suppose for a minute that were true, and of course, assuming that she had no objection to it . . .'

'She would have let you. I could see she wanted it.'

'Well, okay, just supposing. Would that be such a terrible thing? Would it be the end of the world?'

'Of course. It's terrible for me. Because I know when that happens, you will leave me.'

'Leave you! Oh no, Cris. I love you. I'd never.'

'You're staying on with me because I'm the only one you've got. Probably the only girl you've ever had. Once you make love to someone else, I know you will leave me. Anyone, any of those girls at the party tonight – I know you would find it easier to love any of them than me. I've been so bad for you . . .' She held him close to her. There were tears in her eyes. He kissed her eyelids, her forehead, her hair. He whispered softly, 'No, please. That's not true . . .'

By the time they made love and fell asleep on the narrow single bed, the light was already breaking. The cock in the neighbour's yard crowed twice, tentatively. When they were alone together in each other's arms, they were happy. And their love seemed, for once, unchanging, inviolable.

Two Muslim dhaabas were still open at the corner where Jingo turned into Sankli Street. On the pavement outside one of these eateries, a large coal brazier was sparking merrily. A grizzled old man wearing a white knitted prayer cap was seated on a mat beside a large platterful of mince, slowly, methodically shaping handfuls of it into long, cylindrical kababs, sticking them into skewers and laying them over the hot coals to grill.

Jingo thought of the other young people at Dubby's birthday party, many of whom had been at college at the same time as Cris and himself. Such ease, such self-assurance. Most of them had finished college and immediately attached themselves to the big money-spinning wheel of society. They had acquired well-being and style – all of them knew how to keep a conversation going, how to make themselves attractive to one another, flirt yet remain non-committal, making their bids in the game of social contract with one eye on profit, the other on pleasure, without ever faltering or appearing stupid. They knew how to talk to servants and take work from them. Perhaps these were skills that were inherited. The upper classes of all ages have always known the secret of how to look beautiful and unattainable to the rest of society. Wasn't that yet another devious method of domination?

A manipulation of the very notions of beauty and ugliness. Was it some kind of fascist preoccupation to look for a point of coincidence between physical beauty and an inner beauty of the soul? Was it not also a fundamental human longing? Such terrible dislocation then, that spiritual squalor and mental vacuity can flourish under the canopy of an apparently flawless exterior. Or was it plain idealism to expect otherwise? Perhaps it was a failure of modern culture, of the age that invented the cinema – not to mention a thriving cosmetic industry – that the visual faculty be so trusted as a means of obtaining the truth.

Jingo was no different, drawn to that kind of glossy cover-girl beauty himself. Not that Cris wasn't beautiful. But not in any conventional sense of the word, you needed special sight to see her beauty. His flirtations with other women were harmless fun, Jingo believed, no more than a light-hearted curiosity. In spite of his undeniable craving for sexual experience and adventure, he tried never to lose sight of the fact that Cris was terribly special to him.

He had never been in another relationship of such intense involvement, nor could he hope to feel so utterly comfortable in intimacy with another woman. Their minds and bodies seemed to mesh together so perfectly. He knew this rather well for himself, but somehow Cris had never believed it as implicitly as he did. Was it too late now to change things?

Herself, she had always felt ugly and graceless (despite the fact that she was an athlete, who had led her school's volleyball team). Not just in body, but in spirit as well. He blamed her parents for that. Her father had abused and battered his children, her mother had made them feel ashamed for her. But it had to be his own fault, too. He had never quite been able to reassure her that she was worth a thousand times more than any of those wretched togged-up floozies at Dubby's whom she felt so inferior to.

In the end, the logic of her fears about losing him grew so painfully convoluted, so threatening to them both, they stopped going to parties altogether.

He crossed a long railway overbridge which was deserted and slushy with the refuse of vegetable vendors who gathered there every morning. Below him, a quiet railway yard brooded in the dark where several pairs of tracks converged. From the other end of the bridge Jingo saw a lone figure approaching. It was a balloon man, carrying on his shoulder a thick long pole with protruding branches from which were suspended cheap toys, paper masks, rattles, coloured goggles and plastic bags stuffed with candy. A few gas balloons tied to one of the branches of the pole trailed behind him, sagging, their levity expended. As he came closer, Jingo saw that the balloon man was limping.

Where could he be going at this hour, carrying that frivolous cross of his? Home perhaps, to a pavement hut, Jingo decided, after some mela in the church compound. But what mela for parish children went on so late into the night? Maybe he was hungry by the time the fair ended and had stopped somewhere for a plate of sheekh kabab and roti? If so, did he leave his cross of toys leaning against the dhaaba's entrance while he ate inside? Or did he carry it in with him? Jingo was curious about people. He would have loved to ask and find out for sure. But the balloon man passed by dragging his bad leg, without even sneaking a glance at Jingo.

These were the things that intrigued him about the city.

At any time of day or night there was always somebody on the job. On the main road opposite the church, a shed constructed of bamboo and corrugated tin was brightly lit. A painted signboard read 'Lakshmi Commercial Institute: Typing and Shorthand 24 hours'. Inside, bent over ancient rusty machines, a handful of middle-aged men sat among mostly empty rows of chairs clack-clattering away, improving their job prospects at dead of night. Next to Lakshmi Commercial Institute was Shashikant's Hair-cutting Saloon. Its shutters were still up for some reason, though there were no customers. Two glum barbers with closely cropped hair sat lounging in the ostentatious salon chairs smoking bidis.

Under the glow of a streetlamp, a man, a woman and their two small children were weaving buds of jasmine and mogra into short lengths of string. Tomorrow they would sell these at railway stations, offer them to passengers of cars and taxis that stopped at traffic lights. Women on their way to work would buy them for head gear. The clean, fragrant flowers that adorn the hairdos of well-dressed, respectable women are knitted amidst the slush and grime of city pavements in the small hours of morning by haggard women, resentful men and sleepy-eyed children. He must write that down. These were the kind of observations he had filled his journal with. But to make a novel, he told himself, you need story. Not just images and irony.

Now, as he neared home, a long line of makeshift pavement huts began. Most were in darkness, the families in them already asleep. But one of the huts had a candle flickering in a small glass at its door – this was Chandu's discreet signal that he was still doing business. The hut was where he and Lalu slept, usually only during the day.

But, round the corner, was a tiny vacant plot where Chandu had built a makeshift shelter of wattles, twigs and thatch under a gloomy peepul. Jingo walked past the huts and the compound wall of the municipal school they were built against, and turned.

There he was, Chandu, sitting on his haunches, feet swaddled as always in an enormous pair of PVC moccasins. An old calendar picture of the bearded fakir Shirdi Sai Baba was nailed to the tree trunk, above the leafy canopy. A garland of string and withered petals hung by the same nail. A large earthen water pot rested on a stone platform just outside the shelter; and behind Chandu, squatting unobtrusively among the shadows, sat Lalu.

'What, baba?' said Chandu in greeting, inviting Jingo to squeeze in under the shelter. But Jingo preferred to sit opposite them on a cane mat spread out on the ground. 'Very good maal, friend. Come in just today.'

Chandu made a living selling little balls of hashish and opium, frequently ingesting a few himself. But only the hashish, he swore; he never touched opium.

The balls of hashish were wrapped in bits of red cellophane paper and the opium ones in blue. It was Lalu, Chandu's long-time associate, who was honorary custodian of this paltry treasure. He kept it tied around his waist among the gathers of his loongi. When a ball or two were needed, he stretched out his one good limb and raised his midriff towards Chandu, who searched among the folds of the garment until he fished out a plastic pouch; as soon as he had counted out the required balls, he tied it once again among the faded checked patterns of the loongi. Both Lalu's hands and one leg had been amputated years ago when he fell out of a moving train. His dark, small body with its various attached stumps looked like the damaged figurine of some ageless god, very young indeed, the body of a barely fifteen-year-old; but his face was pinched and furrowed with the maturity of an indeterminate, though much greater age. His hair was scant, revealing irregular patches of scalp.

Chandu had already prepared the hashish pipe. Now that he was here, Jingo was asked to do the honours by lighting it.

The street was quite deserted at this hour, except for a few bodies asleep on the opposite pavement. Striking two matchsticks at once, Chandu cupped the flame with his palm, holding it up to the mouth of the chillum while Jingo pulled deeply through a thin damp cloth. He'd had too much to drink at the party; this would help him sober up, he thought. But the smoke was too harsh, or perhaps it went down the wrong way, for Jingo was racked by a paroxysm of coughing. Chandu relieved him of the pipe, rubbing his back gently. He offered him a mug of water from the clay pot, but Jingo shook his head. The coughing had eased now. Meanwhile, Lalu nudged Chandu with his upper arm, reminding him that the chillum was burning up. Chandu took a few deep puffs himself and then held the pipe up to Lalu's lips. Lalu pulled expertly and released a long stream of smoke into the cool night air.

Suddenly, they heard footsteps. A strong smell of cheap liquor filled the air and monstrous shadows engulfed Chandu's dimly lit alcove. Jingo turned his head and saw a drunken swarthy man with a bushy moustache, carrying a thick wooden stick. There was another man behind him whom he couldn't see clearly. But both of them had a squat square build and significant paunches that strained at the buttons on their bush-shirts. Unlikely customers, thought Jingo, a little surprised by the company. Then he noticed their heavy regulation boots. Aha. Cops in civvies.

'Ehh!' It was a guttural declamation, more a summons than a greeting. Chandu saluted and rose to his feet. His other hand dipped into his hip-pocket where he kept his money. Meanwhile the man in the background spoke to his partner in Marathi: 'I'll go down to Dagdu's, then. Catch him before he packs up for the night.'

'Go then, fast,' the first cop agreed, looking at his wristwatch. 'Remember, he owes us two weeks'.'

The man in the background muttered something and stumbled along, disappearing into the darkness. Chandu had fished out some money from his pocket and was holding it out deferentially. The policeman looked at the notes he was being offered and slapped the hand that held them, hard.

'*Yeh nahi chalega*,' he declared. 'Told you last time, didn't I? It's five hundred. Not a paisa less. Or in you go.'

'Sahab,' Chandu said, joining his hands in pathetic entreaty, 'that's all I earn in a month.'

'*Malum hai*, I know how much you earn,' said the policeman with ill-concealed contempt, and spat. His lips and front teeth were stained red with betel juice. 'Five hundred. Or see what happens. My bosses want me to sweep this whole footpath clean. Be thankful I'm a merciful man.'

'Sahab,' Chandu once again pleaded, his palms still pressed together, the notes between them. 'Make it three, and I can give it you right now.'

'Ehh! You fuckin' pimp, you've not understood anything or what?' The policeman leaned agressively on his stick, and momentarily losing balance, staggered forward a couple of steps. He covered up his embarrassment by grabbing hold of Chandu's shirt to steady himself, and then went on to shake him roughly.

'I'll be back tomorrow, same time. If you don't have it ready, see what I do.'

'*Arrey*, sahab . . .' Chandu protested politely and freed himself.

'Saab-baab nothing! Your fuckin' *jopadpatti* and every damn thing goes on the bonfire. And you – inside. For the drubbing of a lifetime. You hear? And this bloody side-kick of yours as well.'

As he glowered at Lalu, his face filled with loathing for the cripple. Suddenly he raised his stick and struck Lalu's naked back.

'Dirtying the fuckin' footpath! Why don't you-all take your ugly butts some place else!'

Lalu screamed. '*Aaie!* Why're you beating? Don't beat me!'

Why indeed, Jingo wondered, why was he picking on Lalu, except for the fact that he was an easy target? The bloody pig was enjoying his display of bluster. 'Bugger has no hands or legs but sits here smoking charas!' He lashed him once more.

Jingo's fuddled brain seemed incapable of reacting to any but sensory stimuli. Then again, *thwack!* That would have stung. The cop had ignored Jingo completely all this while. Yet in some way that final remonstrance seemed to him to be directed not at Lalu alone – the cripple was but a scapegoat for all who sat on pavements in the early hours of morning smoking hashish, and that included him. In that instant he remembered an argument he'd once had with Cris during which she had called him a coward. She was objecting to his laziness, his smoke, his reluctance to take up a regular job. 'It doesn't take courage to be a bum.' He could hear her sharp voice mocking.

He saw the stick coming down yet again and, swiftly, unreasoningly, he leaned forward and intercepted it. It stung the skin on his bare palm, but he closed his fingers around it and wouldn't let go.

'Ehh! *Chhoad! Chhoad rey saala!*' The police-man barked, surprised. Jingo slowly released the stick. Raising it threateningly over Jingo's head now, he cursed again, but couldn't bring it down. The brief moment of resistance had unnerved him. What am I trying to do, wondered Jingo. Too much whisky in your veins, you bum.

'Who's this?' the cop asked Chandu. 'Who the fuck is this wise guy?'

'I don't know, sahab. He came here just two minutes before you did. Never seen him before.' Now Chandu was scared, for Jingo's sake more than his own.

'Okay, come on, get up.' The cop ordered Jingo. 'We'll discuss this at the thana.' Jingo rose slowly to his full height. He was just as tall as the policeman, but less flabby, and broader in the shoulders. He folded his arms in front of his chest and waited.

'My partner's gone down to Dagdu's still. He'll be by in a minute. Then,' he said, gloatingly, 'we'll take a walk.'

'*Chalo*, let's go?' suggested Jingo coolly. 'Police station's that way too.' Then he switched to English. 'You ask for five hundred rupees, then beat a defenceless cripple. I'd like to tell your bosses a few things, too . . . What're we waiting for?' It was a gamble. Jingo was still hoping it would all end peaceably.

'Wah! *Bahut* fancy English *mein baat karta hai*. You're

from educated family. Sitting here smoking charas. Does it look nice? Which college you go? Eh?' asked the cop, speaking in English, too, to show he was no illiterate. Jingo ignored the question. 'Come on then. You tell sahab whatever you want. We'll see.' He grabbed Jingo by the scruff of his collar and marched him along, now reverting to the Hindi he was more comfortable with. 'By the time we're through with you, you won't have any tongue left to speak with. I'll flay the skin off your back, you bloody *souvvar ka bachcha.*'

'Sahab, let him off. Just a kid. He didn't know who you are.' Chandu spoke softly, tentatively, but the policeman ignored him and nudged Jingo on.

The street was lonely; silent, except for the policeman's banter, which had become increasingly abusive. 'Teaching me my job, are you? All you fuckin' rich kids, you go to college and this is what you learn, eh? We'll unlearn you soon enough. Now come along.' They had just turned a corner and come to a dark stretch where there was a vacant lot overgrown with shrubbery and one fluorescent tube that was blinking furiously. The policeman tightened his grip on Jingo's collar.

'Where's the need to push and pull? I'm coming with you, aren't I?'

'Come on, then. Come on,' said the policeman and spat out a red blotch of betel juice.

If the policeman hadn't been so rough with him, none of this might have happened. But, as he walked behind Jingo, he prodded him repeatedly in the back with his stick. A swell of hysteria charged through Jingo as he swung round, stabbed his elbow into the policeman's belly with all his force, then turned and slammed his open palm on the man's sweaty nose, giving it a shove. The last thing Jingo saw before he took to his heels was the sight of a dazed policeman falling backwards. He heard a dull thud and the clatter of the wooden stick as it rolled onto the pavement.

Jingo ran as fast as he could, ducking into a side alley, not looking back until he had crossed two more. Then he looked over his shoulder. No one was following him. Phew! Without slowing down, yet adopting as circuitous a route as possible – only now and then glancing behind but never slackening in speed – Jingo sprinted all the way to Winifred House.

As he entered the building where he shared a small flat with his friend, he stopped for a moment and tried to get a grip on himself. Must breathe slower, deeper. He was stark sober now. Panting hard, he staggered up the staircase in pitch darkness until he had reached the first landing. There he struck a match to find the keyhole in the door, and let himself in.

Gurdeep wasn't there. The small bulb outside the toilet had been left on. Jingo stumbled into his room, kicked off his kohlapuris and, without turning on the light, fell onto the bed. That was painful. The hard spine of a Simenon omnibus got him in the ribs. There were clothes and books everywhere. He got up again, pissed, splashed water on his face and gargled a couple of times. Then he peeled off his shirt and dropped his trousers. He knew he was too excited to sleep; hysteria was slowly turning to exhilaration. He piled the books on his bed in a heap and dumped them on the floor. Then he lay down again in his underwear, still breathing hard.

Well, now you've got yourself into a some kind of crazy fuckin' mess, Jingo-boy. You've given in to your impulsiveness once too often. Bullshit. Says who? That fucker was so pissed he won't remember a thing in the morning.

He'd been lucky, he realized with a shudder. What if the guy hadn't been so drunk and had dodged his blow? What if the other cop, his friend, had come around the bend just then? But what else could he have done? Not got involved in the first place. Lalu had probably taken enough beatings in his time. He'd have groaned over it one night, then forgotten. They do get inured to it, you know. What the fuck're you talking about, man? he argued with himself. That bastard cop needed to be stopped. This was one impulsive act he'd stand by. He felt quite proud of it too. Anyway, once he had got into the fray there was no backing out. If he'd gone along with that maniac anywhere near a cop station, they'd have made mincemeat of him. Torn him limb from limb.

Not frightened any more, he tried to calm himself; but his adrenaline wouldn't cease pumping. He could have been in Dubby's soft Dunlopillo bed just now instead of getting into a bloody scrap with a drunken policeman. He must be crazy. And to think he was actually savouring the memory of his escapade. He felt like laughing aloud, like jumping out of bed and hollering out of the window, 'You fucking arsehole! You fucking Pandu Havaldaar! You wanted five hundred bucks you fucking got it!' It was a great feeling to have cocked a snook at the law and got away with it too.

Across the road from outside his window, he could see the neon sign turning from yellow to red to green, then going dead for a moment before flashing on again, blue.

HOTEL HERITAGE
We take good care of you . . .

From behind the sign, a bird rose irritably every time the sign came on, its sleep probably disturbed by the changing colours. A pigeon. It flapped its wings, hovered in midair for a few seconds and then settled down to try and sleep once more.

There was nothing to it. He must rest. Don't think . . . try and sleep. But that seemed impossible. He could have been in Dubby's bed just now . . . Now *that* was a thought could bear some dwelling on . . . She had wanted him to stay. Her parents had been away in Khandala even that first time. He didn't see the need to tell Cris about that night. There had never been another . . .

On that occasion he'd been randy as hell. But when she undressed, the naked body of the woman he had flirted with so energetically all evening seemed suddenly ridiculous. She was a plump, fleshy woman, but her breasts were incongruously small. So – falsies. The absurd word was trapped in his head. Even as his body lusted, his mind was imprisoned by a comical turn of phrase: 'Like little bells on a cow . . .' It was downright mean, but he couldn't help those words, which kept flashing on and off in his brain, making him want to laugh. When it was over, he felt dyspeptic (he had been gulping down his drinks on that occasion too) and, as he sat sipping the cup of cold milk Dubby got him from the kitchen, he wondered if there was a word for his neurosis. Phraseophilia? Phlegmatomania? Words again. Always words that tripped him up.

But right now he felt anything but phlegmatic towards Dubby, or towards his memory of that evening. A throbbing insistence made him want to kick himself for not being with her tonight. In the dark room he got out of bed and stood by the window looking out at the vacant street – no cops, not a soul in sight – his exposed penis shining by the light of the neon sign which seemed to mock him. 'We take good care of you . . .' Lavishing all his care on those few taut inches of his self, he indulged in his memories of Dubby's tiny breasts, her soft kind body. There was no hurry. He had all night. Yet, soon enough, in that final moment when a tremendous spasm of longing surged through his body and he littered a few million spermatozoa of out the window like a blessing upon the city night, something peculiar happened. His lips uttered a name, not Dubby's, but another, which came out softly like an invocation, 'Crissy . . . ah, Cris . . .'

Only then was he able to sleep. But the darkness that subsumed his consciousness continued to flicker with the static of contradictions and conundrums he hadn't even begun to untangle yet.

Kanara Lunch Home

The next morning, Jingo slept through the trumpeting of elephants, the hungry growls of the big cats, the chittering of birds. The window of his bedroom overlooked a small courtyard and a high brick wall behind which, though he couldn't see it, lay the city zoo. For the rest of the day it would be manic horn-blowing and the non-stop rumble of traffic that invaded his room so he didn't resent being roused at dawn by the salutary cries of awakening birds and beasts. In fact, he rather savoured that bleary, comforting moment that seemed to leap out of his subconscious every morning – enveloping him in a primal embrace, as it were – before receding again like a wave that left behind the tangled, salty remembrance of dreams still stirring inside, as he turned, hugged his pillow over his ear and went back to sleep.

But today it was already bright when he opened his eyes. He had a hazy memory of heavy rain and thunder during the final hours of night. He got up and leaned out of the window. The ground was completely dry and the sky above so brilliant he couldn't bear to look at it for longer than the briefest instant. In that same instant, the crazy events of the previous night came rushing at him:

jagged fragments of a nightmare partially recalled. Over the wall the tall, verdant branches of ancient trees swayed gently against the backdrop of a still white sky. He'd had a late start already. Forgoing the half hour he usually spent mulling over the morning's newspaper, he went in to shower.

When he emerged with a towel round his waist, he first stopped to pull out the *Indian Express* from the mail shaft in the front door, where it had been thrust by the delivery boy. He couldn't resist glancing at snippets in the bottom corner of the front page reserved for just such eye-catching titbits: *'Dead' Man Comes to Life* ran the heading.

> At Lucknow's King George hospital, a man certified dead by the house doctor was shifted to the morgue. No relatives came to claim his body. Eight hours later, the alleged corpse began to stir, and sat up, creating panic among the morgue attendants, who fled the scene in terror. Presently, the man walked out of the morgue stark naked, and went back to the affiliated hospital that had certified him dead. Here, the doctor on duty cancelled the death certificate his colleague had earlier issued; the patient was re-admitted to the hospital for further treatment.

News items like these, reported blandly and without comment, could be hilarious, if not bizarre . . . Gurdeep hadn't been home in three nights. That wasn't so unusual. He and his political buddies were busy in Nehrunagar, a slum *bustee* he'd never even seen, in faraway Ambavali, trying to mobilize its residents to resist a mass demolition of their huts. Tough work. Sometimes Jingo wished he could throw in his lot with them, do something useful. But then, as Gurdeep didn't mind reminding him every time he came home after a late night out, he was just a 'petit-bourgeois running dog who liked to get high'. A lotus-eater. Of course, he couldn't have done what he did last night if he hadn't been so high. He was eager to tell Gurdeep about his fracas with the cop.

Half an hour later when he stepped into Kanara Lunch Home, it was as usual devoid of customers. The old man behind the cash counter was dozing. A folded Kannada newspaper was propped up in front of him against a jar of aniseed. A thin sliver of suspended spittle hung from one corner of his open mouth.

The boy slouching against the kitchen counter didn't come up with the welcoming steel tumbler. Instead, he just stood there in his shorts and vest, grinning, and mumbled something Jingo couldn't catch. He figured the boy had already announced his order for him – that's to say, the usual – and was merely looking to him for confirmation. He decided to rebuff this casualness.

'Oi, Shiv! *Idhar aa!*' he yelled. The boy approached him now, picking up a tumbler of water on the way.

'What do you have for me today?'

The boy, who was little more than a child, stared back at him, as though struck dumb by the senselessness of his question. The menu at Kanara Lunch Home, at least at breakfast, was invariable.

'Well?'

'That only . . . idli, meduwada, uttapa . . .'

The wadas here were rings of mouldy flour soggy with oil, and the uttapa generally came burnt. So idli sambar and chutney it was. The usual. What was all that fuss about then, Shivappa's quizzical eyes seemed to ask.

Jingo was wolfishly hungry, he realized, when his idlis arrived. And for once they were nice and warm . . . What happened last night was outlandish. It was simply out of character for him to get mixed up in sticky situations like that. How drunk must he have been to behave so recklessly?

By sudden association, a bloody image flashed in his mind: one side of a man's skull and a part of his face excavated, dug out. The expression on the face remained unperturbed. He probably didn't even have time to scream, or feel the lacerating pain. Cries of alarm, the horrified murmurs of visitors who had witnessed the accident, drew them to the bear's enclosure. Excitedly, almost boastfully, a man was relating how he had seen it all happen. The drunken fool had been trying to attract the animal's attention by creating all kinds of diversions, feints and silly squeaking noises with his mouth. The bear had ignored him completely. In exasperation, the drunkard had tossed his cap at the bear, still wanting to somehow engage him in play. But the bear disdained to even notice the cap. Then, foolishly, the man decided to climb in and retrieve it. He hadn't seen it coming: one powerful swipe of the beast's paw was all it took to kill the intruder in an instant.

They had been spending a lazy afternoon at the gardens, something he and Cris liked to do whenever she visited him. A pair of zoo attendants reached the enclosure just a few minutes after they did, quickly covering the body with a cleanly laundered sheet, then carrying it away on a stretcher. Two or three other uniformed attendants tried to shoo away the crowd that had gathered. Presently, an official arrived on the scene and declared the zoo closed for the day; watchmen began to blow their whistles early – it wasn't even five – to let visitors know it was time to leave. As they were escorted out, Cris and he, still in a state of shock, were haunted by images of the man's ghastly disfigurement, their disbelief at the body's matchwood flimsiness.

'How horrible,' Cris had muttered, 'to get so drunk and throw your life away like that . . .'

There was no connection, really. He might have been a bit pissed last night, but it was no bear's cage he had entered unwittingly. Had he gone along to the cop station anything could have happened, of course. But there was no point in getting jittery about it now. That cop, who had certainly been more pissed than he, would be sleeping it off this morning.

'Kaaphi?' the boy asked, as he cleared the dishes.

Once he had sipped the strong hot brew, Jingo's head cleared a bit. He started to make mental notes for the tasks he should get on with during the day. First on his list was the cheque he must collect. He had handed over eighteen completed interviews to the agency five days ago. They should have been vetted by now, the data sent on for tabulation and his invoice forwarded to Accounts for clearance. If he could get there before noon, he might be able to pick up the cheque and perhaps a fresh job order as well.

No guarantee, of course, that there'd be more work waiting for him. But it was likely. In recent months, a steady flow of campaigns had kept coming in from the ad agencies, each requiring extensive surveys, and Mrs Hingorani, the woman in charge of farming out work to freelancers, seemed to like him. There were relatively few English-speaking boys who opted for this kind of work. Her other fieldworkers were mostly young college girls out to make some pocket money. After three or four campaigns at most, they dropped out, or were unceremoniously turned away if caught fudging answers. Jingo, on the other hand, accepted everything he was offered without quibbling and completed it conscientiously. In a good month, his earnings were just enough to pay for his share of overheads on the flat and his food bills at Kanara Lunch Home.

What he liked most was that he could do this job in his own time, often working no more than three or four hours in a day, no more than three or four days a week. Sometimes, of course, there was an 'urgent' assignment – he had to deliver on time, or be counted out. Then he would be tramping the streets all day, interviewing dozens of people until all his pencil stubs were blunt and his fingers ached as much as his feet.

And then he liked the work because it was always full of surprises and stories. He was used to having the door slammed in his face by people who were suspicious of strangers. There were others who didn't permit him to cross the threshold of their home and answered his questions brusquely at the doorstep. That was uncomfortable, for he'd have to prop his sheaf of proformas against one arm as he marked it with the other. Still others who'd first ask what was in it for them. If there was a free sample from the client, it usually helped to break the ice. But, reluctant respondents apart, by and large, Jingo found that most people were more than willing to answer questions simply for the pleasure of having someone to talk to.

He found it quite amazing – bored housewives, old men and women, new brides, mothers with whole broods of children to feed and tend to and sometimes an ailing parent or in-law in the back room as well – so many people in the city who were lonely even in the midst of numerical profusion and multiple ties of belonging. Given half a chance, they readily welcomed the random researcher as though they'd been longing for just such an occasion to unburden themselves, to reveal to him some private detail of their lives, even something so inconsequential as the name of their favourite toilet soap.

Why, only last week at the flat of a Gujarati joint-family in a housing cooperative, the husband and children were out. The woman of the house, dressed in a glossy, sequinned sari, was obviously getting ready to go out herself. She agreed to answer his questions provided it didn't take too long.

Jingo soon discovered she meant what she'd said about being rushed for time. After every casually tossed-away answer, she'd excuse herself and go inside, presumably to the dressing table of her bedroom to put the finishing touches to her make-up.

An old woman, slouching on the sofa of the living room, remained glumly self-absorbed so long as the younger woman was within earshot. But every time she made an exit from the room, she leaned towards Jingo and whispered with a tense impetuousity.

'That's the *bahuraani* of the house,' she said. It took Jingo a moment to realize she intended sarcasm in her use of the word; but the level of her voice left little doubt as to the confidential nature of her urgent, parenthetical insertions.

'What will you find out talking to her? Look, does she have time to sit here with you even for a minute? Very busy, oh very busy . . .'

The younger woman emerged for a moment, picked up her handbag which was lying outside and went back in. While she was in the room, the old woman once again assumed her slouch of disinterest. But as soon as they were alone, her eyes narrowed and flashed animatedly at Jingo.

'Where she goes, what she does, nobody knows. Whole world's concerns are hers . . . But cooking? I do it. Provisions? I have to make sure everything's in stock. What does she know about what detergent or scouring powder we use? *Hahn*, ask her about beauty aids – face powder, face cream, lipstick, she'll tell you. In all that she is number one. But to pick up her own teacup and rinse it out after drinking from it is too much work for her. No time. All she knows is to paint her face and go strutting about town . . .'

Amazingly, an old man in a crumpled pyjama-suit was hiding in the passage behind the curtain, listening. He had a sharply hooked nose and was glowering at the old woman. Perhaps he didn't want to show himself to Jingo. For one moment she turned her head and glanced at him. Angrily, he raised a tyrannical index finger to his lips. But the old woman looked away, ignoring the admonition. Meanwhile, the *bahu* breezed in. Mascara and lip gloss highlit her face, the heady bouquet of a strong perfume filled the room.

'Sorry, I'm really late. I have to go now,' she said, slipping into her shoes at the door. 'Anything else you want to know, please ask her – my mother-in-law knows everything.' Jingo wondered if she too had intended sarcasm in her parting line. Her heels made an awful clatter as she hurried out without bothering to shut the door.

The old man could barely walk or even stand upright. He shuffled into the room, and reprimanded the old woman in Gujarati in a deep strong voice.

'*Tunay ketli vakhat kidhuch.* Don't bring up household matters in front of strangers!'

'Then who,' the old woman wailed bitterly, 'who else should I tell them to? Now in half an hour I'll have to go stand in the sun on the main road, waiting for the school bus to drop the children. You'll eat your lunch and start snoring.'

Then the old man turned to Jingo and addressed him in halting English.

'Don't listen her, she talks any nonsense. Whatever comes to her mouth she says. She's not—' and he tapped the temple region on his head to imply, all there. The capricious glint of anger in the old woman's eyes was snuffed out by this ultimate snub. She slouched back once more into her characteristic slump like a straw doll whose cervical splint had been detached, staring dully at the floor.

Who else should I talk to? The old woman's polemical cry, uttered in Gujarati, stayed with Jingo until many hours after.

In the course of his work he had begun to suspect that for the many millions who peopled this metropolis, it existed in effect as no more than an extension of the village they had abandoned, or fled from. The ties they maintained were usually only with people from the home country who had also migrated to the city; the marriages they pledged their sons or daughters into were strictly along caste and regional meridians; the antecedents of would-be in-laws were carefully unearthed and investigated by match-makers from the very village or small town in question. Even pastimes and outings in the city happened only within the small ambit of familiar, well-mapped routes. And the lives of the rich and prosperous were hardly more adventurous, though they followed their own quite distinct lines of movement. And yet the anonymity bestowed by the city on its inhabitants was its most precious gift. For those who lived and functioned within the unbreachable partitions of their past, as also for those who would escape them once and for all.

Sometimes Jingo wondered, had he been less fair-skinned and personable – if he were dark and ugly, with a hunchback, maybe, or a harelip – would the effusive candour of his interlocutors dry up? Probably not. More likely it had something to do with the rigid social structures within which people lived, which made them long to share their secrets with a total stranger. If the stranger was ugly or misshapen, a creature from beyond the pale, he might even evoke darker, more subterranean confessions.

In his early days of market research – during his first weeks in fact, when he had conceived of it as a part-time occupation that enabled him to afford his dates with Cristina – something happened to Jingo which was an adolescent's fantasy come true; though in terms of age he had already left adolescence far behind.

When he had explained his business, a middle-aged housewife let him into her one-room kitchen home. Though most such tenements in the building left their front entrances open to the common gallery, she shut hers as soon as he had sat down – he'd found it odd even at the time, because the room became immediately stuffy – and quietly slid the bolt. After answering most of his questions in a fidgety, nervous sort of way, she excused herself and went into her kitchen. She had been gone for quite a while when she emerged finally, holding a cup of tea in her hand.

He explained that he wasn't allowed to accept it. That was a rule with the agency he worked for. Preferably, not even a glass of water. But her face was tense. His explanation didn't seem to make any sense to her. Quietly, she repeated, as though speaking to a child, 'Your tea. It'll get cold.'

Well, what the hell, thought Jingo, I *have* been longing for a cup of hot tea. But when he had drained it, and stood up to go, the same distracted look of sadness returned to her eyes. She came forward and stood before him, not meeting his gaze. Her sari pallu had slid off her shoulder. Then, one by one, she released the three hooks on the front of her blouse.

A pair of large, luscious breasts heaved a few inches away from his face. Jingo noticed that her smooth tanned skin was covered with a fine down of hair. The odour of perspiration was overpowering and unlike any he had ever smelt before. She took hold of his hands and placed them, one on each breast, still not looking into his eyes. It took him a moment to believe this was really happening. Then he began to caress her breasts and knead them gently, for that was clearly what she was wordlessly asking him to do. He wanted to do more – embrace her, kiss her lips, bend forward and suck her breasts . . . but she wouldn't let him. She held on to his forearms with an unnatural fury, her nails biting into his flesh, just allowing his hands enough leeway to massage her breasts. When he tried to bring his lips into contact with her face she turned away sharply, as though he were the fount of some deadly contamination. Her breath came out in muted gasps now, her grip on one of his wrists was slackening. He released his hand and gently caressed her smooth, rounded waist. But she reacted as though she had been stung by a live electrode and, with great force, knocked his hand away. In the same instant she stepped back and turning her back on him, quickly buttoned herself up again.

'Now go. Please go,' she said. 'Please. Never come back.' He turned reluctantly, lingering still. He wanted to say goodbye, hold her once more, ask her why it had to be like that. But she repeated: 'Go. If you ever come back here, I will have to kill myself.' He left without saying another word.

What was her sense of horror about, he wondered afterwards. Guilt? A desperate, annihilating shame? A fear of the consequences, should she be found out? Or the sheer terror of holding a lighted taper so insanely close to the powder-keg of pent-up desire?

Jingo chuckled inwardly. *Adventures of a Market Researcher*. Title for a steamy X-rated flick starring the irrepressible Jingo Moos. But no, he was no longer looking for adventures of that sort. Even on that giddy occasion, while descending the roughly hewn concrete stairs of that lonely woman's chawl, he had thought appreciatively of Cris. How different she was from any other woman he had ever known . . .

The fierceness of a sexual attraction freely confessed to was what brought them together at first. He was taken aback to meet a girl so utterly ingenuous about love. In the first flush of freedom straight after high school, they had unlocked in each other a gluttonous appetite for self-discovery. Coyness and a false modesty were the normal language of courtship among the young people at college. In Cris he found a girl who was totally guileless about admitting to her desires, about taking her pleasure as much as about giving it. He could hardly believe his own good fortune.

At first, his conscience reproached him: do you care for her at all, or are you only using her to satisfy your baser needs? Soon enough, the question became absurdly irrelevant. They had both grown so passionately involved, so intricately enmeshed in each other's lives, there was no looking back.

Once lecture hours were through, the large stone buildings turned somnolent. Only a handful of students hung about in the canteen, or outside it, but mostly the college premises were deserted.

Cris and Jingo retired to one of several private nooks they had discovered – the choir loft in the chapel; the abandoned attic of the old astronomy department where two rusty tripods stood on which once swivelled, presumably, powerful telescopes; sometimes they would even make their way back to the high-ceilinged lecture halls where only a short while ago they had sat listening to their professors drone on, preferably choosing a classroom at the far end of the long wooden corridor so that approaching footsteps could be heard well in advance. There was always the risk that some prowling peon or lonely Jesuit might peep in, or pass through. But, with the decoy of a textbook open in front of them on a desk, they guarded against unexpected intrusions. Usually, though, they remained undisturbed for hours, exploring their voracious love with a studious diligence, until satiation or dusk set in.

He didn't know at the time that while Cris was too honest to deny her desires, she had to continuously grapple with an overwhelming sense of guilt. Her Roman Catholic upbringing was deeply ingrained – the belief that sex before marriage was a cardinal sin, that there was something dirty about it anyway, except when used for procreation, and that even marriage with a non-Christian was unadvisable. Later she told him that every Sunday before mass she would confess her sins and seek absolution. But that never helped to douse her desperate love. She wanted him terribly. To possess him, to own him. She was ready to fight for him. Any woman who breathed the faintest whiff of interest in his direction became at once her inveterate enemy. As far as she was concerned he *was* her man, and if ever other male friends were mentioned, it was only in retaliation – 'to make you jealous, to make you want me even more . . .'

Only much later, when their relationship was already crumbling, Jingo came to realize that her passion for self-discovery had drawn her into areas of intimacy with others of which he'd had no inkling at the time. This did not anger him so much as sadden him, for he sensed that beneath what he secretly admired as bold overtures into outer regions of her sexuality and self lay a terrible self-contempt which she was acting out. She debased herself by these acts because she despised herself. And she despised herself that much more for having actually undergone the humiliation of enacting them. It was a bizarre logic that compelled her to live up to the foul-mouthed abuse of her parents.

*

Jingo had never really thought of this market research thing as a viable career.

Nor was he much impressed by the pseudo-serious jargon it was cloaked in, which he encountered during orientation and briefings – 'monitoring brand awareness', 'gauging corporate image', 'designing indices for refining product sensitivity'. The actual data he collected was piffle, he knew, later to be hyper-analysed by those pundits in their cabins and applied to the arcane purposes of market manipulation.

Was there a value attached to the kind of work one did? Was it measured by how much one was paid for doing it? Cristina often worried that the kind of freelance pickings he earned would never give them the stability they needed to be able to marry and have children. Admittedly, his income was pitifully small. And yet, he considered himself fortunate, even privileged, to be thus employed.

The men and women at the party last night, almost everyone of them was earning a salary worth tens of times the amount Jingo was paid for doing his market research. But what did they do for it? Client-servicing in ad agencies? Writing eulogies of lyrical praise for some vastly overpriced product in the hope of annihilating the competition? Striving to meet targets set by their managers for flogging a certain number of computers, air-conditioners, or cartons of cigarettes? And then there was the glamorous set – the models who walked the ramp at fashion shows, or fought off one another to corner a press campaign. At Dubby's last night, a debutante Bollywood starlet made a brief appearance. Only after she had left did someone tell him her name, but he'd noticed the buzz of excitement her presence stirred up.

Everywhere, everyone was striving to maximize profit, to live with flourish, stylishly. Was something wrong with him for not being fascinated by the idea of driving his own car, shopping at expensive malls, or throwing lavish parties like Dubby did? Or even planning for a family? Perhaps there was. He would have been more than willing to marry Cristina. Certainly, if that's what she wanted. But kids? Why, they were practically no more than kids themselves!

One thing he knew for sure, though: he loved the city. He loved his work that had allowed him to know it so intimately. In the course of a normal working day, he'd meet people of all ages and classes, from all walks of life, as if just by chance.

Since he moved around a great deal, there was hardly any part of the city he was unfamiliar with. But just when he had begun to believe that was true, he would turn a corner in search of an address and find himself in an unbelievably quiet, soporific street among rows of old houses that stood as if in a time warp, where nothing seemed to have changed in ages, even though only a minute's walk away was a teeming, frenetic city street – or a small market, cheek by jowl with a fish bazaar, that specialized in selling only streamers, bunting, paper masks, whistles and packets of balloons. Some of these places were imbued with a dream-like quality: the auto mill in Sion, where old cars were disembowelled and their parts extracted and packaged for recycling; or the glass works in Kurla – an open field strewn with heaps of broken glass where women workers squatted among the glittering shards, sorting them by colour and thickness with their bare hands.

Most fascinating of all were those little 'villages' that co-existed within the heart of the city: small, rustic communities of people living in self-enclosed isolation, in a maze of narrow, interconnected lanes. Here, hens, pigs and geese roamed freely, and women drew water from a common well. Elderly men or women slouched on stone benches outside their ancient, tiled-roof cottages, engaged in silent dialogue with themselves. Cristina's home, where she had grown up, was part of just such a village. But that was on the outskirts of the city, in faraway Malad, where one might expect to find such places.

It wasn't just being surprised by rare sights that lent an epiphanic dimension to Jingo's work. The incredibly complex array of human relationships he encountered was even more amazing.

An old couple at a middle-class housing society at Chakala was in a terrible flutter when he rang the bell and introduced himself. It was nearing six in the evening, and they seemed to be hurrying out. Profusely apologizing, they made him promise to return earlier the next afternoon.

When they met again the following day, the husband explained: their son had grown up now. Every evening when he and his wife returned from the office, they didn't want to see the old man and his wife around the flat.

'It's an arrangement we have, you see,' lisped the old father, many of whose teeth were missing. 'In the morning they leave by eight. Till they go, we try not to disturb them. Morning-time, going to office, always a terrible rush.'

The old woman beside him sat expressionless. Not that her husband was complaining. Rather, he seemed to be apologizing for the strangeness of this 'arrangement', even justifying it.

'And before six, we have to be out of the house. That's why we were in such a hurry yesterday. Let them come back, relax, have their dinner. It's okay,' he said. 'We sit on a bench in the municipal park all evening, and watch the children play. What else we have to do? They have their dinner early and shut themselves in the bedroom. After nine, they don't mind if we come back quietly and sleep in the hall. But before they wake up, we have to clear up our bedding and sit quietly in the storeroom. What to do, they have grown up now. They want their privacy.'

His wife, whose grey, straggly hair barely covered her scalp, spoke up for the first time. 'He has told us many times,' she said with great bitterness in her voice, 'if you don't like this arrangement you can go. I'll throw you and your things out myself!'

'No, no,' the old man hastened to say, shaking his head. 'He will never do that. He's our boy, after all. He'll never—'

'Our boy, yes,' his wife repeated. 'But that she-cobra! He's completely under her spell. And besides it's your flat – they keep forgetting!'

'Yes, yes,' mumbled the old man. 'In fact, he has even bought a new TV set for their bedroom. Now he lets us watch this one,' he said, indicating the large, old set in the living room where they were seated. 'Only in day time, of course. On Sundays, when they are home throughout the day . . .' He shrugged. 'We have to miss our favourite programmes, but I always tell my wife – after working so hard the whole week they deserve some peace, don't they? So we pack a little tiffin, a flask of tea and spend whole day in the park . . .'

Jingo had come across many strange couples, even stranger arrangements. A woman who was running a brothel in the back room of her own flat; her husband was both procurer and pimp. A woman whose husband had smashed the skull of her infant child against a wall in a fit of jealous rage, believing she was having an affair with a neighbour; he was serving a four-year sentence of rigorous imprisonment. Now alone, she folded and pasted down brown paper into bags of different sizes and sold them to the local grocery. She was counting the days left to her husband's release; she wanted him back.

Then, one afternoon, some weeks ago, he had knocked at the door of a flat in an upmarket area. It was opened ever so slightly by a bare-chested man, perhaps in his fifties. The gap in the door widened, and he saw an opulent paunch overhanging a gaudy, hurriedly wrapped loongi. Jingo realized immediately that he had interrupted something. For in the room behind, he could see a dark naked boy reclining against a stack of pillows; no more than eleven or twelve, even without his clothes on he looked like he had been picked up in the street. The boy was engrossed in a Hindi film that was playing on TV. The man gave him a sickly smile and suggested politely, 'I'm a little busy now. Why don't you come back later? Then we'll talk . . .'

When he had completed what seemed like enough work for a day, Jingo sometimes returned to places that had interested him, to explore them again by dusk. Sometimes he visited the government-licensed country liquor bars wedged into so many inconspicuous corners of these streets. Here, in a small, overcrowded basement or under a stairway, he'd share a Formica-topped table with other customers, a glass of narangi and soda in front of him. Sometimes there was standing room only.

Here, too, he'd met and engaged in conversation with an astonishing variety of characters. By characters he meant, of course, people – workmen, loafers, drunkards, bullies, wimps, spendthrifts, sponges, impatient people who were quick to anger and others willing to submit to any amount of boredom or humiliation if it bought them a drink – each one of them so different and unique they could well have stepped out of a storybook. A storybook that was being plotted and annotated in his head, or so he hoped.

When he had had quite enough to drink, he took his evening meal at a wayside cafe. Often, this was not the sort of place he could have taken Cristina to; even if she herself had no objection to eating there. Sometimes, even if he could afford slightly better-appointed places, he still preferred to eat at these hole-in-the-wall kitchens where the food was simple and basic, and there was no menu to choose from. He liked sitting on a hard bench at a long wooden table eating roti, masala gravy and raw onion with people whose hunger made them relish every morsel they took. He was drawn to the poor, the colourful, the smelly, the outrageous, the earthy. The nature of his work brought him into constant touch with all of these and more, and, for that reason, gave him a kind of high.

It could be that he lacked ambition. The pursuit of wealth, for its own sake, had always seemed to him strangely perverse. Why should anyone work more than absolutely necessary to meet the needs of survival? People were enamoured of the things money could buy, but they never seemed to calculate the 'hidden costs' (to use a bit of financial jargon) of having to work for it. And even if one acquired wealth and all those artefacts it could purchase, would it be possible to enjoy these without raising walls that excluded the reality of life around? Jingo loved using public transport, that is, travelling by bus or train.

Even to imagine driving about in a car gave him a strange feeling of exclusion.

Perhaps work, any kind of work, was its own reward. That's what people said. But often Jingo wondered if there could be any real truth in this. Is it in the nature of man to work, to drudge until his life is finally snuffed out? To labour without questioning – does happiness lie in a simple acquiescence to some such law of the Universe? Are the beaver, the dromedary and the mule the highest of God's creations? Or at least the most content? In that case, the people upon whom it fell to do the really hard work – like cutting stone in quarries, or lowering themselves down manholes to clean city sewers – were indeed the blessed of the earth.

Of course, he knew he'd never have been able to survive in the way he had been carrying on if Gurdeep's father had not allowed his son the use of a spare company flat, and if Gurdeep had not so generously permitted him to stay there without charging him rent.

Nor would he have been able to manage if his own folks' pecuniary position had been more unstable. As the only son of retired parents he would have been expected to provide for them. Thankfully, they always refused to accept any money from him. Instead, when he visited them, his mother usually made a point of quietly slipping Jingo a couple of hundreds when his father wasn't looking.

Even as a young boy, Jingo was keenly aware of his voracious curiosity about the lives of other people. It was this very impulse that had lead him to loiter after dark on the bridge at Bombay Central, gazing into lit windows along the long squat tenement blocks of Dalal Estate, often with an intransigent hard-on. There was nothing much to see, certainly nothing explicitly salacious. A housewife unravelling her sari, then standing by the window in her blouse and petticoat as she neatly folded it, and put it away. A middle-aged man knotting the string on his striped pyjamas. Once, an obese old woman in a muslin sudrah and long drawers, bent double by the weight of her enormous dugs, saying her *kushti* prayers to the last rays of the dying sun that illumined her gloomy kitchen.

Even a tableau of inanimate objects – dining table with chairs around it, a bouquet of artificial flowers in a vase, a radio, an electric toaster, washing drying on a line, scenes of domestic strife and desolation – such brief images filled the youthful Jingo with a surge of excitement whose meaning he had never been able to discover. It was an innocuous enough pastime. But in it lurked, on the fringes of his mind, the terrifyingly possibility of an intense, unnameable pleasure. He knew it from a constriction in his throat, a dryness in his mouth; he was waiting for something to happen. What was it? The unexpected caress of a stranger in the dark, a yell of uninhibited joy, a spectacular burst of fireworks lighting up the night sky? But that elusive something never came to pass.

At last, when it was time to go home, he'd walk back and stand in the great shadows of the abandoned Dunlop Tyres warehouse near his home, as though he had merely stopped to take a pee in the dark – it was a spot frequently used for that purpose by passers-by, the shrubs growing against the godown wall reeked with the strong stench of ammonia – while in fact all he would do was release his erect member from its prison of constrictive clothing.

Awed by its hugeness, he'd wonder about the strange

emotions of yearning that heaved within him. He didn't know yet, at that age, how to intensify those feelings to a point of exultation. He hadn't yet discovered – and perhaps some fear of the unknown kept him from experimenting – a simple technique of sustained agitation that would have taken him to quite extraordinary heights of pleasure and release. So he merely aired his penis to the humid night air. Then, embarrassed that passers-by might notice how long he was taking over a pee, he let it shrink once more, tucked it away in his pants and went home. That aforementioned technique, though, he would discover by chance later and perfect in his years at high school, under the scrupulous instruction of a certain Hippo Gorimar.

'More kaaphi?'

Just one more, then he'd be off. The boy-waiter cleared the cup he had already drained, conveyed the order for the coffee to his pal behind the kitchen counter and ferried it across double quick. As he placed it on the table in front of Jingo, he couldn't resist asking, 'What's up, Pehelwanji? Headache?' Jingo found it easier to nod assent. The boy left him alone after that.

The boys at Kanara called him *pehelwan* or wrestler in deference to his superior height and heft. But he was aware of certain ironic and erotic undertones underpinning the use of that title. For the boys often suggested playfully that the thing to do on a free evening would be to play *koosti* or *kabaddi* – don their G-strings and go wrestle in the sands of the Shivaji Park beach. The idea of rolling naked in the sand grappling with those boys amused him no end, though he had never seriously considered accepting the offer.

As he readied himself to leave, he was nagged by a certain unease, a sense of evasion. All that morning's reminiscing about market research hadn't quite served to deflect it. He had been deliberately trying to postpone any conscious consideration of his most recent adventure in market research: the fantastic coincidence of his meeting with Hoshidar's mother on a rainy afternoon not so long ago.

It had been bothering him. For days he had thought of nothing else. Gradually, the details of his own dealings with Hippo, their joint escapades and adventures, had come back to him. Some day, he'd have to go back and report to Jilla Gorimar. She was waiting for him. What would he say? That he had failed to locate her son's whereabouts? Would she be able to face her disappointment? Would he?

But there was something else, too, about their meeting that had continued to bother Jingo. What was it? Hadn't quite been able to put his finger on it . . . But of course! He had it now. It was the matter of Hoshi's age. The old woman must definitely have got her dates mixed up. Didn't she tell him Hoshi was in her stomach when the big boom happened? But Jingo had come across the news article about the Great Dock Explosion again, and checked the date: 1944. That would make Hoshi a whole eleven or twelve years older than him. He *had* looked quite a lot older than the rest of the class. But by so many years? He felt lighter for having identified the one incongruous detail in Jillamai's story that had been bothering him.

Jingo got up to leave. The proprietor at the cash counter roused himself as Shiv rattled off a list of items consumed by Jingo, making notes in a tattered old copy-book where he kept track of how much credit he was giving his regular customers. Jingo thanked him and left. When he had stepped out of the eating-house, he turned his head and saw Shiv still gazing after him.

He waved. The boy smiled gratefully and waved back.

*

When he first came to the city, Shivappa was only twelve.

One evening he told his mother he was going out to play with the other children on the village common. She stared at him suspiciously. Then she asked him to buy her two litres of kerosene first. 'After, we'll see about your playing,' she added. 'You should be working, earning your keep. Instead, all you think of all day is play.'

A ramshackle one-storey building in the village used to serve as the village school. Shivappa used to look forward to classes. But the school had been shut for six months now, there was no teacher.

He knew of course that when he came back with the kerosene she would find some other work for him to do. If not threshing the *bajra*, then grinding it in the big stone mortar; if not sweeping the house, then plastering the floor of the verandah with fresh cowdung. There was always work, but it was not so much the work he minded.

Just a year ago, his own mother had died. His father married again. Now his stepmother not only made him work all day, she also made up stories. Of disobedience and carelessness, of rudeness and answering back. Why she needed to do that, he didn't understand. It gave her pleasure to tell these stories to his father when he came home tired from the big tanning factory where he had recently found employment, and then watch him beat his son black and blue. It was a daily spectacle, and now his father had become a willing partner in its enactment. No sooner had he had his evening meal, he would ask for a report on his day's behaviour, and then the beating would start.

It was time to move on, Shivappa knew it in his bones. His stepmother was pregnant, and he knew that now his father wouldn't have much time for him anyway. The four rupees she gave him to buy kerosene with was all the money he had in his pocket when he ran away from home. He actually ran, sprinting the best part of a mile until he reached the highway, where he hitched a ride on a lorry to the closest railway station, called Puttur.

While he was riding in the lorry he saw from a distance the fast-approaching darkness and the tanning factory where he knew his father worked. He must be on his way home now, cutting across the mucky fields on his bicycle. Shivappa left the plastic jerrycan his mother had given him for kerosene with the lorry driver as payment for the ride.

At the station he was told there were no direct trains to Bombay. For that he would have to change at Hubli. So he caught the last train to Hubli, climbed onto a vacant luggage rack and lay down.

Now everything that Shivappa knew about Bombay and about travelling ticketless on trains he had heard from Shafi. Shafi had been about the same age as him when he ran away from Hallengdi, which was what their village was called. But six years later, only a few months ago, Shafi had returned to Hallengdi. He had saved enough money to buy presents for every member of his family . . . That was the only way left for him now to prove to his father that he was not so ungrateful as he made him out to be. Perhaps, one day, he too would be able to return home, laden with gifts . . . Rocking to the movement of the train, dreaming of that day of his vindication, Shivappa fell fast asleep.

It was to be his last undisturbed sleep for several days. When the big passenger train from Hubli reached Bombay nearly twenty hours later, he remembered to be alert to Shafi's counsel on how to evade the ticket checkers and the railway police. He climbed off the train on the other side, not where it had stopped at a platform but onto the parallel rows of tracks. He followed the tracks in the direction from which the train had come, until he was no longer inside the walls of the station. He could see the street now, hundreds of cars and monstrously tall buildings. Presently he found a gap in the bars of the railing that cordoned off the tracks and squeezed himself out into the raucous hubbub of a busy sidewalk in the centre of the city he had heard so much about.

He discovered that for the two rupees and small change he had left with him he could only buy a big loaf of soft bread and two fried potato vadas. After he had eaten those, for four days he ate nothing else, and barely slept. Shafi had warned the village boys about the cops of Bombay, too. If they found you sleeping in the streets they'd strip you of every last paisa you had in your pocket. And if you had nothing, then it was the Remand Home for you. That was another story. But most certainly, a fearful one.

Shivappa had been fortunate. The cops didn't nab him and, on his fifth day after reaching the city, he met an older boy who belonged to a village only twelve miles north of his own, and spoke his language, the Konkani of South Kanara. Prasad – that was the boy's name – had been in Bombay for the last two years and was a rag-picker by profession. Prasad, who was himself only about fifteen, inducted him into the trade. He showed him those stretches of the city and outside it – various landfills, garbage dumps – where you could find good pickings; he showed him the retailers' shops in Kamathipura and pointed out the ones which could not be trusted to weigh a fair measure, or pay a fair price; he gave him an idea of how much he could expect to be paid per kilo of plastic, paper or metal, and even found him an old burlap sack in which to collect his 'booty'.

Prasad would start the day's work at 5 a.m., while most of the city was still asleep, and Shivappa would tag along. By eleven thirty or noon, they would find a place to start sorting and then head towards Kamathipura to sell their collection of scrap and claim their earnings.

Often, when the morning's search hadn't yielded enough, they would catch a local train and head for the Malvani dump on Gorai Road. There was always plenty of scrap to be found here, but it was dirty work to dig your way through a mountain of rotting garbage. On one occasion, Shiv chanced upon a light bundle wrapped in a soiled, damp newspaper. He tore it open eagerly, wondering if this was going to be his lucky day, but there were layers under layers of newspaper. He was amazed by the contents of the package when they were finally revealed. For a few moments he thought it was a child's clay doll, until Prasad disabused him. It was a foetus. Clearly so. A girl. Pale blue, smeared with the black stains of dried blood, but well-formed. Handling that unreal object, Shiv felt strange and a little afraid. He wondered for the first time what kind of place he had come to.

After less than a week of this routine, just when Shivappa felt he was beginning to learn the ropes, and also grasp the subtler points of the older boy's strategies for survival, Prasad disappeared. One morning, when Shivappa woke up, he was nowhere to be found.

For days after that, Shivappa roamed their usual haunts keeping one eye peeled for choice bits of scrap, the other, wistfully, for Prasad. But he knew he had gone. On his last night with Shivappa though, Prasad had passed on some information that would prove very useful to him in the days to come. He had told him of a young man called Gopal who hailed from their home state, and who had started out in Bombay as a ragpicker, just like them. But then he had moved up in life.

'Now he has a regular job. Works as a cook in a "hotel" in Byculla, has been for many years. If you ever want a job, go meet him. Tell him Prasad sent you. He'll help.'

'Why don't you?' asked Shivappa. 'Don't want a steady job? Regular meals instead of sorting trash . . .'

'Not for me,' replied Prasad dismissively. 'I like my freedom. Roam wherever I want to. Meet people. Sleep here one night, there the next. I like to be on the move. But you – for you it may be good. You may like it.'

'Why should he help me? This Gopal, you say he's . . .'

'Just tell him Prasad sent you. He owes me.'

'What did you do for him?'

'That's not your business.' By now Shivappa had learnt to recognize a certain edge in Prasad's voice that told him when to shut up. Prasad went on. 'Ah, but he won't give you a job for nothing. If they're paying you something over and above your two meals, he'll want a cut.'

'And if they're not?'

'Then . . .' Prasad gave a queer laugh. He made a gesture with his loosely rolled-up fist, as though he were shaking a bottle. 'Strange fellow, Gopal. Be careful of him. Real madcap.'

Shivappa didn't know quite what that gesture had meant, but he didn't want to ask. He sensed something disquieting in its meaning. So he just smiled, and nodded knowledgeably. In the morning, Shivappa woke early, as usual. But Prasad had risen even earlier and gone. The wander-bug must have bitten him, thought Shivappa. He missed his friend, the only friend he'd made in this city.

It was a whole six months before he took a train to Byculla and began to walk through its streets looking for a 'hotel' whose name Prasad had omitted to mention. He asked at every restaurant if they had a cook by the name of Gopal. Several did. But none of these Gopals knew a Prasad. At last, when he was about to give up the search, Shivappa came across a hole-in-the wall Udipi eating-house called Kanara Lunch Home.

The cubicle that served as kitchen was always smoky and dark.

Apart from the smoke, which the solitary exhaust fan was poorly equipped to dispel, the walls of the kitchen from ceiling to floor were coated with black grime and cobwebs, which formed an oily mixture of almost custardy consistency. There was hardly any room inside, even just for Shiv and Gopal to stand abreast. It was all taken up by the large storage tins containing rice, lentils and sugar, a gas burner and cylinder, two huge Primus stoves, sacks of onions and potatoes, innumerable pots, pans, skillets and glasses. Except for the few which were in daily use, the rest were filthy and rusting from not having been scoured in ages. At the back was a kind of scullery where dirty dishes were stacked.

The regular clients of Kanara Lunch Home came in batches at approximately fixed hours. At seven thirty in the morning, while the large kettle of tea was still brewing, came the daily-wage workmen – masons, plumbers, carpenters, painters, with their small cloth bags that contained their few tools – stopping by for a misal and a 'cutting' chai on their way to the Kabutar Khana opposite the Jain temple. Here, like the pigeons who flocked to the grain which the devout fed them, they would mill around until a client approached them and they were hired for the day. Not all of them, however, were lucky enough to find work every day.

Again, at lunch time a few dozen people came in for the Kanara thali, which was served with puris or rice, and the day's vegetable, along with a thin lentil soup and a small dollop of sour curd. It was the most inexpensive meal, though not the most wholesome, you'd be able to find anywhere in that area.

The next swell of business was between four and six in the afternoon, when Shivappa was kept busy ferrying orders for tea to neighbouring offices and shops. For the evening meal there were hardly ever any customers, except the odd bachelor or a bunch of drunks who had tanked up at Dagdu's country liquor still and came there to eat like hogs, chomping noisily and messing up the table, even spilling food all over the floor.

At night, the rolling shutter in the restaurant's front

was pulled down and padlocked, sometimes by the old man, more often by his son, who came there in the evenings to relieve his father and take away the cash receipts. Once that was shut, Gopal and Shiv heaped a few benches on top of tables and spread their bedding rolls on the floor space thus cleared, under the breeze of a ceiling fan. There was a back door leading out from the kitchen into a small courtyard behind, where they had the use of a latrine. There was a radio on a shelf in the wall, above the cash counter, which they were allowed to listen to. The rotary dial on the phone was kept locked. As though, Shiv remarked, they had anyone to make calls to.

By ten in the night, it was lights out at Kanara Lunch Home. The Boss didn't mind if they listened to the radio, but he was very strict about saving on electricity bills. Having been on his feet all day, Shivappa often fell asleep as soon as his head touched the rolled-up towel that was his pillow. Then Gopal turned off the radio and went to sleep himself. Sometimes both of them fell asleep curled up together, and the radio remained on. But the older boy usually woke up in the middle of the night with a start, to switch it off. He knew the Boss would be terribly annoyed if ever they were found asleep with the radio still on. Both boys made sure they were awake well before that awful clangour of the rolling shutter being thrust up shattered the early morning quiet.

At six, or latest by six thirty, Gopal would have the Primus lit and potatoes on the boil for sukka bhaaji. He knew the Boss felt pleased if he found them already at work. Shivappa kneaded the dough for the afternoon's puris, chopped up onions for the day's vegetable, or cleaned the rice. And if a customer walked in by chance, he'd step out of the kitchen and double as waiter. It was a long day for both of them.

Today, when Shivappa finished his afternoon tour of offices and shops in the vicinity, Lalu hailed him from the clearing outside the huts. Shiv still had two glasses of tea left in his wire-mesh glass-holder.

'Is it hot?' asked Lalu.

'Hot enough . . . Where's your mate?' asked Shivappa, holding the glass up to Lalu's mouth, as Lalu slurped up the tea thirstily.

'Asleep inside,' said Lalu. 'You know that big fair fellow, don't you, who eats at your hotel?'

'Who? Pehelwan?' Shivappa asked.

'Yes. Pehelwan baba,' Lalu confirmed. 'Did he come today?'

'In the morning,' replied Shivappa.

He returned the empty glass to its holder. There was some small change lying on a stone beside him. Lalu gestured to Shivappa with his head to help himself to it.

'If he comes again, tell him . . . No, never mind. I'll catch him myself . . .'

Why was the cripple asking after Pehelwan, Shivappa wondered. When he returned to Kanara Lunch Home, the Boss first counted the number of glasses he had brought back in the holder; then he counted the small heap of coins which Shivappa slapped onto the counter.

Evenings could be terribly gloomy at the Lunch Home, especially since the Boss didn't believe in turning on the lights – unless there were customers. Sometimes the dreariness began to weigh on the old man himself and, if he knew his son was due to arrive soon, he would leave some petty cash with Gopal and head for home. Now Gopal was in charge, until Janardhan arrived. But the boys found the place even duller with no bosses around. Sitting side by side at the last table in the darkening, vacant Lunch Home, they felt bored and tired. A melancholy film song was playing on the radio.

'Want to go see a movie?' asked Gopal idly.

'Are you dreaming it's Sunday?' asked Shivappa with indifference. Sunday was their half-day off.

'Nice fighting picture's come to Kismet,' said Gopal, wistfully. '*Zakhmi*. Saw the posters this morning on my way to market . . . If Janardhan permits, we could catch the night show.'

'Close early to see a movie?' said Shivappa, still unexcited by the plan. 'No chance! Better wait till Sunday.' But Gopal could not sit still. Putting one arm around Shivappa's neck, he began squeezing it, while pinching and jabbing the boy's ribs with his other hand. 'Okay, it's Sunday, then. *Pucca*.'

Presently, Janardhan walked in and switched on one light. Gopal went into the kitchen and began pottering around to look busy. Shivappa remained seated where he was.

Without Gopal's help, Shivappa might never have got the job at Kanara, he knew. When the old man had agreed to hire him, he sent him into the kitchen so Gopal could acquaint him with his duties. But before assigning him any work, Gopal asked the boy to sit down. Then, holding his face with both hands, he asked him, 'You'll be my friend, won't you?' And Shivappa had nodded.

From the very first night of sleeping beside each other in the shuttered Kanara Lunch Home, Gopal's hands had begun to explore the younger boy's body. For a few nights, Shivappa pretended to be in deep sleep. He even simulated a snore or two. But then one night, there had been no longer any question of pretending – he was betrayed by the stiffening of a muscle, which made Gopal sit up in delight. After that night, Shivappa, too, began to enjoy this pastime. There was little else they had by way of recreation. Once, Gopal had tried some rough stuff on him, which hurt. But now he didn't stand for any of that. If ever Gopal got into that overheated state, he knew exactly what to do. The right pressure at the precise point would have him moaning, 'Not so faast . . .' and end the nuisance in a jiffy.

*

Jingo had had quite a successful afternoon at the agency. Not only had he got his money, he had been able to persuade the accountant to issue it by cash voucher instead of the usual cheque. Moreover, he had secured a new lot of fifty proformas researching the prospects of a new toothpaste that was going to be launched in the market – a simple questionnaire that shouldn't take more than fifteen minutes apiece, with three weeks to complete the lot in.

Outside the station, where the vegetable and fruit market spilled onto the pavement, Jingo bought a dozen green bananas to take to the flat. If by some chance Gurdeep was in today, maybe they could go out for a drink together, thought Jingo, and after, a somewhat superior dinner than the usual Kanara slop. But no sooner than had he turned off the main road to head in the direction of his lane than he heard a voice hail him: 'Baba! Baba!'

He didn't know how he managed it, but somehow, manipulating himself with his one good leg, and the one arm that was only an elbow-length stump, Lalu could get around quite a bit on his wooden trolley.

'*Arrey*, Lalu! What're you doing here? Are you okay?'

'I'm okay. But that Chandu is lying on the mat groaning.'

'What happened?'

'Two cops came in the morning and took him to the station. They knocked him about a bit. To make him tell where you lived. Fortunately, it wasn't so bad. He really doesn't know exactly where you put up. So they believed him.'

'My God!' Jingo turned cold.

'I waited here to warn you. That cop is out to get your ass. When you pushed him, his head struck a stone. Had to take four stitches on his scalp. He's hopping mad.'

'I'll go see Chandu.'

'No need, just make yourself scarce – for a few weeks, few months – how long, I can't say. But they've decided to keep a watch out for you. Starting tonight. Just don't come anywhere near our place. Okay? Take care . . . Sir, I can never forget what you did for me.'

'What?'

'You stood up for me against that dog of a policeman. I won't forget.'

'Oh that,' said Jingo, throwing his hands up in embarrassment. 'Didn't know what I was doing . . . Anyway, thanks. You-all take care, too.'

For the second time in two days, Jingo followed a circuitous route to Winifred House. He was walking fast. He was frightened. Anyway, for all his well-meant gratitude, what could Lalu do to help him? There was a light on in the flat. He ran up the stairs and nearly embraced Gurdeep with joy at finding him in.

'Oof, man. I've got myself in some kind of crazy mess.' And he told him of the events of the previous night and the news Lalu had passed on to him just a few minutes ago. Gurdeep listened quietly, without saying a word. Then, contrary to Jingo's expectation of some word of approbation from him for having stood up to a bully, he abused him roundly.

'You fucking arsehole, who do you think you are? Do you know what you've done? You've assaulted a police officer! That's a very serious offence.'

'Yes, I know,' said Jingo, sheepishly. 'But I didn't know you were on the side of the cops.'

'If an attack is to be launched on the state apparatus, it has to be at the right time and place. A lot of planning is called for. You can't just knock down a cop in the street and expect me to applaud your revolutionary fervour!' He was a stocky, clean-shaven Sikh whose eyes grew bulbous whenever he was angry. Gurdeep was furious now and his eyes were practically bursting out of their sockets.

'Now this will take some sorting out,' he said. A moment later, though, his anger had subsided and he was lost in thought.

For a few long minutes, Jingo maintained an embarrassed silence. Then he said, 'I was thinking, maybe we can go out and get a drink. Some dinner. I've got some bread.'

'I have the best solution. Here's what you must do,' said Gurdeep. 'Just pack a few simple clothes in your haversack. Nothing fancy, mind, or you'll stick out like a sore thumb. Tomorrow I'm taking the 6 a.m. fast to Ambavali. You come along. I have a friend there who's working with us. He'll put you up in his shack. Nobody'll dream of looking for you there, in Nehrunagar.'

'But I don't want to be – don't want to feel like a fugitive . . . How will I do my work? I've just got a new assignment which has to be delivered in three weeks' time.'

'What? Oh, you mean your . . . Whereabouts do you have to be for that?'

'Starting address in Sion.'

'So that's perfect. You'll get a fast train to Sion from Mankhurd.'

'Which means I'll have to commute every day.'

'So? You've always wanted to find out how the other half lives.'

'Okay, fine. Done. Now how about that drink?'

'So what's this new assignment you've got, eh?'

'Oh, routine. There's a new toothpaste being launched. They want me to—'

'You see now why I call you a capitalist running dog? You're a minion of the toothpaste industry. And you're running from the cops!' It was an unexpected flourish of humour, coming as it did from Gurdeep, and eased the tension that had gripped Jingo. He laughed heartily and Gurdeep grinned. 'Okay,' he said. 'I'll go out and get something.' Jingo handed him a fifty-rupee note. 'But you start packing. We have to be up at five.'

'Five it is,' said Jingo. 'We'll sleep early. Always did want to see this Nehrunagar of yours.'

'It's not mine. Bloody anarchist!' That was Gurdeep's exit line. He slammed the front door behind him.

Half an hour later, they shared a nip of rum diluted with tepid tap water. Jingo wished Gurdeep had bought a quart instead of a nip, but Gurdeep reminded him they had to be up before five. Then they tore open two little plastic bags that contained mutton biryani and shared it.

The biryani was oily, full of chilli and spice that set their mouths on fire.

Slumming

With his stick, the railway policeman prodded a sleeping figure on the platform. A dishevelled old man sat up, startled; clumsily, he began to fold his threadbare sheet.

Dozens of people got off the train, among them Gurdeep and Jingo. They walked past the beggar, now wide awake, the policeman, who had strolled on languidly, the handful of commuters taking their morning tea at a refreshment stall, and others waiting for trains to take them to Mumbra and beyond.

Emerging from under the grimy stone portico of Ambavali Road station, Jingo and Gurdeep picked their way through a huddle of kiosks: a newspaper vendor, a florist, a milk-'n'-curd seller, numerous nameless others that were still shut. A low smog hung in the air. The sun was out but its heat had not yet become oppressive. Where the kiosks ended, hawkers had their wares spread out on the tabletops of large-wheeled carts; others with wicker baskets of vegetables and fruit were squatting on the uneven ground. A growing stream of pedestrians negotiated the narrow path through the impromptu street mall. Gurdeep would have liked to hurry on, but they were moving against the drift of commuters heading for the station.

It was only when they reached the open tarred road running parallel to the railway lines that the police van came into sight.

A jumble of chaotic thoughts coursed through Jingo's mind in that instant: will the nemesis of my folly pursue me to the end of the world? Wouldn't it be better to give myself up and take the punishment? With measured casualness, he made a slow about-face and started back in the direction they had just come from . . . It took Gurdeep a moment to realize that Jingo was no longer walking beside him. He looked around and stared in disbelief at the somnambulistic figure of his friend drifting slowly down the road back towards the station.

'Oi, Jingo!' he called out in surprise. Jingo had stopped behind the last kiosk, out of sight of the police van.

'What's up? Feeling sick or something?' asked Gurdeep, catching up with him quickly. Jingo's face was bathed in perspiration.

'Cops,' he whispered tiredly.

The monosyllable floated out of his lips like a soap bubble. Gurdeep didn't react immediately. But a moment later, he broke into a ridiculous chortling.

'*Those* cops? You think they've been hot on your trail from Byculla to Ambavali? Someone's surely tipped them off on the whereabouts of the dreaded gangster, Jingo Moos!'

'You don't think . . .?'

'They're probably here just to stand by and watch while the BMC's goons start ripping up the wretched homes of Nehrunagar. Just in case the residents pluck up enough courage to resist. I told you, we were expecting something of the sort. Nobody's interested in your drunken misdemeanours of the other night, Mr Moos.'

The saw-edged churning in Jingo's stomach ground to a sudden halt. A wave of relief flooded his body. He wanted to laugh aloud with Gurdeep at his own foolishness. But in the interests of self-esteem, he only mumbled crossly, 'Okay, okay. I'm not thinking straight, I know. Haven't slept enough . . . Couldn't we have taken the next train out? It's humiliating, you know, to be woken with a pitcher of cold water in your face.'

'Sorry, but you were dead to the world . . . Floating on cloud nine of some hashed-out Xanadu, I expect. Anyway, you see now why it was important to get here early?'

They'd had a hunch there might be trouble today, Gurdeep explained. Just two mornings ago, the 'R' Ward Officer had issued a strict warning that all first shift workers must report for duty on time or face penalties. Their contact man in the municipal Ward office, a garbage-collection worker himself, found this rather unusual since no one ever bothered how easy they took it, or if they turned up for work at all. He communicated his suspicions to Thiru.

'One can't be sure, of course, but every block leader in the slum is on alert. These municipal *baboos* probably wouldn't dare to contravene the court's injunction. But one can never say . . . And now, to find the cops waiting . . .'

'So you-all run this place like an army intelligence outfit, eh?' said Jingo. 'Block leaders? Informers? Spy versus spy . . .' Even before the frivolous observation had tripped out of his mouth, he regretted it.

'For one thing, we don't run this place,' snapped

Gurdeep, coldly. 'For another, if you're planning to stay here, try not to be facetious . . . It'll be embarrassing as it is to explain to my friends the circumstances in which you happened to slug a cop.'

Jingo hitched his haversack higher up his shoulder and they proceeded to walk on in silence.

'You'll have plenty of time to catch up on sleep,' Gurdeep continued, in a more conciliatory tone of voice. 'Not much else you'll find out here to do . . . In the afternoon, if there's no trouble, I'll show you around. Once you've met Thiru and the others, and settled in.'

'Actually, I'd prefer to discover the place for myself.'

'Ah, the romance of the pathfinder . . . Mr Moos goes a-slummin'.'

While Mr Ahluwalia, the working-class hero, fights pitched battles with the powers-that-be! thought Jingo, but he kept it to himself.

Had it been sensible, Jingo wondered, to put himself so completely under Gurdeep's protection? How would this arrangement work if the average level of snobbery among these activists was anywhere close to Gurdeep's? Jingo could have moved to his parents' place instead. But that would have entailed other forms of nagging – and being in the heart of South Bombay, just a stone's throw away from Gamdevi police station. The actual threat of being hauled up by cops, however, now seemed suddenly remote. Still, he was better off taking his chances with Gurdeep's pals.

The level crossing was closed. They had to wait practically cheek-by-jowl with the police van which was parked one side of the wicket gate. Other vehicles were waiting, too, for the gate to open. In the distance, a train was approaching fast. A couple of youngsters decided to make a dash for it. The man in charge of operating the wicket gate yelled after them angrily,

'In a tearing hurry to die or what? Arseholes!' He was an elderly, red-faced man with a muffler wrapped round his head. He continued to mutter disgustedly to himself even after the boys had bounded across the tracks to safety.

Meanwhile, the cops in the van were enjoying their breakfast. One of them held out a plate of knobbly-brown pakoras to another seated across.

'*Arrey, ghey, ghey*. Don't be shy. Take one from my hand. Open your mouth . . .' The policeman who was being urged to eat was very young indeed, no more than a boy. He didn't want it, he was quite content with his glass of steaming tea.

'Feed him this banana also,' remarked another beefy policeman, breaking one from a bunch of plantains in his lap. 'Here . . .' He touched the banana to the boy-cop's lips. The boy turned red, and everyone else in the van who had been following this drama of seduction cracked up.

The train whooshed past, raising dust. The gates had opened now, half a dozen cars, three-wheelers and some cyclists overtook them as they crossed the tracks. The police van, however, remained parked.

Once on the other side, Gurdeep and Jingo took a detour off the tarred road. At the fork where they turned off, an old Koli fisherwoman was squatting, her scale-sodden wicker basket buzzing with flies. She was discarding fishheads and entrails, feeding a bunch of stray cats.

There were more stalls ahead, cubicles, roughly battened out of jungle wood with inexpertly painted signboards: 'Girish Tailor, Alterations'; 'Dhunvijay

Lottery Centre'; 'Laxmi Auto Garage'. All these were still shut, except the last, where a mechanic in overalls was disembowelling an upturned auto-rickshaw. A vegetable monger had just thrown open the shutters of his shed. Touching both pans of his weighing-scale piously, he joined his palms. Wisps of smoke from a pair of *agarbattis* impaled in a small purple brinjal curled upwards.

This was the last shop, at the very edge of the settlement.

It was like crossing into another world, a dull, discoloured realm where everything existed in shades of grey and dun. The very air seemed to grow stale and murky. For a moment, as they careened down the rocky slope into the low-lying slum, Jingo caught a glimpse of its vastness. The panorama of endless tin and plastic roofing filled him with awe. In the distance, beyond the smoggy haze, he could see hills.

The crudely built pathway that led into the maze-like interior was bounded on both sides by runnels of waste water that gave off an acrid sour-sweet stench. The path curled and ran between a dense thicket of huts, shanties, lean-tos, all manner of tentative shelters that abutted and spilled into one another, a veritable mangrove of intertwined living spaces leading deeper into the jungle of scrap.

An uncanny hush hung over the settlement. It had grown hotter now. Hard sunlight was diffused by clouds every few minutes. Hardly anyone was about except a few women and children and even they seemed preoccupied, staying mostly within the shaded spaces of their huts. The atmosphere seemed charged, but perhaps only to his own quickened imagination?

The path was not broad enough for the two of them to

walk abreast comfortably. At sharp corners he had to watch out for the jutting edges of rusted tin roofs. He felt ill at ease, as though conscious of trespassing on someone's private property. But no one stared, no one asked them what or who they were looking for, hardly anyone took notice of them at all. There was a sense of intimacy about this form of impoverished, huddled living, a sense of free access. Besides, Gurdeep was known here.

An infant was wailing loudly as his mother splashed him with water from a pail and scrubbed his rump. The puddle of bathwater meandered into the gutter by the side of the road.

'It was Thiru's idea,' Gurdeep now remarked, speaking to him in sidelong, punctuated bursts, 'to organize residents in area-wise blocks. A group chief for each block – most are women actually, since the men are usually out at work – a strategy for quickly mobilizing resistance, in the event of a surprise raid. The poor can be so easily cowed, unless they have a framework to fight from, you see.'

A young man with slicked-down hair, in the neat blue uniform of a janitor or office peon, hailed Gurdeep. Gurdeep waved back, but didn't slow down.

'Boss – one minute.'

'*Kya*, Kishan*bhai*? Some problem?' Gurdeep stopped to speak to him.

'That's just what I want to ask. Police van at *phaatuck* since seven in the morning. Saw it?' Gurdeep nodded. 'Some rumpus again today, then?'

'We just have to wait and see, Kishan. Court order's with us – judge has stated clearly, no *toad-phoad*. At least for now. Anyway, we-all are here the whole day. But what guarantee is there with those municipal devils? You go on to work, if you have to. We're here.'

'That's what I was wondering. Should I phone in and take an off? My Mrs and the little one will be alone.'

'What will you do even if you're here? The men they'll arrest right away, if there's any *tamasha*. And you'll simply lose a day's wages. But in front of the women these eunuchs turn weak-kneed, haven't you noticed? It's up to you really . . . Don't think there's any cause for worry.'

So word *had* spread that there was trouble brewing. It wasn't as if people weren't moving about just as they might on a normal morning, but everything seemed a little subdued to Jingo, deadpan. As though the residents were expecting the worst to happen – but then, the worst was just another of the routine hardships that they had grown accustomed to living with.

Kishan seemed relieved at not having to ring up his boss and beg the day off. He stooped and put his head in at the door of his hut to take leave of his family. Gurdeep and Jingo moved on.

They had been walking for about five minutes when they came to a sort of clearing where numerous alleyways met in a stony slush. At its centre was a dark green pond overgrown with weeds. On the other side of the stagnant pool stood the shack they were headed for.

'Do they know we're coming?' Jingo asked Gurdeep.

'I phoned Menezes last night, when I went out to pick up the grub. He should be here already,' replied Gurdeep.

'*Malcolm* Menezes?' asked Jingo, incredulous, though he already knew the answer. 'Our basketball coach?'

'Brother Malcolm,' nodded Gurdeep. 'Only now he's a brother in a much wider sense of the term.'

Jingo remembered a tall man with a high forehead striding determinedly through the wide, wooden-floored corridors of their old college building. Usually wrapped up in his thoughts and an oversized cassock, he was also sometimes seen in shorts, darting about the basketball court with a whistle between his lips, refereeing the engagement of two student teams. A few months after Jingo dropped out of college, he had heard to his great surprise that the ex-seminarian had followed suit, chucking in the study of theology to devote himself full-time to social activism.

The CPSDR (Committee for Protection of Slum-Dwellers' Rights) was an NGO that had been registered some time in the 1970s. It had lapsed into inactivity for some years until revived by Gurdeep and his friends in the mid-1980s. Vijay Thirumalai, one of the few educated residents of the slum, was now its general secretary. Nehrunagar itself had apparently been in existence for nearly fourteen years. The threat of demolition was relatively recent. Jingo was familiar with some of its history, which Gurdeep had related to him on numerous late nights over a quart of rum.

At first the demolition was mooted on account of some civic engineer's hare-brained scheme to build a massive flyover stretching from Mankhurd to Thane, which would also touch down in the area occupied by Nehrunagar. Of course, this gigantic bridge never got off the drawing board. But now, mysteriously, other departments of the municipality had been issuing more demolition notices on the hapless slum-dwellers for a spectacular variety of reasons. Such as that there was danger to them as their huts had encroached too close to the railway tracks; that pollution caused by effluent from the slum was poisoning the fish in the nearby creek; that complaints had been received by the police that the local populace had taken to spitefully hurling stones, garbage and even fissile bags of human excreta at passengers hanging out of passing trains.

Twice before, the demolition squads had acted on these alleged complaints, smashing a few huts and making off with whatever building materials and personal belongings they could grab. But the locals had fought back and turned away the marauders. Though officially deemed an 'illegal' slum, Nehrunagar had been in existence for too many years already for the municipality to simply raze the huts. What was more, the CPSDR had gained temporary respite for the slum-dwellers in the form of an injunction. They had convinced the magistrate that the reasons for the proposed demolition were confused and mala fide. No alternative site was being offered to relocate these slum-dwellers, many of whose names were on electoral rolls, whose families held ration cards, and some of whose children attended the Tamil- and English-medium primary schools in the area. A recent Supreme Court judgement calling for a stay on the wholesale demolition of slums, especially during the monsoon season, worked in favour of the CPSDR's petition. As it was the monsoon would be breaking over them any day now.

'I know these people. They have enough problems of their own as it is to want to throw stones at passing trains. It's just propaganda,' Gurdeep had claimed indignantly while chatting with Jingo one night.

'I saw that report in the papers,' Jingo had said, slightly diffident about contradicting Gurdeep in a matter so close to his heart.

'The media in this country is totally biased against the poor,' replied Gurdeep scornfully. 'Only fools blindly believe whatever they read in the press.'

'But there was even a photograph of this guy with a bandaged eye along with the report,' Jingo had persisted.

'Sure, someone must have got hurt. And they printed a picture. So the newspaper-reading public turns indignant and writes in to the editor calling for an end to the menace of slum-dwellers,' replied Gurdeep. 'But did any of those reporters bother to investigate if it was really a slum-dweller who chucked the stone, or an outsider? Provocateurs are employed, you see . . . The battle in Bombay is for land. It's an insidious struggle that's being waged by the builder-politician lobby. These blokes will do anything to give a bad name to the slum-dwellers. Then bulldoze their huts and grab the land.'

For a moment, the galvanized-tin facade of the CPSDR's shack caught the sun and dazzled Jingo's eyes. Larger, more sturdily-built than the other huts, it wasn't pocked with the ubiquitous brown-red rust that was the reigning pigment of the township.

'Oh, by the way, I'd better tell you, before we get there,' said Gurdeep, slowing down as they picked their way over a series of flat stones placed in the slush around the pond. 'You'll be meeting Gloria. She's quite a woman. Had a hard life until recently, with a brute of a husband. But she's got her divorce, and now she's with Thiru . . . Don't go making gooey eyes at her.'

'What?! For heaven's sake,' Jingo protested, almost losing his balance on the stones and slipping into the slush. 'You *do* have a one-track mind, don't you?'

'*I* have?' Gurdeep repeated smugly, and laughed. 'You've never been able to resist anyone who likes you. And I know Gloria's going to fuss over you like a baby.'

'Really, man – what d'you take me for? A walking prick?'

'Just thought I'd warn you, since you'll be staying here. They might like some time on their own. Besides, Thiru's a very jealous person.'

'Maybe this wasn't such a good idea, after all. Does she spend her nights here, as well?'

'No, no. The place is big enough, you'll see. Gloria lives in Sion with an aged mother whom she can't leave alone for very long. Thiru won't mind at all your putting up here for a few days.'

As they approached the shack, they heard voices, at first indistinct. It seemed like a regular row was in progress. A deep male voice appeared to be dominating the argument, which had become more audible now.

'I clearly told you – don't call up *Mid-day*. Wish you'd pay attention sometimes. That damn tabloid is so anti-poor, they'll print any nonsense.'

'But the pictures!' the woman complained hurtfully. 'You also said we can't afford to neglect free publicity! Anything I do is always wrong.'

A short dark man with a thick beard was scolding a tall woman in an ankle-length skirt and a loose T-shirt. This must be Thiru and Gloria. Thiru's voice grated and rumbled as he chewed with annoyance on a curly strand of his beard.

'Well, never mind,' the bearded man said, indicating Gurdeep and his guest with an outstretched hand. Her face was distraught when she turned, but she quickly regained her composure and smiled.

'Come in, come in,' said Thiru. He had a sharply aquiline nose and piercing wide-set eyes. They entered, Gurdeep first.

A simple office desk, a portable typewriter, a couple of folding steel chairs and a small Godrej cupboard took up most of the room. In the far corner, a wooden stringbed and a large iron trunk. A curtain that needed washing hung on a wire, dividing the bed area from the office space. Overhead, a fan whirred noisily. Just as Gurdeep finished introducing Jingo formally, first to Thiru, and then to Gloria, one more person walked in.

'And here's Malcolm,' said Gurdeep. 'Somebody you know, Malcolm . . .'

Menezes's vacant expression showed no recollection at all of the person he was being introduced to.

'Hello,' said Jingo with a smile.

'This is Jingo. Remember him?' asked Gurdeep. Malcolm narrowed his eyes and frowned, evidently searching his memory.

'Brother Malcolm?' Jingo tried again, and Menezes smiled.

'Ah, college,' he said. 'I was wondering where I'd seen you.'

Presently, Gurdeep took his chance and launched into a humorous account of the circumstances that had led Jingo to seek 'asylum' in the CPSDR's office. His narrative was both patronizing and tinged with mockery, as Jingo might have expected it to be. But Menezes and Thiru caught on quickly to Gurdeep's vicarious discomfort, and heightened it by feigning astonishment at what they called his 'decadent secret life'.

'Smoking dope at street *addah*s in the middle of the night, eh?' exclaimed Thiru.

'Really! We didn't expect this of you, Gurdeep!' said Menezes, pretending shock.

Rather fatuously, Gurdeep protested that he disapproved entirely of his friend's habits and wasn't even present when the incident occurred.

'Anyway,' he added limply, 'all that's just by way of background.' For the others had burst out laughing, and he realized a little late they had been kidding all along. 'Jingo's a cool guy, really. Thought the best thing would be for him to come along and – if it's no problem – spend a few days here . . .'

The others didn't make such a big deal of it anyway. Thiru said he was most welcome, if he wasn't too squeamish about living conditions.

'The place suits me fine,' said Jingo. 'Thanks very much.'

'Oh, he's young,' said Menezes. 'I'm sure he'll manage quite well.'

'We should be moving outside soon,' muttered Thiru.

'I figured let him have a taste of real life,' said Gurdeep. 'It can only do him good after all these years in Bohemia.'

Nobody seemed to register that comment except Menezes, who thought that Gurdeep was stating that his friend had just come from abroad. His confusion was glossed over, though, for Gloria began to speak:

'Amazing how much the cops get away with, really,' said Gloria. 'Their extortion racket is such big business, they're willing to bribe their way into the force. It's like a one-time investment . . . That was a brave thing you did, Mr Jingo.'

Gloria was probably close to forty, thin and large-boned, with a frizzy mane of hair that made her look rather attractive. Her intense involvement in Gurdeep's dramatic rendition of Jingo's tussle with the cop had been apparent. From the expression on her face, Jingo fancied that she had mentally enacted a much severer punishment for his adversary than he had actually inflicted.

'By God, I'm glad you really gave it to that bastard,'

she said, still preoccupied with the story. But Malcolm Menezes cleared his throat softly, and frowned. He seemed unhappy with her conclusion.

'Actually, it's all rather sad,' he said quietly. 'Those two corrupt policemen will certainly keep their eyes peeled for you. Not so much because they want to nab you, but perhaps because they would hate to have another run-in with you.' He bared his teeth in soundless mirth. 'Anyway, I doubt very much if they'll officially report the incident. The stitches in Pandu's scalp will heal. I think you'll be quite safe out here . . .

'But when something like this happens again – and I hope you will not take it amiss, my saying this,' he continued, in the fastidiously precise manner of speaking that recalled for Jingo the collective diction of all the priests who had lectured to him at school and college, 'we must realize – after all, the suffering of the poor is immeasurable. If they demolish this slum, how much the people will suffer! We cannot bear it – none of us can bear to think about such suffering, let alone witness it. But does that mean we should pick up a stick and start breaking all the policemen's heads? It's all wheels within wheels. That's what's so sad about it. The policeman would not have been so corrupt if his senior inspector did not expect a cut of whatever he received. It's true. They are victims of the system just as much as your dope peddler. *You* may have got away scot-free. But the *system* will continue to function in the same way. And it's the system that we have to change.'

A familiar conclusion, thought Jingo to himself, to a rather long-winded polemic. He was about to clarify, just for the record, that he wasn't in the habit of going about smashing policemen's heads, but he didn't have a chance.

'Personally, I don't think he should have got involved at all,' said Thiru, in a deep undertone which barely muffled his growing irritation. The reference to him in the third person made Jingo uncomfortable. But, the next moment, Thiru addressed him directly: 'For all you know, the policeman enacts this little drama every time he comes to collect his *hafta*. You probably just made it worse by interfering.'

Gloria was clearly disappointed by his statement. 'What would you have done in his place, Thiru? Sat back and watched a cripple getting bashed up?'

'That's hardly the point. Individual acts of heroism are all right for the movies, but they change nothing. This kind of tomfoolery with cops can be dangerous. You're lucky,' said Thiru to Jingo. Then, looking away, he continued: 'I had a friend once, who got picked up one night for questioning. From this very camp, during the Emergency. Suspected him of being a wanted Naxalite, they strung him up by the legs, broke his knuckles, gave electric shocks to his balls . . .' Here he paused for effect, and adjusted the thick black frame of his spectacles on his nose. 'After three days in lock-up, when he was practically done for, they realized it had been a case of mistaken identity, and let him off. But to this day, he hasn't recovered. He limps. Stammers terribly, if he speaks at all. And he's become totally impotent.'

For one awful instant, Jingo remembered Chandubhai. Were they giving him the third degree right now to make him reveal Jingo's address, while he was safely ensconced here, in this ghetto?

'Anyway, all that's beside the point,' said Thiru, getting up, very businesslike suddenly. 'I think I'll go outside. There's work to be done.'

'I'm coming too,' said Gurdeep, 'but couldn't we have some tea first? I'll ask Pandit to bring in – how many, five cups?'

'Okay,' nodded Thiru. 'But tell him, make it snappy!'

'Oh yes, Mr Jingo,' Gloria continued, as Gurdeep stepped out to order the teas, 'you did the wise thing coming here. But you better not go out much for the next few days. We're expecting some trouble. You be careful not to get involved at all. Just stay out of sight. As it is, you do look a bit conspicuous – like a foreigner.'

'Please don't call me Mr Jingo,' mumbled Jingo, grateful for her concern. 'I could use a haircut, I'm aware, maybe a shave as well. Do you know of any place around here?'

'That'd certainly help,' agreed Gloria. 'There's a barber somewhere not far from here, isn't that so, Thiru?'

But Thiru wasn't listening. Maybe he'd heard approaching voices, footsteps . . . For at that very moment, a group of boys and women rushed up to the door of their cabin calling to him to come and help. The BMC squad had arrived, they said, with their crowbars, pickaxes and other instruments of destruction. In the meantime, Gurdeep, too, returned, looking hot and bothered.

'Fuckers have already started tearing down the huts close to the tracks,' he swore. 'How come nobody alerted us earlier?'

At the open door, one woman was ranting breathlessly, beseeching Thiru to *do* something.

'Come soon, oh see, just see what they've done. My father-in-law is in plaster, with a fractured thigh. I begged them to let him be, but they wouldn't listen.'

'So, Dattu wasn't wrong to smell a rat,' said Gurdeep.

'They're really asking for a contempt action to be slapped on them,' said Gloria indignantly.

'Let's move,' said Thiru and rushed out, with Menezes and Gurdeep following him.

'Hurry, do something! They've pulled him off his cot,' said the first woman, trying to keep up with the men. 'The old man is weeping in pain.'

The small crowd at their door was growing by the minute; some women were waiting for Gloria to accompany them; they were all speaking at once.

'My cot, my blanket, my stove' – a dazed old woman was enumerating her losses – 'my jerrycan filled to the brim with kerosene . . . How will I explain to my son when he gets home?' Then she remembered, 'They even stole my kitchen knife!'

'Scoundrels threw everything in their van, *didi*,' a companion of hers was trying to catch Gloria's attention. 'She's lost everything, but worst hit of all is poor Hamida-bi.'

'Hamida is ruined,' said another woman. 'She had pawned her gold earrings to buy new schoolbooks for her son. So proud she was that he had been promoted. Those swine took everything, even her trunk of clothes, even the tarpaulin over her head.'

'And the things they had no use for – like her son's schoolbooks – they threw in the slush! Her husband doesn't even know that she pawned her earrings to buy those books. They were her wedding gift . . .'

'*Didi*, come soon, oh come, please. Our own *jhopdi*s are next in line.'

As she followed the others out, Gloria called over her shoulder to Jingo: 'If you're coming pull the door shut. But just stay in the background.'

Jingo watched from a distance. Amidst the shrieks of outrage and the cries of protest, he recognized Gurdeep's loud voice trumpeting slogans against the injustice of the government and its lackeys, which the women picked up and chorused in shrill unison:

'Give us our homes, we're human, too! Don't snatch-smash what don't belong to you!'

'No warning, no notice, nothing. Like it's their father's *raaj*,' an old man standing near Jingo was muttering to himself.

'*Arrey*, one of them I saw,' said a woman who heard him, 'sticking up the notice *now* – after the job is done!'

'That too in English,' said another.

About a dozen dazed and tearful people were picking up the scattered remnants of their belongings, in a state of shock. But seventy or eighty others – perhaps even a hundred – emerged from every side of the slum to support the victims of the onslaught, encircling the demolition workers. Thus hemmed in, there was no way the BMC men could even approach the next row of huts, leave alone wreck them.

The police van had crossed the tracks and was now parked outside the settlement, since there was no proper road further in. Until now, the cops had remained aloof, leaning on their sticks and watching. Surprised by the concerted resistance and hampered by the fact that they had no policewomen in their midst, they tried to disperse the women by flailing their sticks. The officer in charge was yelling orders to his subordinates in Marathi: '*Gheoon ja, gheoon ja, sarvaana gheoon ja!* Take them all to the station.' But the policemen were wary of actually laying hands on the angry women.

Thiru, Gurdeep and Menezes were engaged in a

heated argument with the Ward Officer in charge of the municipal staff. Thiru was waving a copy of the court's injunction order, but the official refused to look at it, dismissing it out of hand as an obsolete order that had been 'vacated ex-parte' by the High Court. The three of them, along with a handful of other male obstructionists, were then arrested and bundled into the van. Meanwhile the women continued to yell abuse, demanding their possessions back.

'Pimps! Scoundrels! Have you no wives or children, no families of your own? How would you feel if we came to your homes and started smashing and robbing them?'

'We have to do as the big sahabs tell us. We'll be sacked if we refuse to be on duty.'

'Is it your duty to kick the poor in their bellies? Better to pimp for your mothers!'

'And if we get the sack, will you fill our stomachs by whoring?'

Somebody threw a stone which hit one of the workers on the head. The skin on his forehead split and he began to bleed profusely. A cop tried to give chase to the youth who had flung the stone, but he disappeared into the warren of narrow pathways inside the settlement. The rest of the workers, protesting inadequate police protection, withdrew. The cops felt there weren't enough of them to engage in a full-scale battle, and the Ward Officer decided to call off the operation. The BMC van revved up its engine and drove away, with the injured worker in the front seat beside the driver, a bloodstained handkerchief tied to his forehead. The police van followed, carrying in it some of the more vociferous males, who were led by Thiru, Gurdeep and Menezes in protest songs that continued to be heard from a distance, even after the van had driven out of sight.

> This won't do, this just won't do –
> Not o'er our dead bodies – we won't let you
> Smash our homes and snatch our bread
> All we want is the right to livelihood!

A few minutes later, two other police vans arrived with more men in them, this time armed with rifles. One of the vans also carried a dozen policewomen. But they merely parked on the path outside the slum, and an officer used a megaphone to urge the crowd to go back into their huts and maintain the peace. Reluctantly, seeing that the BMC van had gone, people began to disperse.

*

What was it that had startled the crows at this time of night?

A few strangled squawks at first, mutedly hesitant, as though it were the little ones who were roused first and thought to alert their elders. Of a sudden it rose to a fierce caterwauling: a hideous chorus of cawing and screeching that swelled for a full minute or more before abruptly succumbing to an eerie silence.

In pitch dark, Jingo cupped one hand over the faintly luminous dial of his wristwatch. He stared at it for a long while before it gave up the ghostly outline of the hour. Ten to three. He hadn't been able to sleep much. His mind was seething with impressions of his first twenty hours in Nehrunagar. He would have liked to write them down but he'd forgotten to bring his journal.

What a day, what a night! Earlier, as evening descended over the slum, there was still much noise outside.

A distant shrillness of women talking animatedly as their menfolk came home, a sudden clanking and hammering on tin, the sounds of people reconstructing their dismantled huts, the crackling of wood fires and, periodically, the low rumbling of a passing train.

The activists had been detained for about three hours before being released by the station house officer, who had been given the court order to peruse by Thiru and the others. Evidently he was a slow reader. A few reporters and press photographers arrived on the scene, rather late (Gloria had needed to make some more phone calls) and talked to the distraught slum-dwellers. They had taken pictures of the broken huts, the angry, tearful women recovering their strewn pots and pans, the children picking their way through the debris.

By the time it was dark, things settled down and life in the slum was about as normal as it could possibly be under the circumstances. Gurdeep had gone back to the flat to attend to an urgent personal matter. His sister-in-law, he explained, was in hospital, having a baby. There had been complications. Gloria was worried about her mother who had been left alone for far too long. She was probably waiting for her to return and prepare the soup that was all she ate for dinner. And Menezes, who lived in faraway Jogeshwari, decided to spend the night in Nehrunagar with a friend and sympathizer by the name of Ranade.

After a delicious hot meal of khichdi, which Thiru prepared himself over a Primus stove and garnished with green chillies and onion rings, they chatted for a while. Ranade, a middle-aged man who worked as a welder at an industrial unit close by, dropped by for a moment with Menezes. But they left soon after and refused to partake of the khichdi. Thiru borrowed a spare charpoy for Jingo from a neighbour.

He told him of the time he came to Bombay at the age of nineteen, from a town in Tamil Nadu called Mettupalyam. He had an uncle in Bombay who had invited him to come and seek his fortune in the city. But when he got here, he discovered that the business in which his uncle and his uncle's children had made their fortunes, and in which he had intended to co-opt Thiru, was an illegal one, involving the large-scale adulteration of edible oil. Thiru decided to look for some other job of his own and found one as a forklift operator in the docks of the Nhava Sheva.

After four years of working at the dock, he had still not been confirmed. Then he, along with two other probationers, was summarily dismissed on charges of wilfully destroying dock property.

'The charges were completely trumped up. The real reason for wanting us out was that we had just started a new union to press for certain basic demands. The official union was affiliated to the GSF, whose office-bearers were known to be in the pockets of the management. Since ours was an autonomous and internal union, we had a lot of support from the workers. So they decided to nip us in the bud.'

After a whole year of picketing at the service entrance of the dock, Thiru decided to call it a day. Of the two other dismissed workers, one had already taken up employment somewhere else, and the other had gone back to his village. Thiru himself had been offered another job, which appealed to him. He joined the CPSDR as their resource person and liaison man in Nehrunagar. Subsequently, he was appointed honorary secretary of the organization. He received a modest, if erratic, salary from the NGO, but found the work more fulfilling. The other members of the NGO were all doing voluntary, unpaid work.

'When I first got here – long before the CPSDR was born – this was all marshland. Now they're talking of building a flyover here, or God knows what . . . The mosquitoes in those days were huge – something unbelievable. The residents came together and got truckloads of landfill dumped here. Gradually, the place became liveable.

'Later, we got ration cards made for the families living here. CPSDR ran a small savings scheme. Schools in the area were not willing to admit children from Nehrunagar. They would say, this is no proper address. We don't want slum children in our schools. We took out *morcha*s, picketed them. It's been a long struggle, but the lives of these people are a little more settled today.

'And now, with the development of New Bombay, this land has become valuable real estate. Some bloody councillor or builder is trying every dirty trick in the book to drive us out and grab the land. Don't know if it's an individual or a cartel. But one thing's sure. The struggle and sweat of the people have made this place what it is, and we're not about to give it up in a hurry.'

It was still quite early when they turned out the lights and got ready to sleep. The last train had gone to the yard by then and a calm silence had descended over the settlement, when suddenly Jingo heard screaming, the sound of blows and drunken abuse from a neighbouring hut. It was all in a southern tongue which he didn't understand at all – probably Tamil – but the meaning and desperation of the cries came through quite clearly, or so he imagined.

'Save me, someone, oh save me, have mercy!' A woman seemed to be crying out. A man was abusing her violently, flinging metal utensils, presumably at her. '*Rungalinga naleya . . . Kandarvoli tendiya!*' the man was screaming hoarsely. It was all gibberish to Jingo. But Thiru suddenly shot up in bed and shouted equally harsh, vile-sounding imprecations in the direction of the hut from which the screams were coming. He spoke their language, but his threats seemed to have no effect on the hysteria that had broken loose next door. A child's frightened wailing commenced, adding mutinously to the sad uproar. Muttering under his breath, Thiru got out of bed and went out. A few minutes later, he was back. Miraculously, he had managed to restore complete silence in the neighbouring shack.

'Tonight of all nights! Fucking freak,' Thiru said, back inside. 'You awake?' He turned on the light, and saw Jingo sitting up in his cot. 'Beats his wife black and blue, every other night. Every time he's drunk, he's certain she's been entertaining men in their room during the day, while he's out working. If she saves up a little money, he's sure she's made it by spreading her legs. And then demands it for his drinks. Now he's sitting there weeping, feeling sorry for himself.'

That was the first instance Jingo witnessed of Thiru's authority in the slum. In the days to come, there would be others. He was an educated Brahmin, and people respected the years of work he had put in for the community. Whenever there was anything to be read, or filled in – legal notices, municipal circulars, school admission forms, even personal letters – people came to Vijaysaab, or Un-nah, as he was respectfully called by other Tamilians. He never charged them for this service.

Thiru turned out the light once again and retired. For a while, mosquitoes buzzed noisily around Jingo's ears, keeping him awake. The tin roof was still radiating the day's absorbed heat and there were curious hothouse aromas trapped in the torpid air of the poorly ventilated room. Thiru began snoring almost immediately. But there was another sound which bothered Jingo even more, stirring up primal fears and memories. It was the sound of a soft, steady grating on wood.

It sounded awfully close. It would cease for a few moments, if he stirred, and then resume again. Could it be a rat sharpening its teeth on the rough-hewn frame of the very bed he was trying to get some sleep on? He had seen a few huge ones prancing about in the clearing by the green pond that evening. Though probably no more than an old wives' tale, he still remembered the impression the story made on him when his father told it to him one night while stroking him to sleep at bedtime. A story about how cunning and vicious some of these big bandicoots could be. They were known to nibble at the toes of sleeping children who live in slums, his father had said, or on pavements. But, he said – and this was the remarkable thing – at the same time as they are biting away, they have a knack of blowing a gentle, cool draught of air from between their fangs that soothes the very lacerations they're inflicting; so the hapless victim continues to sleep peacefully, while Mr Rat indulges his savage craving. Now that he thought about it, it seemed a strangely inappropriate story to tell a child at bedtime. But then his father was like that – always full of strange stories about animals and people and places – and perhaps there had been some moral intent in its telling which he had now forgotten.

For a brief, sad instant he saw his father's face. He was much younger in this image than when Jingo otherwise remembered him, and happier. A long time had passed since he had last seen his father looking like that. Gradually, things had changed and his father had stopped finding time to tell him animal stories. Now, every time they met, there was only unpleasantness and resentment. There had been times when he had looked to him for support, when driven to rage and exasperation his eyes had searched for solidarity and even sympathy from the only other male in the house. But even that was long ago. And since he'd never quite known how to respond to that look, his father had retreated further and further into a stony silence.

Again that scraping, gnawing sound. Again the intermittent silence. What the hell was it? For a moment, it occurred to Jingo that in various ways this was exactly what Cris and he had done to each other for months, even years; this rhythm of alternately gnawing and soothing, inflicting and easing, and neither had woken out of their stupor for a long long while.

Thoughts of Cristina were never far from his mind. He felt at times that he had still not recovered from the trauma of their relationship. At times he felt liberated, happy it was over. At other times, he found himself wishing that she had given them more time. He believed that after the storm was quelled and the heartaches soothed, they could have been happy together. Some day, perhaps. Now, however, in the new environment he found himself in, his sense of regret and longing had receded considerably. He was feeling both stimulated and dazed by the events, the people and places he had seen during that day.

It was not as though he had never stepped into a slum

before or had been totally ignorant of the poverty that existed in such places. In childhood perhaps, and as long as he had lived at his parents', he'd never had occasion to enter one. But later, his search for adventures of the mind often led him to speakeasies and hash-smokers' *addah*s in just such locations. But even then, as customer, he'd never had to be up so close to it, never had to muddy his own feet in its slush. This was the first time probably that he had been witness to such distress as he had seen on the faces of the women who fought the municipal workers to save their homes. Lying there on his *khaat* in the dark, he felt quite overwhelmed by the awesome weight of misery and deprivation he was surrounded by, the incredible agglomeration of lives that had no choice but to accept these conditions of living.

One woman whose hut had been demolished and her tin sheets carried away couldn't find her child who was separated from her in the melee. She was shrieking with horror, running this way and that, aimlessly, as though she had quite lost her bearings herself.

When she couldn't see her toddler anywhere, a terrible thought must have struck her. She rushed to the pond, wailing. People attempted to restrain her from wading into it, not because it was very deep, but because a rumour had started a few months ago and since gained currency that its water had turned poisonous. They pulled at her sari, tried to drag her out, but she stood waist-deep in the pond, plunged her hands in it and splashed about, as though expecting to find her missing child entangled in the weeds; then, with a heartrending wail of despair, amid protests from the gathered crowd, she dipped her own head in the noxious scum, as if to drown her grief.

Someone brought a long bamboo pole and began to stir the water in the pond to reassure her that there was no child-corpse floating beneath its surface. But she refused to stop searching and began wading further in. Just then, someone else reminded the woman that her child had been sleeping, wrapped up in a blanket, when the demolition began. Could he not have been carried away by those scavengers? She charged out of the pool, dripping with muck and wailing pitifully, for now it seemed certain to her that her little bundle of joy must surely have been tossed into the waiting truck along with her other belongings and carried away to the municipal warehouse.

A group of neighbours and well-wishers got ready to go with her to the warehouse and demand their baby back. But just when they had started marching up to the access road to hail an auto-rickshaw, a little child with long curly locks came wandering up to its mother from nowhere, quite unaware of the commotion his absence had caused. The mother picked him up and embraced him tightly, her body continuing to shake with sobs.

Well, it's a different world I've entered today, thought Jingo. Overstimulated by the day's events and the numerous glasses of dark, double-brewed tea consumed, Jingo was resigned to the prospect of a relatively sleepless night. This is the world I'd like to write about, to contrast it with my own, the world of the Mooses, the Dubbys, the Juggys and Bablis, the advertising agencies, the corruption and sleaze and inhumanity of this appalling and beautiful city.

For a moment he remembered his father's opinion of the work he did. He's probably quite right, thought Jingo, it *is* meaningless, silly work. But then Dad didn't understood why he preferred it to other, more regular kinds of jobs: for the chance it gave him to explore the crevices and by-lanes of the city, feel the furtive caress of its faceless streets while ringing the doorbells of strangers; to wallow in their warmth, imbibe their joys and anonymous sorrows, pretend not to have heard their gross eructations, nor noticed their embarrassment, evasions or falsehoods – it was a very special kind of intimacy – while all the time collating the scenes and images he knew would figure in the novel he would one day write.

The other itinerary, the one his father had charted for him, seemed unreal and remote. To go abroad, for more academic plodding. Then the slow ascension of the ladder of middle-class success. He didn't have the drive in him to want to succeed in that way. He knew he wouldn't be able to make it work for him. Of course, he had never travelled outside his country. Nor had his father, for that matter. But Jingo had always believed, from the time he dropped out of college, that the primitive face of cruelty he had glimpsed in his city would continue to haunt him wherever he went. It wouldn't leave him in peace, especially if he tried to adjust to the aseptic, well-ordered cities of the West.

On the other hand, perhaps the truth was, as Gurdeep had once summed up for him dispassionately, that he had become a drifter, a defaulter, incapable of any form of sustained effort. Somehow he had lost his enthusiasm for most things. His psycho-social theories were only a manner of justification for something very particular that had happened to him – the souring of his love relationship, his reckless experimentation with booze and hash and grass, his innate disinclination for work.

But there was something else. Something perhaps

Gurdeep, too, would appreciate, if he were willing to give it some thought. Jingo's lack of motivation to become a successful chartered accountant, or even for that matter a successful writer, was inextricably enmeshed in the miasma of deep hopelessness that seethed everywhere beneath the surface of this city. One had to only step out into the street to be witness to a hundred forms of social cruelty and degradation institutionalized into the very fabric of daily life. Who was he to compete with? What forms of failure and suffering was he to base his own success upon?

It was there for everyone to see, yet nobody spoke about it. No one allowed himself to think of it, for that would mean, as in his own case perhaps, paralysis, a capitulation to despair. On the other hand, there was an unexpressed covenant among the successful and the middle classes to lobotomize that cancerous half of reality from consciousness. So that finally one strode past the most mangled forms of tortured and ailing humanity without batting an eyelid. The price one had to pay for this blindness, for adjusting to this form of social schizophrenia, had perhaps not been discovered yet, or was only just beginning to become apparent.

Gurdeep's own beliefs were without doubt honourable. Perhaps the only way to evade the despair Jingo sometimes felt overwhelmed by was to join the struggle, fight to change society. But he just couldn't see himself adopting that stance with any conviction. Would he be able to live here, for instance? He was here for now, of course, but for a longer while? To live and work here, like Thiru? Embrace the cause of social justice, identify with the masses in their campaign for a better world? Logically, it made irrefutable sense. And yet, whenever Jingo had found himself in the midst of activists, he couldn't but sense a suppressed hysteria in their fervid preoccupations which immediately made him want to exclude himself from their missionary embrace. He'd never been able to exactly identify his objections. Perhaps he didn't have any. Perhaps their idea of human happiness was just too strait-laced. Somehow he'd never felt at ease with a view of reality rendered so starkly simple. In fact, at times their self-important ways made him feel like giggling.

Perhaps it was he who was hysterical. Gurdeep was probably right. The world *was* stark, the issues were horrific. It was just his self-indulgence that prevented him from making the correct choices. Compassion and empathy were all very well, his friend had once declared angrily, but one needs courage to be able to change things for the people who excite your compassion. His logic was unimpeachable, Jingo's own position indefensible, if he had one at all. Pressure had been brought to bear on Gurdeep, too, to go abroad to a business school and do an MBA. But he had resisted it. His work was here, he said, among the people. And yet, Jingo knew with unqualified certainty that he'd feel like a fish out of water if he were to throw his lot in with these guys . . .

He couldn't remember when he fell asleep, but such were the thoughts that flapped about his mind during those dim-lit hours of morning when the querulous crows began the colloquy of their search for food.

Haircut

Dusk, sulphurous. Everywhere a fog of smoke.

Traffic, chaotic, interminable. Cars move in every direction, spewing great clouds of exhaust. Absolutely no chance for a pedestrian to even dash across.

In the small crowd waiting at a traffic light, a man stands puffing at a bedi. His own jaws begin to crave for a smoke. He takes out a cigarette from a pack of ten in his shirt pocket – how did that get there? He never bought more than a couple of loose ones at a time – holds it between his lips and taps the man on the shoulder for a light.

The man turns and flicks open a cheap lighter. The flame leaps high, and nearly singes his nose. He recoils, and the man laughs. With a shock, he realizes he's staring at the mocking face of the portly plainclothes officer he'd knocked down in the street a few nights ago.

Perhaps the packet of cigarettes in his pocket was some kind of ploy, a carefully laid trap.

Suddenly he's running, zigzagging through the endlessly slushy aisles of Nehrunagar, pursued by the stomp of several pairs of heavy boots.

He doesn't recognize anything around him, he isn't

even sure if this is Nehrunagar or just another slum. An ocean of huts stretches on both sides of him, merging into darkness. But there are no people in sight.

He knows then, even as he races through it, that this is the landscape of his own emotional indigence. He knows he is guilty, certainly, but he cannot remember the exact nature of his crime. He tries to glance over his shoulder to see how close in pursuit the posse of policemen is. He can't see them, but he can hear them. They're cheering and yelping like delirious hounds. Perhaps this is some kind of game they're playing with him?

He turns a bend and then they're all gone – no slum, no slush, no cops. He's found an exit, after all.

A tremendous sense of space envelops him; cool, fresh air. The night sky is clustered with millions of bright stars. There are fields of glistening paddy on both sides of the road. Not a soul in sight, and everything's lit up by a large, round moon.

Why, he knows this road . . . If he follows it further, it will lead to a small beach and a ferry crossing, then across the brief lagoon to a seaside village called Manori; Cris's grandma and grand-aunt live there. He sniffs the air. He can already smell the sea, the sharp tang of drying salt-fish.

Feeling utterly relaxed and happy, he traipses down the empty road. But something in the distance causes him to slow down. He feels afraid. Looming large against a white sky is a cross built on a concrete pedestal. There is somebody there. As he approaches cautiously, he can make out a figure kneeling at the foot of the cross. He sees her more clearly now. He is dismayed, even a little angry, but not surprised. What the hell is she doing out here alone at this time of night? He calls out: 'Cris! It's me . . .'

Even as he says these words, some instinct warns him of danger. In the same instant, a wandering cloud blots out the moon and, for a time, there is utter darkness. He moves forward, slowly. The cloud passes and everything is suffused in white light again. He finds himself at the foot of the cross. But there's no one there! He didn't imagine the kneeling figure. He could have sworn it was Cris . . . Suddenly he hears a rustle among the shrubs and steps back, just in time to see a thickly sinuous snake slide into the vegetation.

On the altar at the base of the cross are the residual blotches of several burnt-out and half-burnt candles. Among them, lying face down, is a little wax doll. He picks it up, turns it over. He is repulsed. The doll is smeared with fresh blood. Its eyes are alive; they're staring at him . . .

When he awoke, Jingo sat up wearily in bed. What remained with him was the moon-washed vision of Cristina hunched in prayer, and a dull ache of sadness in his heart.

The shack was empty. The ceiling fan was whirring noisily. Already he could feel the heat beginning to bounce off the corrugated roofing.

The sheet Thiru had used to cover himself with in the night was lying crumpled on his bed. On the table was a lock and key he had been told to secure the door with whenever he went out. By the window was a plastic bucket, half-filled with water, with a pink plastic mug floating in it.

One afternoon, many months ago, he had dropped in

at Cris's place in Orlem without warning. Her father had answered the door. Shushing the barking dogs in the yard, he called to Cris to come out. Domasso, her father, was holding a bunch of electrical wires in his hand and a pair of pliers.

'Signalling system malfunction,' he said to Jingo, pointing inside. He was referring, Jingo knew, to his personal train set – a vast, motorized assemblage of rail tracks and bridges, stations and signal-posts, permanently laid out on a large oval table in their living room. Cristina had switched it on for Jingo the first time he had visited her. Now her father was ill and never went out, but when he felt well enough he amused himself with his train set.

'Not safe,' he muttered, getting back to work. 'Goods train, express could ram each other. Has to be synchronized . . . Cristina!' he yelled again, for she seemed not to have heard him the first time. 'Go on, go on in . . . She's in the kitchen, I think.'

So she was, standing over an enormous pair of mackerel sizzling in a pan on the gas. Delighted to see Jingo, she hugged him tightly and kissed his lips; but, releasing him at once, she stepped back – for an instant she must have imagined her father was following.

'What a wonderful surprise!' she said, recovering her poise. 'If you had come any later, you'd have missed me.'

'Thought you said you were going to be home all day,' said Jingo.

'You should've phoned, anyway.' She shook her head. 'But I'm so glad to see you . . . Come with me, oh please do. It'll be such a lovely picnic. And you've never ever met my granny, or auntie. It's such a beautiful place where they live. Look, I just need five minutes to get this packed, then we can leave. Unless you'd like to eat something first? I think you'd better, if you haven't . . .'

The fried fish was to be a treat for her grandma and grand-aunt who lived by themselves in a cottage in the village of Manori. Cristina had thought of visiting them only that morning when she saw how glisteningly fresh the mackerel was that the fisherwoman had brought to their door in her basket.

'Auntie's a little younger, about eighty-two, I think,' Cristina said, stepping out of the boat onto the stone jetty. 'She can even see a bit, when there's enough light.'

Granny, on the other hand, was eighty-nine and almost completely blind. Nevertheless, with a little help from the younger sister, the two of them managed their own affairs pretty efficiently. Neither ever went out, and hardly anyone came to see them, except one of the neighbours who dropped by every morning before setting out to the market to ask if they needed anything. Their cottage was a bit isolated, closer to the beach than the rest of the village houses.

The old women recognized Cristina's voice as soon as she called out to them at their open cottage door.

'Cristina!' they both gurgled at once. 'You've come?'

Granny was reclining against the bedstead of a heavy antique bed that seemed to have had a few inches sawed off its legs – it was unusually low. Cris held her head in her hands, kissed her wrinkled forehead, her puffy eyelids, combed her scanty white hair with her fingers. Then she turned to her grand-aunt and hugged her warmly as well.

'Who has come with you, Cristina?' asked Granny in a creaky, quavering voice. And her younger sister answered for her, 'She has brought a friend along, Irene. Come, don't mind anything,' she said to Jingo. 'Please take a chair, sit.'

'Wait,' said the old grandma. 'Let me meet him first.'

She held her hands in the air. Jingo walked up to the bed and pressed them in greeting.

'Hello, dear. I'm Cristina's friend, Jingo,' he said.

But, disengaging her hands from his, she reached for his face. She felt his nose, his lips, the wispy fuzz on his cheeks. All the while she touched him, he kept smiling embarrassedly into her unseeing eyes.

'Ah, you have a beard, young man,' she said, with a giggly croak.

'It is the fashion these days,' said Auntie.

'I keep nagging him to shave it off,' said Cristina, 'but he refuses. He thinks it makes him look sensitive, like a poet. And keeps the girls chasing after him.'

The elder women both chortled at that.

Then Grandma lowered her arms, placed them in her lap and said, 'It's true. He has a handsome face.'

'Oh my,' Auntie muttered, opening the round, insulated tiffin-box Cristina had brought them. 'So much fish . . . Irene, Cristina has brought us two big baangras, fried. Where shall I put them?'

'You shouldn't have taken the trouble, Crissy,' the old woman said to her granddaughter. Then turning to her sister, she chided, 'Now don't be childish, Phyllis. Put one away in the meat-safe, and bring me a piece of the other. With some *pao*. I'm feeling quite hungry again. Don't you want to taste it?'

Phyllis said she didn't believe in overloading her stomach. Meanwhile, Irene picked at the half fish that was handed to her on a plate. She felt it for bones, found one, extricated it with great dexterity and popped the flesh into her mouth.

'Mmm,' she murmured appreciatively. 'Very nice, very fresh . . . it's still warm. Thank you, my dear. Over here we never get to see fresh fish. Export-wallas bag the whole lot even before the boats touch the shore. And only the stale, soft-boned rejects are sold in our village market . . . Mmmm, what a treat this is. Phyllis, try some.'

For some reason, Auntie was feeling cross with her. She snapped irritably, 'There's a full one and a half in the meat-safe. I'll have some at night.'

In a very short while, conversation dried up, and Granny said she wanted to rest. Auntie suggested to Cris and Jingo that they could take a walk on the beach if they liked. But, she said, be sure to come back for a cup of tea. While walking them to the cottage door she murmured, in a low voice: 'Eat and sleep. Whole day, eat and sleep . . . Poor thing, what else she'll do? Sometimes I think it's not right for God to make us live for so many years . . .'

Cristina turned and looked towards Granny. Her eyes were already shut.

Over an undulating expanse of tawny beach, they had walked for a long while. It was clean sand, unblemished except for millions of tiny crab holes along the shoreline. Jingo had his arm over Cristina's shoulder, but she shrugged it away and, slipping off her moccasins, waded in the cool shallow water. After some time, Jingo decided to hold his leather kohlapuris in his hand, and followed barefoot behind her.

They didn't see anyone, except a wiry old fisherman in a loincloth; he was walking in the direction they had come from, carrying an enormous skatefish slung over his sun-darkened shoulder.

Once, a bullock-cart passed them with unhurried ease, laden with sacks of grain and vegetables. Its driver seemed to have fallen asleep. They had watched the cart grow steadily in size as it proceeded jauntily over the hilltrack that came down from Gorai, the neighbouring village.

Once they had left Manori far behind, Cristina pointed ahead. 'You can't see it just yet,' she said, 'but at the bottom of that hillock, there's a new luxury resort that's come up. Very pricey, patronized mostly by foreign tourists.'

The villagers resented its flashy, pearl-white presence, she told Jingo, which had definitely aggravated already scarce conditions in the village. The hotel tended to corner the best vegetables, fish and seafood produce, offering outrageous prices for them to local sellers, thus triggering inflationary trends in the village market. Not to mention the receding levels of groundwater which they sucked up ruthlessly through borewells, using powerful pumps.

In the way she spoke about the problems of the local people, Jingo could tell Cristina completely identified with them.

'My ancestors come from here. These *are* my people,' she said. Manori had been her mother's birthplace. Granny was her mother's mother, Auntie was her mother's aunt. Her father hailed from a village further north along the coast, called Uttan.

'Whenever I come here, I feel so totally happy,' said Cristina. 'Nothing would give me greater pleasure than to rent a cottage and live here . . . Would you like that,

Jehan?' That was the abbreviation of his name she preferred. She thought Jingo sounded rather clownish.

'Live here? That'd be great,' said Jingo. 'On peace and
fresh air?'

'I'd cook you scrumptious meals,' she mused. 'Maybe I
could persuade some fishermen to supply us with fresh
fish. In my spare time, I want to start painting again. And
you'd have all the time in the world to finish your
novel . . .'

'Sounds wonderful,' said Jingo, quite willing to indulge
her fantasy.

'We could take long walks every evening, watch the
sun go down . . . then go back to a warm, early dinner,
and straight to bed.'

'And we'd wake at sunrise, with the birds,' Jingo
laughed, knowing how much Cristina hated to wake up
early.

'Don't you think it could work? We would be really
happy and so much in love, don't you think, if only,
somehow, we could exclude the rest of the world? I mean,
in a place like this it's possible . . . It's not even so far from
the city. It would just take us half an hour longer to get
into town than it takes me from Orlem. Not that we'd
want to go in so often . . .'

She was more than half serious, he could tell.

'Things are cheaper here anyway, than in the city. Of
course, you'd have to continue working till your book is
published. If you think it's a good idea, I could even make
enquiries in the village about a cottage to let.'

Moved by the beauty and remoteness of the place, they
talked in this fashion, fantasizing about a great getaway,
a quaint, sparsely furnished cottage which would become
their home. And if there were children, wouldn't it be

so much nicer for them to spend their early years in the midst of nature, rather than the hurly-burly of city life?

But the rest of the world has a persistent way of impinging on one's dreams of seclusion . . . What was it that lay ahead on the sands, glistening in the sun? The carcass of some dead animal? Bleached-out bones of a big fish? It turned out to be neither.

Another minute's walk, and they realized it was only a couple of white-skinned women lying beside each other on a mat. They had plastered their bodies with oil and were exposing themselves to the sun. Jingo noticed that one of them looked quite gorgeous, at least from a distance, with a long mane of curly hair and the briefest of bikinis.

They were close now to the point where the hill began its upward climb. Not far from them, a thick grove of coconut palms practically camouflaged the imposing wrought-iron gates and cobbled pathway that led to the Samara beach resort.

'Shall we turn back now?' Jingo asked Cristina.

'Not just yet. I'm a bit tired. Let's sit here for a while.'

'Shouldn't we move back a bit? I mean, give them some privacy.'

'It's not a private beach,' said Cristina, annoyed by the suggestion. 'Just because they've stopped at Samara doesn't give them special privileges.'

'Oh well,' said Jingo, and they plumped themselves on the sand not far from the sunbathing women and their sandy towels.

Presently, one of the women sat up and untied her bikini top. Instantaneously, enormous pale orbs bloomed, a generous libation to the oblique rays of the sun. Then she turned over, and lay down again, sunning her broad back. After a while, the other woman did the same.

There was still at least an hour before the sun would dip below the horizon. But the tide was crashing in closer, more insistently. Jingo and Cris sat in wordless awe, watching the deep orange preside over the ferment in the sea.

Later, when Jingo thought about it, it seemed obvious to him that by continuing to sit there Cris had been trying to prove something. To him, to herself? But what? He recalled a palpable tenseness in her, and even suggested once again that they should be heading back. Maybe he should have just reached out at that moment, pulled her close to him and kissed her.

The two women meanwhile were completely unconcerned by their presence. Then, the curly-haired one stood up: on one leg. She bent the other at the knee and rested its heel on the knee of the first. Then she joined her palms above her head in obeisance to the setting sun, maintaining this yogic pose for maybe a minute or more. Balanced on one leg, toweringly still, there was something quite Gorgonesque about the woman's harsh profile, her curls flying wildly in the sea breeze. Jingo kept glancing at her, half expecting her to lose her balance. For him, the sight of her topless and top-heavy posture was more amusing than alluring. But before he could find the words to entertain Cris with a suitable observation, she had already reached her flashpoint. She shot up suddenly and, without a word, started walking away, but not before kicking a clump of sand in his eyes.

'Owww!' he screamed. 'What did you do that for?'

Cris continued walking, but he heard her hiss: 'Stare, stare, till your eyes pop out! Never seen a naked woman before, have you?'

Jingo's heart sank to hear the pain in her voice. 'Cris, it was you who wanted to sit here.'

Suddenly downcast, Jingo remained seated there for about half a minute, nursing his smarting, watering eyes. He had expected to be able to easily catch up with her. Now, opening his eyes wide and searching, Cris was nowhere to be seen. He jumped to his feet, yelled out to her, but she had simply disappeared. The sunbathers may have heard something, too, for they had got up and, with towels wrapped around their bodies, were repairing towards the gates of Samara.

'Cris!' he called again, as loudly as he could. He made a dash towards the sea from where he had an uninterrupted view of the beach; he turned, stopped, stared in disbelief, ran again, but there was no sign of her. He thought of going back to where they had been sitting and searching for her footprints in the sand; but it became obvious to him now that Cris must have cut through some field or copse on the private land adjacent to the beach, taking one of the inner footpaths back to the village. He knew that even if he tried to follow her, he'd lose his way. All he could do now was find Granny's house again, and maybe she would be there, waiting for him. After all, they had promised Auntie they'd be back for tea . . . So this was Cris's idea of punishing him, he supposed, kicking sand into his eyes and disappearing before he could open them again.

It had grown quite dark by the time he found Granny's cottage. A dim bulb had been turned on outside the cottage door. Unlike in the afternoon, the door was not wide open, but slightly ajar. He peeped in. The old women were sitting quietly at the table, eating fried mackerel with pao. There seemed to be no one else around.

Just to make sure Cris wasn't sitting somewhere inside, Jingo listened intently at the crack in the door. Then he nudged the door ever so slightly. The room was vacant, except for the two old women at dinner. Auntie heard a creak, and called out: 'Who's there?'

But she didn't get up to investigate, and Jingo quietly moved away without replying. Then he took the road back to the jetty.

It was already noon when he locked the door of the office and set out. As he wandered through it, he was once again amazed to see in broad daylight how vast the slum really was, how different its mood from what he had imagined it would be. How different, too, from the slum in his dreams, that dark labyrinth of his despondency in which he became the hunted, and was nearly run to ground. Which reminded him: if he came across that barber's stall, he should take a crop and a shave, for whatever it was worth.

During the sleepless night, Jingo had felt crushed by the black misery of this condensed assembly of people in which he had sought refuge, but what he now saw by day were people who didn't seem at all burdened by any such encumbrance themselves. True, the aggression of the demolitionists had only touched the fringes of the slum, and even there, the destruction had been largely contained. But at least some of these people had been witness to yesterday's mayhem, and yet seemed unaffected. As though nothing special or remarkable had happened.

Jingo walked at a leisurely pace, stopping to peer into huts wherever he could. People glanced up at him from their work, smiling with faint amusement. Children waved. Perhaps they imagined he was a tourist, soaking up the sights and smells of poverty, or a loafer in search of a bottle of hooch.

Except for maybe a few months at the beginning, his relationship with Cristina had always been tortured by a precarious vulnerability. She could never trust him somehow, never completely believe that he loved her. Was she being utterly irrational in this? Did he share some of the blame for making her feel so insecure? On the other hand, on the beach that afternoon, surely his punishment had been undeserved. Yet the entity of the 'other woman', no matter how implausible or far-fetched, had begun to stalk them; with time, it grew into a large, brooding shadow in their lives.

'Can you swear to me you'll never make love to anyone else?' she'd often ask. 'Well, say it, then, if you love me so much as you claim to.'

'Never ever?' He laughed, but his laughter was forced and hollow. To make such a sweeping claim sounded absurd to his own ears. 'Of course I won't,' he said. 'But, really, how can anyone say something so categorical about the future? How do I know what may happen years from now? I'm no Nostradamus, for heaven's sake. I can say quite definitely I don't want to ever make love to a woman I don't care for. And I simply can't see myself falling in love with anyone else, considering what we have between us. It's such a very very remote possibility. And after all these years together, do we still need to drag each other down discussing such an implausible scenario?'

'Then say it, if you're so sure.' She waited, tauntingly. 'You can't, can you?'

He had realized perhaps a little too late that all she wanted to hear from him was a certain no. A make-believe asssurance that encompassed eternity. His own response, or the lack of one, was always predicated to philosophical uncertainty: the impossibility of knowing the future, his obsession with being precise in his use of language. Yet she wouldn't have minded even a straight white lie.

Moreover, her obsessive fears of losing him made it impossible for him to confide in her, or even admit to himself, that a whole continent of feeling lay unexplored within him – the inexpressible feelings of tenderness he felt towards so many women, even some men perhaps. Was that wrong? Was it some kind of narcissistic self-delusion to feel like that? Surely life was bigger, more expansive and wonderful than these narrow corridors of possessive fidelity? He had always felt there was an abundance of love in his heart to go around. But he had to admit all this was only abstract yearning, something he had never been able to act on. His one true love *was* Cristina, and he knew that if it ever came to it, he could never bring himself to hurt her.

Yet, how much of his repressed promiscuous longings had she sensed? When accused of a crime that hasn't actually taken place, except in the realm of thought, and at that, only for an instant, the mind is nevertheless dismayed, startled into an admission of guilt as though it actually had transgressed . . .

In one hut, a man with an impressive handlebar moustache was bent over an anvil on which he was tapping at something with a small hammer. Seeing Jingo watching from outside, he invited him with a wave of his hand to come in and see the work he was doing. Jingo hesitated. The man repeated his invitation.

Leaving his footwear outside their door, Jingo stooped a little, and entered the hut. The man was creating artificial jewellery from beads, tassels and lengths of thick wire. The shiny, coloured beads were in a box in front of him. His tools consisted of a wire-cutter, pliers, a box of glue and a small burner which served as a mini-furnace, presumably to bend and mould the metal wire. The burner hadn't yet been lit, but there was a small tin box on the floor in which lay some pieces of finished jewellery.

The man's wife was cutting a sheet of pink cardpaper into small squares, with a small pair of scissors. A sheet of blue cellophane had already been cut into slightly larger sized squares. The card and the cellophane were being used for packaging the bangles, earrings and nose studs which the man manufactured. Their son, no more than eight years old, helped his mother to staple the cellophane paper on the cards once the jewellery had been enclosed in it. A strip of red ribbon, folded into a bow, was also stapled on one corner of the card. All in all, when packaged, it made an attractive little item.

Thanking them for letting him see their work, Jingo spoke in Hindi. He felt pleased at the discernible surprise this caused. The man with the handlebar moustache had been behaving with Jingo as though he were dealing with a foreign tourist.

'Where you from?' asked the man, still pursuing his query in English. Jingo explained, once again in Hindi, that he had lived all his life in this city, that he was no tourist, but a Parsi from Bombay. Ah, Parsi – the man had heard of his tribe, but seemed a little disappointed, nevertheless. Jingo offered to purchase a set of pretty earrings as a souvenir. It was priced at only five rupees, the man told him, but theirs was not a retail business.

They sold these pretty ornaments to a middleman who collected advance orders from shops in the markets and railway stations all the way down to Kurla. If Jingo wanted a large quantity . . . the man offered him tea instead, but seeing the entire family was busy, Jingo politely refused. At which the man and his wife insisted on giving him one set of earrings free of cost as a token of goodwill toward the unusual visitor. A memento for him to take back to wherever he had come from. Perhaps they still didn't quite believe he belonged to this city.

When he left their hut, Jingo slipped the packet of earrings into his pocket.

As he wandered about in this manner, he was the object of much curiosity, but most people were too polite to accost him with questions. Quite soon, though, a giggly bunch of children began to follow behind him. They were of all ages, ragged and barefoot.

A very old and withered woman, not much taller than the children herself, barred his way with outstretched hands. She said something to him in Tamil, or Telugu, he wasn't sure which it was, but the interrogative gestures she made with her gnarled hands conveyed her meaning. Who do you want? What're you looking for? He himself tried to indicate by a gesture and a phrase of Hindi that he was roaming about aimlessly, just looking around. But the old woman refused to accept this for an answer. She assumed he was completely lost or searching for something he was too ashamed to admit to. She rolled up her fist keeping her thumb sticking out and raised it to her lips. No, no. Jingo shook his head, realizing what she meant. He really didn't want a drink at this hour.

He tried to walk on, shaking his head from side to side emphatically now to make it clear that he needed no assistance, nor did he have anything to offer the children, some of whom had started asking for alms. But the old woman wouldn't let him pass, insisting on knowing the object of his peregrinations in Nehrunagar, unreeling a string of further questions in her language that sounded distinctly offensive. The stragglers began to giggle with even more unrepressed hilarity.

As the small crowd attracted more and more attention, Jingo began to feel distinctly uncomfortable. On impulse, he told her he was looking for the barber. Which was true in a way, though he would have preferred to visit him later in the day. With sign language, bringing his index and middle fingers together, he mimed the act of cutting a lock of his hair. There was immediate comprehension. The old lady began to point and gesticulate giving directions excitedly in her tongue. The children had understood him too, and now they set up a chant, 'Shankar-dada, Shankar-dada!' They bossily took over and led him away, assuring the old lady they would take him to his desired destination. One of the smaller children gripped Jingo's wrist, clutching it firmly to ensure that he didn't stray.

From the old days when he would walk morosely down the hill at Khareghat Colony to Good-Luck Gents Haircutting, a small salon in a by-lane off Babulnath, once every other month, haircuts had always been a source of distress for Jingo. Acutely aware of his powerlessness to exercise any control over the devil-may-care approach of scissor-happy hairdressers, an unpleasant feeling of passivity overcame him, which had remained unchanged to this day.

Now, too, in the little hut in Nehrunagar which served as its official hairdressing salon, Jingo once again felt hopelessly victimized. Perched on a low wooden stool in the poorly lit interior, peering at a jagged, mildewed mirror, Jingo knew he couldn't expect much coiffurial finesse from this dark southerner whose name he had learned from the rag-tag procession of kids who had led him there.

They had followed him in to watch the shearing, but Shankar shooed them off, vowing forcible tonsure for all who lingered without work. They dispersed, reluctantly, and once they had gone, Jingo noticed a girl sitting on the floor behind him. Evidently, the threat didn't apply to her. When the barber had draped him in a fusty white sheet, the girl stood up for a moment, as though merely to get him to notice her, and then settled once again on the floor, arranging her colourful skirt neatly all around. But this time she had placed herself differently, at a strategic angle from where she could gaze at his reflection in the mirror unobstructed.

She was probably about fourteen, but tall and very thin. Somehow, Jingo felt he had seen her before. Could she have been among the crowd of women gathered at the site of the demolition yesterday?

She may have been too old to play with the children outside, perhaps, but there was something about her face, small and blunt-featured, that suggested a mind fixed at a stage of childhood that her body had long outgrown. She sat there idly pleating the folds of her skirt, apparently disinterested in anything else, yet surreptitiously stealing occasional glances at Jingo. How oddly she was dressed for a girl her age, in a florid purple ghaghra and a pink choli. Her nails were painted, her eyes vacuous and lined with kohl, her hair tied with ribbons in two neat plaits. She was wearing a thick coat of bright red lipstick which looked entirely incongruous with her child-like face – all the more, since the same brightly painted lips were making puerile blubbering sounds every now and then, blowing a fine spray of spittle distractedly in the air. And yet, Jingo had to admit, there was something curiously attractive about the girl – that tensile relationship between the child in her and the woman? – which she seemed to be aware of, and even, perhaps, flaunting.

The barber's breath smelt heavily of aniseed, which only partly disguised the stale reek of country liquor. His eyelids were drooping. His manner was rather brusque and disgruntled, as though he had been just about to take a nap when the children brought in the customer. Jingo shut his eyes in resigned anticipation of a stylistic disaster, wondering how his vanity would weather this one, but presently Shankar squirted his hair with cool water; Jingo was pleasantly surprised by the gentleness and efficiency with which he launched into a preliminary head massage. The barber's own hair was short and flecked with white but uniformly neat, which was a good sign, Jingo thought.

'Once they have tasted the caress of my hand, people come back to me. Even from far-away places . . . Mornings, I conduct my business outside, by the bazaar road. Plenty of custom – shave, haircut, armpits, massage. Afternoon, evening, mostly local peoples coming . . . But who was it sent you to me?'

Jingo told him he was spending a few days in Nehrunagar with a friend, Vijay Thirumalai.

'Thirusaab? Big man,' he said impressed by the reference. 'For eight years now, he's my regular customer.' As he spoke, Shankar began lopping off Jingo's locks with a pair of scissors and a fine-toothed comb.

Meanwhile, the girl in the mirror seemed utterly absorbed in herself. Or was her peculiar grimacing and snorting intended to catch Jingo's attention? He couldn't tell. Shankar largely ignored her. Once, when she burbled too long and loud, he cleared his throat to show his displeasure and raised his right hand threateningly in the mirror. Jingo saw a moment of frozen fear in her eyes; after that, she was silent for a while, then she began again, softly puckering her lips and pulling hard on them, as though sucking on an imaginary straw.

Shankar said he was so used to barbering the poor and uncouth he was glad to have a real gentleman for a customer once in a while. 'Eight years is a long time . . . This camp has grown so much in eight years. Every day peoples are coming from village to join some relation or friend here – thinking, once they are in Bombay, their lives will improve . . . So they land up in Nehrunagar, or in some other wretched slum . . . As for me, I'm trying to find some place . . . just to get out of here . . .'

Shankar paused a moment to check if he had clipped both sideburns to an equal length. 'You know how it is, sir,' he continued, 'biggest problem in Bombay is space. People are willing to fight, kill for it . . . If I find a nice *gala* in a good locality, may be in Thane or Ghatkopar, just see – I'll set up such a tip-top saloon, it'll be the talk of the town . . . But prices are high . . . For a hut like this in a godforsaken hole, I can get fifty thousand. Imagine! But that's not enough . . . Even for a small room in Thane or Badlapur, they're asking three lakhs, four lakhs!'

The girl in the mirror was screwing up her features, crinkling her nose, pursing her lips, now pretending disinterest, now smiling furtively, now nodding approval at the outcome of the haircut. But every time Jingo tried to meet her gaze, she looked away with dreamy-eyed affection. It was impossible for Jingo to be certain whether she was bored, distracted, sending him messages of endearment, or just curious about this light-skinned stranger who was unlike all the other customers she had seen her father barber. Once, Jingo thought she winked at him, but too quickly for him to be sure it had been a deliberate gesture. Shankar saw the flicker of a smile appear on Jingo's lips.

'You like it, then?' he asked, assuming it was his handiwork that had brought the smile to Jingo's face. 'Wait, I'll show you,' he said, holding up a small hand-mirror to display the rear portion of his head to Jingo. Jingo secretly wished he had instructed him at the start to retain a reasonable length; but he nodded approval. It wasn't bad. Anyway, he'd wanted a more conventional look.

'It's a strange place, you know, full of surprises,' said Shankar thoughtfully. 'When you *saab-log* visit us, what you see? Shit-hole, no? Real WC. Stinks like one, too. But there's more to Nehrunagar than meets the eye. Would you have imagined you could get such a first-class haircut in this place?'

'Why not,' said Jingo. 'Thiru said you were good.'

'Like a small-sized city,' continued Shankar, 'fine hooch, charas, ganja, cheap and tasty food, even women – there's nothing you won't find here. You could say it's the underside of your city. The arse . . . That's why it stinks. Did you expect shit to be perfumed?'

He picked up the sprinkler and sprayed Jingo's hair thoroughly. Then he gave it a vigorous rub and brushed it down again. 'Drunkards, gamblers, layabouts – all kinds of third-class people live here. Many work from morning till night. At the docks, in the industrial estates, others ragpicking. Whole families set out each morning to clear the streets of junk. And yet they all remain poor . . .'

Now he began expertly snipping at uneven tufts, adding finishing touches to the haircut.

'You see that notice, sir? Very clear, no?' He pointed to a hand-painted sign inside the doorway which said: Haircut – Rs 10. Shave – Rs 5. 'Yet, all kinds of loafers come to me, "Shankar dada, I have five rupees less, three rupees less, two rupees less . . . Tomorrow I'll give you, promise." Who has seen their tomorrow? It never comes . . . I'll tell you one thing, sir . . . I'm used to poverty . . . I've lived with its stench all my life . . . But now, it nauseates me. Cannot take it anymore . . .'

Jingo looked at the barber in the mirror, expecting to see a face contorted with bitterness, there had been so much anger in those last words. But his face remained dead-pan, expressionless. Shankar fell silent, as he commenced massaging his neck and shoulder muscles. Ah, that's nice, thought Jingo, feeling the knots of tension dissolve.

He noticed the girl behind them stand up; then she sat again with a flourish to make the gathers of her ghaghra fall evenly about her.

'Is she your daughter?' Jingo asked.

'Yes,' answered Shankar, after a moment's hesitation. Then he ordered the girl, roughly, 'Shanti . . . Go tell Rafiqbhai: two 'pecial chai.'

Shanti made her exit sourly, ignoring Jingo as she passed him. The barber whipped up a generous lather and rubbed it on his cheeks. Then he lowered his voice to a whisper as he stropped his razor on a belt of leather.

'What to tell you, she's our misfortune. Everyone knows her story. Wife was a charitable-minded person.

Insisted on taking her in . . . But that girl's strange. You saw now . . . Likes to dress up like a doll, but doesn't have the brains of a sparrow. We thought she'd grow up. Now, my wife's dead and I'm alone with her . . .'

After every swathe, he wiped the razor against the side of a small pewter basin; a soft mound of white froth mixed with black particles of hair collected.

'They were our neighbours' children. Her brother lives close by, too. Boy's smart; he was too young when the thing happened – doesn't remember at all. But this poor half-wit, Shanti . . . Now she has only me . . . How much can I see to her needs? You tell me.'

Shankar expertly swabbed a streak of red that suddenly appeared on his throat, wiping it away so swiftly that Jingo hardly noticed he had been nicked. He continued: 'Father was a hard-working fellow, electrician at a welding works near the station. One fine morning: electrocuted! Employers said he died of his own carelessness, so no compensation. Union made a big noise, and they finally gave the widow something – five thousand rupees. But the poor woman was practically a child herself, not yet twenty, and illiterate. At the time, even those relations who've adopted the boy were not in Bombay. No one to turn to, couldn't speak any language except her native Telugu. Now five thousand rupees was a big sum for her. Where to hide the money? She gave it to one of her neighbours for safekeeping . . . Two days later, she found that the neighbour had packed all his things in the night and disappeared. Nobody saw him again. She lost her courage and ate rat poison.

'This girl, Shanti, was only five. She was alone in their hut when she saw her mother die a horrible death . . . Some hours later my wife went in with a pot of kheer –

just like that, didn't know anything was the matter – and she found the little one whimpering to the corpse of her mother . . . Her little infant brother was bawling his head off from hunger, trying to suckle the dead woman . . .'

The barber shrugged, but Jingo could see he wasn't unmoved. 'No family connection . . . still, we took her in. Later, her father's relation came to Nehrunagar from Telengana and adopted the boy . . . but he didn't want the girl.'

Now Shankar sprayed Jingo's face with water for a long time. The cool water stung and refreshed. The barber wiped away the excess drops with a napkin.

'She's not very bright.' Shankar shook his head regretfully. 'Her mind is full of boys. Plays with herself all day. Shamelessly . . . Not with other children – with herself. You know what I mean? I've thrashed her many a time, but it's all she can think of doing. Have to get her married off, soon as I find someone who'll take her. She'll get into trouble if she fools around with anyone at all, she's old enough to have a baby. Try to look after her, keep her happy. But alone, how much can I do? She doesn't understand anything, she's just a child.'

Shankar rubbed a piece of alum on Jingo's grazed skin, and then dabbed it gently with the napkin. The shave was complete. Jingo was pleased with his well-groomed look.

Shanti brought in the 'special' tea herself. It was very sweet and quite deliciously fragrant with crushed cardamom. Jingo drank it quickly and left, tipping Shankar generously, over and above his charges for the haircut and shave.

Earrings

All that week Thiru and the other office-bearers of CPSDR were busy trying to fix up an appointment with Gajanan Ghaag, elected representative to the Greater Bombay Municipal Council.

The elusive councillor from Ambavali was difficult to contact by phone, and even more difficult to meet. But doing that was probably the first step towards finding a solution to the vexed problem of Nehrunagar. For less than a year ago, Ghaag, while canvassing for the post, had promised that his party would ensure basic civic amenities for the slum, even negotiate a title deed for residents who could prove occupancy prior to 1983. Now was the time, CPSDR felt, to put pressure on Ghaag: bring him to account for promises that had won him votes.

Thiru, Gurdeep and Menezes were kept busy working out strategies towards this end – contacting sympathetic reporters to do stories on the plight of the slum-dwellers, investigating Ghaag's record of non-application and apparent breach of trust, planning for a public protest outside the Council office – Jingo hardly saw them. Thiru would leave his office-home early, and wouldn't return until evening. Neither Gurdeep, Menezes, nor Gloria had come around since that day of the attempted demolitions.

For Jingo, who didn't have much to do with all this himself, the hours passed slowly. Of the interviews he was to conduct for the agency, he'd only brought along half a dozen sheets, and even those he felt disinclined to start on. The rest were at the flat; Gurdeep had promised to fetch them whenever they were needed. He reckoned the whole lot would take him no more than ten days to complete. Not looking forward to commuting on crowded suburban locals, he decided to take it easy for a while, enjoy the enforced sluggishness of his sojourn in Nehrunagar.

After his first days of blundering through the maze of Nehrunagar, Jingo believed he had a rough layout in his head of by-lanes which made for the shortest way out of the settlement. And another, of more wayward routes which took longer – and could be disorientating, but definitely more rewarding: the same instinct of exploration which animated his forays in market research now stimulated him.

The more he walked around, the more apparent it became to him that the monotony of the huts was an illusion of his own inattention to detail. Not all were equally bedraggled or blighted by poverty. Even the most wretched-looking were decorated with calendar art or good-luck charms – pin-ups of film stars, kitsch deities, an inverted swastika – and occasionally his spirits were lifted by the sight of a cosy little room built with bricks and cement that had a TV antenna perched on its tiled roof and mud pots of curry leaves or basil shrubs flowering outside. Here, too, in a desert of deprivation, people were striving to create their own private oases of respectability.

The heat inside the corrugated tin shed grew oppressive indeed, driving Jingo to wander the narrow pathways of the slum. Several times a day, he left the cabin and returned to it. It wasn't less hot outside, but occasional breezes brought relief. He knew there was a world within these huts he hadn't even begun to discover. In the early part of the evening, while it was still light, Jingo went for a longer walk, looking for an expanse of open space. This wasn't easy to find, obviously, unless he crossed the tracks and walked on the relief road alongside the highway to Panvel.

Around the vast semi-circular periphery of the densely packed slum, the land was dry, amorphous and empty. At its rear end, a rocky incline rose and then undulated gently towards the creek. If he stood at the highest point overlooking the shallow water, in the distance he could see hills, not entirely barren – looking really quite pretty as the evening set in.

Before it turned dark, he found his way back to the shack. Switching on the one naked bulb that hung over it, Jingo spent some time at the desk, mulling over a notebook, ball-point in hand.

June 28
Ever since that first burst of heavy showers, it's hardly rained at all. Sometimes the clouds thicken and it looks like the monsoon is about to break. But then the sky turns bright again. People have begun to fret: will the rains play truant again this year?

And even if they don't, the season brings its own special torment for these poor folk. The whole of N'nagar is so low-lying, it floods up

like a basin. In years when the rains are good,
Thiru says, people have had to climb up onto
the roofs of their huts to sit out the night.
Until it stops pouring and the waters subside.

Bought myself this 100-page notebook from
the provisions store. Putting down a few
sentences every now and then helps me feel
more focused. The notebook carries a picture
on its cover of a new hero of the Indian
cricket team – his name is Mohamed
Azarhuddin, I think – very rugged and
determined-looking, wielding his willow with
aplomb.

June 30
Shanti, the barber's foster child, has grown
exceedingly fond of me though I've done
nothing to elicit her affection. (I can imagine
Cristina sniggering at that – she's always
accused me of projecting myself as a better,
nobler person than I actually am, merely to
win the affection of others.) But it's true. Ever
since my haircut, hardly a day passes without
Shanti dropping by at the CPSDR office.

She brings along a friend, another child
younger than herself. They chatter softly in
what I presume is Kannada. Maybe it's me
they talk about, for sometimes I catch them
sneaking glances at me, then they burst into
giggles.

If I'm cooking, Shanti insists on taking over,
claiming some sort of no-nonsense sisterly
authority. Of course, when it comes to

chopping onions or dicing tomatoes, her
efficiency sharply improves on my fumbling, so
I have no reason to object. Apparently she's
picked up her cooking from watching Usha
Kakee, who she says has been like a mother to
her. Early in the morning, she cooks a meal for
her father, and bakes chapattis. On occasion,
I've asked Shanti and her friend to eat here, or
at least taste the food they've helped prepare,
but they wiggle their heads as if I've suggested
something preposterous, and mirthfully scoot.

The younger girl attends some sort of
literacy class in the afternoon. Apparently
Shanti herself, and presumably her guardian,
too, have no interest in schooling.

July 1

She's an overgrown child. Her fascination
for me becomes embarrassing at times; I
confess I do end up thinking about her a lot
myself.

She's alert, not 'slow' at all, nor
unintelligent. At times, however, terribly
withdrawn. Something about her small head,
her well-oiled plaits, her crimped features
suggests a trace of mongolism, perhaps. I
know next to nothing about the subject so
that's not a fair observation to make –
probably even that term is considered
politically incorrect now and might well
enrage some Mongol nationalists – but if she
could be examined by a qualified child
psychologist, one might learn a bit more about

what goes on in her head during those spells of intense self-absorption.

Sometimes it's as if she weren't present in the room at all, as if her mind had quietly effected an escape. And quite often, of course, she resorts to that awful blubbering and spraying of spittle – is it some sort of autistic pastime, a defence mechanism against the world, or just a bored diversion?

At other times, when she's cheerful, she seems entirely normal. More than once, she's offered to show me around Nehrunagar, to meet her friends. Tentatively, I've agreed to a guided tour, but put off fixing a date.

July 3

Today was that day. Started on our tour around 11.

First stop: Babu Attarwalla's. 'Very important man, richest man in all N'nagar!' Shanti's intriguing pronouncements led me to expect a house of brick and plaster at the least, but we knocked at the door of an average-sized shanty.

It opened about six inches, and a bare-chested, white-haired man peered out. If he recognized Shanti, he didn't give any indication of it. Presently, he stepped back into his room and returned with a pair of spectacles installed on the ridge of his bulbous nose.

This time the door opened wider. Humps of soft, hairy flesh bulged at unexpected corners *of a large rotund body. Slipping his hand under a tight-fitting vest, Babubhai scratched his stomach vigorously, and yawned.*

'What's it, baby?' *he asked Shanti, staring inquisitively at me.*

'Thirusaab's friend . . .' *she said, with a gesture in my direction.* 'Staying here with Thirusaab . . . Just showing him around . . .'

'Come, come in please . . .'

'Babubhai, we won't,' *Shanti declined.* 'Only just began our tour, brought him to your workshop first. But, if you can' – *she held out her thin wrist shyly, and suggested –* 'if you could . . . just a dab . . .'

Her request brought a smile to Babubhai's face. He knew exactly what she was asking for. Stepping inside a moment, he returned with a small jar of dark green liquid in his hand. The plastic stopper of the jar had a protruding straw; with this, he daubed Shanti's wrist in the region of her pulse. She held her wrist to her nose, and gave a deep sigh of pleasure. Renu was waiting her turn patiently, wrist extended. Next, the plump old man turned to me.

'Try, sir . . . Best perfume. Khus. Very good . . . Cools the brain in this hot season.'

'Very nice,' *I gasped, overwhelmed by the powerful scent.*

'I thought, Shanti has brought along some exporter to meet me,' *Babubhai continued.* 'This is my lab'ratory, sir, where I mix and blend my fragrances . . . Wife and child stay in*

nice two-bedroom flat in Mahim . . . But I'm a
simple fellow – I go there only to sleep. Nose
very important in my work. Somehow, my
nose works best here – in Nehrunagar, where I
started my career, twenty years ago . . . Come
to my showroom in Mankhurd. There you'll
see all the popular brands – Topaz, Poison,
Chanel 5, you name it. Just by sniffing at each,
I create ditto original. Delicate job, but God
has given me this gift, this big nose. Dabba-
batliwallas provide empty bottles, and I create
the perfect blend to match the label. But my
friend Shanti here, now she still prefers my
attar to all those "foreign" perfumes. Always
comes to me for a little touch of khus . . .'

The attar's powerful fragrance was less
boggling than the irony of finding a spurious
perfumery in the malodorous alleyways of our
slum.

Creek's accessible from two points, the girls
pointed out, offering to take me down to the
water. It's quite filthy, they said, but in one of
these gullies somehow clothes come out
looking miraculously cleaner. That's where all
the women take their clothes to wash, slapping
them on the rocks.

We turned back towards the slum. Four
boys in shorts and faded T-shirts were
lounging outside one of the huts. They called
after Shanti by name, and said something to
her in her language. She deliberately ignored
them, and all four burst into paroxysms of
laughter.

They're not good characters, she said, as we walked on. Just layabouts, whose only form of self-employment is trapping rats and bandicoots. They own two large traps which they use for this purpose; and they like to torture the poor creatures before handing them over to the local BMC office. Apparently, the Municipality offers 25 paise per head, dead or alive, as an incentive to involve slum-dwellers in controlling the burgeoning rodent population. Often, she says, these boys barbecue and eat the rat meat, if they're hungry, or in the mood for it. Once, they gave her some to taste, saying it was mutton tikka. Since that day, she doesn't speak to any of them.

We've been wandering around for at least an hour when I make an amazing discovery: at a short distance from the slum proper is a single-storey wooden structure. Very old and rundown. Squat, and built into a slight depression, I might never have seen it if Shanti hadn't brought us walking this way. It's an abandoned soap factory, she tells me. Goes by the name of Suryavansh Chawl, after the popular and inexpensive bath soap that once used to be produced here.

Follow the girls into the barn-like structure. Very quiet and dark inside. Lit by a single beam of skylight, the whole scene's very atmospheric. The entire shopfloor of the factory is divided into neat little cubicles made of plywood. In various corners, thin nylon ropes have been stretched out, over which clothes are carelessly slung. Good clothes, intended for re-wearing, are more neatly suspended on plastic hangers. There must have been people inside some of those cubicles, but I didn't see anyone. Though I could smell some delicious food cooking.

When the girls pushed aside a curtain and entered one of the cubicles, I waited outside. But only a minute later, they were back, Shanti unwrapping a peppermint drop, which she popped into her mouth. Renuka put hers away in her pocket. Apparently Usha Kakee, whom I never got to see, was asleep. The sweets were courtesy of Manisha, her daughter-in-law, who was busy cooking a meal.

'She's asked us to drop in again tomorrow. It's some Maharashtrian festival, and there'll be more sweets,' Shanti said. 'Usha Kakee always makes me sit down and gives me something to eat. Then, while I'm eating, she loves to tell me stories of long ago ... Of the days when there was no one around for miles and miles. And Suryavansh Soap was the only bath soap poor people used. And the creek below had such clear sparkling water, it was possible to even see the fish swimming in it.' Her cheek bulging with the sweet in her mouth, Shanti chattered on.

We made only one stop on the way back. Shanti had to pick up a bottle of jeera for her father. Joachim, a thin, weedy man in shorts, distils the hooch in a closed cabin behind his *shack, just five minutes up from Suryavansh Chawl. Judging by the pervasive odour, he probably dumps the dregs of his handiwork in the gutter that flows past his back door: an olfactory advertisement that leads customers straight to him by merely following their noses.*

Picked up a bottle myself for twenty rupees. Shanti assures me it's of the best quality; her father regularly purchases a bottle. It's a light country liquor flavoured with cumin. Joachim claims he uses only natural fermenting agents and that his jeera, if consumed regularly, will certainly improve my digestion. I'm willing to give it a chance. Interesting day.

Just as Jingo was planning to set out for his evening walk, Ranade dropped in. Thiru wasn't back as yet; he decided to wait for him. Jingo made them some tea. In conversation with him, Jingo was surprised to discover that Ranade's association with Nehrunagar went even further back than Thiru's. When he was still a young boy in his teens, his father had been employed by Suryavansh Soap Factory as a watchman!

Unlike the rest of the settlement, which had mostly South Indian Muslims and a few Christians, all thirty-odd families living in the Chawl were Hindus. The factory used to be owned by an orthodox Hindu called Dattatreya. An enlightened employer in many ways, according to Ranade, except in that he was willing to hire only Hindus, preferably Maharashtrian-caste Hindus. He gave his employees regular food rations and medical aid. As a businessman, though, he wasn't very successful, and eventually had to stop production. A few years after it closed, as a final act of goodwill, he allowed his ex-workers to squat the premises of the abandoned factory – he had no intention of restarting it and no children or family to take over, after him. By that time, of course, he was a very old man, practically on his deathbed. The Suryavansh factory antedated even the slum itself, which gradually came up at a short distance from it.

Ranade's father, and his polio-stricken sister, still lived in the Chawl. Ranade himself spent most nights in their room, unless he had some work in south Bombay, in which case he stayed with Menezes in Jogeshwari. Jingo told him that by a strange coincidence, he had seen the Chawl for the first time that very morning. He'd probably never have spotted it on his own, if the girl Shanti hadn't taken him walking that way.

It *was* very isolated, agreed Ranade. A few Hindu individuals and families lived scattered in other areas of the slum, but these were just a handful. In fact, an uncle of his who was an RSS man had strongly urged his father and sister that, for their own safety's sake, they should relinquish their room in the Chawl and move to a more Hindu area like Ghatkopar. But Ranade's father didn't share his brother's prejudices about the villainy of Muslims. His sister had been quite annoyed by the suggestion, in fact: 'We have lived with these people like brothers and sisters for years and years!' It was true, said Ranade, even during times when the city had seen tension between Hindus and Muslims, Nehrunagar itself had always remained calm.

Ranade had finished his tea and was wondering aloud whether to wait longer for Thiru, or meet him the following day, when somebody knocked.

'Hi!' said Ranade, pleased to see Gloria push open the door and enter, but when no one followed behind her he was disappointed. 'Isn't Thiru with you?'

'I couldn't make it to Ghaag's office, Mum's not well again . . . But Gurdeep and Thiru – not back yet? Their appointment was for four!'

'Either they're thick in discussion with Ghaag,' said Ranade, 'or the blighter's stood them up again.'

Ranade decided he wouldn't wait any more, and left. Gloria picked up a chair from the stack leaning against the wall and unfolded it under the fan. Settling in it, she said, 'Thiru's going to be hopping mad if Ghaag has ditched them yet again.'

'Could the councillor have been late for his appointment?' Jingo suggested. 'He could be talking to them now.'

'Unlikely,' said Gloria. 'Public servants aren't known to work long hours; besides, this guy seems a master of evasion . . . Anyway, for whatever reason, Thiru's decided to put his trust in him . . . for the moment at least.' Her voice was subdued and thoughtful. 'The thing about Thiru is, he's – an idealist, I guess. When he decides to trust someone he puts all his faith in him. And if that person falls short of his expectation, he's enraged – cuts him off completely . . . He sees that person's failure as a personal betrayal.'

'So if this Ghaag's playing a double game, he really doesn't know what he's in for: Thiru's wrath! Waving a red rag at a temperamental bull!' He was getting carried away, Jingo realized. 'I mean it, of course, not literally.'

Discounting Jingo's attempted retraction with a wave of her hand, Gloria burst out laughing. For some reason, she found the description terribly amusing. Caught up in the moment's frivolity, Jingo went on: 'Well, I *can* imagine Thiru as the bull in an animated cartoon, repeatedly jabbing Ghaag's butt with his horns, while the rascal screams, "Aargh! Aargh!"'

Gloria found this even funnier; Thiru must have heard her loud guffawing for at that very moment he walked into the room. He gave Jingo a stony stare, then turned to face Gloria.

'Well, did you get to meet him, Thiru?' she asked.

'Waited for one hour in his office,' rumbled Thiru in a deep voice. 'At five o'clock he phoned to say he was sorry, but he'd be there within fifteen minutes. Waited another hour and a half, and then we gave up on him. And what happened to you?'

'Couldn't leave my mum until Auntie came over, and *she* was late. Mum's in terrible pain.' She turned to Jingo for a moment and explained. 'She's severely rheumatic. Obviously this Ghaag is playing games, Thiru, don't you think?'

But Thiru didn't reply. He had put his briefcase on the desk, and quietly left the room.

The days grew hotter and more humid. The next evening, Thiru told Jingo he had spoken to Ghaag on the phone. The councillor was profoundly apologetic about not having been able to keep his appointments on two occasions. But he had made one more for the next morning.

Gloria had intended to go along with them but, as usual, she was late. When she arrived at the CPSDR office, they had already left without her. She decided to proceed to the Ward office, and catch up with them there. She must have been in the CPSDR office for no more than two or three minutes, but in that short time, Shanti dropped in, too, clearly in some state of agitation. For the first time, Jingo felt she wanted to talk to him about something, maybe confide in him. But, on seeing Gloria there, alone with Jingo, she wouldn't even enter the shack. Before Jingo could ask her what the matter was, she was gone.

That afternoon, Jingo hadn't felt like cooking. After knocking back a small tot of the jeera still remaining in the bottle, he crossed the railway tracks and went across to the eatery where he consumed three loaves of bread with a plate of mutton masala. The meat was very tender and deliciously prepared.

During his first days in Nehrunagar, Shanti had warned Jingo against eating meat at the dhaaba. According to her, a gang of five hooligans, who worked at night, bludg-eoned stray dogs to death on the marsh, every time they managed to catch one. The mutton masala and mutton shahi kurma dished out by the dhaaba were really dog-meat masala and dog shahi kurma. Shanti loved animals passionately. Since that day when she tasted rat meat, believing it was mutton tikka, she had turned vegetarian.

It was a believable story, so far as Jingo was concerned. The mutton dishes were priced far too low. But Thiru had pooh-poohed the idea. He said they were just bony ribs of beef, cooked with a special tenderizer prepared from papaya and passed off as mutton. In any case, it had never disagreed with him, so what the hell?

When he got back to the shack he found Gurdeep and Thiru in a jubilant mood. They had just had a successful meeting with Gajanan Ghaag. Gloria had been present, too, and Thiru said her feminine charms had definitely rendered the councillor more pliable. She had gone home to her mother now, since she was already late, but her presence had really helped.

They had managed to secure a promise from Ghaag that he would personally see to it that there were no more demolition raids on Nehrunagar till the matter was settled in the courts. It was right and proper, he had agreed, that the council wait for the judge's final decision. He even went so far as to assure them that if there was any more harassment, he would himself lend his name as co-plaintiff in a contempt-of-court action. He had persuaded Gurdeep and Thiru not to file any complaint about last week's incident and to let him handle the matter internally. In any case, it was on record, since the *Indian Express* and the *Blitz* had published pictures of the damaged huts.

'Not that I trust him completely, but at least we should give him a chance,' said Thiru. Despite Thiru's doubts, the mood was cheery, and Gurdeep asked Jingo if he had any of that jeera left. Jingo offered to go fetch a new bottle.

'He hasn't changed a bit,' kidded Gurdeep, 'ever ready for highs! But let's wait a bit, until after sundown?'

Though he didn't know it, that was to be Jingo's last night in Nehrunagar.

The three of them polished off an entire bottle of jeera between them that evening. The jeera was light, and induced high spirits. The boys talked about many things, including Jingo's indolent and easy job, the problem of the migrant influx into Bombay, which after all was responsible for creating slums, the pastimes of the privileged, and cricket as a street sport.

Earlier, they had packed some food from the dhaaba,

but most of it remained uneaten. Gurdeep, taken in by the jeera's smoothness, had consumed a lot of it. When they finally retired for the night, he seemed to fall asleep even before Thiru could turn out the light.

A few minutes after midnight, Jingo fell asleep too. But he was aware of a terrific storm that had broken outside. There was thunder and lightning, and it was raining hard. He couldn't be sure he wasn't dreaming it, for later he also remembered a hammering on the door in the middle of the night. A voice which sounded vaguely familiar called out, 'Thiru! Thirusaab!' a few times, and then stopped calling. Thiru didn't stir, and nor did Jingo, but the storm continued to rage.

In his sleep, Jingo heard the pitiful and prolonged yelping of a dog. Then he dreamt he was in the fishing village of Uttan where Cristina had taken him to attend the wedding of a cousin. The pig that had been fattened for the feast escaped just as the cook was getting ready to stick him. With much laughter and a caterwauling that was meant to mimic the shrieks of the terrified pig, the villagers set off in pursuit. It was all part of the sporting merriment. In his dream Domasso was quite well, and cantering after the pig. Jingo was there too, joining the village boys in the chase. The pig was quickly caught, and with a deft jab of a knife his shrieking silenced. The warm blood from the pig's neck was collected in a sort of chalice, and passed to Domasso, the guest of honour at the wedding. Domasso glugged it down and burped loudly.

When Jingo awoke, he didn't open his eyes immediately. Thiru and Gurdeep were arguing. He heard Thiru's deep voice muttering, 'Nice friends you have! Just tell him as soon as he gets up to pack his things and fuck off! And you've seen her. She's barely thirteen.'

'I had no idea all this was going on. But I'm not sure it's fair to blame him without giving him a chance to explain,' said Gurdeep, circumspectly.

'It's not a question of blame or explanation. What kind of impression does it create? Bloody pervert!'

When Jingo sat up with a start, he saw that there was two inches of water inside their shack. But the look on Thiru's and Gurdeep's faces told him something else had gone terribly wrong.

'What's up?' he asked them.

'Plenty,' said Gurdeep.

Thiru glared at him as though possessed by a demon of rage. 'We trusted you!'

Jingo had no clue as to what they were talking about. 'What have I done?'

'Good question,' said Gurdeep, trying to maintain some measure of equanimity. 'Thrice last night, Shankar the barber was here, hammering at our door. Finally he woke us up early in the morning. My head is still throbbing.'

'That jeera is only deceptively smooth. I warned you.'

'That's hardly the matter. Shanti, Shankar's daughter, has been missing all of yesterday and right through the night,' said Gurdeep. 'He believes you had something to do with her disappearance.'

'I? I had something to do with—' Jingo couldn't complete the sentence. 'But I've been here with you guys. And you – you actually believed him?'

'She was spending a lot of time with you, everyone knows that,' said Thiru.

'She was never here alone. Her friend, Renuka, came along always. I never ever asked her to be here. She came because she wanted to pass her time that way,' said

Jingo in his defence. 'She was just looking for compan-
ionship, I suppose. Of an innocent, childish kind. I didn't
encourage her to be here . . .' But doubt clouded his mind
even as he protested his innocence. Could he have, perhaps, without desiring it, fuelled her romantic longings,
which is what had made her want to run away from her
oppressive foster-father?

'Well, you should realize this is not your Khareghat
Colony flat,' said Gurdeep. 'Everyone here knows what's
going on in the next hut.'

'Oh, but really, this is too sick for words. And what do
you think was going on? She's a child! Do you really
think I would do anything – to harm her?'

'Tell him. Tell him about the earrings,' said Thiru to
Gurdeep.

'Shankar found the earrings you gave her. He knew
they were the type that Rana makes. So he showed them
to him. And Rana told him he'd sold you that pair only a
few days ago.'

'So? What does that prove? They were given to me as
a gift by this Rana, I didn't buy them. And I gave them to
Shanti because I had no use for them. I thought she might
like to have them. And she did.'

'Whatever it is,' said Thiru, 'we're willing to give you
the benefit of the doubt. But do you know how long it has
taken us to build up the trust and confidence which the
local people have in us? And then you come here and in
one shot you destroy everything! Naturally, they will
identify you as one of our members.'

'What did I do?' said Jingo. 'Just tell me, what did I do
so wrong?'

'You should have had the sense to tell her not to come
and meet you every day. Now Shankar's planning to file a

missing person's complaint with the cops, as soon as it stops raining, and he's sure to name you and the CPSDR in it,' said Thiru.

'Look,' said Gurdeep, 'perhaps you had nothing to do with it. But I think it's best you leave now. Maybe if you're not here we can persuade Shankar not to mention you in his complaint. That may be better even for you.'

'Sure, I'll leave,' said Jingo. 'Right now. Nothing gives me greater pleasure than to go away from where I'm not wanted.'

Apparently this last statement irritated Thiru even more. 'Listen to him. Just listen to him,' he said to Gurdeep. 'After you saved his skin, and kept him here for nearly two whole weeks . . . It's a matter of character really. When a person lives like a parasite, he has no compunction about doing anything. That's why I even warned Gloria not to hang around here when he was alone.'

'What!' exclaimed Jingo, and looked daggers at Gurdeep.

'I have nothing to do with this,' said Gurdeep. 'Look, there's no point in getting abusive, Thiru.'

'And what about poor Shanti? Is no one worried about what might have become of her?' asked Jingo, taking out his haversack from under the bed.

'You don't need to worry about Shanti. Her father will, and the cops,' said Thiru.

'For all you know,' said Jingo, 'she's only run away from her foster-father. He used to beat her. I wouldn't be surprised if he tried to physically pile on to her or something, while he was drunk.'

'Look at the bastard. Look at the way he talks,' said

Thiru, enraged. 'We don't want to hear your fancy theories. Just get out, before they lynch you.'

'I'm going ,' said Jingo, shoving his towel and tooth-brush and loongis into the haversack.

'Wait,' said Gurdeep. 'You have the key to the flat?'

'You know I can't go back there so soon. I'll find some other place. Don't worry about me.'

So saying, Jingo waded out of the tin door. The flood waters were rising fast. The cemented pathway was bare-ly visible. All manner of unspeakable filth and scum was being carried in the current.

Squall

'Get me the hammer, will you, Khorshed?' called Boman, wrestling with the bolt that had stuck. 'This won't budge . . . and screwdriver, too, please,' he called. 'No, no, the long one – Papa's, with the red handle.'

A regular storm was raging; the first blast of furious winds had slammed the windows hard against their frames, and one pane had cracked.

The reckless gusts had taken both of them by surprise. But Khorshed had recovered first, running from one window to the next, shutting and fastening each before any further damage could be done; while Boman fidgeted with the jammed bolt on the one that had already cracked.

Boman's father's set of English carpentry tools had withstood years of corrosive humidity, preserved by regular greasing and the large wooden box with clamps in which they were stored. Boman liked to use the tools whenever opportunity allowed, and even prided himself on his carpentry skills; now, with just two or three measured taps of the hammer, he was able to get the bolt to slide again, But, to his dismay, he discovered the aperture in the frame itself had worn out and wouldn't hold the bolt in place.

'This is more complicated than I thought,' he said, a note of exhaustion creeping into his voice.

'Look at it tomorrow, when it's light,' said Khorshed, who had in the meantime fetched a length of white drawstring to secure the window by tying its handles together.

Boman reluctantly settled back in his easy chair. 'Short-term solutions . . .' he muttered, wrinkling his face to show that Khorshed's neat bow didn't appeal to him.

'There'll be time enough to fix it tomorrow. We'll call in Jairam, if you like. Anyway, the glass needs replacing.'

'No need. I'll take the measure and send him to Ebrahim's to buy a ready-cut piece. Then I can change it myself.'

'But why? He'll be happy to do the whole job for just thirty rupees.'

'It's not the money . . . such shoddy work . . .'

In the dark room, Boman didn't notice Khorshed's eyebrows rise ever so slightly.

'Besides, you know I like working with my hands.'

'As you please . . . Shouldn't you put on a shirt, first?' she asked her husband, who was wearing only his sudrah and pyjama. 'You don't want to catch a chill.' Obediently, he rose and put on the bush-shirt that was hanging on the backrest of a nearby chair.

It was still early evening, but there was a distinct drop in temperature, and it had grown very dark. The winds had been a mere prelude to the histrionic display the heavens now unleashed. Bursts of sheet lightning illumined the sky. Timpanic rolls of thunder detonated with a suddenness that made the elderly couple start. A torrential downpour lashed the facades of buildings, washing away months of dust from shuttered windows and sills, lintels and terraces, drenching compound gates and garden paths, flushing the foliage of trees and shrubs thoroughly, resolutely, as though it never intended to stop.

'What a night it's going to be,' said Khorshed wistfully. 'Wonder where our Jaungoo might be tonight. Somewhere safe and indoors, I hope.'

'Umm,' grunted Boman, after a pause. 'He hasn't phoned or anything, has he, after Behram Roje?'

Khorshed didn't feel it necessary to answer. A moment later, she sighed.

'There's no call for any lamentations, please,' said Boman with a hint of anger. 'The bloody fool is probably getting drunk somewhere with his cronies. I've washed my hands of him. Ungrateful wretch.'

'I wonder . . . I feel, perhaps,' said Khorshed hesitantly, 'we haven't dealt with him in quite the right way.'

'What's right and wrong about it? He's not a boy any more, he's a grown man. He's made his choices in life. He doesn't want to work. God help him.'

'I'm not sure. I'm not sure he knows what he's doing at all. He seems so –' she hesitated again – 'lost. And helpless.'

'Ha! Helpless,' repeated Boman sarcastically and said no more on the subject. The silence between the elderly couple grew palpable.

'Don't you want to turn on the lights?' he asked irritably.

'I thought you'd prefer to sit in the dark,' said Khorshed apologetically, getting up. 'The storm . . . lightning flashing outside. A few years ago, you'd have picked up a pencil and scribbled out a verse on the splendour of the monsoon's first evening.'

'Turn on the lights,' said Boman decisively, and Khorshed did. The yellow glow of bulbs brightened the room. Briefly, deferentially, she joined her hands and bowed to the light. Boman did the same, but he kept his eyes shut.

'That whole business with the girl, you know,' began Khorshed again. 'Perhaps we opposed him too severely.'

'Did we, now?' said Boman, surprised more than sarcastic. 'You've always complained that I wasn't firm enough.'

'But who could have known she would become such an obsession?' said Khorshed. 'It's not natural for a young boy to give up home and all concern for his future, like that. All for the sake of a Catholic wench? She wasn't even so good-looking or anything.'

'We've been through all this before,' said Boman impatiently.

'All I'm saying is, it's not natural. Why on earth would an intelligent young Parsi boy who has his whole life before him get so hooked on a dark-skinned slip of a girl like that and ruin his whole life? Unless –' she paused here for effect – 'unless there was some trickery involved, something underhand.'

'Careful what you say at dusk,' warned Boman, grasping immediately what she was hinting at. 'It's the hour for kindling of lamps.'

'Shouldn't we at least consult somebody?' Khorshed persisted. 'He used to spend so much time there at her house in Malad. It would have been easy for one of them to slip him something in a cup of tea or a hot curry . . .'

'Now really, enough, I say. Enough!' said Boman raising his voice.

'Don't be angry, please,' said Khorshed. 'If that is indeed the case, I'm just saying, there are ways to reverse such mischief. Tell me, which Catholic family can hope to find a Parsi son-in-law? Just fifteen years ago – why even today – they'd be glad for the position of a cook, or an ayah in a well-to-do Parsi home!'

'Thank your lucky stars your son is not here to hear you speak,' chuckled Boman quietly. 'Or there would have been an explosion of disgust! "Scratch a Parsi, and you'll find a bigot underneath . . ."'

'But it's true,' said Khorshed. 'He has to face facts . . . There are ways of achieving such things. They-all still have tribal connections. How else could fisherfolk even dream of netting such an eligible Parsi in-law—'

'Eligible, my foot,' said Boman. 'He's not even a graduate. Lazy, good-for-nothing bum.'

'Oh, the family has lots of land and money. What do they care about education? Just any Parsi would make a good catch for them. That Dastoorji Framroze, in Udwaada they say he has special mantras to reverse such evil . . .'

'Oh, please . . . Where do you pick up all this information?'

'Don't you remember? One of the members of the Circle we met at Rusi's place was praising him. Rusi himself would know how to contact—'

'I should have guessed. Spare me the torture of having to hear that name spoken in my house. Bloody charlatan! Fraud . . .' Boman swore, and continued to mutter inaudibly to himself for a while.

'No need to get excited, Boman. All that is past, it's

over,' said Khorshed, hushing him placatingly. 'This is a practical matter.'

'Past? But the past doesn't go away,' said Boman. 'It stays with you. And do you think I'm not aware you've persisted in keeping touch with that man?'

'What? I haven't. I swear I haven't, Boman,' cried Khorshed, shocked by the accusation. He seemed to accept her denial, for he said no more. 'If you mean Baba, that's different,' Khorshed continued, reverently. 'I still believe Baba has been helping us all the time, in His own way. I'm grateful.'

'For years I believed he was a friend. I actually liked him. But he turned out to be more fiend than friend! I can never forgive him,' muttered Boman bitterly. But he was speaking only to himself. Then he looked towards Khorshed and spoke louder. 'And as far as Jaungoo is concerned, get one thing straight. Nobody's cast a spell on him. He's dug the trench of his ruination himself.'

Just then, the telephone began to ring. Khorshed got up to answer it.

'At this hour? Who could it be?' she wondered aloud. 'Hello? . . . hello . . . hello . . . Who is this? Hello? . . . Jaungoo? Where are you? We were just talking about you . . . Of course. But of course. Why do you ask? This is your home. You can stay as long as you like . . . Hello . . . hello? HELLO . . .'

But the line had gone dead. When Khorshed replaced the receiver and turned, she saw that Boman had shut his eyes again. She didn't say anything to him, and he didn't react. Maybe she should say something to him or he'd be angry that she didn't even ask his permission.

'The line was so bad. Got cut. I think Jaungoo was

saying something about wanting to come back for a few days. You don't mind?'

Boman didn't answer, he didn't even look up.

Presently, Khorshed covered her head with a clean white cloth and knotted it below her chin. Then she sat down with her prayerbook, as she did every evening, to softly intone hymns of praise and thanksgiving to her Creator.

Part 2

Post-Partum

There is a glass. Short, wide-bottomed, like a whisky glass; octagonal perhaps, within the hazy shimmer of its cut-glass contours.

It is three-quarters filled with oil. At its centre is a cotton wick kept afloat by a wire contraption clipped to the rim of the glass, and a small cardboard disc. The lamp burns with a smoky orange flame. All else is shadow.

When my mind courses back to its remotest beginnings, the shadows converge in a solid black tunnel. At the end of the tunnel flickers this lamp-in-a-glass. It is placed on a small square table that is covered with a checked maroon-and-white tablecloth. It is always there. Always lit. Behind it, in a vertical photo-frame, stands the black-and-white close-up of my elder brother, Rumi. He's only two years old in the photograph, looking slightly bemused. Perhaps there's also a hint of mirth in his eyes as he self-consciously poses for the lens: right index finger placed firmly on his dimpled chin, curly mop of hair delightfully dishevelled.

Twice a day, once early in the morning and once more before retiring at night, my mother would replenish the oil in the glass. Custom dictated that such a lamp be kept lit for ten days after the death of a family member. But in the case of my star-crossed brother, who died while I still skulked in my mother's unhappy belly, the lamp remained lit for a full fourteen years. Until that fateful evening when my father snuffed it out in fit of rage and forbade its re-kindling. He had just realized with a measure of pained certainty that Rusi Hansotia, the well-known spiritualist, and would-be family friend, who had for years been acting as a medium for Rumi, was an utter fraud and an irrepressible scoundrel. Mother disagreed with him, of course, but for all her bossiness, she was always a little frightened of his temper on those rare occasions when he showed it.

Still, the incandescence of that oil lamp remained a constant flicker through the years of my growing up, in sometimes annoying and insistent ways.

'Put on a shirt! Rub your hair dry!' Mother would shriek, aghast to see me stepping out of the bathroom in my thin muslin sudrah and cotton pyjamas. As though I were about to embark on an Arctic expedition clothed in such flimsy vestments; instead of already

*beginning to perspire in my sultry peninsular
city.*

*Not for me those crisp, slightly burnt deep-
fried samosas served with chutney on a leaf
platter outside the school gate; nor the little
pink ice-cream cones (rolled out of blotting-
paper, it was rumoured) with their creamy
green and yellow toppings, nor even the neatly
cut squares of delicious crushed mango
pancake: all the street food which made
school-life bearable for my confreres was
strictly forbidden to me. Mother had glanced
over it once and, for all time, declared it
swarming with contamination and disease.*

*A rainy day on which I came home from
school with damp socks would result in a
mandatory half-hour footbath in a white
enamel basin specially designated for this
purpose – hot water mixed with a
tablespoonful of ground pepper and turmeric,
and Mother re-emerging from the kitchen
periodically, holding aloft a kettle of
simmering water to ensure a just bearably
scalding temperature for the solution.*

Anything to keep me from catching a chill.

'Not counting the mumps and measles, has he ever been
down with anything more serious than a mere sniffle?'

'Touch wood, touch wood,' Mother whispered, horrified by the implied hubris in these words, and often
Father would oblige her by rapping his knuckles on a
handy table rather than argue.

Sometimes, however, he muttered under his breath,

'But the boy's growing up nicely, strong and stout. It's perverse, Khorshed, *perverse* to be so fearful about the dangers of being alive.'

'We can't be too careful, Bomi,' Mother pleaded.

'But at least be realistic,' father snapped, irritably. 'Everything doesn't always turn out for the worst!'

Khorshed was aware, of course, that her anxieties about Jaungoo's well-being were excessive, given the evidence of his ruddy good health. But then, excessive by what measure? The savagery of the practical joke life had played on them still clawed at her helpless grief. It was as if she had entered into a devilish bargain without reading the fine print on the reverse. In her obsessive concern to do everything right for the child whose birth they had so eagerly awaited, she had allowed herself to neglect the blessing that was already theirs.

After all, Rumi had been in the best of health too, hadn't he? Until – oh yes, Boman still refused to admit it, but what sensible person will deny the dark powers of envy? – until two months after he put in that entry for the Murphy Baby Contest.

Boman took the black-and-white photograph himself with his sturdy Leica. Rumi won second prize – a large and splendid-looking radio called the Murphy Maestro. The sad irony was that only a few weeks after it came home by special delivery, the Maestro was silenced forever. Even Boman who loved music so much never dared to turn it on again. Now it reposed dourly in the loft, among assorted *tapeli*s that had sprung a leak, burnt-out *kaansia*s, derelict saucepans and abandoned, ornate gourds that hadn't been used in decades. While Khorshed continued to be tormented by an unanswerable question: why, oh why, for God's sake, had they not worried more about those patches of red in Rumi's throat, as soon as they appeared?

Partly ignorance, partly her own sluggishness brought on by having entered her eighth month of carrying Jaungoo. Boman was working long hours at an office job which he subsequently quit. But in those crucial moments when she needed him most, she didn't have him at her side.

At first, both had agreed that frequent salt water gargles should take care of an inflamed throat. They gave Rumi cumin and rock sugar to chew on for relief. But the patches grew more painful till he couldn't swallow at all, and the fever rose. On the third morning she took him to see Dr Lalkaka, while Boman went off to work.

Fidgety as always – spinning the paperweight on his desk, shifting the angle of his pen-holder – the elderly physician swung from side to side in his swivel chair like a distracted schoolboy while listening to the details of the case. Then he examined Rumi on the Rexine-covered cot behind the partition, narrow as a stretcher, and scribbled out a prescription on his pad. While the swarthy compounder mixed the concoction in his cabin, the doctor didn't forget to enquire after Khorshed's own condition.

Two days later, half of Lalkaka's raspberry-coloured mixture had been consumed by Rumi, but there was no improvement. Khorshed phoned the doctor and asked him to come home. During the home visit, Lalkaka remained genial and unhurried as always. But Khorshed was alarmed: the doctor advised her that the boy be shifted immediately to Parsi General Hospital.

That was the day the city newspapers reported an epidemic of diphtheria. Khorshed saw the headline in the afternoon paper only late that night when a visibly shocked and exhausted Boman rushed into the children's ward – followed by an agitated nurse hushing him to be quiet for the children were all fast asleep – carrying the day's *Bulletin*. Though he had purchased the copy of the paper earlier in the day, even Boman had seen the report only while riding home on the bus in the evening.

Trudging up the hill tiredly, he was surprised to see their two-room-kitchen flat in darkness. That, in itself, was unusual. But what had further alarmed him was that even the additional wire-mesh windows, attached to prevent stray cats from entering the flat, had been left open: Khorshed was terrified of cats, and it was unlike her to forget to fasten them before going out.

Then, approaching the verandah of their ground-floor flat, Boman saw the padlock on the front door. And Khorshed's note in a sealed envelope stuck under the nameplate, telling him where to come.

The first two days spent in the otherwise pleasant environs of the Parsi General Hospital – her days at Rumi's bedside, her nights on the wooden bench in the corridor which overlooked the vast, sombre garden – had a deceptively reassuring effect on her. When the house doctors began to frown and mumble regretfully – some even reproachfully – that the boy should have been brought in earlier, she wondered what on earth they could possibly mean. She had brought him as soon as her family doctor suggested it, hadn't she? And she was willing to go to any lengths to nurse him back to health again.

Fortunately, a pharmacy was located just outside the hospital gate, so Khorshed didn't have to leave her son alone for long, and the nurses were very kind. When time-tested formulations failed to produce results, the doctors pinned their hopes on newer drugs, the latest. As for Khorshed, she pinned her hopes on God's boundless mercy, which she had invoked many times in the past, but never with such beseeching desperation. In the past, He had never failed her.

On his thirteenth morning in hospital, Rumi began to experience difficulty in breathing. His skin had turned distinctly sallow, and doctors suspected the onset of tox-aemia. He was shifted to the ICU. By the end of the day, he went into a coma.

Here, the nurses were stricter about hospital rules regarding visitors. She spent most of those last forty-eight hours waiting outside, praying, helpless, sometimes with Boman beside her on the upholstered sofa at the end of the corridor; more often alone, besieged by her worst fears.

No, there was no point in appeasing her own guilt by nudging a portion of blame on to Boman. She alone had been responsible. They were newly married and he had been working himself to the bone – for whom? For her and Rumi, for their family's sake, of course.

Just weeks before the illness, Boman had had to seal off all the electrical plug points within Rumi's reach, using up an entire roll of Johnson's sticking plaster. But the little monkey was climbing on sofas, knocking down vases, often going for a fearful toss himself while making a desperate snatch at some object quite outside his reach. The folding red-and-blue playpen they had bought to keep him cooped up had clearly outlived its purpose. The child had learned the knack of climbing out of its tentative enclosure in ten seconds flat. At Boman's own suggestion, Khorshed had started making enquiries about a good kindergarten or nursery in the neighbourhood – a little young for school perhaps, Boman had argued, but at least he'd be kept out of harm's way.

It was difficult for Khorshed to attend to the cooking. Boman's lunch had to be packed and ready before the tiffin man came pounding on the back door with a vehemence that always made her hackles rise, arousing in her as it did an unconscious dread of inauspicious tidings – though she knew by the punctuality of his summons it was only the impetuous tiffin-carrier. So then how was she to keep an eye on the little imp to ensure he didn't bring himself to some grief?

And if by chance she apprehended him just in time to avert a disaster, like when she found him with his face coated with the thick gluey contents of a jar of Australian honey – what good fortune that the glass container had not shattered when he knocked it over, and only its lid flew open – he'd burst into an infectious giggling.

'But, Mama,' he said on the occasion of his orgiastic honey-guzzling, 'I thought you'll be happy I've become so tall. I can even reach the honey bottle myself.' She could never forget the gentle voice that lisped out those words, cleverly drawing attention to his achievement of growth to distract her mounting exasperation.

What was the point of memories? What was the sense in remembering that which could never be re-lived?

Just a few days before Rumi fell ill, the organizers of the Murphy Baby Contest had announced the prizes. They gave it a big spread in all the newspapers, with the names and addresses of the winners printed alongside their respective pictures.

What a terrific hoo-ha there was about Rumi's victory among the residents of the Khareghat Colony. Scores of people from the Colony, even persons who had never spoken to her before, dropped by to congratulate Khorshed; and so many of them kept harping on about how much prettier Rumi looked than even the first prize-winner, whose name escaped her now. How much of the gushing had been well-meant, how much of it was born of sheer envy, she had tried not to speculate. But her fingers reached nervously for wood every time she heard out their golden paeans of praise, nodding her head politely with a fixed smile on her face.

What irked her most at the time, and Boman as well, was the evident unfairness of the jury. Never mind that the child who had won first prize was nowhere as pretty as Rumi – that was a matter of opinion. But he had even posed for the photograph with his *left* forefinger on his chin, instead of the right one, a clear travesty of the original Murphy mascot's pose, which the contestants had been urged to emulate. And Boman heard, just a few days later, from someone in his office, that the first prize-winner was the child of one of the directors of the ad agency that was handling the Murphy account!

But very soon all those considerations became irrelevant. Nothing mattered. Take back your damned prize, she felt like screaming, we don't want it. Just make my Rumi well again, please God . . . But it was too late for that. The envy in a million admiring eyes (to which they had so thoughtlessly exposed their son) had congealed to form a membrane in his throat that smothered the poor blameless child, and curdled forever the happiness of a young couple.

On that Sunday afternoon, by the golden light of the waning sun that bathed the small procession of mourners plodding up the terraced hill, with the tiny white bundle that was her Rumi, Khorshed solemnly swore with her hand on her swollen belly that she would never be careless again, never with the other one who was due any day now.

Her torment temporarily soothed by the sonorous chanting of the quartet of priests, she begged forgiveness of the Almighty for the terrible crimes she must have committed, perhaps in a previous existence, to have merited such a devastating punishment. And also for the violent discontent she had given vent to, just a few hours ago, against His divine will.

Minutes later, the prayers ended, and the procession moved out of sight . . . The baby corpse would soon be relinquished to the garden of vultures on the hill from which none returned, except the gnarled and gnomic corpse-bearers for whom it was all in a day's work.

Two weeks later, Khorshed went into labour prematurely and was admitted to the maternity ward of the very same hospital where her first son had died. Word had spread among the nurses of her recent loss and they were all, without exception, the epitome of kindness and sympathy. But the more they urged her to take consolation in the effortless birth of her immaculate second child, the more repugnant he grew in her eyes. She couldn't help it. Even weeks after she had returned home and was entirely preoccupied with the business of feeding and burping, cleaning and changing and scrubbing the newcomer, she still had to contend with that feeling of a gaping void in her being, which this squint-eyed, colicky, near-bald interloper, who had usurped Rumi's cradle, would never, never be able to fill.

But she was wrong to think that, of course.

Condoling neighbours, unctuous relatives, everyone remarked with unfailing regularity on the resemblance.

Though she withheld them, Khorshed had her reservations about this.

Rumi had been her dream of perfection. In his looks, his good humour, his loving kind nature, in every way he had been the flowering blossom of her life itself. This Jaungoo was morose and taciturn. When he wasn't mewling, he was napping. That piteous bleating, once commenced, could easily last an hour, racking her nerves and setting her teeth on edge, until she pacified him (and herself – though she knew this was a bad habit to inculcate in an infant) by thrusting a teat into his mouth. It wasn't hunger that made him cry, for within a few minutes he would drowse back to sleep. He displayed none of the playful effervescence of his late elder brother who, even when just a few months old, had been lean and energetic. Jaungoo, on the contrary, was overweight, and rather sluggish. Sometimes she felt sorry for him, and then she would be kinder, more patient. For in her heart of hearts she knew that his vague, causeless whimpering had much to do with the grief that he had surely soaked up like a thirsting sponge, during the final hours of his coming forth into the world.

The dull irrevocable ache of sorrow had annulled memories of those first years. She remembered so little of that time now, except its endless, grinding routine and her isolation. She felt crushed, hopelessly incapable, inept. She avoided meeting the neighbours, and even stopped inviting them in when they rang her doorbell to help her pass the time, or offer some practical help. For in their eyes she invariably saw a smirk of pity that accused her of being too stupid to save her own child's life. In her polite refusal of all assistance, they saw arrogance, and further stupidity. Boman was workng harder than ever

before and had no time for her, though he made it a point
to cuddle Jaungoo and play with him for a few minutes if
he was still awake when he got home in the evening.
Somehow the days passed.

If there had been anything in her youth that had been
gay and carefree, it was no longer in evidence. Sometimes,
stretched out on her bed in the daytime beside a sleeping
Jaungoo, she remembered her own childhood that had
been spent in the lap of luxury. Her father, Merwanji, was
a rich man, but he too had decided to leave the world
when she was still no more than a child.

It must have been around Divali-time, for her first
impression on being startled awake by the loud report
was that a cracker had exploded somewhere very close to
their house. But for many years after that, the sudden
reverberation of a pistol shot ricocheted in her dreams,
awakening her with a start. Only much later, after she
had been married for a while, did that auditory nightmare
stop recurring.

But even when lost in thought, the slightest movement
or whimper of her child would snap her out of her rev-
erie. She didn't allow her depression to affect her efficiency
at all. In fact it seemed to heighten the obsessive particu-
larity with which she managed her home. Everything was
kept in order, in its right place, controlled by strict inven-
tory. She performed her duties without shirking. But all
the while, even when she seemed fully composed, a thick
gloom was seeping through the very pores of her being,
settling in her life like a sediment. Gradually it calcified in
an implicit belief that she had been cursed by ill-luck. In
her heart of hearts she knew that both she and Boman
would be dogged by misfortune to the end of their days.

Everything in her world was tinged with a sense of doom, like a pustule only waiting to ripen and burst.

On certain mornings, when Boman kissed her good-bye, a black thought winged through her head – it was no more than an instant really, for as soon as she recognized what it was she frantically brushed it aside – that he would never come back home alive. A fatal accident would strike him down on his way to work. What was most frightening was the vividness with which her mind produced these unwanted images of disaster. She saw him lying on the road, his skull crushed under the huge tyre of one of those lumbering BEST behemoths.

Even in matters of relatively minor importance, the same pessimism infected her outlook. If Parbati, the *bai* who came to sweep and scrub, was a little late, she'd assume that the woman had done the bunk again and she would be landed with doing the dishes. Or perhaps, the thought invariably occurred to her, the woman had stolen something from their flat and would never show up again.

If little Jaungoo sneezed a couple of times, she would say *jivsey*, or 'may he live long', repeating it to herself a dozen times, though even the ritual blessing did little to dispel the sense of impending dread that was immediately aroused in her.

In the evenings, if he was quite well, she took him to the open ground in the Colony where there were a few concrete benches and other children playing on the see-saw and the swing. But if she saw one of the neighbours whom she disliked in the distance, she immediately turned back to avoid any encounter.

In this manner, Khorshed lurched through the darkness of those days, incessantly sparring with the demons of suspicion and fear that lurked behind shadows in every corner of her mind. Soon the unhappiness in her became a habit she embraced unabashedly. Her acceptance of it made her calmer, her fears of insanity receded. She decided that she may have found no great happiness in her marriage, but *she* was certainly not mad.

Then, one Sunday afternoon, in a spare moment while Jaungoo dozed, she read an article that had appeared in an old edition of a weekly Gujarati tabloid, the *Jame-e-Jamshed*. It told the true story of a young couple who had suffered a devastating car crash on their way back from their honeymoon. The husband survived the crash with multiple fractures and severe head injuries. The wife could not be saved. When he came out of hospital, many months later, a broken man, his nascent business had collapsed, and hospital bills had rendered him practically bankrupt. Physical disabilities resulting from the accident and the tragedy of his recent loss left him too weak-willed to find his feet again.

It was around this time that he met – the article was written in the first person by the grieving husband himself – a *farohar*, a guardian angel, by the name of Rustom Hansotia. Hansotia was a spiritualist and a healer who employed various arcane lines of treatment, such as gemstone therapy, colour-ray therapy, radio-wave therapy and homeopathy, besides little-known yogic *asana*s. There was a paragraph in the piece devoted to the miraculous efficacy of his treatment, but that apart – and here was the remarkable angle to the story that made Khorshed sit up and take notice – this Hansotia had acted as a medium for the husband, making contact with and conversing with the spirit of the dead wife, sometimes for hours on end. Her love for her husband had remained undiminished, and she had remained constantly in touch with him – through Hansotia, of course – sending him heartwarming spiritual advice, encouragement and practical tips pertaining to his business affairs, even efficacious home remedies and recipes for powerful nostrums until he was able to completely rehabilitate his health as well as his business. Not only that, by the end of this period, once she was satisfied that her husband was prospering again (and it was time, she communicated, for her to depart from this sad realm of suffering and undertake the next lap of her celestial progress towards planet Jupiter), she placed her seal of approval on her husband's hitherto platonic relationship with his secretary, selflessly urging him to marry this girl who had served him faithfully through his illness and, in days to come, would certainly bring him much good fortune. And so, the article concluded, for the past one and a half years, they had indeed been very happily wed and the gods of success had begun to smile upon him once again.

At the bottom of the page, in one corner was a small box advertisement which read: 'Ye who think that all is lost, Do Not Despair!'

Below, in smaller type:

Why do we always blame God for every misfortune? What is written in our destiny cannot be avoided. BUT – whether ill-health, tragic loss, failed business or prodigal son – Ahura Mazda has given us the means to repair our lives. All we need to do is believe in His Goodness. Contact Rusi Hansotia: 367829 or meet personally by appointment at Sans Souci, Forjett Hill Road, Gowalia Tank, Bombay 12.

When Khorshed pointed it out to him, Boman admitted he had already read the piece. But he tried to discourage his wife from taking it too seriously.

'How ridiculous that a so-called spiritualist should suggest that everything in this world doesn't always come to pass by God's will! Or that we can alter the course of our destinies,' he scoffed. 'The fact that this article has appeared on the same page as his own advertisement makes it highly suspect. Some humbug out to milk the gullible for their last penny.'

'I don't know what makes you so cynical, Boman,' said Khorshed, a little angrily, 'but I have a strong feeling there's something special about this man. He's worth checking out, at the very least.'

'For heaven's sake, Khorshed, I will not have you getting mixed up with some godman-type! God knows, you have suffered enough already. Let us accept once and for all what has happened, that it was nobody's fault, least of all your own. This Hansotia is not going to make our son alive again.' Perhaps Boman said this rather more strongly than he should have, for it only strengthened a stubborn streak in Khorshed to follow her own resolve.

'I know that nothing and no one can bring my Rumi back,' said Khorshed. 'All I said was, it may be worth checking him out. You know it yourself, when I have a gut feeling, I'm hardly ever wrong. Besides, perhaps you haven't noticed the date on this publication . . .'

That was the clinching argument that undermined Boman's refusal to pursue the matter further. It was a startling coincidence, he admitted to himself privately, but he had missed it completely because he, too, had read the article not on the day it was published but a few days later, and hadn't noticed the date of issue. The article had appeared in an edition of the *Jame-e-Jamshed* dated exactly seven months from the day of Rumi's passing.

Reluctantly, not without a sense of foreboding, he

agreed to phone Rusi Hansotia and make an appointment to meet him. But he insisted on meeting him alone the first time. 'If he's a fraud, I'll be able to see through the man more clearly. If you and the child are with me, I'll be distracted,' he insisted. He also made it clear that if he remained unconvinced, or if his misgivings about the man were confirmed in his first meeting, there was no question of arranging a second.

It was a Saturday when Boman set out at 10 a.m. sharp, dressed in cleanly laundered white trousers and a white shirt.

For most of the two and a half hours that he was away, Khorshed was kept busy, attending to the baby's needs. Then she put some white rice and a pot of mauri daal to boil in the pressure cooker. But all the time she went about her chores mechanically, chopping onions, tomatoes and brinjal for the afternoon's *paatya*, she kept murmuring to herself, sotto voce, the ancient scriptural incantations recorded by her forefathers for posterity. She didn't really know quite what they meant, but she charged them with the emotional fervour of obsession, praying that Boman's first meeting with Mr Hansotia should turn out to be an auspicious one, that his own prejudices shouldn't affect his appraisal of the man, and that only what was right and good should ensue from it.

Her prayers may have had some effect, for Boman returned home remarkably chastened, more humble and contrite than she had seen him in years, somehow also more relaxed and lighthearted.

'I'm sorry, darling.' He plunged straightaway into an apology. 'I have to admit: you were right, after all.'

'Tell me what happened!'

'First thing he asked me was the date of Rumi's passing. He, too, was impressed by the fact that the article that brought us in contact with him was published exactly seven months after. He said that seven was the number of spirituality, and it would be foolish to ignore such a striking coincidence . . .'

'What else did he say?'

'Well, Khorshed, I'll tell you exactly what he said. I'm still a little sceptical about this part, but I'm willing to go along with it if you are. Somehow, I couldn't help trusting the man . . . He said that in his experience, and according to certain esoteric texts which he mentioned, the souls of children who die very young remain close to their families for a while. They don't traverse those vast cosmic expanses of space and time like the rest of us – since they've had so little opportunity to create bad karma for themselves – so there's no period of wandering and self-cleansing. They remain close at hand, nearby, in a sort of spiritual anteroom reserved for the very pure' – the punctuated cadence of Boman's concluding words seemed to suggest that he was not unaware of their dramatic impact – 'waiting to be quickly reborn.'

'Yes?'

Khorshed was impatient for him to go on, but in her mind, she was already reciting a prayer of thanks to the Almighty for their incredible good fortune in having encountered Rustom Hansotia.

'Now, don't get too excited, Khorshed. So far it's all just talk,' cautioned Boman. 'Well, what he was basically urging me to do – he said I came to him not a day too soon – you see, he wants us to try – wants you to try, that is – to conceive again as soon as possible. He said that if he has our permission, he'll try and make contact with

Rumi and perhaps Rumi himself can guide us as to the precise date and time when his conception can be enabled. He said it was risky to wait too long, for the child may easily tire of his insubstantial existence and, longing for form again – even though he loves us very much and wants to be reunited with us – willy-nilly slip into some other womb.'

'Oh my God,' said Khorshed, dismayed. 'And then he'd be lost to us forever?'

'Not quite, dear,' said Boman. 'He also said that karmic ties are inviolable and, some day, some place, per-haps when he has grown up, he will meet us again to repay his debt of gratitude to us. But that could be a very long time away and perhaps not even in this lifetime . . .'

'Oh darling,' said Khorshed, with a gasp of joy, throw-ing her arms around Boman's neck and pressing her lips to his. 'Let's try . . . let's please try.'

'I love you,' said Boman, responding to her passionate kiss as he had not in a long time, with his tongue. His hands cupped her swollen breasts. Flushed with pleasure she had begun to enjoy his touch, when from the next room came a wail at once irascible and forlorn.

'Now look at that little chimp,' said Khorshed, break-ing free of his embrace.

As she changed his urine-drenched nappy, Boman told her that Rusi had invited them next Sunday to attend a seance at his place where, with some luck, he'd be able to pass on to them more specific instructions – if they were interested in pursuing the matter, that is. He had to phone and let him know.

'Of course we'll go,' said Khorshed. Then she put to him a question whose reply, to her mind, would constitute decisive proof of Hansotia's genuineness. 'And did he say anything about how much it would all cost?

'Not a word about money. I didn't even feel the need to ask him. And when you see his flat you'll realize – it's filled with such beautiful antiques and paintings and the quaintest old furniture – I don't think he needs it at all. But having said that, I'd just like to emphasize,' said Boman, sounding a note of caution once more, 'that there's a side of me that's still not one hundred per cent convinced—'

'Now stop it, Bomi!' interrupted Khorshed. 'I know of your need for rationality in everything. But you have to have faith.'

'But I'm willing to go along . . . I said so, didn't I? In the meantime, he wants us to keep an oil lamp burning day and night at the head of his cradle. He said it would act like a beacon to reassure Rumi and keep him from wandering too far.'

'Right away,' said Khorshed. 'I don't think I have any wicks left in the house, but right after lunch I'll go down to the grocer's and get some.'

The following Sunday, they hired a taxi and set off for Forjett Hill Road. Boman was carrying the baby, bundled in a soft cotton quilt.

It was an old house, snuggled against the side of Forjett Hill. Illegal quarrying had defaced much of the hillside, leaving gaping holes below the protruding rockface of its forehead, like the vacant sockets of gouged-out eyes.

Hansotia occupied the entire top floor of the three-storey building that was called Sans Souci.

The door was answered by a lean old man with prominent cheekbones and dark circles under his eyes. He wore a hangdog look and a rather dirty curry-stained apron. The man stood there dumbly, blocking their way. But a moment later, they saw a short figure emerge from the dark corridor behind him. Before she even saw him clearly, Khorshed heard his booming voice. He had a deep, rich baritone that reverberated through the entire flat.

'Come, come, please come,' he said. 'Why are you all waiting outside? So happy to see you both . . .'

Introductions followed, which Boman handled deftly. But Hansotia's thunderous welcome had roused little Jaungoo, who protested shrilly at the stranger. Khorshed was shown into a room where she could suckle her baby in privacy. Then, summoning the grumpy-looking cook, Hansotia gave instructions: 'Michael, we'll be in my prayer room – not to be disturbed. Child will be sleeping inside there,' he said. 'Once he's fed, he won't bother you. Leave the fan on, and just keep an eye on the little fellow. Okay, Michael? No matter if lunch is a little late today.'

Michael had a very doubtful look on his face, but he grunted and left them.

It wasn't long before Jaungoo dozed off again. Khorshed laid him in the centre of a wide settee, and barricaded him with bolsters to prevent him from rolling down. Presently she joined the men in the living room.

'So the little fellow's asleep?' said Hansotia to Khorshed; then, consulting his wristwatch, 'We must begin at once, before the sun enters Rapithvan Geh.'

He led them through the corridor into a small inner room, which was darkened by blinds and perfumed with incense. It was fully carpeted and, following his example, they slipped off their footwear outside. One section of a wall was almost completely covered with pictures of saints and prophets, holy men, mendicants and miracle-workers, including Zarathustra, Jesus Christ, Gautama Buddha, Guru Nanak and the Shirdi Sai Baba. At least these they easily recognized. But the largest picture of all was a beautiful painting on silk of Hansotia's adoptive guru, Framroze Funibunda. In the portrait he had long hair, a short beard and searching eyes. He was smiling ever so slightly at the world. An oil lamp burned with a small flame under the portrait. Hansotia bowed before it reverently, and Khorshed and Boman followed suit, paying their respects to the portrait as a matter of form, though they had never before seen the remarkable face, nor even heard anything about the man.

While waiting for Khorshed to finish feeding the baby, Hansotia had briefly told Boman about this wondrous man who trod upon the earth not so long ago. Now, he told them some more.

He had never had the great fortune of meeting his Master in the flesh, he said, since he was born in 1940 himself – just a few months after the Master gave up the shell of his human body and became unfettered spirit. The important thing was that Framroze Funibunda's writings had been collected and published by his youngest disciple, who was still alive and all of eighty years old! For more than ten years, Hansotia himself had been pursuing his one real passion in life – the study of the occult and metempsychosis – but his search seemed to be leading nowhere, until he came across Framroze's writings, quite by chance, at a second-hand bookstall. He began his own investigations into the life of Funibunda. And he discovered that there were many who still revered him as a saint and told awesome tales of his miraculous healing powers.

Himself interested in alternative healing therapies,

Hansotia found Framroze's unpublished notes on the subject fascinating. A series of dreams came to him in which Hansotia received tuition directly from Framroze Funibunda on methods of healing the spirit-body. Thereafter, he was granted an out-of-body experience during which the spirit of Framroze took him on an aerial tour of the entire globe, pointing out to him in detail the extent of misery in this world. Other communications from the Great Soul followed, which convinced him that he, Rustom Hansotia, had been entrusted by the saint to advance His mission of increasing the quantum of happiness in this world, which had been cut short by His untimely departure, by acting in the capacity of a trance medium for the spirit of Framroze Funibunda.

For some time now, in a most mysterious and mystical fashion, others too, had begun to approach him, people who had heard of Framroze or read his teachings, or simply those who were suffering and seriously in need of help. A band of faithful disciples had congregated once more – now numbering close to forty, which was the number of the Inner Circle that the Master had maintained around him while he still occupied his human body. The activities of this spiritualist group were guided at every step by their perfectly endowed Master, who had always been lovingly known among his followers as Fali Baba.

'Just like an empty vessel, I am the earthen pot that resounds with the beautiful rhythms of love my Master taps out,' said Hansotia, once again bowing his head humbly towards the painting of Fali Baba. 'And now, let us pray . . .'

With these few words, Hansotia entered into meditation. For a long while, he sat in silence, his eyes shut, his hands with their white patches of leucoderma lying passively upon the table. He had instructed the couple that as sitters at a seance, they had an important role to play and would have to cooperate with him by remaining silent and focusing their minds on the Universal Love while keeping them free of any extraneous and irrelevant thoughts. Once, Khorshed peeped through half-shut eyes, but seeing Hansotia's face immersed in deep meditation, and Boman, too, with his eyes shut taking his part seriously, she tried to follow instructions as best she could. The fragrance of the joss-sticks burning under the portrait of Framroze was calming.

The minutes passed slowly and there was not a squeak from Hansotia. Then there was. A little squeak, like the distant sound of a child crying out in delight. It made Khorshed start; but no, this was not Jaungoo's voice, she realized, keeping her eyes shut. It was Rusi Hansotia who appeared to have uttered the sound. A moment later, he continued in the voice of a child:

'Mummy . . . I'm so glad to be here with you, Mummy . . . At last . . . I'm so glad to talk to you again . . .' This was incredible. It was the same gentle voice she had heard so many times in her dreams. It did in fact sound like – Rumi! And he was addressing *her*!

'I'm very happy here, Mummy . . . I love you so much, Mummy . . . I can't express how much . . . There's nothing to worry about . . . I'm very happy . . . Baba looks after me . . . Baba looks after us all . . . I have many friends here . . . I'm more happy than you can ever imagine.'

Khorshed couldn't believe her ears. Could it really be Rumi talking to her? It must, it must be. Tears of gratitude welled up in her eyes. She wanted to believe, she was ready to believe completely. Heavens be praised! It was true! It had to be true. She would give her everything, every ounce of faith she could summon, to be able to talk to Rumi again. In her mind's eye, she saw him again. She wanted to open her eyes and look at Hansotia's face, as her child's words poured out of his lips. She felt deeply grateful to Hansotia, the man who had made all this possible, and wanted to express her thanks to him, but he had warned both of them very strictly that the channel of communication would break abruptly if there was any interruption. Moreover, something else kept her eyes shut. She feared, perhaps without consciously knowing it, the ludicrousness of actually seeing Hansotia's long jaw and pert goatee as he lisped out those words in a child's voice – that it might in an instant shatter the tenuous bulb of belief that was growing in her.

Suddenly, there was soft and very pleasant laughter. And a deep, warm voice continued in place of the child's.

'Rumi is with me, my dear. He's safe and very happy. Don't worry, I will look after him and guide him at every step. I would help you, too, in every possible way. And your husband, dear Bomi. If Ahura Mazda wishes it, perhaps you can all be reunited once again. But for me to be able to do that, you must love me. Trust and love me . . . For only love can open the way . . . Love is everything . . . Love is all . . .' The voice trailed off.

Once again, a child's crying impinged on the silent spaces of Khorshed's bemused and dazzled imagination. She heard it as though coming to her from light-years away, across the firmament. But this child seemed to be mewling. Then the crying grew louder and more insistent. No, this was no spirit-child. It was Jaungoo. And he was crying! She opened her eyes and in the same instant there was an urgent rapping on the door.

'Saab . . . saab!' Michael, the cook, was calling urgently. Khorshed jumped up and was moving to the door to open it. But a peremptory voice, Hansotia's, stopped her in her tracks.

'Wait!' he called sharply, and a moment later, got up himself. 'What you did just now is dangerous. My sitters must never leave the table while I am still in communion. The link is broken.'

But the banging continued, as did Michael's imploring agitation.

'Please, saab! Open!' And Hansotia unlatched the door to see what the problem was.

Hunched and stooping, the lean Michael stood framed in the doorway holding up a naked Jaungoo, who was crying and kicking his stubby feet. Michael was carrying the infant gingerly by his underarms, holding him away from his own body; despair and fatalistic forbearance combined on his face in an expression of shocked self-pity. A strong, unmistakeable odour overwhelmed the incense-fragrant room.

'There's so much I want to ask Rumi,' said Khorshed, taking the child from Michael's outstretched hands. How she wished that Jaungoo hadn't chosen this time and place to demand her attention. 'Can we go back, please?'

'It may not be possible to contact him again, not twice in one morning. For one thing, it would be quite exhausting for me,' said Hansotia, wiping his forehead with a handkerchief. 'But at least we've made a beginning today. You heard: there is hope . . .'

For a while, the humdrum routine of Khorshed's daily life was animated by the cosmic dimensions of her intrigue with Rusi Hansotia and Boman for the reclamation of

Rumi's wandering soul. The lamp at the head of the cradle was never allowed to go out. By means of abstruse astrological calculations, always finalized in consultation with Fali Baba, and sometimes even Rumi himself (Khorshed, too, naturally, for she was to be the recipient of their grace), a list of dates and propititious hours was compiled. Initially, it worked wonders for their sex life. But then, the need for punctuality which Hansotia stressed, the odd hours of night or small hours of morning during which they were sometimes enjoined to copulate – not to mention the irritating awareness at the back of Boman's mind that Hansotia himself might well be visualizing their amorous engagement at that very moment since he was so anxious about its success – and the brief but mandatory prayer he had asked them to recite before making love which Khorshed kept muttering ritualistically even during intercourse, considerably diminished the joys of love-making and soon rendered it a chore.

Her husband's acquiesence to this spiritual conspiracy had been, at first, good-humoured and enthusiastic. He had been entirely charmed by his first meeting with Hansotia, and had taken an instinctive liking to the man. His subsequent meetings with him, in the company of his wife, had been somewhat different. Now Boman began to feel embarrassed by many things: the low lighting in the room, the incense, the atmosphere of 'holiness' that had been deliberately rigged by Hansotia in his den. Of course, it could all be justified, he supposed, as 'setting the scene', creating the right environment for communing with the dead. But there was a side of Boman that detested humbug and was quick to detect it. And more than anything else, just as he had feared, Khorshed was going a little over the top in her adulation of the man.

He couldn't help the way he thought. He wasn't terribly impressed by Hansotia's voices. He had heard a ventriloquist during his college days who had done a much better job, and hardly moving his lips! Yet he restrained himself from expressing any of his misgivings to his wife. He knew that when it came to this matter, she would be entirely headstrong in her pursuit of irrationality. And to forbid her outright from having anything more to do with Hansotia could be disastrous. He knew that she was capable of disobeying him and might even begin to see him without his knowledge. It was more strategic to play along until she discovered the truth for herself.

So he only grumbled a bit, voiced his doubts none too strongly, but allowed her to persist in her fantasies of a reunion with Rumi. But more than anything else, in the end it was the total absence of any tangible result that finally made Boman give vent to his aversion to their folly. His disgust steadily grew with every urine report from the pathologist's that proved negative.

'There's something quite unnatural about all this, dear,' he'd say, shaking his head tiredly. 'I told you I was willing to go along. But for how long? Has there been any proof of substance in his crackpot theories? I mean, it's all very well to long for Rumi to come back. I mean, even if it's not Rumi and some other child is born to us – that would be great, too—'

'Please, please, Boman. Can't we go on trying a little longer? He did say it may take a while . . .'

But more often than not, consultations with Hansotia now took place over the phone. Sometimes he would ring up Khorshed while Boman was at work and encourage her not to be disheartened.

'Just think of it, Khorshed,' he said once. 'What we are attempting is so audacious – just think of the odds – billions and trillions of souls all floating out there in the Grove of Serenity, and we want to entice one of them back into our world! It may take some time, and persuasion. But we have to be patient . . . By the grace of Baba, it will all work out. Is Boman being quite regular? . . . Hello? Hello, are you there?' He interrupted himself, unnerved by Khorshed's silence.

Embarrassed about having to discuss her sex life with this inquisitive, albeit well-meaning man, Khorshed made excuses for her husband. 'Well, sometimes if he's very tired after work, or if he has to wake up at 3 a.m. or something, he can't quite . . .'

'No, no! It's very important to keep at it regularly. Do observe all the timings I give you, every month,' said Hansotia. 'And the other thing that's even more important – now I know how difficult this is for us Parsis – no meat! No meat on the day you have sex and the day before . . . Animal flesh may be creating a sort of aversion in the little soul.'

When he finally rang off, Khorshed sighed and went in to prepare lunch for herself and Jaungoo, who was still asleep. She rather liked this man and enjoyed the gentleness of his concern for her. She believed that he was sensitive enough to see through Boman's selfish and egocentric nature. In fact, Boman had become rather suspicious of her relationship with Hansotia. He had warned her that he would be able to tolerate a great deal, but under no circumstances would he allow her to join the band of Fali Baba's disciples. Khorshed found herself very much drawn to Baba. She even made time now to read some of the literature supplied to her by Hansotia. If only she could have paid a visit to His ashram in Nargol. She would have taken Jaungoo along, of course. That wouldn't be as difficult as trying to get Boman's permission to go.

Time had passed quickly, and Jaungoo was growing up. Now Boman had very little to do with Rusi. Hansotia himself was away for many months at a time, travelling. His travels took him to various cities in Europe and the USA where he provided largesse and encouragement to the far-flung disciples of Fali Baba to set up their own branch organizations. Once, he even went on a lecture tour to eleven different cities and towns. Money seemed to be no object to Hansotia, and he always came back from these overseas trips laden with expensive gifts for Khorshed, for Boman and even Jaungoo. Boman was embarrassed by the extent of his generosity, but he was happy to have such a well-to-do friend, who was also rather well connected. Khorshed was truly grateful and began to appreciate his altruistic nature more than ever.

Gradually, though, she grew resigned to the sadness of never becoming pregnant again. She realized with a shock that in her intense yearning for this fantasy of rebirth to be enacted, she had been behaving like a childless mother craving for an offspring. When God had in fact compensated her fully well, and almost immediately, for the loss of her first-born. She felt remorseful when she remembered the vow she had made on the hill of the Towers of Silence, never to neglect her second son. Now she decided to dedicate herself to him with a renewed interest. She helped with his homework. She took him to the neighbourhood municipal park at Babulnath in the evenings, pushed the swing for him when it was his turn to sit on it and baked him custards and bread puddings.

She avoided any mention of Rumi when speaking to him. But the feeling of an absence in her life persisted. Now, whenever Hansotia phoned, or if she called him up for some advice, she avoided mentioning it to Boman, if she could help it. There was really no point in exacerbating the issue. Anyway, she and Boman had drifted further apart than ever before.

In spite of everything, she continued to believe in Baba's grace. She felt protected. She felt He was watching over her every minute of the day. The sense of gloom that had weighed her down for so many years now seemed to lift and she felt she had something to look forward to in life, after all. Boman, meanwhile, had accumulated enough clients of his own to venture into setting up as a private consultancy. Though he remained very busy, working out of a friend and partner's office, they were much more comfortably off. Secretly, he felt somewhat relieved that Khorshed's obsession with Rumi and Hansotia had taken the pressure off him and left him free to work.

Little Jaungoo was growing up really very charmingly sweet. Things were easier for Khorshed too, because she didn't have to budget and penny-pinch to make Boman's salary last through the month. The impatient tiffin man no longer came pounding at the back door, giving her a start every morning at eleven, for Boman had decided to order his afternoon meals from a small cafeteria below the office.

As a concession to her past longing for Rumi, Boman agreed to let her keep the lamp lit. When he became a little older, Khorshed assigned Jaungoo the task of refilling the glass with coconut oil. Sometimes she would ask him to nip down to the grocer's for a fresh batch of wicks. Fortunately, the grocer's shop was right outside the Colony gates. No roads to cross, no traffic to negotiate: she was sure he would be quite safe.

Schooldays

While he was still eight, his mother had already begun to warn Jaungoo of the decisive drawbacks of latter-life obesity (though secretly she delighted in his plump rolls of fat). She urged him to go easy on the butter that he plastered thickly onto his slices of broon every morning, and scolded him if he reached for more than three of the oil-rich naankhatais he ate with his afternoon tea.

These biscuits, baked in Surat but available at the corner Irani's cafe, were a favourite with his father, too. Boman ensured that a glass jar was always well stocked at home. Impelled by a voracious post-school appetite, it was difficult to stop Jingo from gobbling down large numbers of these Surti cookies.

'Expense apart, look at his size,' Khorshed complained to Boman, and thenceforth rules were laid down to regulate how many times a month Boman was permitted to refill the jar.

But the years passed, and time had a surprise in store for both parents. For on completing his twelfth year Jingo's physique went through a remarkable transformation. It was as though a lever had been depressed and a spring released – he shot up in height dramatically, in a relatively short period, until he stood just six inches short of his father's stature. His voice had only just begun to crack. Now there was no more talk of juvenile obesity. Stretched over larger bones, his flab became taut and power-filled. He began to take part in all those outdoor games which until now he had abstained from under the influence of his mother's anxious buffering.

Boman was distinctly pleased by this turn of events. He claimed a direct genetic lineage for Jaungoo from Savaksah Dhunjisah Moos, his own father, a bank teller who was also a celebrated bodybuilder. Savaksah's boyishly handsome figure hung in a photo-frame over Boman's writing desk. In the foreground was displayed a large shield which Savaksah had just won in the Western India Body-Beautiful Statue-Posing Contest.

Jingo had never seen his grandfather alive. He imagined him in death as he appeared in this photograph: stark naked, but for a G-string, and fully coated in a shiny white paint intended to enhance the alabaster effect . . . sinews magnificently tautened, body arched and straining as if to perform some feat of Herculean proportion, a diabolical grimace frozen on his face.

Of course, he was only posing as a statue. A few motionless moments later, the statue came to life amidst tumultuous applause; then, bowing awkwardly, exited the stage. Jingo had replayed this routine over and over again in his head, but what was rather more difficult to imagine was the cruel absurdity of this powerful bodybuilder being felled by a massive cardiac arrest, no more than two months after that photograph was taken. That was to be his final bow before the irreversible stiffness set in, the authentic rigor mortis that no amount of imagination could resuscitate nor turpentine wash away.

Jingo's childhood abounded with stories of Boman's struggle as a young man to provide for his mother and his little sister. He had been in his last year at school when Savaksah collapsed one night, just as he was getting ready to go to bed, and within minutes, passed away. Boman's final exam had been no more than a week off when the tragedy struck. Somehow the boy managed to keep his wits about him and grief at bay, presenting himself for the school-leaving examination at the appointed hour. He finished with flying colours and even won a scholarship that would pay for his college education.

But what he needed more urgently was a job that would keep the kitchen fires burning. He opted for evening college instead of regular day college, which the trustees of the scholarship fund kindly permitted, given his special circumstances. After a nine-hour stint at reading proofs in the overheated print shop of an evening paper, six days a week, he procceded to a well-known institution at Flora Fountain called Daavar's Classes to apply his mind to the principles of commerce and cost accountancy.

Especially after Jingo grew up, Boman's stories were laced with a strong moral content. Often their narration bore a direct relationship to Jingo's own restricted capacity for study, or any form of sustained application. The stories commenced at the point of Savaksah's untimely death, but went on through the early years of their married life, sometimes bringing tears to Khorshed's eyes, for they reminded her of the old days of their struggle, of her husband's sterling character and his spirit of never-give-up.

But all that had changed now, for both Boman and Khorshed. For Khorshed such stories now prompted only tears of irrational vexation; she was frightened by the comparison her husband made so often between his father's physique and Jingo's – Savaksah had died when he was just thirty-three.

'You have a twisted mind to think such things!' Boman reprimanded her. 'Papa would have lived to be eighty, just like my uncle Causi. If only he hadn't pushed himself so hard. He was preparing for his big moment . . . the greatest show on earth,' said Boman, a hint of wistful melancholy now entering his voice. 'And he would have won it, too, hands down! But only a day before the contest, bloody Fate beat him to it . . . Poor Savaksah would never fulfil his dream of becoming Mr Universe.

'Now Jaungoo's case is completely different,' Boman went on, more sternly. 'He's not even lifting weights! The simple exercises I've shown him – *dund*, *baithak* – even those he won't do regularly. He's a strong boy, but lazy. Do you understand? When I speak of genetic lineage, it doesn't mean that *every*thing has to follow in exactly the same pattern, or that—'

But Khorshed would not permit those words to be spoken, even if she had to clap a hand on Boman's mouth. She snapped her fingers loudly, muttering *ovaaryu*, *ovaaryu*, and Boman let his sentence remain incomplete. For what was the sense in belabouring a parallel which he himself perceived as dubious? On the evidence of physical appearance, his father's line of genes seemed predominant in Jingo. But there was also a unmistakable feebleness of spirit – and Boman could only guess which side that had been inherited from.

Driven by compelling ambition, his own father had tried to mould his body to perfection. He wanted to be the best. But Jingo's lack of rigour in all matters was in worrying contrast. Boman had tried to inspire him with edifying aphorisms gleaned from his *Thesaurus of Memorable Quotes*, on the virtues of perseverance and ambition – *A man without ambition is like a boat without oars, adrift on a choppy sea* – but his son's inability to see tasks through to their conclusion frankly dismayed him. It seemed to him that the boy lacked spine. Too willing to find friendships, too easily swayed by ill-chosen ones, he was prone to distraction, always willing to forsake his own path at the very first diversion.

In the grudging respect his schoolmates now accorded him, Jingo sensed his own physical prowess. He had never really had to work for it, nor was he particularly proficient at games. But his general bulk and height were impressive enough to exempt him from bullying at the hands of his seniors – or, for that matter, those lanky hulks known as 'repeaters': boys who had failed to obtain passing marks, and were therefore constrained to stay behind in the same class with a younger lot of boys, newly promoted.

There were always one or two in every class. Being that much older than the rest of the boys, these specimens of academic ineptitude were not difficult to identify. Among teaching staff and the priests who ran the school, they had a justifiable reputation for being vile, cynical creatures who could stoop to shocking levels of disorderliness, disobedience and downright brigandage.

Undoubtedly, the most dreaded among the repeaters was a boy called 'Hippo' Gorimar.

Part-boy, part-man, his chronological age was a matter of intense speculation among his mates who put it anywhere between sixteen and – on the outside – twenty-two! His nickname, though universally acknowledged for its aptness, was not one to be carelessly bandied about. The boys lived in terror of his savage retribution should any of them be overheard mouthing that awful insult. Even some of the masters quailed in the face of Hippo's hulking insolence, hesitating to exact punishment for misdemeanours whose culprit it was possible to pinpoint beyond a shadow of doubt.

To be sure, there was something quite ridiculous about Hoshi's physical appearance, rather than wicked or nasty. His large face was curiously smooth and oafishly inexpressive. The small forehead and high cheekbones were attached to a disproportionately large body without evidence of any conjunctive neck. A splay-footed, ambling gait conveyed unhurried tranquillity, rather than the impression of a body slowed down by corpulence. Massive forearms and muscle-thonged upper arms hung languidly at his side, except when in assault mode. His thickset eyes were small and uninteresting until one noticed how they darted from side to side with a restless agility, an icy aggression. A patch of baldness, perhaps congenital, shone in the middle of his pate, surrounded by sharp short quill-like hairs that gave him an air of dubious venerability, as of a depraved friar too quickly past his prime.

There was an avuncular jollity about him, too. His outrageous humour, his brazen daring, were much admired by the boys. He had the aplomb of a power-crazed dictator, commandeering around himself a detachment of aides, foot soldiers and cheerleaders, each with specific duties to perform.

Some boys were expected to finish his homework for

him, while others (selected for their neat hand) were permanently engaged to transcribe 'notes' dictated by teachers during school hours into his exercise books. Hoshi didn't mind if they took their time, doing it over weekends, so long as his books were up-to-date when the teacher called them in for checking. Variations in script caused comment sometimes, but Hippo's explanation was simple: 'Sir, my handwriting changes according to which pen I use. I have a very changeable personality.' Most of the time, teachers preferred to overlook this kind of thing, rather than enter into confrontation with Gorimar.

A number of other boys, selected for the variety and taste of their menus, were expected to share their tiffin lunches and snack-time relishes with Hoshi. Never greedy, he always ensured that his donors had enough left for themselves and never went hungry.

On days when the boys had PT and were required to run several rounds of the football ground, Hoshi would try to excuse himself by feigning a limp, or suddenly shrieking out loud – a swear word thrown in to add conviction to his claim that he had only just, in that very moment, clumsily sprained his ankle. Should none of these ruses convince the physical trainer ('Aflatoon' Irani) that Hoshi should be exempted from his fair share of rounds, there were always a couple of boys who obliged him by massaging his legs during the lunch break. Though the stench of his nylon socks was powerful enough to stun a horse, these chores were carefully rotated by Hippo to ensure that his appointees did not rebel against his regime.

There was only one context in which Hippo didn't mind his nickname being used. In fact, he had suggested it himself when it came to him in a flash of inspiration.

'Hippo-long Gorimar', he had called himself, after the cowboy action comic hero Hopalong Cassidy. Hippo was obsessed with penile length and boasted frequently about his own, even offering to prove its superior dimensions with a footrule. After school hours, a very select few boys – and particularly one effeminate puny fellow by the name of Percy – were entrusted with the dark privilege of providing Hippo with secret pleasures in the cubicles of the vast student latrine.

Going by build alone, Jingo could easily have been mistaken for a 'repeater'. But by demeanour he was different. Quiet and thoughtful, he deplored a ruckus and was not himself inclined to bullying. He had a strong desire to be regarded by his teachers as above average in maturity and exceptionally well read. For this reason, unlike some of the hyperactive rowdies in his class, he always behaved with a dignified and admirable circumspection. It was not as though he didn't crave friendships, but an essential timidity kept him from seeking any adventure that seemed too temeritous.

Jingo quailed in the face of violence. No doubt Hoshi, who was taller, could easily have licked him in hand-to-hand combat. But it never came to that. For Hoshi, too, kept a safe distance from Jingo, treating him with guarded respect. Perhaps it was Jingo's image of self-contained circumspection that drew Hoshi to him. As might be expected, for all his wild bravado, Hoshi, too, lacked companions.

To begin with, Jingo didn't find any basis for reciprocity to the chumminess Hoshi was offering. Then one day he heard from a fellow student that Hoshi didn't have a father and had been brought up by his widowed mother. This revelation disposed Jingo more favourably towards Gorimar. In some way he could identify with him now; himself, he had a father and mother, but he didn't have a brother. And his mother's attempts at communing with the spirit of her dead son never allowed him to forget that. Rumi's untimely death at the age of three had permanently transfixed him in his parents' mind in an aura of beatific goodness. When Jingo considered his own nature in contrast, he felt inadequate and even guilty.

He knew quite well that friendship with Hoshi could lead him into all kinds of trouble. On the other hand it would give him status, privilege and protection as a buddy of the school's worst bully. Besides, Jingo had reached an age at which he felt his mother's protective cloistering was positively tyrannical. His association with Hoshi held promise of excursions and campaigns which were simply outside his spirit of boldness to venture into alone. He was apprehensive, but certainly fascinated by what Hoshi had to offer.

Now, it was around this same time that a spaghetti western was released at the New Empire cinema called *The Return of Django*. The New Empire was conveniently located no more than a hop skip and jump away from school. The film ran for a number of weeks. Before long the similarity of the hero's name to Jingo's own sobriquet was spotted and he was dubbed Duh-Jango by all and sundry among his schoolmates, though Jingo himself knew that the 'D' must remain silent. Like most of the other boys, Jingo himself had not seen the film. So, when Vispy, Kayomus and Hoshi came up with a plan to cut school and see a matinee show, even offering to subsidize the cost of his ticket, there seemed to be no sensible reason to refuse.

'But is it safe? What if Father Dias or Father Bulchand sees us entering the movie hall?'

'And what would Dias or Bulldog be doing at New Empire during school hours, dumbo?' the others argued back with faultless logic.

Was it the effect of the company he began to keep? Something of the brazen bravado inherent in the hero's name must have rubbed off on him, or perhaps he felt obliged to live up to the daredevilry of his adventures, for it was around this time that Jingo turned maverick with a vengeance.

One afternoon, Hoshi invited him to bunk the last two periods of the day – Ghanshyam's language class – and hop on a 69 bus with him. This bus passed Jingo's home and, later, even Hoshi's. But after that, it followed a slow, circuitous route through the lanes of the city's red-light district, Kamathipura. The bus was fairly empty when they got on, and Hoshi picked choice seats for them, right in front, on the top deck.

When the bus sped past Khareghat Colony, Jingo ducked. Hoshi chuckled and pretended to hail an imaginary Mrs Moos, drawing attention to her son slouching deep in the seat beside him. But soon they turned off at Gowalia Tank, and Jingo straightened up again. Within minutes, the bus was moving jerkily through the traffic-logged streets of Kamathipura.

'Just look at all those sleepy-eyed *rundee*s,' cried Hoshi gleefully, pointing out the women lounging outside the brothels, some preening their long hair, others peering into a hand-mirror while applying make-up on already caked faces. 'They're getting themselves ready for an evening of non-stop fucking. Oof, just looking at them I've got a hard-on. Feel it, man, just feel it. It's hard as wood! It'll tear open my pants in a minute . . . Just look at those boobs bursting out of her blouse! Aaah . . . By God, I love this!'

It was an extraordinary afternoon for Jingo, who was seeing the cages and their inmates for the first time. Later, they got off the bus and Hoshi wanted to stop for a glass of taadi. He ordered one for Jingo as well, but Jingo couldn't finish it. It was too sour for his liking. He tried puffing at the Wills Navy Cut cigarette that Hoshi offered him, but with even more unpleasant results. He couldn't stop coughing.

There was something distasteful about allowing one-self to be led by a friend whose tastes and sensibility he didn't completely share. He felt he was betraying his parents in some way, besmirching the pure goodness of their true Parsi character. He had to admit that the for-bidden fruit wasn't always as delicious as it was supposed to taste, but he was glad that at least it was no longer so inaccessible.

Nevertheless, he began to discover the heady charms of freedom. The thrill of narrowly escaping capture and punishment by donning a persona of decency and utter innocence, then the pleasure of recounting the close shave to the others in highly dramatized detail. Since Ghanshyam, their Gujarati instructor, was a soft target for the form of sadistic mischief that Hoshi excelled in, Hoshi harassed the life out of him. And Jingo, too, was gradually drawn into the same venal pleasures.

Many years ago, Ghanshyam had authored a treatise on Sanskrit grammar that had earned him the reputation of being a scholar. Heavily built and tall, G. Ghanshyam was not at ease with his large body and conducted himself rather clumsily. Essentially a nervous sort of a man, he was clearly not in the best of health. Under stress, he broke out in facial twitches. Moving from classroom to classroom, often having to climb several flights of stairs in a day, he was always huffing and puffing. He was irreverently called Ghunto, or 'danglers', by the boys. Partly this was just a meaningless nickname of the sort schoolboys excel in providing for those whom they cannot openly disdain. Partly it was a reference to the enormous bulb that sprouted between the elderly teacher's legs every time he sat down in front of the class. This, of course, may not have been any more than the result of poor tailoring in the 'fork' region of his trousers. But the more knowledgeable boys claimed that Ghanshyam suffered from a chronic ailment called hydrocele, which meant that every time he drank water, instead of going down to his stomach it went down to his balls, which then swelled up. Sometimes, if he drank too much water, they became as huge as footballs.

Ghunto was a gentle soul, whose reputation of being a sacrificial goat preceded him, communicated unfailingly to every fresh batch of students by those satiated gremlins who reluctantly moved out of his academic ambit. For years, he had been routinely subjected to every form of harassment that classroom boredom could concoct.

He managed to reinforce his own image of being a helpless, foozling clown by losing control over himself every time he couldn't keep control of the class. Hysterically hurling abuse and blows at the young monsters who took spiteful pleasure in making him chase them round the classroom, his facial twitching took on an exceptional vigour. His agitation gave him a marked limp as he dodged the deliberately outstretched feet of students between rows of desks and benches, in a kind of St Vitus' dance of bungling rage.

He was subjected to all this harassment by the boys as they tried to make instruction in a language they were neither fond of nor interested in learning more entertaining. Being a third language, they knew it would make no difference to their overall percentage of marks at the high school exam. And it gave them a kick to be able to inflict such merciless punishment on this elderly teacher with so much impunity. It was a vicarious pleasure which compensated them for all those hours they had had to spend with the more implacable and disgruntled teaching staff. For Ghanshyam they knew was essentially feeble and, despite all the odds, even kind-hearted.

Ink stains on the rear of his shirt, chewing gum stuck on the seat of his chair which then attached itself to his trousers, feats of ventriloquial farting, shrieking and guffawing – Ghanshyam had withstood them all for generations with noble forbearance. But finally, one day, he outdid himself and physically hauled Hippo to Vice-principal Dias's office, while raining blows and slaps on his head all the way down the corridor. He had caught him red-handed peeing into the wastepaper bin which stood in the corner, behind the class cupboard.

'Couldn't control, couldn't control,' sang Hoshi, warding off the blows, as Ghanshyam pushed him along. He hadn't expected Ghunto to catch him peeing in class, for the teacher had been busy explaining some abstruse clause of Gujarati grammar. The metal wastepaper bin was too full of scrap paper and pencil shavings for his stream of urine to create a din. It was the uncontrolled tittering of the boys which gave him away.

Father Dias showed no mercy, even though Hippo feigned tears and told him of a weak bladder on account of which he often wet his pants unless he urgently relieved himself.

'We'll discuss that with your mother,' he said and sent Hippo home to fetch her. 'In the meanwhile, I'll keep a pink card ready to hand over when she comes along.' This pink card was the punitive weapon the Jesuits wielded in the most extreme instances of indiscipline. Three pink cards – which were equivalent to one grey card – meant expulsion from school, and everyone knew that Hippo had already earned one such pink blot in the early years of his school career for seriously injuring another boy in physical combat. So Hippo went home before lunch break, ostensibly to fetch his mother, but didn't return for the rest of the day. Later, he told Jingo that he had spent the afternoon drinking beer with Sakuntala, the kindliest harlot at Pila House who, he claimed, was so fond of him that she never charged for her services.

The Education Ministry had drafted a proposal to introduce sex education at secondary and high-school level. I remember my father reading this out approvingly from the newspaper one Sunday morning. Perhaps the proposal took longer to implement than it was supposed to, because our lot remained completely ignorant. Even Hoshi, for all the knowledge he claimed to have about sexual matters . . . It was in the VIth, or was it VIIth, that he sidled up to me one afternoon during breaktime and said, 'Do you know how babies

are born? Do you know how you were born?
You're so ignorant about the essentials, man.
Your father put his popo into your mother's
popee and pissed inside. That's how babies are
born. That's how you were born, too!'

I remember my feeling of disgust and horror
at this statement. Outrage, at the audacity of
his lies. Yet somehow there was a ring of truth
about it, and I couldn't discard the
information outright. I felt ashamed for my
parents, for their indulgence in an act so
putrid and disgusting. I must have felt some
anger against my father for doing something
so vile to Mother. Much later, when I realized
that this was perhaps what Father suspected
her of doing with Rusi Uncle, my anger was
redirected towards her.

At least another year or two must have
passed before I saw at close quarters Hoshi
trying to push his engorged cock into Percy's
retching mouth. This was more of the same
ugly behaviour he had described for me a
couple of years ago in connection with my
own parents. I felt a great deal of sorrow to
realize that this was what people were all
about, that this was what they meant when
they spoke of having sex – this act of emission
in another's orifice.

The next day, Hoshi came to school as usual with his
satchel of books, pretending nothing unusual had happened, but Father Dias was waiting for him at the gate.
He sent him home at once, telling him not to return with-

out his mother. This time, Hippo knew he wouldn't be able to escape his second pink card. All the way home by public bus, he plotted revenge on Ghanshyam, muttering to himself, '*Maaderchod* Ghunto can spit his blood-red paan-juice in the wastepaper bin whenever he likes, but so much fuss over a simple piss.'

The real joke about the whole episode, which would have escaped Father Dias, though not the students of IX B, was that it was in fact Ghanshyam who had a weak bladder and would, on occasion, excuse himself with a wretched, crimped look on his face, making a dash for the staff toilet which was down the corridor and up a flight of stone steps. Hoshi was not frightened of Dias or his pink card, but he knew that his mother would have to apply for a day's leave from the post office in order to accompany him to school. And then there would be tears and curses and lamentations about the misery and trauma he had brought on her head, and how she had gone grey worrying about what would become of him once she was no more, considering that he had already strayed so far from the path of decent living.

Feeding him a sandwich garnished with broken bits of shaving blades, preparing a cocktail of sulphuric and other acids stolen from the chemistry lab and offering it to him in a moment of extreme thirst (just as he's released from a classroom where he was locked up overnight without water), a commando-style assault on him while on his way home after school – all these and many more means of exacting revenge on poor Ghanshyam had danced through Hippo's mind. Jingo knew, for Hippo had discussed some of them with him. But when he finally decided on his course of action, he kept it entirely secret from everyone, including Jingo.

His only concession to candour was to ask Jingo if he could fetch him a bottle of oil from home.

'Oil? What kind of oil?' asked Jingo. 'What do you want it for?'

'Any kind of oil – cooking oil, hair oil,' said Hoshi. 'Just don't make too much noise about it. Can you get it or no?'

At Jingo's, apart from cooking oil and hair oil, there was always at least a litre of coconut oil kept in stock to refill the lamp-in-the-glass beside Rumi's crib every morning and evening. Jingo readily agreed to smuggle out a bottleful for Hoshi. Handing it over to him in school the next day, he once again asked Hoshi what he meant to do with it. A raffish wink was all the reply he got but he knew he was about to witness the unfolding of a vendetta.

It was just as well that Hoshi didn't involve him further in his plan of revenge on Ghanshyam. For when the accident occurred, the priests hushed it up publicly, but spared no pains in conducting a thorough internal inquiry. They cross-examined all the troublemakers and tormentors that Ghanshyam had named from his hospital bed, from every class that he taught. The list extended into scores of them and Jingo's name featured prominently on it too. But gradually, they shortened the list, zeroing in on the most hardened types and even threatening to hand them over to the police if they didn't confess. Of course, Hippo Gorimar was prime suspect. But in the end, they were unable to break his defences with any of their bullying threats. Hippo had covered his tracks well.

It had been a simple plan that hinged on accurate timing and a general knowledge of Ghanshyam's teaching timetable. Hoshi, like most of the other students, was aware of Ghunto's bladder-control problem and knew that during every break and sometimes even between classes, he would make a quick dash to the staff loo. There were two routes by which he could do this. One, through the staffroom and into the annexe building where the staff washroom was located in a separate low stone structure. The other route was to climb a short but steep flight of stone steps that led directly to the staff loo from the main building. It was this route that Ghanshyam mostly preferred, perhaps because he was embarrassed by his frequent need to go, which he imagined the rest of the teachers kept count of while lounging around the staff-room during their free periods.

At the end of the short recess during which the staff drank their coffee, he knew that Ghunto had a class with IX A. Hoshi also knew that before entering IX A, Ghunto would pay a quick visit to the loo, using the shortcut.

He was waiting at the end of the corridor when the electric gong shrilled, announcing the end of short recess. He saw Ghunto entering the loo through the swing-doors. By now all the corridors had cleared and the boys had settled in their seats. The coast was clear for Hoshi. He poured his entire stock of oil on the stairs outside the staff loo and then raced back to his classroom and settled in his seat.

The school had quietened down, except for the humming of voices from IX A, which meant that Ghunto hadn't arrived yet. Some of the teachers had already commenced their lessons, including 'Jakes' Furtado in IX B, when the boys heard a series of dull thuds and a soft cry of pain that seemed to come from very far away.

Many minutes after classes had resumed Vice-principal Dias set out on his rounds and discovered poor Ghunto lying in a heap, moaning, at the bottom of the short route to the staff washroom. He had fractured a wrist and hurt his head.

The Jesuits were much alarmed by the accident, as also were the sweepers and cleaners of the school who were naturally the first to be summoned and questioned about the slippery, sticky mess on the stairs leading to the staff loo. Soon, it became evident that this was nothing short of a case of premeditated sabotage. The investigation began the day after, which gave Hoshi ample time to dispose of the empty oil bottle.

Now Jingo, shocked by the violence of Hoshi's revenge, thanked his stars that the old man had not broken his neck instead of his wrist. Incidentally, Ghanshyam recovered quickly, and was absent from school for only a week, after which he reported for work once again with an adhesive plaster on his forehead and a more substantial one around his wrist. Jingo was frightened that being the supplier of the oil that had caused the accident he would be implicated. But Hoshi kept his secret – as Jingo kept Hoshi's – and both came out of the incident unscathed. But the parents of all the troublemakers who had been named by Ghunto were called to school and lectured at by the Vice-principal on decent behaviour befitting the students of a good school.

'I can understand if boys from the Bhikubhai Nanavati Technical School next door behave in such a rowdy fashion,' he said. 'But you lot! Studying at St Joseph's! We expect different kind of behaviour from boys of good families.'

This was the very first time that Khorshed had been summoned to school in this manner to hear complaints about her son. She was scandalized. When the priest had finished speaking to her, she turned to Jingo: 'What will I tell your father in the evening when he comes home from work? This is how you study in school? Aren't you ashamed of yourself?'

'Bad company, madam. One rotten mango can spoil the whole basket,' said Father Dias. 'Your Jahangir needs to be more careful in choosing his friends . . . How much these boys trouble poor Mr Ghanshyam,' Father Dias went on. 'You should hear the ruckus they make during his period. Oh yes, they're quite capable of reducing the poor man to tears!'

Jingo kept his eyes turned to the floor during the diatribe. But what he heard now startled him and he looked up.

'And what do you know, Jahangir, of poor Mr Ghanshyam's personal problems? Do you know about his wife who has been in hospital for the last six months, dying of cancer? Do you know that last week, because of his own injuries, for the first time in six months Ghanshyam wasn't able to visit her?'

A current of electric remorse shivered through Jingo's body. He had heard some rumours before now that Ghanshyam had a sick wife who was in hospital. But they had seemed remote and apocryphal. Now for the first time this information had been confirmed. So she was dying of cancer. And he had heard it straight from Father Dias's mouth . . . And all these months while they were making life miserable for Ghanshyam, just for a lark, a giggle, a distraction, privately he had been trying to cope with something much bigger. Something that was probably quite beyond their comprehension . . .

After that day, gradually Jingo began to distance himself from Hoshi, without making it evident to Hoshi or anyone else. Soon, the academic year drew to an end, and the distance between them increased until Jingo had hardly any contact with Hoshi at all. For Hoshi failed the final exams and was asked to repeat a year in the IX form.

I can see how it's always been like this with me – a part of me longs to be appreciated for my goodness, my sensitivity, my ability to empathize and be compassionate. It is not as though these feelings are not real. It's not as though I fake them. But there appears to be a motive behind them that makes it all suspect. I want to be admired and loved . . . Just as I sought popularity among my schoolmates by befriending Hoshi and creating mischief in class, just as I needed to prove to Cristina that I could understand the private hell of her suffering and love her in spite of everything she had been through – and everything she made me go through – she instinctively sensed it, and said as much to me – I have a need to be admired for my goodness.

This shortcoming is surely the fulcrum of the see-saw on which my manic and depressive sides pivot. In both versions of myself – the high and the low – I find lurking an enormous, if unspecific, guilt.

What this guilt is about, I've asked myself a hundred times. To say it's to do with the lamp-in-the-glass, the most abiding image of my life, seems simplistic. Can a three-year-old brother who died even before I could see him or speak to him play such a crucial part in my life? I've

spent hours wondering what he might have
been like if he had grown up. But there's no
way of knowing. For reference I only have the
barbaric idealizations my mother constantly
draped him in.

Or, for that matter, did this unnameable
guilt burrow deep into my being in that
moment when I learned from Father Dias that
Ghanshyam's wife was fighting cancer in a
public hospital? While I, unthinkingly, was
ladling out even larger helpings of despair
onto the poor professor's plate? But I wasn't
alone in having fun at Ghanshyam's expense –
dozens of other boys were in it with me – and
unless I'm once again trying to make a case
for my special sensitivities, I don't believe
even one of them was at all affected by this
news.

An awareness has begun to grow in me, too
late perhaps to be of any use . . . of the pain I
must have caused Cristina every time I was
frivolously attracted to another woman. In my
heart of hearts I knew it wasn't important, a
mere amusement, that Cris was my real
partner, my one true love. But how could I
have been so vain as to expect her to know it
too? She had become so much a part of me, I
assumed she would understand, and often
made no attempt to even keep it private . . .

The mindless ease with which I aided and
abetted the voiding of a life from her being . . .
There's some guilt there too. We went into it
like children, not realizing there was a high

price to pay. *Forget the moral issues: a clod of
tissue that could have been a fully fledged
human being, flushed down the drain . . .
Cristina said it wasn't mine anyway, but how
can she be so sure?*

*The guilt could be derived from any or all
of these sources. But one thing I have
understood more clearly now: at the core of
my sickness is vanity and self-love. Like
Narcissus, too engrossed in his own reflection,
I have lost touch with the outside world. With
humanity – even my own.*

*In the IXth, my last year with Hoshi, he
came closest to wanting us to be real pals. Not
sure who I was, or what I wanted, I played
along. His most generous gesture of friendship
was to invite me to the toilet block after
school where he had a rendezvous with Percy.*

*Horrible sight: to see Percy snivelling as
Hoshi tried to force his swollen penis into his
mouth.*

*'If even a single tooth grazes Hippolong's
thing,' he warned Percy, 'I'll knock it out with
my fist, just see . . .'*

*My turn was next. But at least that once I
did protest and showed my disapproval by
walking out. My gesture wasn't enough to save
Percy. I should have complained to the priests
and brought an end to his torment.*

*Even at this juncture I had sensed the evil in
Hoshi and decided to gradually dissociate
myself from him. But perhaps that is never
enough. If I'd had the courage to challenge*

him right then, perhaps the evil in him
wouldn't have grown so monstrously. Perhaps
my own life, too, would have turned out
differently from what it has.

Two nights later Jingo was in bed, about to fall asleep, when he heard raised voices from his parents' room. He was too sleepy, and at first assumed that the quarrel was over his bad behaviour at school which, as far as he knew, his mother hadn't yet communicated to Dad, who had been extremely busy over the past few days trying to meet the deadline for filing his clients' tax returns.

In the daze of impending slumber – his parents would have assumed he was already fast asleep – he realized their quarrel wasn't exactly over him. It was something quite different and far more serious. Boman's angry accusations and sarcasm, Khorshed's quiet pleading, sudden bursts of wailing and smothered sobs . . . he pieced together the circumstances of the quarrel, but wasn't entirely sure he had heard everything right, or interpreted it correctly.

That afternoon Boman had come home at two o'clock without any warning to pick up some important papers he had left behind. He hadn't had time for lunch, and was hoping to pick up a bite as well. He was utterly amazed to find that Khorshed was not alone, as he had expected her to be, but was having lunch in the company of Rusi Hansotia.

Years had passed since they had last been over to Hansotia's place, and many months since they had even heard from him or spoken to him on the phone. He was supposed to be away on one of his European jaunts. Boman turned cold at the sight of this apparition from the past. In fact, at first, he almost didn't recognize him, for Hansotia had grown a long, thick beard and let his hair hang down in tresses. Now he looked more the part of the spiritual legatee of Fali Baba that he claimed to be.

Khorshed's own consternation at having her lunch party interrupted by Boman was even more evident. Hesitatingly and evasively she began to give him an explanation for Hansotia's presence, but Boman curtly cut her short, collected his papers and left. He came home very late that night and hadn't even bothered to call.

'How do I know that you haven't been having an affair with him, all these months, all these years, for all I know?' raged Boman in the silence of the night. 'How do you expect me to trust you ever again?'

Khorshed was pleading with him to believe her, that she had never cheated on him or lied to him about anything, and that is why, even now, when he was so angry, she was sticking her neck out to tell him the truth. But the truth angered Jingo's father even more than his own wildest suspicions. He threatened her that he would not rest until he had exposed Hansotia and completely quashed his circle of spiritual phoneys.

'I was shocked, too, and angry, when I heard his proposal. As soon as he finished his lunch, I asked him to leave and never contact me again! The very thought of it makes me sick. And now you add to my suffering by suspecting me!'

'Tell me again how that bastard happened to be here having lunch with you. If he wanted to discuss anything, why didn't you tell him to call when I was going to be at home?'

'Well, he specifically suggested that it might be better if he talked to me in private.'

'Ha! And you so conveniently obliged.'

'He said it was very important.'

'Of course! And so it was, wasn't it? You should have carried out his suggestion right away, as soon as I went back to the office! Perhaps that's exactly what you did. Or did he ask you to wait for the right *Geh* to begin?'

'Stop it, Boman. Oh, please stop this, Boman!' She was sobbing with exasperation. 'I told you! I told him, too, in no uncertain terms, there was no question of it. I sent him away.'

'Oh, thank you, thank you so much for remaining faithful to your husband.'

Hansotia had contacted Khorshed that morning, unexpectedly, after many months, or so Jingo understood. He had insisted on seeing her that very afternoon. He said he was carrying an urgent message from Fali Baba and Rumi, which had come to him in a dream while he was flying over the Atlantic. And the message was for her ears only.

When he came there, he told her that Rumi was waiting to be reunited with his mother. But the poor child was losing patience. This was their last chance. In the event that his rebirth did not come to pass, he would remain in the Beyond, evolve to a higher spiritual plane from which there was no return. He would continue to work with Fali Baba, as his young helper. Anyway, he was extremely happy where he was, but the time had come for her to decide.

The communication hadn't ended there. Fali Baba had gone on to explain that unfortunate seminal complications had developed in Boman's constitution which were preventing the incarnation from coming about. He had himself suggested that Hansotia could provide the semen that would make Khorshed pregnant once again. It was the only way. Rusi had arrived in Bombay just that previous night, but felt this was important enough for him to see her the very next day, even though he was still jetlagged.

'Incredible! This is the most incredible confidence trick I've heard of. Didn't I tell you from the beginning it's best to keep away from these bloody godmen?'

Boman's fury didn't translate into decibels, but his voice was fierce enough to give Jingo a terrible fright. 'I'll strangle that man with my own bare hands. If I had some proof to show, I'd go right now to the Tardeo police station, file a complaint and have him arrested.'

Khorshed was frightened and weeping.

'But I didn't do it, I didn't do anything, I sent him off,' she cried. 'Please stop it, Boman, we need never see him again. Please stop . . . The neighbours!'

'To hell with the neighbours!'

'Jaungoo will wake up!'

There was a lull in the argument. Jingo would have liked to get out of bed and go into the next room, say something to his parents that might ease their pain, soothing words that would magically repair the breach that had suddenly ruptured their lives in the middle of the night. But what could he say? And how much interference from him would they tolerate? He'd heard his parents quarrel before now, but there seemed something terribly final about this one, which frightened him. He continued to listen for voices, afraid that if he fell asleep he might miss something crucial. But there was silence now; and sleep was the more comprehensive solution to anxiety. All his heedfulness only hastened his bewildered slide into oblivion.

The next morning, when he woke up, the lamp was missing. Even the crystal glass in which it flickered day and night had been put away somewhere.

His father had already left for work. His mother didn't speak to Jingo as he got dressed for school and ate his broon-pao and tea. He had almost forgotten about the disturbances of the previous night. Then he noticed her swollen eyes.

'I heard some noises last night, Mama,' said Jaungoo, 'just as I was falling asleep.'

'What kind of noises?' asked Khorshed.

'You and Daddy were quarrelling,' said Jaungoo. 'Daddy doesn't love you any more?'

Khorshed was too stunned to reply.

'You don't love him either . . .' Jingo continued, despondently

'Nonsense. Of course we love each other. You must have had a bad dream . . . Papa's been a bit tense lately. He's overworked. Now, you'd better hurry, young man,' she said to him sternly. 'I don't want to see any more late remarks in your calendar.'

Jaungoo picked up his bulky haversack of books and left for school.

Part 3

Bitterness

Boman stared with open-mouthed disgust at the figure of his son. Seated, with his back to him, he was calmly tearing pieces of crunchy broon from a round brown loaf. Occasionally, he sweetened his morsels of fried egg with a lick of strawberry jam from the dollop on his plate. It was past eleven now. Boman had had his own breakfast a long time ago.

He was sorely tempted to say something rude – a few stingers had already crossed his mind, but there they remained, sourly simmering. He had promised Khorshed before the boy got up that he would let him sleep as late as he liked and wouldn't lose his cool when he came out. Well, there was nothing to say that hadn't already been said before. It wouldn't make the slightest difference anyhow.

Shamelessly, the prodigal slob had returned home. No word of apology, no explanation – 'Just for a few days,' was all he had to say, 'till I find something else' – and ever since, his daily routine, his personal habits, the way he ate, the way he dressed, everything about him made Boman see red. Dr Soonawalla, the cardiac specialist, had urged him to stay calm in all situations if he didn't want his blood pressure to skid into danger zone. The doctor had warned him of the real possibility of a stroke and prescribed three separate pills for daily consumption, besides a general tonic.

Well, he was taking them all as conscientiously as possible. But what pills can safeguard against the ultimate provocation of watching a degenerate son fritter away the best years of his life before one's eyes? And purposefully too, with the smug dedication of one engaged on a secret mission of enormous and cryptic meaning.

He woke up late every day, but never too late to skip the hearty breakfast that his mother was quick to provide. Then, shortly before noon, he left the flat, carrying his worksheets self-importantly in a cloth slingbag. Boman had glanced through the file one morning while he was still asleep. Such utterly meaningless waffle! Did he spend his entire day questioning people about such irrelevant aspects of their lives and then recording their responses in all seriousness? He returned home late at night, tired, still carrying the clumsily overpacked slingbag, and sometimes with the smell of booze on his breath. Usually, he'd have had something to eat at a wayside cafe.

Once, Khorshed found an empty packet of cigarettes in his shirt. He never smoked in front of them. Boman had always believed that his son would have the good sense to never take up that vile habit. Zoroastrians worshipped fire. They didn't pollute its searing purity with their lips and spit and phelgm! But the thought had occurred to Boman even then, when Khorshed showed him what she had found, that the boy might well be on drugs for all they knew. That was certainly one explanation for his utterly irresponsible behaviour. He still thought of him as a boy, but he was a full-grown hulk behaving with the neglectful insouciance of an adolescent.

Well, there was another explanation, too, though Boman had never dared to speak it out loud: a line in the family was tainted. The use of drugs was surely a logical offshoot of the kind of emotional make-up that the Mehli Kavaranas of the world represented. The one weak link in their family history. In any case, there was no way he could ask Jingo about drugs and expect an honest answer. The boy had grown too far from him.

At first, Boman refused to let him have the key to the flat. But during his first few days there, he had shattered their slumber with piercing, impenitent blasts of the buzzer well after midnight, and poor Khorshed had been forced to stumble out of bed in the dark to let him in. The next morning, Boman had told Khorshed that he would switch off the buzzer when they locked up and retired at ten, and the boy could bloody well spend the remaining hours of night on the landing outside if he came home later than that – but Khorshed was horrified by the idea: 'What will the neighbours say if they see him sprawled out on the landing when they open their doors in the morning to take in the milk?' she argued. 'What will they think of *us*?'

'That he's a bloody good-for-nothing loafer, obviously,' replied Boman without hesitation. 'A conclusion they'd have reached on their own anyway. And I don't care a damn what they think of us. What d'you think I say to them when they ask where he's employed, what salary he brings home? How much can one conceal from the world around?'

'These prying, meddlesome neighbours,' muttered Khorshed. 'If they sense some trouble in the family, they'll become even more shamelessly inquisitive. Anyway, Jaungoo said he's going to be here only for a short while.'

'Short while?' repeated Boman disgustedly. 'Six months have passed!'

'Six months?' said Khorshed, counting discreetly on her fingers before correcting him. 'Four and a half.'

'Well, seems a lot longer to me,' grumbled Boman.

'Far as I'm concerned, the longer the better,' said Khorshed matter-of-factly. 'At least we can keep an eye on him.' Then she appealed to Boman more persuasively: 'It's safer . . . At least this way we'll come to know what he's up to. So while he's here, let's try not to make him feel oppressed in his own home.'

'And do we have no rights at all? It's *our* home, too,' said Boman.

For a fraction of a second, a picture flashed in her mind of Temu Kaka, her eccentric painter uncle to whom the flat had originally belonged. Khorshed didn't think this the right moment to remind Boman that the flat had been a wedding gift to her from Temurus Kavarana, who retired to his cottage in Udwada shortly after the wedding. He wanted to be close to the Iranshah Fire Temple. Temu Kaka must have sensed that the end was coming, for only a few weeks later, he passed away quietly in his sleep.

'At least, after we're gone, it'll be Jaungoo's . . .' murmured Khorshed, reflectively. Imperceptibly, Boman stiffened.

She realized immediately how thoughtless it was of her to talk like that. As it is, Boman was showing signs of depression, having taken Dr Soonawalla's prognosis to heart. To talk now of death and Jaungoo's inheritance was ill-timed, to say the least.

*

Some telepathic exchange must have taken place in that moment when Khorshed remembered her favourite uncle. For Boman's mind, too, had wandered back to the time of their wedding, and just after.

In his lunchbox, which Khorshed faithfully dispatched to the office every day with the tiffin-carrier, they had exchanged little love-notes. She had no time to scribble more than just a sentence – 'Come home safely, your true love, Khorshed' – for that rascal of a Dhondu who collected the box from her was always in such a tearing hurry. But after he'd taken his lunch, Boman would sit back and compose a verse or two in praise of her beauty, her noble character.

One of them came back to him now: 'Each day brings new hope, New light in darkness where I grope. Walk ever with me, by my side, Philosopher, Friend and Guide.' There had been a second verse, too, but he couldn't remember even a line of it; in any case, the feeling behind those words had turned rancid like stale food. Scribbled long ago, while he was still in love, and she was still carrying Rumi, they seemed infected now by an overwhelming rancour. After their first son was born, they were still very happy. But before long, everything changed.

Sullenly, he had clung to the idea that Khorshed could never violate the implicit pact they had observed for so many years, of preserving a simple modicum of decency in their relations with each other, of never wilfully deceiving the other. He should have put his foot down right at the start, understood how risky it was to allow someone of her weak temperament to tangle with an inveigling trickster like Hansotia.

Then again, perhaps he had allowed this rigmarole

about contacting Rumi to continue for purely selfish reasons. He found no other way to shrug off the weight of her brooding, insatiable grief, to keep her distracted so he could get on with his work. And all those years of work had been worth it, definitely. For one thing, they had kept him sane.

He would have liked to go on working for another ten, perhaps fifteen years. But the things Dr Soonawalla had said, and the results of the pathological tests he had submitted to, had frightened him. A month ago, with encouragement from Khorshed, he had finally relinquished his share in the firm to Vaijubhai, his younger partner. After all, it did make sense – they were quite comfortable as it is, and there was no one to take over the firm after him. But on the day he put his signature on the agreement, he felt like he had amputated an arm.

The office premises on DN Road he had rented at only 60 rupees a month thirty-five years ago were worth a lot more now. The company itself, Moos and Shah, had built up a reputation for reliablity and trustworthiness which probably couldn't be computed in figures. But he hadn't really felt like haggling with Vaiju over the amount. It was substantial. And, besides, he didn't want to make the mistake of leaving behind too much for Jaungoo. That would be a sure recipe for disaster, of the kind that had befallen Mehli Kavarana. He must apply his mind to working out some sort of deed of trusteeship which ensured that his son wouldn't be able to withdraw a single rupee of his inheritance – even after he and Khorshed were dead – unless he could prove he was earning more of his own.

He was aware that morbidity was staking a claim on him: his frame had shrunk, his step was faltering, even his firm was no longer in his control – that sly fox Vaiju had kept saying he was welcome to come back any time his health improved, as though gloatingly confident it never would! – but worst of all, his thoughts were becoming obsessively preoccupied with the past, with memories not always pleasant. And he felt frightened by the detail with which his most irrational fears were stirring to life again.

He imagined a newly widowed Khorshed telephoning members of Hansotia's Inner Circle immediately after he was dead – though not necessarily for the purpose of communicating with her late husband! The whole motley crowd of disciples would probably turn up at his funeral – as if to celebrate the removal of an obstacle in the path of Khorshed's spiritual upliftment! This thought angered and humiliated Boman. And as for Hansotia, that Rasputin who was feathering his nest in some European city right now, God knows what he would say and do to Khorshed once she was alone. The bastard would probably catch the first available flight and rush to her side to soothe her grief!

And instead of dousing him with a sober and reflective calm, Dr Soonawalla's prognostications had the effect of making Boman even more irascible.

'He'll bloody well follow the rules of this place so long as he stays here. And if he doesn't like it, the door is open . . . Just look at the way he dresses, the tramp! I'm surprised people let him into their homes at all. And those old kohlapuris he drags his feet in, wherever he goes.'

'It's the fashion, these days, dear,' Khorshed said indulgently, making an effort to put him in better humour.

'Fashion?' rumbled Boman angrily. He disliked being talked to like a child. 'And is it fashion that tells him to discard his sudrah and kashti? What's become of that heap of new sudrahs you stitched for him when he left home? God alone knows to what unholy purpose they have been put to use.'

'Now, now, Boman,' Khorshed placated him. 'Don't get worked up over things we can't change.'

'He drinks, he smokes . . . God knows what else . . .'

'Okay, okay, we know all that. But don't forget Dr Soonawalla's—'

'Soonawalla, Soonawalla, all the time!' shouted Boman. 'I can depend on you-all to realize his prophecy.'

'Stop it, now. *Ovaaryu*,' said Khorshed, and snapped her fingers.

'I won't tolerate this blackmail,' he muttered, more quietly. 'It's nothing but a form of censorship!' He was damned if he was going to let Khorshed boss over him on the pretext of monitoring his health. The boy had been spoilt, utterly, beyond restitution. No call to get excited? Well, so long as he had been staying on his own it was okay. What you don't know won't hurt. But now to stand by and watch his mother still coddling him . . . and not be able to protest!

While these thoughts spluttered and crackled in his head, Boman suddenly became aware of his mouth agape, and shut it. Jingo was still munching on his fried eggs and broon. Presently, Khorshed came out of the kitchen with a cup of steaming reheated tea and placed it on the table before her son.

Jingo himself wasn't unaware of his father sitting behind him on the sofa with an open newspaper spread out at his side. In earlier days, it would have been most unusual to find him at home at this hour, except on Sundays. Poor guy. This was his second attack of angina – the first one had happened while Jingo was still at college. Now two months' bed-rest, the doctor's fearful pronouncements and strict regimen had quite shaken up his dad.

He sat home through most of the day, going through the newspapers – the *Indian Express*, and the Gujarati *Mumbai Samachar* – with a fine comb. Reviving an old habit of his college days, he once again began writing vituperative letters to the editors of these publications whenever he felt strongly about something.

After typing them out in fair on his portable, he got Khorshed to post them for him, rather proud of the fact that they were almost always printed in full. At last count, his published letters totalled something like 147. These letters, sometimes indignant and full of fury, gradually became mellowed by irony and even an eccentric sense of humour. They commented on the corruption and cynicism that had contaminated Indian politics from top to bottom, on the garbage-clogged sewers of Bombay, the unchecked plastering of posters and raising of hoardings in Bombay, especially during election time, the amplified noise pollution during Ganapati and other festivals, and so on. A thick old scrapbook, in which Khorshed pasted every clipping of these published letters, was not quite up to date. Tucked into its back cover was an accumulation of three or four recent letters. They had been ripped out of the papers in which they had appeared, but hadn't been pasted down as yet.

Jingo's attention was focused on his plate. He was hoping to finish breakfast as quickly as possible and leave the flat without being drawn into any bickering.

'There's more bread if you want,' Khorshed said to him in a whisper, not wanting to disrupt the uneasy silence that hovered over the living room.

Jingo declined, with a shake of his head.

'Or a piece of cheese?' she continued, adopting a slightly more natural tone of voice. 'There's an open tin in the fridge.'

Jingo shook his head once more. But the moment had come when Boman felt he could no longer ignore this hush of maternal solicitude. Was he some kind of three-headed demon sitting there waiting to devour them that she dared only whisper in his presence? He mimicked her with pleasant sarcasm.

'A bowl of hot oats porridge, perhaps? Why not a well-done cut of steak, grilled with tomato and onion? I'm sure there's still plenty of room in his excellency's ample tummy?'

'Now, Boman,' said Khorshed, chiding him gently.

'No, no, I mean it. And why not? The kitchen is open twenty-four hours in this hotel,' said Boman, rather pleased with himself at having hit upon a suitably controlled tone for registering his protest. Besides, he had been feeling a little left out of the closeness he sensed between mother and son.

'Let him eat in peace,' said Khorshed. 'You know he won't get a decent meal once he steps out on the road.'

'Yes, of course. Quite so . . . That's what I'm saying too,' said Boman. 'And besides, the poor boy won't be home until after midnight . . . Give him some dessert, too, Mama. Fruit salad topped with cherries? Or apple pie, if you please.'

The flicker of amusement on Jingo's lips widened as he chewed on, listening quietly to the options on his father's elaborate and imaginary menu. The ghost of a smile appeared on Khorshed's pinched face, too. She lingered a moment to reassure herself that the peace of her flat was not going to suddenly erupt in hysteria. Satisfied, she returned to the kitchen, making a sound that was somewhere between a snort and a chuckle.

'Sorry, Dad,' said Jingo at last, turning his head towards where his father sat behind him. 'Woke up very late today, I know. I'm going to try and get up a little earlier.'

'No problem, no problem at all. Please feel at home . . . Of course, you were up most of the night,' he said, nodding with exaggerated sympathy. 'Working hard at your book?'

'Just couldn't sleep,' said Jingo lamely, bracing himself for more jibes. But this morning Boman's bitterness seemed to have found an introspective vein, rather than its usual belligerent one.

'So many things I wanted to do when I was younger,' he said with rueful nostalgia, addressing the wall behind the large frame of his son. 'You wouldn't believe me if I told you . . .

'In junior school, I fancied I'd become a sailor. Imagine! My dream was to sail to every port in the world . . . As I moved to high school, I grew more studious. My interests shifted to archaeology. History was fascinating . . . I wanted to delve deep into the past. Later it was birds, animals. I was already studying and working by this time. But, just as a hobby, I started collecting books on rare birds and animals, endangered species . . .'

There were two cupboards full of books in the flat. The one in the living room, glass-fronted, had works of fiction, which Jingo had read and re-read several times. The other, in his father's bedroom, was of polished wood. You couldn't see the books unless you opened both doors of the cupboard. A few old bound volumes of zoology and ornithology, mostly stuff on accounting and taxation laws, and, on the bottom-most shelf, files that contained old bills and yellowed correspondence.

Nearly through with breakfast, Jingo chewed his last mouthfuls less noisily, in deference to his father's soft musings.

'There were a hundred things I wanted to be. I was good with words, too. I could have been a writer myself. Some of those things I can't even recall now,' he said almost apologetically, with an abstracted smile. 'Where was the time to do all of it? Papa died while I was still at school. That put paid to all my dreams . . .'

Yes, thought Boman, even Jingo's back and the shape of his head reminded him so much of Savaksah.

'Papa had a passion for bodybuilding, as you know . . . Without begrudging it, his bank manager would sanction any number of days of privileged leave, whenever he was taking part in a tournament . . . The whole office supported him and came to cheer!

'When he died, I had to work very hard. But I didn't regret it. Those were the best years of my life. I was restless, I changed jobs, always trying to improve our circumstances. It was years before we reached this level of stability – to be able to send you to a good school, to acquire these few creature comforts for our family. And now I'm practically retired . . .'

Jingo wiped his plate dry with a last crust of bread and was about to put it in his mouth, but something made him turn in his chair to look at his father, who had left his sentence incomplete. The sight of the old man hunched on the sofa, lost in thought, came to him as a shock.

His hairline had receded till he was almost bald now.

The white sudrah and pyjama, loosely draped about him, showed how much weight he had lost since his attack. A frown of unfathomable regret creased his vast, gaunt forehead. Jingo felt a twinge of pity for his father, but only for a moment.

It was best not to say too much. It would take very little to put his father back in the throes of outrage, and that wouldn't be good for his blood pressure. Besides, Jingo *had* nothing to say in his own defence. He didn't think he could be held responsible for the old man's troubles but still, his own life had taken twists and turns he couldn't claim any control over. The years had passed too quickly, showing up the hollowness of his claims, revealing everything he had said in the past by way of self-justification – about becoming a writer, about writing a book that would chronicle the times – to be no more than romantic self-delusion, fantasy, an excuse for inactivity. He had to face it himself. The dream had receded considerably, and he didn't believe he'd ever have the energy to pursue it any more.

'How old are you now? Thirty-one? Thirty-two?' asked Boman, but he didn't wait for clarification. 'It's still not too late, son. I was older than that when I gave up my bank job to enter into insurance broking, a totally new field. In just a few years' time, you'll be too old to acquire new qualifications, or be eligible for any kind of real job . . .'

After a pause, Jingo spoke: 'How much does a man need to live on?'

'What do you mean?' asked his father suspiciously.

Jingo drained his cup of tea, and turned sideways in his chair to face his father.

'There are people who survive on far less than I earn,'

he said. He sincerely meant what he was saying. 'I have seen how people live . . . Don't worry about me, Dad. Please. I'll manage.'

'Yes, of course there are people who survive on less,' answered Boman angrily. 'But they are wretched and poor to begin with. Okay, so you dropped out of college . . . even now you can complete your graduation. Even now we can approach Golwalla for that loan. There's no rule saying you're too old.'

'But there's no way I could get interested once more in those dreary textbooks. Just to acquire a degree. I couldn't possibly clear any more exams even if I tried to. Honestly, I can do without those creature comforts you spoke of. The important thing for me is – well, my sense of freedom.'

'Now you really make me laugh, Jahangir,' said Boman, though his face showed more anguish than amusement. 'Freedom? What freedom? Do you mean like those American hippies who come here to loll about on the beaches of Goa? That kind of freedom – to be a hippie? *Arrey*, most of them have rich fathers back in the States to bail them out, big businesses to take charge of once they tire of aimless living. And they all do. Let me tell you, by the time they're thirty, they all do.'

'I didn't mean that at all. I mean the freedom to lead a simple, uncluttered life . . . To retain a creative perception of it, be fully aware of one's surroundings . . . I mean, to resist that unthinking suction that pulls one onto the conveyor belt of class, slowly dragging one towards prosperity. And numbness.'

'And what's wrong with prosperity?' asked Boman, dismayed. 'Just because you were born in a poor country doesn't mean that you are obliged to remain poor.'

'But when a person begins to do well, make money, he automatically closes his mind to the plight of others – to those millions around him who haven't the slightest chance of replicating his success. That's when he becomes blinded, starts losing his sense of reality. Do you see what I mean? When a man starts becoming preoccupied with money, he has no other way but to be split, schizoid.'

'I don't know whether to laugh or cry,' sighed Boman in exasperation. 'I can't believe anyone can be so naive at your age. You only know how to use big words, but maybe it's you who needs to see a psychiatrist. Not those people who work hard and earn good money for their families . . . Look, Jingo,' said his father, remaining silent for one moment before making a desperate attempt to reach out to his son. 'There may be a speck of truth in what you're saying. I won't deny it. Please don't think I don't understand you at all. Maybe there's a generation gap . . . But this is all romantic dreaming. You're a dreamer. Who do you see yourself as? Some kind of Jesus Christ? Is it your Catholic girlfriend who's been putting all these ideas in your head?'

Jingo thought it ironic that he had been through the same sort of argument with Cristina several times.

'There's no need to feel guilty about other people's poverty. We do what we can. Charity is an essential part of our religion. But even more than that, our religion enjoins us to work hard and become prosperous. Zarathustra said so himself: "Do not renounce the good things of life. Enjoy God's gifts in good measure and be happy",' said Boman. 'I'm paraphrasing, of course.'

'Yes,' said Jingo, beginning to enjoy the debate, 'but invariably those gifts of God come to us at someone else's expense, don't they?'

'What do you mean? Speak clearly,' his father growled.

'We prosper only when we start exploiting others,' said Jingo. 'It's built into the way our society is constructed.'

It may have been an ill-chosen phrase or an argument too abruptly introduced, but Jingo hadn't expected his father to become so infuriated.

'Yes, indeed!' Boman spluttered. 'If I worked hard for forty years, to be able to send you to a good school, to give you a head start in life, I was in fact only exploiting others!'

'I didn't mean you, Dad,' said Jingo, alarmed that he had made his father so furious after all. Boman was shouting now.

'And what are you doing, may I ask? When you drink and smoke, live like a pariah, a parasite on society? Are you not exploiting others? All that doesn't worry you? Because, of course, it's all at my expense! Right?' Boman was quite out of breath now, and talking fast. 'You have no problem about living off your aged parents. Not to mention the cost of driving us all round the bend with your fancy talk. Shame on you for spouting such poppy-cock at your father!'

Khorshed came rushing out of the kitchen.

'Now what are you-all on about?' she complained. 'Can't I cook a simple russ-chawal without ten interruptions?'

'You stay out of this!' He yelled at her as well. 'My hair has turned white and most of it is gone. But I haven't heard such drivel and nonsense in all my life!'

'You promised to leave him alone, Boman. Let him be.'

'But I am! I'm leaving him alone . . . You tell me when *he* will leave *us* alone, for God's sake?' asked Boman, a shrill note in his question.

'I'm sorry, Dad,' said Jingo. 'I guess I've overstayed. I'll move out as soon as I can. Maybe tomorrow.'

'Why tomorrow?' yelled Boman. 'Move today, if any of your friends will still take you in!'

'What are you saying?' screamed Khorshed, aghast. 'You know he doesn't have anywhere to go . . . Wait, Jingo. Your father doesn't mean it that way.'

'I meant it. I'm saying it again, let him go . . . What does it matter where he lives, if he wants to live in this fashion? It doesn't matter,' repeated Boman, breathing hard. His hands were trembling with agitation.

Jingo went inside to fetch his things. What was there to argue about? Why couldn't he be humble and admit he was confused, that he had never felt more confused in his life? Within a few minutes he came out with the slingbag on his shoulder. He said goodbye to his parents – not waiting for an answer, and not receiving any – shut the door of the flat behind him, and left.

'Now see what you've done,' lamented Khorshed quietly, without any hint of recrimination in her voice.

'He'll be back. Where's he going to go?' muttered Boman softly, privately regretting his intemperate behaviour. The more so because he hadn't seen the outburst coming. And just a moment before he erupted in anger, he had in fact been feeling rather glad that, for once, he was engaged in a real conversation with his son. For a moment, he felt like rushing to the door and calling out to him to come back in. But he desisted.

'If he wants to be one of the wretched of the earth, let him! Why won't he say that he's just a lazy pig who doesn't want to work? Instead of giving us all this philosophy . . .'

Long after Khorshed had retired to the kitchen to conclude her preparation of the afternoon's simple meal of rice and meat gravy cooked with fried onion, Boman continued to mutter and brood. Jingo had gone. Now he was having a conversation with his wife, saying things to her that he would never have dreamt of saying if she had been listening.

'Well, what do you expect? There's no doubt about it, Khorshed, he does take after your father, Manecksah. I'm not saying this just to hurt you, because I know you will be hurt. But what did Mehli do with his own tragically brief life? Was it tragic? Or simply meaningless? . . . Genes do matter, let's not underestimate their importance. They are the pointers on the crossroads of life that determine which fork in the road we take.'

The Kavaranas had been quite well-to-do for a couple of generations already. Such pretensions they had to being 'cultured'! Manecksah had inherited a thriving business from his father as a racecourse bookie. They even owned a couple of race horses, apparently. But what kind of work is that, racing horses, betting on them?

One night when he was barely forty, Manecksah had a dream. In it, he saw and remembered the names of all five winning horses at the Derby jackpot races. He didn't take much heed of the dream, but in the course of the day he found that all the five had indeed made it to the winning-post. A week later, he had another dream. This time, again, he saw the five winners, a new and absurdly unlikely lot of horses. He mentioned the dream to a friend, but some essential cynicism – or was it just laziness? – made him feel that it would be too much of a coincidence for such a dream to come true again. That Sunday, he was more distraught than ever and cursed his faithless inertia – for all five horses he had seen in his dream won!

On the night before the races of the third Sunday, he prayed that he should see the winners again. And once again, a dream came to him with great clarity of detail. As soon as he got up, he wrote down the names of the winners and then, right through breakfast, he was on the phone to his various accountants and brokers urging them to liquidate for him a very large sum of money from his personal funds, a great deal of what his clients had asked him to bet for them, and even raising loans from professional moneylenders.

He put it all without blinking an eyelid on the five horses who had appeared to him in the night, convinced beyond a shadow of doubt that he would at least quadruple his fortune by the end of the day. Alas, as anyone with even a slight sense of irony might anticipate, this time his dream run was over. The winning list turned out to be quite different. Not one of the five horses he had bet on won. It was a vicious twist of fate. Manecksah lost everything, even his self-respect, and his brokers were laughing at him. Early next morning, while his two small children and his wife still slumbered, he shot himself in the temple.

What can you say about a man like that, thought Boman, except that he was a coward? Okay, if he hadn't decided to do what he did, he might not have been rich any more, he might have had to face some hardship, struggle a bit to sustain his family. But why was his mind wandering like this into the past, Boman wondered? Why was he thinking about others' lives, and what had gone wrong for them? Quite enough had gone wrong with his own.

Of course, it would never do to say such things to Khorshed. She had been just twelve when her father died, and very attached to him. He had never said anything like this to her, though he had often thought about it. And he certainly wasn't planning to say it today of all days. Now that the morning had been quite ruined by his quarrel with her son, to have to deal with a lachrymose mother on top of everything else would have been the proverbial last straw for Boman.

Destitute

The old stone stairway was the shortest way down the hill, though also the steepest. With every step Jingo took, the Colony's secluded hush was frayed thin; as he descended the concluding flight, a surge of traffic on the thoroughfare tore it to shreds.

This route led to a small side gate left half open at all times. Nearby, where the hill's steep incline evened out, a giant banyan luxuriated. Involuntarily, Jingo's eyes searched beneath its branches for a figure he didn't expect to see. He had first set eyes on her years ago, while he was still at school.

Every morning, when he left home to wait for his school bus by the petrol pump on the main road, he'd see her; every afternoon, when he returned from school, she'd still be there. The brief clearing beneath those knotted aerial roots was her home. Sometimes he'd see her eating some watery slop from a leaf platter, using her fingers to slurp it up, sometimes drinking tea bought at the tea stall outside the temple. The *bhatt* didn't hand her the glass of tea as he did his other customers, but poured it for her into the rusted tin mug she carried along. She'd sip it very slowly, as though it were much too hot, but probably only to make it last longer. Mostly, she just lay there under the shade of the banyan in a stupor. Rarely did their eyes meet. And if ever she noticed him pass by, it was he who became self-conscious and looked away.

She was one of those unfortunates so far gone in her degradation that she seemed beyond the pale of human contact, unapproachable. She seemed to have lost her will to be physically active. Her hair was dry as straw and knotted in dreadlocks. A cleft lip gave her mouth a permanent grin that displayed a pair of blackened, decaying teeth. She had no other obvious physical deformity, it would seem, yet hardly moved at all from her chosen arboreal abode. Most of the time she would be lying there on raw earth, eyes open, gazing fixedly at the creepers in the sky as though puzzling over the secret of their ancient ravelling.

With only a threadbare cloth wrapped around her midriff, she was not embarrassed by her nakedness; she seemed barely aware of herself or her surroundings. Jingo found himself transfixed by the sight of those lean, pendulous breasts. Her miserable condition seemed to have stripped her of her sexuality, though she was probably not that old or unattractive. She had a tall, Dravidian build, Jingo observed, on those rare occasions when he saw her walk down to the tea stall by the temple. But her shoulders were hunched, her dark torso turned in on itself. Unwashed and layered with grime, there was yet something striking about her face. After much guarded observation, Jingo sensed a quiet dignity in the high forehead and wide-set eyes that seemed to derive from uncomplaining self-absorption. He even began to perceive a strange beauty in her disfigured face.

As far as he knew, she had never made any attempt to move closer to the temple, where begging would have had more lucrative results. But despite her reticent location, a few people did climb up the steps to her bower to offer alms. She never acknowledged the odd, oil-stained packets of food wrapped in newspaper that were left at her feet, though presumably she survived on these hand-outs. Fortunately for her, not too many other people used that gate or the stone stairway. Perhaps because of the steep gradient of the hill at that point, most residents of the Colony preferred the alternative path which was broader and sloped more gradually down to Hughes Road. Even so, Jingo found it amazing that for so many years no officious trustee of the Colony buildings had tried to shoo her off.

Why was he thinking of her now when he had so much else to think about, and do? Maybe he'd romanticized her while she was still around; but now, especially since she was gone, she had become a symbol of his own failure.

A rank despair was fermenting in him, like a mould. To begin with, it had only been an experiment: the negation of middle-class aspirations in the hope that something else would flower in their place. He had been seeking a more dedicated, a nobler way of life. For a while, the dream of being a writer had captivated him – the search for beauty and meaning through the medium of words. Perhaps he'd never quite understood what that choice involved. So taken up by his own perceptions, his ostensibly penetrating insights into life and people, he had believed he had something unique to say that had the potential to touch people's lives. More than anything else, what enthralled him was the romantic notion of an anarchic freedom which he associated with the artist's way of life. Somewhere along the line, things had gone very wrong. In his understanding, perhaps in the method he chose to apprehend that beauty and freedom for himself.

It was as if he had left a fungoid culture overnight in his lab in order to observe such changes as might take place. He had meant to leave it there for just one night, or at most two, to keep it under observation. But he had quite forgotten to check on it for a long while. What he now saw was a disaster he hadn't even been aware was brewing. The fungus had proliferated arbitrarily, monstrously, overwhelming its tray and spilling out to occupy the entire room. His indolence, his apathy, his cowardliness, his failure to reach out and act – call it what you will – had infected everything in sight. God help him. The impulse to live might itself be threatened if he allowed this malignancy to flourish unchecked. He would need to thoroughly dredge the laboratory of his soul in order to discover what it was that had generated such a fecund expanse of emptiness, such a disinclination for effort in the real world.

The truth was that he had never had any clearly conceived course of action for himself, not even for pursuing his putative career as a writer. There must be a more systematic means for laying claim to those rich tracts of creative alluvium he believed he had once glimpsed in himself. Was it arrogance that prevented him from writing? His literary ambitions were too vast; he had wanted to capture the entirety of life and society in his work. Through his writing, he had wanted to subvert the feeling of powerlessness he felt crushed by in real life. But he had never proceeded step by step, never had faith in himself.

On the other hand, the problem was perhaps that he was rather good at most things he tried his hand at. Which gave him a false sense of complacency about the future. Later was as good as now. In fact, later was probably better, because he would be able to accomplish the task in question even more satisfactorily – for the present he was already feeling quite bored with it. The moment something seemed achievable, it didn't seem worth the effort. Gradually he developed a fear of any kind of sustained application, a loss of belief in the value of tangible achievement.

It was this very trait in him that angered Cristina, though at one level he was quite sure it also made him attractive to her.

'You're so vague,' she'd reproached him more than once. Jingo recalled one occasion in particular when she had hit out at him: 'Don't you want to do something, get somewhere in your life, become somebody? If you were a character in a book, I'd have lost interest in you long ago . . . I'm disappointed, frankly.'

Her dark brows were knitted together. Her long lashes, usually fluttery, were motionless, her round face hard with the effort of distancing herself, thinking critically. She watched him pull at the loosely refilled cigarette in his hand. They were speaking in whispers, in deference to the tombstones around. He had made her stop at the cemetery behind Paradise cinema so he could buy a couple of balls of hashish from the keeper of the graveyard to smoke later that night. Then he'd changed his mind and decided to have one right there, before catching the train to drop her home.

They were sitting on a bench in the gravelly path that cut through the burial ground. It was too dark to read the inscriptions on the gravestones, but they were mostly in Urdu anyway. Cristina was late, and found herself increasingly irritated by the deep draughts of scented smoke Jingo pulled and released, slowly, rhythmically. A half moon was rising in the sky.

'I guess concealed in that there's a threat somewhere.' Jingo smiled at her, releasing another cloud of smoke.

'Threat?' Cristina asked, genuinely puzzled.

'That you'll start looking for more interesting, more successful men.'

'But, for heaven's sake, you've got so much going for you,' Cris said. 'I believe in your talent, Jehan. It's you who don't. You need to strive, realize it through hard work. The vocation you've chosen for yourself is a difficult one, but you chose it. No one forced you to want to become a writer. And I do believe you can do it still. But you're just letting it all go up in smoke instead. You've become so complacent, don't you see? You're happy to be an underachiever. As if in just such an adjustment to ordinariness lies your most cunning triumph.'

'That's really quite eloquent, you know,' said Jingo. 'Do you want a puff of this to keep going?'

'No, thanks,' she replied crossly. 'I don't need that shit, believe me. Let's go. This place gives me the creeps.'

While leaving, Cristina tripped on the base of the graveyard's wrought-iron gate. She could have hurt herself if she hadn't caught hold of Jingo's arm in the nick of time.

In that instant, he had the first glimpse of a truth about himself. It was something he would dwell on in the days to come. But for the moment, it was just a passing thought: he had been pursuing a phantom art. Not one that was creative, intensely lived, but a mere conceit, an affectation, whose only purpose was to stay sheltered from any real experience. He had been ducking all along, preferring to take the back seat and let someone else do the driving. He had gone to such lengths of rationalization merely to avoid hard work. Not least the work that remained to be done on his inner life, the crying need he felt for some insight into himself that would enable him to change and grow.

It was an important key, an intuitive flash. It could have been the beginning of a journey into self he sorely needed to undertake. But at that moment he was feeling pleasantly stoned and at peace with himself. No sooner had they turned onto the main road leading to the station than he was attracted by the sight of a tall woman heading in the direction of the Mahim Church – long-legged, mini-skirted, in high heels. Evidently a Goan or an East Indian Christian, possibly on her way to attend a late-night Novena service? In a mini-skirt? It was too dark to see if she was really so beautiful as she seemed to be, but the introspective gravity of a moment ago was deflected by another flight of speculation: ah, why have I never had the courage to break off with Cristina? Well, for a short while at least? There are so many beautiful women in the world I could get to know. I've been afraid to experiment . . . Jingo was probing another aspect of the same line of thought, or so he chose to believe, but in fact he had side-stepped its seriousness altogether, distracted by a pair of legs.

Unfortunately, most of the writing Jingo had done remained at the stage of notes, or early drafts. The one story he had actually completed – which won him a prize at an inter-collegiate story competition – had been in the form of a conversation between three drunks in a country liquor bar who express regrets about what their lives have become. Spurred on by one another and a lyrical, if temporary, lucidity, they fervently resolve to find adventure and escape from numbing routine, and fantasize about how they'll go about it. The story ends with them being turned out at closing time. Staggering into the street, they are caught in an unexpected shower of rain. It was a funny story, whose main protagonists, after reaching quite hysterical heights of drunken glee, are drenched in the cool wash of sobriety – they return to their respective homes and wives and start snoring. It had been published in his college magazine. Jingo still had a copy somewhere.

The series he had planned on occupations – brief vignettes from the lives of a butcher, a tailor, a coolie at the wholesale market, a dabbawallah, a domestic maid-servant – remained mere sketches of no more than three or four paragraphs each. His detective thriller, set against the backdrop of Bombay's sleaze and corruption, never got beyond its dramatic opening. The screenplay (about a man from a small town who comes to Bombay with the hope of making it big in Bollywood, but is unhinged by his experiences here, so that when he goes back home he slips into delusions of power and star status, believing in an imaginary fan-following) consisted of five complete scenes; at which point Jingo had abandoned the idea altogether. It seemed absurd to believe he could ever find a producer to back it.

All these and other exertions had come to naught. Even his novel, that grand opus for which he had scribbled copious notes (some illegible, when he tried to read them back later, such was the rush of excitement in which they had been jotted down) – somehow every construct melted into tedium and irrelevance even before it was complete, just as soon as he imagined it in some detail. Jingo felt wearied by the thought of actually writing and rewriting those stories bit by bit until a final product emerged which came approachably close to what he had first envisaged. And even that, he knew, even if he worked hard and finished it, would be no more than a distant echo of the subtle polyphonies he had first heard in his heart.

Drawn to the worlds of the poor – the inconsequential, the feeble, the maimed – for his subject matter, Jingo noticed that defeat and despair were able to stir his imagination like nothing else. But perhaps he had himself been infected by that very despair he imagined his characters must feel . . .

Perhaps even more than the imagined despair of his characters, it was his own despair about the act of writing that disabled him. The work was too demanding, his ambitions too grandiose and idealistic. No matter what the final outcome, the process of creation could never be more than a compromise, a dissimulating patchwork designed to cloak its own inadequacies.

A short tubby man, Furtado, had taught them English language at school. He was quite passionate about his subject. Every composition class would begin with a strong exhortation from him:

'Write what you know best, boys . . . Dip your pen in the pigment of your soul, and write your heart out . . . No matter if it reads like rubbish later on, but at least it's straight from the heart . . .'

This was the formula old JX Furtado had touted. He had gone grey trying to teach the boys of St Joseph's how to parse a sentence in English, how to write an essay on a stated theme or compose a story on a given outline. But what was it that he, Jingo, knew best about? What was the given outline of his story? Nothing. He felt he hadn't lived. He was a nonentity. An anti-hero, if ever there was one.

Now that he considered it, he had probably acquired much less experience than those of his peers who had pursued the beaten path of university degrees, job-hunting, plum salaries, early marriage (possibly arranged), and kids. The obedient sons had scored over the rebel. His own prodigality had simply petered out. Was this really so? Or was he just feeling rotten after the row he'd had with his father? Was he a shirker who had allowed devious slothfulness to dictate his choices in life? A burnt-out case?

Even in earlier days when Jingo was smoking hashish quite regularly, it wasn't often that he began his mornings with that sensual scattering of pressures and priorities. The euphoric haze of unreality – well, distanced reality – was difficult to sustain through the day, anyway, and by evening he would be feeling quite dull and tired. But today was different, marked by a reckless grace. It was six months since he had had his last smoke. He needed to soothe his jangled nerves. Well, why not? He wasn't going home tonight, come what may. Even if he had to crash out at a railway platform, he'd rather do that than annoy his father. He cared for his dad. He really did.

Temptation is the devil of convenience. Just a few feet ahead of him, it stood waiting at a traffic signal – a 42 route bus that would take him to Byculla. The signal turned green before he could make up his mind. He sprinted a bit and jumped on.

'Raani Bagh,' said Jingo, putting a coin in the conductor's outstretched palm.

While he was still a child, Jingo had devised a game to help him pass the hours. He picked on people who lived in his own building, or in neighbouring blocks of the Colony, and endowed them with fantastic characteristics and private lives that nobody else had any inkling of.

In his game, Dadi Vesavewalla, who owned a store called Vesawe Medicals at the corner of Hughes Road, became a villainous homicidal maniac. The poisons he concocted in his pharmacy worked slowly, over months and years, so the murderer had never once come under suspicion. So impressed was Jingo with his own mental portraiture of this serial killer – thick eyebrows, thin face, long, delicate hands that clutched at you with creepy tenderness, if you crossed his path in the Colony, and wouldn't let go – that if ever he was sent out to buy a bottle of emetic or a strip of aspirin, he always went to Kemps, the other pharmacy at the far end of Hughes Road, preferring to walk an extra furlong rather than risk a confrontation with Vesavewalla, who might somehow read in his eyes that his secret had been uncovered – and then his own life would be in danger.

There was old Mrs Silla Saklatwala, on the floor above them, who always unfurled a large black umbrella the moment she stepped out of the house, especially if the sun was shining brightly. People generally called her Silla 'Satakia', or Silloo 'Screw-loose', but in Jingo's lexicon of the imagination, she had most certainly discovered the secret of aerial locomotion. Perhaps her umbrella was a gift given her by some wizard in the distant past, for it gave her the power to disappear quite suddenly and turn up once more where you least expected to see her. The umbrella's thick wooden handle contained an ingenious device of technological far-sightedness that allowed it to function as a mini sky-jet and also, when unfurled, as a parachute. Sillamai was relatively harmless, though, a kind of aging Mary Poppins who liked to mischievously bombard her neighbours with bits of orange rind, old slippers, broken eggshells or dead rats, while cruising through the clouds. She did this to spite them for calling her names and for teasing her ever so rudely.

But Tehmton Dumgoriwalla, who had a government-licensed agency for Plumbing and Sanitation Works, was the most frightening of all of Jingo's gallery of rogues. He was a scout master who emerged from F-Block every Sunday morning at 9 a.m. sharp, dressed in khaki shirt and shorts and cap, decorated with epaulettes, medals, rope and all the other paraphernalia of his scouting career. Tramping loudly over the flagstones of the Colony sidewalk he was on his way to drill his troop of boy scouts at the grounds of the Jamshetji Jeejeebhoy School. No one ever suspected the truth: that, on occasion, this man abducted young boys, making use of his intimate knowledge of the city drains.

Suddenly, while walking home, a manhole would open unexpectedly, just as he was stepping on it, and the startled boy would be whisked away through the sewers, to emerge finally from a trapdoor that opened in the home of some strangers desirous of becoming foster-parents; they had informed Dumgoriwalla of their 'requirement' earlier. The kidnapped boy would then be cajoled and pressed into years of slave labour as a domestic servant, while all the while being made to believe he was their rightful son and heir.

During his years of middle through high school, there were days when Jingo felt enraged by his mother's cold selfishness. Earlier, she had taken an active interest in his studies, but abruptly her manner had changed; she began to reiterate that she wanted him to become 'independent', work hard and make a brilliant career for himself. Perhaps she was clumsily compensating for those years of overprotection. But Jingo never failed to notice that such high scholastic expectations were stressed only on Thursdays, his midweek holiday from school, when for some reason his mother needed to spend a large part of her day out. Never once did she agree to take him along; instead, she insisted on leaving him alone in the flat, having assigned him a whole series of exercises in Maths – his weak subject – plus a great many household chores as well.

She never ever told her son where she was going or what her work was. But he suspected it had something to do with Uncle Rusi's spiritualist group. Without obviously stating it, or having the humility to seek his compliance, she depended on him to avoid mentioning her absence from home to his father. Jingo had preferred to keep her secret. Because even without having once divulged it, there were the most terrible rows. Always late at night, always after they thought he was asleep.

At times like these, when Jingo felt burdened by the cruelty of a domineering mother and a preoccupied but essentially weak father, he fantasized that perhaps one summer's day long ago, Tehmton Dumgoriwalla had spirited him through the city sewers and passed him on to the Mooses, with whom he had no real family connection at all. They had lost their first child to an awful disease called diphtheria, and their real son's photograph stood there on a table in his father's study. (Once, in a fit of vexation Khorshed had even described him as 'but a second-rate replacement for my Rumi'. Later, she apologized profusely and covered his face with tender kisses, but Jingo had never been able to forget those words.) So, perhaps he never had a real brother at all, not even a dead one. He was quite alone. As to the identity of his own true parents, he had absolutely no clue. Were they still grieving the loss of *their* son, who had simply disappeared into thin air one fine day (thanks to the villain, Dumgoriwalla)? Perhaps they too kept his photograph by a lamp in their living room? Or had they stopped caring soon after he was lost and given up on him?

Such fanciful ruminations added interesting perspectives to the cheerless, quotidian reality of a lonely boyhood. Between Khorshed's otherworldly preoccupations and Boman's hard-nosed practicality about this one yawned a chasm – an open manhole – one in which Jingo was still falling.

Instead of making up weird stories about his neighbours, Jingo now began to wonder about the mass of silent people around him of whom he knew nothing. Whose stories never figured in the books he had read. The *bai* who came to scrub their dishes, the *jamadaar* who swept the Colony compound with his long broomstick, the *mali* who on occasion trimmed the hedges along the pathways in the Colony, the *rama* who came in whenever there were any odd jobs to be done, such as moving furniture, or replacing a glass pane that had been shattered by an errant cricket ball. He wondered about the lives of these people and realized that they too must have their own stories to tell.

In fact, he couldn't help a growing feeling that became

more powerful with time as he discovered more of it – that the streets of his own city were pregnant with stories and images far more astonishing and fantastic than anything he could recall having read in books he had borrowed from his father or his school library.

Filth had never revolted Jingo. He didn't think anything of wading through flooded gutters during the monsoon, or tramping over slushy heaps of uncleared garbage. It made him feel more real, down to earth. He would have liked to get to know the wretched woman who sat in his path outside the Colony's side gate. Maybe even to touch her, cup her elongated breasts in his palms and gently lift them.

He often fantasized about bringing her home on a Thursday, when his mother was out, and giving her a long, hot bath in his bathroom. It was a wildly exciting thought which he often indulged in, making up long conversations with her – to persuade her not to be frightened, reassure her of his love and genuine concern. But he never attempted anything like that, of course, knowing instinctively it could be as dangerous as uncorking a bottle with a genie in it.

After he switched courses at college (against his dad's wishes, for Boman had wanted him to opt for something more practical, like Commerce, instead of Eng. Lit.) the thought came to him that he would indeed be breaking new ground if he were to write a story about the destitute woman. To be able to get under her skin, see the city through her eyes, tell her story from *her* point of view – the perspective of a person who had been diminished by poverty to a point of no-return and who, it would have to be assumed, was still a thinking, feeling creature. It would be one way of loving her, touching her, restoring her to humanity. It would all be done in words, of course.

Imagining her life and writing her story would be the closest equivalent he could imagine to making love to her. A sanitized equivalent perhaps, but not sanitized in literary terms, he hoped. He wanted to embody her despair in his prose, the seething anger which must surely exist beneath her soulful equanimity, the filth and stench of her unwashed body – in all their rawness.

For a while, the ambition engaged his mind entirely, even to the detriment of his college studies. The idea grew in his head and he thought he could make it into a fully fledged novel which would allow him to bring in the city and its people, and a character who represented himself as her self-seeking, lust-filled benefactor – who takes the woman up to his flat and tries to make love to her in his bathroom. In Jingo's plot for the novel, the woman very nearly kills this benefactor by smashing a porcelain vase over his head, before making her escape. Jingo started making notes.

It was around this time that he thought of dropping out from college and finding PG accommodation, somewhere far from his parents' place. What he earned from market research would allow him to subsist while he worked on the novel. He made more notes, outlining what he imagined to be the woman's background, her reasons for coming to the city. Once, only once, did he feel the need to research his subject and made an attempt to speak to her.

It was one afternoon, just a week since he had found an affordable room in Mahim. To assuage his mother's resentment about his decision to move, he had dropped in to see her – but his real purpose for visiting Khareghat Colony had been to talk to the destitute woman. He stopped in front of her and waited until she became aware of him. Her half-shut eyes travelled from his shoes to his jeans and up to his face.

'*Aapse baat kar sakta hoon?*' he asked her, bending down.

She stared at him, her eyes open wider now, haunted by incomprehension and perhaps fear, but she wouldn't speak. He persisted. Just for a few minutes . . . I don't mean to cause you any trouble, he stammered in Hindi. But she only made some kind of strange moaning and grinding sound with her mouth, clicking her teeth and shaking her head. Maybe she didn't understand Hindi? Then he realized, a moment later, that she couldn't speak. She opened her mouth and showed him the bizarre sight of a brief, lopped-off tongue. She wagged it for him.

What dreadful course of events had ended in such a vicious excision? It didn't seem like a natural deformity. Was it some macabre medieval punishment inflicted on her during her past in a remote village? For betraying a secret or telling a lie? For abusing a powerful landlord, or infringing rules of caste? What monster had committed this foul deed? Or could it possibly be self-inflicted? Some sort of penance? No, he couldn't probe further. He gave her a rupee instead.

In the past his mother had sent him to her with a bowl of stale rice or leftover lentils, or some cooked vegetable wrapped in a leaf or a newspaper. On one occasion she had even sent an old sari, for the woman's indifference to her own immodest exposure annoyed and alarmed his mother quite a bit. But Jingo had never seen her wear it. Perhaps she had put it to some other use, or exchanged it for a few rupees. This was the first time in his life that Jingo had given the woman money. The silver coin lay there in her motionless palm but she made no gesture of gratitude. She had already lapsed once more into her world of non-communication.

Jingo could have asked the row of itinerant beggars seated outside the temple steps about her, or the *bhatt* at the tea stall, if they knew anything about the woman. But he didn't really have the stomach for such an investigation. At the time, he had fooled himself into believing that his imagination would be equal to the task of inventing the details. Actual facts didn't matter.

Later, he found he was quite wrong. It was possible to describe poverty from the imagination, certainly, even if one hadn't experienced anything like it oneself. But to imagine a world that is completely without hope is terrifying. The meaning of the very word is just that – forsaken, devoid of. One can deal with the problem of poverty by feeling charitable and compassionate towards its victims. But who can delve into the mind of a person who has lost all hope, the dark unpropitious fiend who does not have it in him to be grateful for the uneaten crumbs on one's plate? That is why we're afraid of the destitute, thought Jingo: because he lurks somewhere within all us, making rude faces at our smug optimism.

Perhaps the hopelessness of the woman's situation had been so overwhelmingly complete, so irredeemable, that Jingo gave up even before he could start. In any case, she disappeared one morning, or at least that's what his mother told him when on subsequent visits to the Colony he couldn't find her. For all Jingo knew, she might have died, her body quietly bundled onto a handcart and carried away by municipal workers. But there were hundreds like her dotting the streets and by-lanes of the city, living out various degrees of stuntedness, amputation, disease and despair. To write about such a reality with earnest soulfulness, Jingo knew, would make for a ridiculous compilation – an encyclopedia of the grotesque, which left the reader untouched. For, in life if he has successfully banished the horror from his consciousness, how will art ford the deep moat of his defences? Unless, by some bizarre yet gut-wrenching magic, the writer is able to tom-tom the obscene comedy of it all?

It was a difficult enterprise. In any case, Jingo's own writing had always suffered from the same malaise: imprecision, loose ends, the lack of conviction in his words, the mountain of work that remained to be done to come anywhere near conveying what he had wanted to. He was never able to persevere and polish, never able to pursue like one possessed the goal of completion, of sparkling clarity. Invariably dissatisfied with anything he wrote, Jingo didn't find the energy in him to do better, to gradually improve on his own handiwork. He was more of a 'fantasist' than a real writer, he'd have to admit, and had never outgrown the games of his childhood.

Still dawdling, still unproductive as ever, he had opted for an easy life. A mere market researcher, going from door to door, prying into people's household affairs, picking up fragments of stories, gathering impressions, observations and ideas which he then tossed about in his head like a salad during intoxicated and idle reveries – the pieces of a great jigsaw which, once completed, would astound the world with its beauty and meaning. But he knew he was never going to be able to complete it. Unambitious, he would always remain satisfied with basking in the imagined greatness of momentary insights, fleeting empathies.

For even if his sympathies were in the right place – with the small people of the world, the invisible and the irrele-vant – actually writing about them was a different matter. Writing was essentially about hard work. And hard work was anathema to him. He'd never put up a fight, never been able to struggle with anything in life. It hadn't seemed worth the effort. Far easier to let oneself sink in the common miasma of indifference. Face it: in his case, wanting to be a writer had been no more than an alibi for dissolute living, and now he needed to think clearly. He needed to decide what he wanted to do with himself, what he *could* do, given the fact that he had so prematurely burnt all his bridges.

As it approached Bombay Central, the bus was slowed down by handcart-pushers, cyclists and swarms of pedestrians. Where the driver saw a clear stretch of road, he sped up vengefully, twice failing to halt at designated bus stops. Since it was already full, the conductor didn't bother to remind the driver of his oversight, but the crowd of men and women who had been waiting impatiently at the roadside roared with indignation as the bus sped past.

Suddenly, it stung Jingo like the cold water that months ago Gurdeep had splashed on his face to rouse him from a deep slumber at 5 a.m. – what was he thinking of, jumping on to a bus headed for Byculla to get stoned? At three o'clock that afternoon he had to be in town, at the MIRA office! He had quite forgotten about the special briefing he was scheduled to attend. He consulted his watch. It would take him another ten minutes to get to Chandu's. Then maybe twenty more to prepare and smoke the pipe. He might still be able to make it there in time. Anyway there was no point turning back, now that he was almost there. And then of course, after the briefing, he could start worrying about where he was going to spend the night.

Mira

In times past, it had sustained him. Though Cristina often blamed his habit for their problems, he'd never have been able to go on with her for so long if it hadn't been for those little black balls of resin.

They gave him an emotional distance from the unpredictable upheavals that were the only constant in their relationship. The breadth of mind to look beyond immediate provocations and deceptions, to be able to glimpse the panoptic perspective which alone elevated life's sordidness, made it bearable. Most of all, they allowed him to forget, and start anew each time. But just when he thought he knew all about her, she would reveal a side of herself he had never imagined existed, or disclose an incident from her past she had never mentioned before.

He got off at the traffic signal opposite the church, just before the cinema hall, and walked down a street he had once come to think of as home ground.

Past the row of huts propped against the compound wall of a municipal school, ambling in what he hoped was a nondescript fashion, he came to a peepul tree where the pavement ended. But there was no one here – no Chandu, no Lalu. Even the earthen pot of water and the picture of Sai Baba were gone! Well, thought Jingo, slightly alarmed but also, for some reason, relieved: there have been some changes here. Perhaps it's better this way. He could do without the smoke if he had to. Of course, even in town, where he was heading, there were any number of places where he could buy the stuff. But most dealers adulterated a speck of hashish with unimaginable rubbish. Chandu's stuff was more reliable, since he smoked it himself.

Jingo was walking back towards the bus stop on the main road, when he heard a voice call: 'Baba! Pehelwan baba!'

He stopped and looked in the direction the voice had come from. In a niche between two buildings, at the far end of a small lane on his left, was a makeshift shelter. There they were, reclining on their haunches, looking almost exactly like they had when he last saw them: Chandu, a little older, perhaps, with more lines of grey in his wavy hair; and Lalu, still as dark and inscrutable as the earthen pot that stood on a flagstone outside the hut. There was the picture of Sai Baba, adorned with a freshly strung garland of flowers. Jingo was quite delighted to see them. He grasped the hand Chandu offered and squeezed Lalu's shoulder, affectionately.

'Everything all right?' he asked by way of greeting.

'*Hum log to theek hai*, baba, thanks to the blessings of you, *saab-log*. But what about you? Long time no see. I thought of you only yesterday . . . Some very good maal I have, baba. Afghani, "pewr" Afghani. Show, Lalu . . .'

Jingo noticed that Chandu peered searchingly into the distance before fetching the maal from the folds of Lalu's loongi. Smoothly, he slipped it into his own pocket and stood up.

'We'll have to move inside, baba. Come.'

Jingo bowed low and followed him into the hut, which was smaller than the size of a double bed, almost completely bare except for a cane mat spread out on the floor.

'Times have changed . . . what to do? Those days when we could sit out in the open and smoke are gone. See this . . .' He offered him the black chunk in his hand. It smelt fresh and deep and resinous and sent a shiver through Jingo's body. Jingo passed it back to Chandu. Lalu came inside, too, and sat down on the mat.

Before long, Chandu had got down to the ritual of preparing a pipe. Jingo lit it, and took a deep breath. It was good, mellow stuff. He felt his muscles relax, his nerves soften. A smile of well-being appeared on his face as he passed the pipe to Chandu.

'Now this place per-ma-munt,' said Chandu, using his own unique flavour of Hindi peppered with pidgin English. 'Very good place. No one push us from here. Morning, night, come any time, baba . . . We're here . . .'

Jingo had been feeling slightly nervous. Until then, he had avoided any direct question about the cops. But what Chandu told him now came as joyful manna to his ears. Some sort of routine transfer, he said: the two cops who had been so unreasonable with him were no longer on the beat.

'Worst kind of vermin,' said Chandu. '*Paanso lao, ek hazaar lao*. Always grubbing for more. New in-charge is decent fellow. Call me to station, explain all rules: this special place for *addah*. Inside *gully*, no one bother. Big *jhamela* of *charsee*s no allowed. Keep inside *kholi* . . . Of course, I have to pay separately for this position. Wanted eight thousand, but very reasonable man: settle for six.'

Jingo felt incredibly elated. The wonderful hashish he

had just smoked after so long had given his world a wash of roseate softness. And now this great news. It was as if he had just heard that a long sentence he had been serving was commuted. Now there would be no problem about staying at Gurdeep's.

In all these months Jingo had spoken to him just once, over the phone. And Gurdeep had repeated that the place was still open to him, whenever he felt it was safe to move back. Jingo felt a wave of affection for his friend who shared his flat so unselfishly, without ever making him feel like a freeloader. He still had the key to the front door in his wallet, the key he'd never had a chance to return. But it would be more decent to forewarn Gurdeep before simply moving back in.

Now where and how was he to contact him? He took out his wallet to pay Chandu.

'No, no . . .' said Chandu. 'Nothing doing . . . Don't insult us, brother. It's been a long time. Here, keep this.'

He broke off a small piece from the lump in his hand and gave it to Jingo. Jingo touched the palm of his hand to his chest in a formal gesture of gratitude. Then he dropped the piece in his pocket.

As he walked away, Jingo raised his hand in farewell to them.

Over the years it may have slowed him down, made him disinclined to strive for money or success. But the hashish had given Jingo something else instead, immeasurably valuable: the awareness of an extra dimension to reality – the dimension of mind. One that he always knew existed, but had never before experienced with so much lucidity and vividness.

When he was stoned, connections sprang to life that

linked the humdrum with the outrageous, the sensual with the sublime, the grubbily mundane with the grandiose. Fields of barrenness sprouted orchids of breathtaking meaning and colour, illuminating the unlikeliest patterns of interdependence and causality. An entire universe whirled into significance out of the nucleus of the minutest phenomenon, electro-magnetic orbits whose paths lit up like the wired model of an atom Jingo had once seen at a science exhibition. Often dazzled by the grandeur of his perceptions, he felt he should transcribe some of the feverish activity of his brain on paper, and sometimes tried to – but, reading his words later, they never quite captured the flashbulb of experience that had ignited in his moment of epiphany. Jingo remembered the essential feeling for a while, but then it dimmed, and was lost.

The bus he rode back into town moved torturously slowly down Mohammed Ali Road. Jingo had been fortunate to find a vacant window-seat on the upper deck, which gave him a comfortable overview of the convulsive disarray of traffic and people darting about and around the halting, weaving passage of the bus.

Several times the driver stepped on his brakes to avoid hitting dreamy-eyed schoolchildren or reckless cyclists: each time, the bus and its passengers lurched dreadfully. It was completely absorbing, this living theatre of the street to which Jingo had a top-angle ringside view.

The bus was moving slowly past endless rows of residential houses on both sides of the broad asphalt roadway. Many of them were badly in need of repair, re-plastering or a fresh coat of paint. These were the dwelling places of large Muslim families. Occasionally he caught glimpses of darkened interiors, too. An old man, surrounded by children kneeling in prayer on a mat. A young woman in her kitchen wiping stacks of shiny steel thalis and glasses with a cloth. A child shrieking with all the power in her lungs; but the sound of her scream drowned by the uproar of traffic.

In most buildings, the ground floor was occupied by commercial establishments, cafeterias, bakeries, doctor's dispensaries, sex-and-VD clinics, tailoring outfits, cinema halls, timber marts, wine shops. Sweet shops with multi-coloured sweets stacked high in attractive heaps on tables that protruded from shop facades, encroaching onto the pavement.

What month was this? Ah, November end. No wonder the streets were so festooned and colourful. The month of Ramzaan must have begun already, and Divali, too, would be around the corner. In two hours from now dusk would set in and the streets would come alive in preparation for the breaking of the fast that had begun at daybreak.

Up ahead, there was some commotion. A fire engine was parked to one side of the road. For a few moments, traffic ground to a halt. From a manhole on the edge of the road, two firemen were extracting a body. Either unconscious, or dead.

A garrulous, moustachioed know-it-all, in the seat behind Jingo's, was addressing his co-passengers on the upper deck. 'They'll take him to KEM when the ambulance arrives,' he observed, as the bus circumvented the gathering of avidly curious pedestrians, and moved on. 'Chances are very small . . . for these conservancy fellows, it's an occupational hazard. Go down to clean a clogged drain and never come up again . . . carbon monoxide . . .

deadly poison . . . By the time their mates go down to find out what's happened, it's too late . . .'

For a few hundred metres, the bus picked up speed. Jingo looked at his watch. He might still make it. Mrs Hingorani had told him when he phoned her two days ago not to miss the briefing. They were trying something for the first time, so Madam had issued strict instructions that all her researchers must be present.

Just as the bus entered Victoria Terminus square, it was held up for almost fifteen minutes by a procession of political activists carrying banners and shouting slogans.

It wasn't such a huge gathering, but the demonstrators were bent on stalling the traffic to register their protest; some of them even climbed on to the bus and exhorted passengers to disboard in the name of Ram. 'Jai Shri Ram! Jai Shri Ram,' the protestors shouted. 'Ram's name be praised! Ram's temple *will* be built in his birthplace!' Some were carrying tridents and ceremonial swords.

Only after the police intervened did the traffic begin to move again. By the time he reached the Army and Navy building, an old wooden structure in the heart of the city's business district, the briefing was just over.

It was four fifteen. The dozen or so plastic chairs that had been specially squeezed into the office reception area were vacant and disarranged. Mrs Hingorani was inside her cabin. She was probably annoyed with him for coming in so late, Jingo thought, for she completely ignored his mumbled apology.

Some of the researchers were still there. A couple of them who knew Jingo by name hello-ed him as they finished collecting their sets of proformas, guidelines and addresses from Nancy. Nancy, Hingorani's secretary, was making entries into a ledger as she handed the material to each of them in a bulky paper folder.

From the next cabin Chief Accountant Gangwal was calling out a string of figures to his assistant Bhangera, who was busy keying them into a large-sized office calculator. He had a raucous voice, and was practically shouting. 'One-jeero-two-five-six-seven; three-seven-eight-nine-jeero-jeero-three; one-two-three; no, no, *bhai*, only one-two-three . . .'

Jingo wondered if they were totting up profits, or payments due from clients. There was so much confidence money gave you, even when you were only handling someone else's accounts. Should he have become a chartered accountant himself, like his father wanted him to? Behind the disdain he felt for people who made pots of money – and knew how to go on making more – did there lurk a festering envy? If he had been in a position to do so himself, would he have soon tired of the routine, experienced the same soul-killing despair which he so dreaded? Or would the inflow of crisp notes have provided its own bulwark against such despondency?

Mrs Hingorani turned to Jingo at last, and asked him to shut the cabin door. The cackly voice of Gangwal now muffled brought back calm to her cabin. She asked him to sit.

'Lucky, Madam Mira left just a few minutes before you came,' she said. 'Others who walked in late got quite an earful from her!'

Fortunately, Jingo never had to deal directly with Mrs Shivadasani, the founder-chairman of the agency. A pugnacious woman in her early forties, she was known to be hard as nails, patronizing to employees and arrogant. The acronym she had devised for the firm (Market

Investigation, Research and Analysis) was based on her own first name: Mira.

In the twelve years or so that the agency had been in existence, two or three smaller competitors had sprung up in the city, offering the same kind of consumer survey at cheaper rates. But MIRA was by far the most established of the lot. And now Madam Mira had stolen a march on the competition by securing contracts with two leading newspapers to conduct opinion polls for them on current political matters. This was a first even for MIRA, and today's briefing had been called to orient field-workers to this new task. Mrs Hingorani was the coordinator – older than Mrs Shivadasani, but very nice. She handed Jingo a set of printed guidelines and said, 'In fact, Madam said she didn't want anybody who was absent at the briefing to take on the survey. I guess she meant among the newcomers . . . But just go through this paper first and ask me if you have any questions. It's different, but actually very simple. I don't think you'll have any problem.' She smiled at him, and shrugged. 'But all the nice areas are gone, I'm afraid. I can only give you Chinchpokli. Or Lalbagh-Parel.'

'That's great! Thanks a lot. Nothing new about that,' said Jingo good-humouredly: over the years, he had developed a reputation in the agency for being one of the few willing to take on working-class areas. Jingo was still reading the guidlines when Mrs Hingorani rang for the office-boy and asked him to fetch a coffee for him.

There were four basic questions he would have to ask:

i) Do you think that a Ram Temple existed in the place where the Babri Masjid now stands?

ii) Do you think a Ram Temple should be rebuilt on a nearby site?

iii) Do you believe that this controversy has been raked up by political parties and has little or no bearing on religious sentiment?

iv) Do you think the *Rath Yatra* from Somnath to Ayodhya was a political gimmick, intended to inflame communal passions in the country?

Each question was followed by a choice of three responses, one of which was to be ticked: Yes; No; Can't Say.

The guidelines gave a fixed ratio of income groups the agency was to maintain among respondents. His would be a low income area. Researchers were urged not to enter into political arguments with respondents, given the volatile nature of the questions. At the same time it was recommended that they keep abreast of current political affairs.

'Won't be much of a problem, I shouldn't think,' said Jingo to Mrs Hingorani, when he had finished his coffee.

Since he was sitting in front of a phone, he asked Mrs Hingorani's permission to use it. He had tried Gurdeep's number once while still in Byculla, but it had just kept ringing. He dialled the number again, expecting the same result. This time, however, he was amazed to hear Gurdeep's voice answer after the very first ring. His friend, too, was pleasantly surprised to hear his voice.

'Hey, you're lucky to find me in, man,' he said. 'How are you? I just stopped by for a few minutes to pack a few things. In two hours' time, Thiru and me are catching a train to Delhi.'

'Delhi? Whatever for?' asked Jingo.

'Well, lots has been happening. I don't suppose you know anything about it?'

'I don't,' said Jingo. 'But listen. I was hoping to move into your flat later this afternoon.'

'So go ahead. You have the key, right?' said Gurdeep. 'I'll fill you in once I get back, but things haven't been going too well for us at Nehrunagar.'

'Like what?'

'For one thing, the High Court threw out the stay order. The municipality's getting ready to start demolitions again in a big way. You see, we're trying to get a Supreme Court lawyer in Delhi to file a writ petition to stop them . . . Other things have been happening, too.'

'Ya?'

'A bunch of thugs offered Thiru sixty thousand rupees to close down the CPSDR office and move out. Then they offered him a lakh. He still refused. Then they threatened him with dire consquences. That's why I've been staying out there for the whole of last week. The cops refused to even file an FIR.'

'That's tough,' said Jingo. 'Wish I could be of some help.'

'We'll see what you can do when I get back,' said Gurdeep. 'Meanwhile, look after the flat.'

'I will.'

'And oh yes – I have a message for you from Thiru.'

'What?'

'He said to apologize about the way he lost his cool with you over that girl, Shanti. A few days after you went away she was found among a group of minor girls rescued from a brothel in Chembur. She told the cops it was Shankar, the barber, who sold her to the brothel keeper for 5,000 rupees.'

'Amazing. And where's she now?'

'They've moved all the girls to a Remand Home in Kalyan.'

'Shankar?' Jingo asked. 'Have they charged him?'

'The barber's absconding. Cops are mad at him, not so much for selling his kid into prostitution, but for faking a missing person complaint. Apparently everyone in Nehrunagar knew he was looking at places to let in Thane, collecting money for his fancy hairdressing salon. Crazy . . . Thiru's said he's sorry he gave you such a rough time while you were here.'

'Tell him to forget it,' said Jingo.

'I have to go now. We'll talk at length when we meet.'

'Good luck with the lawyer in Delhi.'

'Ya, thanks. See you, then.'

'And thanks for letting me stay.'

'You're welcome.'

Gurdeep rang off. Just as he was leaving the office, Nancy remembered to give Jingo a message: 'Oh by the way, there's a Mrs Gorimar who been calling for you,' she said. 'I explained to her that you didn't come to the office every day. But she goes on ringing up every now and then.'

'Sorry,' he explained. 'Someone I met on a survey. Wants me to help her contact a boy I knew a very long time ago. I'd left my card with her, unfortunately.'

'It's no problem,' said Nancy. 'But maybe you should call her back. She sounded quite upset.'

'She doesn't have a phone. I'll have to look her up.'

'Well, when she calls again,' said Nancy, 'I'll tell her I've passed on the message.' Jillamai seemed to have won her sympathy. That was Nancy's subtle way of nudging Jingo to respond. Had Nancy sensed some real distress in the old woman? Or was it only her longing for her missing son, which the old woman hoped to assuage by meeting his school mate again? Jingo supposed he had some reason to feel guilty about all this. He *had* promised to get back to Jillamai. But then, what on earth was he to tell her? He had absolutely no news of Hoshi to give.

Vada-pao

When Gopal first suggested they ask their boss's permission to sell vada-pao on the street outside the lunch home after closing time, he had been only partly serious. But Shivappa thought it was a brilliant idea.

Unless he found some way to earn something extra, how was he ever going to save enough to shop for presents for his family, how was he ever going to be able to afford to visit his village again? Of course, it'd only be a short visit, a week or ten days at most, just to let them know he was doing well for himself, make peace with his father. Then back to Bombay. Truth to tell, he'd had enough of Hallengdi for a lifetime.

Over the last few months, business had become increasingly dull at Kanara in the evenings. At night, there was practically no custom at all. A couple of guys dropping in to share a cup of tea, or a misal-pao; on rare occasions, an order for a single thali, or a soft drink. But can you run a fully fledged lunch home on titbits like that? Finally, Janardhan, the old man's son, persuaded his father to shut early, by seven thirty.

'Think of the amount we'll save on food that's wasted, Papa,' he said. 'Our peak hours are morning time, and lunch. Let the boys eat the day's leftovers, no cooking again in the evening. Think of the saving on gas and electricity bills!'

His keen distaste for the old eating-house was evident; Janardhan intended to completely refurbish the lunch home some time very soon. Shiv and Gopal had overheard the father and son discuss their plans for a posh speciality restaurant – serving, among other things, traditional fish curries and seafood preparations from the Konkan – and were afraid they might be laid off. So when, hesitantly, they mooted the idea of a vada-pao snack stall they could run at night after closing time, they were taken aback by Janardhan's fulsome praise for their spirit of enterprise.

Yes, he said, it was an excellent idea. In the early part of the evening, the locality was quite dead. But later at night, they might do well selling some lightly fried and low-priced snacks. A sizeable crowd of late-shift millworkers, returning home from the station, passed that way. Encouraged by his response, Gopal asked him if he would forward them a small advance towards purchases for the venture, even offering to share their profits with him until the loan was repaid. But Janardhan laughed at the idea.

'*Arrey!*' he exclaimed, as though astonished at their stupidity. 'Who do you think you are, big hoteliers already? Do you know how much every new utensil will cost you?'

Janardhan proposed an alternative: he would allow them the use of the old Primus stove in the kitchen, one big stainless steel thali and the large iron kadhai. They could also borrow half a dozen saucers in which to serve their vada-pao. For all this he would only charge them a nominal rent of a hundred rupees a month.

'What more do you need,' he said, 'to start off? Just pitch your things outside the shutter. The asbestos awning over the signboard will even protect you from the rain . . . Well, what d'you say?'

They remained tongue-tied, slightly amazed by his sudden generosity. He was not doing this for money, he said, but only because he approved of their desire to work hard and improve their station in life. 'First start making good profits, *then* you can buy your own equipment, no? What's the big hurry?'

He would even have waived the rent on the utensils, he said, but that would not be quite right, for they must learn that nothing in life came for free; one had to value the things one took for granted. They would of course be fully responsible for all these items, which were strictly on loan and must be scrubbed and put back in the kitchen every night. The rent for the same would be deducted from their salaries, fifty-fifty.

Before the matter could be finalized, however, Janardhan had to have several discussions with his father, whose growing deafness made it difficult to have a private conversation with him. Clearly, the old man had several misgivings.

'How will you keep a check on what items they steal from our kitchen to cook their vadas?' he argued with his son, not caring that he was being overheard.

'Don't worry, Papa,' Janardhan replied. Then, in as low a voice as the old man's hearing could tolerate, 'I'll keep a strict check on them . . . When renovation starts, and the place has to be shut down for two months, then you'll understand my logic. Once they've set up with something of their own, they'll learn not to expect any more help from us. And Papa, a hundred a month is no loss. It'll more than take care of petty pilferage. Right now there's only outgoings.'

Nevertheless, on their first evening, when they had got the spicy potato balls rolled and ready to drop into the kadhai of hot oil, Janardhan issued a strong warning to Shiv and Gopal: 'It's only thanks to the kindness of my father that you're being allowed to conduct this sideshow at night,' he said. 'What we're deducting from your salary for all these facilities is nothing, peanuts. Just to help you out. So make very sure you never take anything from this establishment that's not part of our agreement. If I ever find you have abused our generosity . . . if even one potato or onion or chilli is missing from the kitchen, both of you'll find yourselves out on your backsides in the street the very next day! Make sure you buy your own kerosene, pao, whatever else you need,' he said. 'Don't think this is your father's property to dip into as and when you like. Keep your things separately in that corner. And don't leave the main shutter open for even a minute unless you're inside.'

There were several other instructions, but Shivappa and Gopal went on nodding, cheerfully willing to accept every condition.

Shivappa sat on his haunches before the heap of dishes that had to be washed, thinking excitedly of the developments of the last few weeks. The scullery, if it could be called that, was no more than a niche in the rear of the kitchen, partitioned off by a plywood construct to conceal from view an open drain, a tap and the foot-high parapet on which he squatted. The dishes, piled on the floor in front of him, smelt of decomposing food. He turned on the tap. Cold water splashed on dry grease and bare feet. He shivered momentarily – this had been an unusually chill November for Bombay, so everyone said – but his own mind was engaged in making calculations.

A few days ago he had seen a terycot cut piece in a shop window near the market. It was of a rust-brown colour he instinctively knew his dad would love. Only 225. Not impossible to acquire. The last ten days had brought in a cool 310 rupees between them. That was only from vada-pao; starting tonight they were planning to offer tea as well. Between them they should make at least seven or eight hundred per month . . . Mustn't forget to get a cheap sari or a blouse piece for his stepmother as well, maybe some *khilona* for the baba . . . Was it a baby or baba, even that he didn't know . . . But they'd better not forget to set aside the fifty a week they had promised that Vichare bloke, or things could get nasty. Shivappa felt hot around his neck thinking of the man's crude insolence, but decided it was better to write it off as an incidental expense of running a nocturnal business . . .

It was a little after half past midnight on the very first night. They hadn't done so badly. Having just extinguished the Primus, they were carrying in the thalis, the saucers, leftover mash of spiced potatoes and gramflour batter, when this Vaman Vichare and his two buddies accosted them. At first Shivappa was frightened and Gopal, too, had lost his voice. All three of them looked like real hoodlums; a moment later, they were still not so sure. The leader began shooting questions at them as though he were a plainclothes cop.

He asked their names and which part of the country they came from. How long had they been in Bombay, how long had they been running this business? Finally came a key question: why were they not paying their weekly donation to the Ghorpad Shakti Fauj? Gradually, the man's tone became more pedagogic, even pleasant.

'You must have heard of Dada Ghorpadey?' he asked. They nodded assent. 'Who hasn't? He's our leader. A very enlightened soul. He ensures that there are many advantages for all those who pay their dues and join the Fauj. Fauj exists only for people like you, who have no one else to protect them. You and your vada-pao business will be protected once you enlist. Not even the police will dare to harm you,' he said, picking his nose intently. 'And Dada always likes to help out youngsters like you. 'Specially Hindu boys. He has a special soft spot in his heart for all Hindus. He'll have no truck with Mussalman traitors, mind you. The type who burst crackers and distribute sweets when Pakistan wins a cricket match against India. If you were one of those *kuttoo*s selling kababs or bheja fry—'

'*Gurda!*' said one of his associates, 'gurda fry! Their own!' And the goons laughed. But Vaman didn't like being interrupted, and continued only after directing a cold stare at his ebullient friend '– or something like that at a street corner, you would have had to pay through your nose. And no guarantee of protection.' With that, he flicked a shred of something he had managed to extract from his nose into the air. Shiv tried to follow its trajectory to see where it landed, but it was too dark.

Since it was only very recently they had started the business, Vichare said he would overlook the arrears they owed him. But from next Monday onwards, he would drop by every week to sample their vada-pao. And for now he would charge them a flat reduced rate of 50 rupees a week, though the normal rate for such vada and snack stalls ranged from 10 to 30 rupees per night depending on profit margins and location. Shiv was fuming inside. Seeing that Gopal was only nodding his head cravenly, agreeing to Vichare's terms without a word of protest, he felt it was up to him to speak out:

'Fifty's too much,' he piped up in a nervously high-pitched voice. 'We don't make much – a few rupees every night. On top of that, we have to pay the boss for these thalis and stove and everything.'

'I like his spirit, this fledgling's,' said Vichare after a pause, looking straight at him and pinching his cheeks hard, as though he were a bonny baby. Shiv brushed away his hand. The man was smiling at him, but it was a glazed smile and there was menace in his eyes. 'Leave the calculations to us, *pilloo,*' he said, indicating Gopal and himself. 'I wasn't born yesterday. You're not even Maharashtrians, still we accommodate you in our Mumbai. You come here to make money, by all means. But give the party your share, and see. Dadasaheb will be kind. If you're loyal, I'll even take you to meet our Division Head. He's a big man, close to Dadasaheb and his sons. He'll advance you a loan to buy your own equipment, your own four-wheeled cart. He's fixed up so many others like you in good locations near the station where they're earning three times what they used to. Only thing Dadsaheb expects in return is a little loyalty . . . Right?'

The question was directed at one of his henchmen, who repeated after him, 'Only a little loyalty, that's all . . .' and Vichare nodded, before continuing: 'There were some who thought they could outsmart us, change locations, hide from us. We ran them out of town, with a few broken bones, eh? What am I saying?' He turned again to his sidekick for confirmation, and the lackey repeated: 'A few tried to hide . . . but they got their bones broken instead.'

The other sidekick laughed and said, 'And believe me, we know what bones to break.'

Meanwhile Vichare had commenced digging into his other nostril distractedly. 'Don't worry, sahab,' said Gopal, 'we'll do whatever you say.'

'I don't need to worry,' said Vichare venomously, and spat. 'It's *you* who need to – think – clearly!' Then he flicked a fresh string of nose-goo in the direction of Shiv and strode off, arms swinging, goons following a step behind. This time the shred of mucus from his nose had fallen right in the middle of the Formica-topped table they were clearing up to take inside. Bastard. He would have liked to take on that creep, refuse to comply with his extortion. Shivappa bristled with annoyance at the memory of that night. If only he had some help, someone to support him in his fight. For one instant he thought of Pehelwan Baba, who had disappeared without a word more than six months ago. Somebody like him would have been able to advise him on what to do.

For three days in a row, since he had moved back to Gurdeep's, Jingo had been working very hard indeed. From nine thirty in the morning until late evening he'd been out of the house. He had agreed to interview a list of fifty-two men and women, and promised to deliver his results back by the 2nd. That gave him only two days.

'Any time on the 2nd,' Hingorani had said. 'Even if it's ten in the night. Pankaj and the other execs are planning to work late and finish tabulation. The *Express* will need a couple of hours to write up their own report based on our findings.'

Fifty-two individuals needn't have taken so long, considering he had only four questions to put to them. But most people, he found, were fairly ignorant about the temple-masjid issue, or else uninterested. And those who already knew something about the matter found it necessary to make lengthy justifications for the positions they took.

'It's a matter of national pride,' some said, echoing the catchphrases of the politicians. 'Of course a Ram temple must be put up in the birthplace of Ram.'

'It's time for us to put our foot down. Historical proof is not relevant. We don't need proof. It's a question of faith, of Hindu sentiment!'

But Jingo met, among others, a skinny, bespectacled Maharashtrian gentleman called Ekbote who was remarkably down-to-earth. He was a retired rationing officer, and also a stamp collector.

'When politicians start making a hullabaloo,' he said, 'you can be sure it's time to cast your vote!' Then, absent-mindedly, he started drumming a jaunty beat on his desk with his knobbly fingers, as if to announce an impending election. 'Actually, I used to be a government servant. If you had met me six months ago, I would not have been able to speak like this. Now I'm retired,' he explained, 'I just look after my stamps . . . and I speak my mind.

'Ask these fellows who are agitating for a temple,' he declared, 'eighty-seven people have died so far in UP of the cold wave. Will the *poojari*s fill the bellies of these unfortunates who are dying of cold? Will they offer them shelter under the sculpted *gopuram*s of the Ram mandir? It's purely a matter of stirring up passions; people need to believe they have something to vote for. Otherwise, on a hungry stomach, who feels like casting a vote?'

When Gopal had got the coffees ready, Shivappa carried them out to a front table at which Janardhan and his guest were seated. The other man had a paper in front of him and was busy doing some calculations. A little while ago, he had whipped out a roll of metal measuring tape from his pocket and noted down the dimensions of the lunch home in some detail. A contractor, Shivappa had presumed; over coffee, Janardhan and he discussed the kind of tiles he would use for the flooring, they selected from a shade-card the colour of the paint he would use on the walls, and so on. Janardhan asked the man to be quick about sending in the final estimate, and to remain reasonable in his quotation.

The bosses had assured Gopal he would be re-employed in the New Kanara, or whatever it was they were planning to call the fancy restaurant, but they hadn't mentioned a word about Shivappa, until Gopal asked if they meant to keep him on as well. Of course, of course, Janardhan had affirmed, but Shivappa was unconvinced. He doubted if Gopal himself would be re-employed. For one thing he was just not good enough to prepare those delicate fish dishes they were planning for the menu – they'd have to get a fancy cook, too, to go with the new restaurant. And as for waiters, he reckoned they'd want some guys with a little more education, who could speak a few words of English at least.

Surely this was what had inspired Janardhan's largesse. The shrewd fop was making a virtue out of renting them a lot of old junk that was littering up the place, and making a hundred bucks a month on it as well. When the time came, Shivappa was expecting him to give them the boot without any qualms.

That's why it was important to tolerate Vichare, much as he hated him. At the rate they were earning, it would take them at least two or three years before they could afford a cart with wheels and an awning, a stove of their own and all the other equipment they needed. Eventually they could diversify their menu to offer bhaaji-pao, biryani, maybe even Chineez, all of which would bring in better profits. But in the meantime, if the lunch home was shut down for renovation, they'd be out in the street again, having to start from scratch. Yet, if they could trust the claims and promises Vaman Vichare had made last week, some sort of loan would be arranged, and they'd be in business sooner than he hoped.

The building Jingo was tackling in Parel had a mixed lower-middle-class population. Next on his list was a Mrs Fonseca, Ekbote's neighbour on the floor above. Her front door was open, though the room inside was shielded from view by a grubby printed curtain. He rang the doorbell, and a dark Goan woman with a curly mop of hair moved the curtain aside.

She was perspiring profusely and seemed very harassed; it took her a long time to understand who he was and what he wanted.

This was not a random survey like the ones Jingo usually undertook. All the respondents had been selected out of the phonebook, first questioned about income grouping/religion/community, and then informed, if they fitted the requirement, of a date on which the agency's representative would visit them to ask a few questions. But Mrs Fonseca could remember nothing about such a phone call. From inside came the shrieks of several children crying at once.

'I'll answer anything,' she said. 'Whate'er you want to know, I'll tell you. But you'll have to wait one hour, man. At least one hour, while I finish cooking and give my children to eat.'

She drew the curtain open wider to show him the single room that was her home. A large worn-out cane mat was spread on the floor, and on it, five children of various ages were sprawled – lying down, sitting, crawling, and the two eldest, a girl and a boy, who must have been about nine and ten respectively, brawling. There was a large crucifix on the wall, and under it, a sideboard on which sat a plump black telephone.

The little girl shrieked on receiving a well-aimed blow on her chin. This was repeated several times, until her mother screamed even more hysterically, 'Conan! I'll bash your brains out, man, if you touch Priscilla again. I'm telling you, no vindaloo for you today. I don't care if you bloody well starve, you hooligan!' To Jingo, she said, 'Too much *churbi* the bugger's got.' On hearing this threat spoken with so much severity, Conan protested that it was Priscilla who punched him first. Just then, the phone began to ring and, quite forgetting about the argument, Conan rushed to answer it. Not able to recognize the caller's voice or understand what he was saying, he declared, 'Wrong number!' and replaced the receiver.

His mother shouted at him for not giving her the phone. Now Conan too began to cry, softly, resentfully. Within minutes, the third, fourth and fifth child had also joined in the chorus of snivelling. Jingo noticed that both hands of the mother were stained with the fiery red masala she must have just finished grinding for their curry when he had interrupted her.

'Actually they're all bloody hungry fellows, man. That's why they're crying,' she explained. 'And this pork also is taking so long to cook.'

Just then the whistle of a pressure cooker shrilled.

'Ah,' said the mother. 'Now only three more . . . Better to let them eat and fall asleep. Then we can talk in peace. You want to go somewhere else and come back later?' she suggested.

Later that afternoon Jingo met a man called RP Malani. Elderly, but very dapper, he was wearing a clean white T-shirt and padded sports shoes. He had a toothbrush moustache, and spoke in a dignified and civil manner. But very soon he seemed to take a dislike to Jingo, or to the nature of the survey he was conducting. With every question he was asked he grew increasingly belligerent.

'Definitely, temple is a must,' he declared with grave pomposity. 'Muslims can't have everything their way. Congress Party has been appeasing them at the cost of the Hindus, just to get their votes. But this is a Hindu *rashtra*, let no one forget. If they want to live here, they'll have to be put in their place.'

As he went on, he grew more and more abusive of Muslims and Jingo couldn't resist asking him (contrary to his guidelines) if he believed like Jinnah in the two-nation theory. His eyes grew large and more furious.

'Don't mention that shyster's name to me!' he roared. 'Two-nation? Bharat is one and always will be *akhand* Bharat! If it weren't for that hypocrite Gandhi . . .' At first Jingo had been slightly amused by the histrionics, but now he felt afraid as he witnessed the rising hysteria.

Malani's voice, as he continued his ideological ranting, had risen to the pitch of a man addressing a large rally of supporters: 'If they don't want Ram's mandir in Ayodhya, they can pack up and go to Pakistan! We will not tolerate them any longer.'

Perhaps the man had sensed that Jingo wasn't entirely sympathetic to his views, for he couldn't resist adding: 'These butchers and carcass-handlers should have gone long ago. And anyone else, too, who wants to arselick them. Let them all go!'

Jingo was aware that people who felt like Malani had grown more vociferous of late. But this was the first time he had been face-to-face with a rabidly fundamentalist Hindu. And he hadn't really tried to provoke him or anything.

He wasn't even very sure what he felt about this temple-masjid dispute himself. Born and bred in Bombay, a city which had for generations attracted every kind of migrant and trader, where cultural differences were taken for granted, Jingo had never thought of Muslims as 'the other', and his own impression was that most people in the city didn't either.

Come to think of it, his people, too, belonged to another race. They had come to India not as invaders but as refugees, 1,200 years ago. Was it only a matter of time before they would be labelled 'outsiders', too, if this business of a 'Hindu nation' was carried to its illogical extreme? What about Cristina, and her clan of East Indians? They were Christians by faith, and meat-eaters, too, like the Muslims. But they were the original settlers of Bombay, and had lived there since the time it was just a small cluster of fishing villages. Would Hindu zealots like Malani soon be calling for their expulsion too?

His next stop was at the flat of one Mr Jadhav, a senior engineer with an offshore oil exploration company. Here, too, he found the front door open. The living room was crowded with people, some standing, an old woman sobbing into her hands; a body bedecked with garlands and flowers was laid out on the bed and a thick smoky incense enveloped the room. A young man came to the door and introduced himself as Suresh Jadhav. He wiped away tears as he explained politely that Mr Jadhav, his father, had passed away just an hour ago.

'You're too late,' he said, as if apologizing for his father's inability to keep the appointment. 'He had been complaining of some uneasiness. He was expecting you, he told us you were coming. But before we could even call a doctor . . .' He broke down. Wiping away his tears, he collected himself and explained: 'Massive heart attack . . . No chance.'

'I'm so sorry . . .' said Jingo, and shook the boy's hand before retreating. He was disturbed by the wails of collective grief that rose and fell in waves from the smoky room behind, an unexpected reminder of human mortality. That was one man's opinion on the temple-masjid controversy he would never find out.

Around 8 p.m., he went back to the office and added the fifty-one opinions he had polled to those of the other researchers. The lights were all on in the office. Pankaj and the others were busy at their computers.

The following day's *Express* carried the 'results' of the poll: 672 people or 53% were in favour of building the temple for Ram at the disputed site. 12% wanted it built somewhere close by, without disturbing the mosque; and

35% had answered that they couldn't say what should be done.

Jingo, reading in bed, was disturbed by these findings, because they quite contradicted his own, in which most people didn't have an opinion and, among the ones who did, most felt it was only a ploy of the Hindu political formations to corner Hindu votes in the coming UP assembly polls. But then most of the people he had interviewed belonged to a particular economic segment, working class and lower middle class. God alone knew by what reasoning or mechanism these results were finally tabulated. And other researchers would probably have tackled more prosperous respondents.

After glancing through the report, Jingo turned over and went back to sleep. When he woke up again it was past noon. He was feeling lazy, a little tired from his exertions of the last three days. He decided to have his lunch at a place called Arvind Restaurant that provided slightly better food than Kanara. Later, he dropped by at Kanara for a coffee to find out how things were going with Shiv and Gopal.

'There's a guy outside you might want to see,' said Gopal to Shivappa, as he entered the kitchen. 'Go take his order . . .'

There was a coy insinuation in his tone which puzzled Shiv. The first person he thought of was Vaman Vichare. Could he and his hoods have turned up at the lunch home to try and frighten them again? But then what was Gopal acting so mysterious about?

'*Arrey*, go, take the order,' repeated Gopal more emphatically.

But Shiv deliberately took his time, first washing his

hands, then wiping them dry on the rag of a napkin that hung in the kitchen before going out to see who it was.

His eyes lit up spontaneously. A smile would have appeared on his lips if he had let it. Instead he nodded casually at Jingo, as though he had last seen him only yesterday, and went up to take his order. Pehelwan Baba had some explaining to do.

When the coffee was ready, Gopal brought it out himself, all smiles. It took Jingo a little longer to dispel the younger boy's cold indifference. But when he told them about the trouble he'd landed in with the cops, Shiv dropped his resentful manner and even showed concern.

Anyway, they were eager to tell him about all the changes that had taken place in their lives: about Kanara's impending renovation, their vada-pao stall, about Vichare who had enrolled them as members of a party called the Ghorpad Shakti Fauj, which was a fine party, they said, whose main objective was to help the poor, and especially Hindus. And about the Chief Division Head of the party Vichare took them to meet one evening. A big man called Olundaz.

'He's much nicer than Vichare,' said Shivappa. 'A real man-mountain, Olundaz-saab, more *pehelwan* even than you. His skin colour is *gora*, too, like yours. But each of his arms is a ten-kilo hunk of mutton, no less! He's agreed to advance us two thousand for the cart as soon as we find a suitable location. Boss may give us the sack any day. Imagine our situation if we didn't have the Fauj to help us . . .'

All in all, they were quite pleased by the turn of events, and hopeful about their future, Kanara or no Kanara.

Already they were feeling loyal to Dadasaheb Ghorpadey, the Commander-in-Chief of the Ghorpad Shakti Fauj, not to mention Olundaz, his lieutenant.

By the time he got up to leave, it was almost five. Jingo was feeling oddly depressed. He promised Shiv and Gopal he'd be back some other evening, soon, to try their spicy-tasty vada-pao.

Victoria Gardens

The tumultuous chorus of awakening animals didn't disturb Jingo's sleep that morning, but Poonjwani's deep bellow had much the same effect.

'Brahmanand!' his second-floor neighbour rumbled tetchily, calling to the Nepali watchman who mostly sat out the night in a wooden cubicle at the other end of the Winifred compound. 'Oi, Brahmanand Singh!'

'*Haan*, saab,' cried the watchman, hurriedly presenting himself below their balconies.

'Ah,' said Poonjwani, 'you're awake? And where were you last night at ten?'

Jingo looked at the alarm clock on the table beside his bed. It was ten to seven and day was just breaking. The soft twittering of birds made pleasant counterpoint to Poonjwani's throaty harangue.

'I was there,' replied Brahmanand.

'Now don't you dare start lying to me,' his neighbour declaimed with operatic suddenness in a strongly accented contra basso.

'Maybe gone for dinner, saab,' mumbled the watchman.

'When I came home at ten, I passed your cabin,' said

Poonjwani, who was also the Secretary of the Winifred Housing Cooperative, 'and there you were inside, snoring away. Not just that, two outside cars were parked in our compound! Were you sleeping when they grabbed that space? Or did you accept some chai-paani to provide it?'

'*Nahin*, saab. I didn't accept anything. I didn't see any cars . . .'

'Ah, so you admit it? Such golden dreams you must have to believe I pay you to sleep!'

'*Nahin*, saab, I stay up all night! Only sometimes, by chance . . .' pleaded the watchman.

'I heard you, snoring loudly as a bison, with my own ears!' Poonjwani yelled. 'Now go on, you lazy son-of-an-owl, switch on the pump quickly! It's past seven and there's not a drop of water in the taps!'

It was a ritual vilification, frequently enacted, though the issues and the ferocity of dispute varied from time to time. Jingo had never met Poonjwani but had seen him often enough: an elderly bachelor living alone on the second floor of C wing, right above Gurdeep's flat, to the left. Sometimes from their balcony he could see the big, flabby man lean over his own balcony rail to grumble at the watchman, sometimes pacing the length of his living room like a caged beast, then out onto the balcony, then back inside. He was probably very lonely, and picking on the young Nepali watchman was Poonjwani's favourite pastime.

Usually, when he came out on his balcony for these slanging matches, Poonjwani would be quite naked, except for a pair of extra-large undies and an extravagantly curly hirsutism. Perhaps it was his way of advertising his solitariness, his freedom. These frequent verbal punch-ups with the watchman made Jingo wonder if perhaps what Poonjwani really wanted was to clasp Brahmanand tightly to his chest and smother him with kisses. Instead, he only upbraided him while in a state of partial undress.

Jingo got out of bed and stepped out onto his balcony wearing only a florid printed loongi himself. He glanced up at the second floor, but it was deserted. Most of the buildings in their lane were old structures that had been built more than twenty years ago. There had been one wedge-shaped plot of land at the far end of the compound, beyond a makeshift fence, which had been vacant for years, but during the six months he had been away some construction work had commenced even on this pitifully small piece of land.

Reinforced concrete pillars stood at intervals with twisted black rods sticking out of their napes, like so many stiff-necked Medusas. A crude wooden casing had been hammered together all around the projected first floor, awaiting the pouring of hot concrete into its cavity. A cement mixer brooded silently in one corner of the plot. Construction workers living on the site had erected a couple of huts by the edge of the property. From an iron tank filled with water, one of the workers was bathing her child.

Well, vacant land never remained that way for long in Bombay, did it? Still, he'd grown rather fond of that little patch of open space in the distance. There had been some undergrowth on it, a few trees. Now it had all been shaven clean, even the trees had been felled.

Jingo returned inside, filled the electric kettle and switched it on. Immersing a teabag into his mug of hot water, he opened the newspapers. Up north, in the dusty temple town of Ayodhya, there was trouble brewing. The papers spoke of a convergence of thousands of *kaarse-vak*s, not counting those already camping in the town, who were awaiting their chance to make a voluntary contribution of manual labour for the construction of Ram's temple.

The wily politician whose party had never succeeded in capturing power in all the years of its existence, had thought up a clever ruse. The so-called Chariot Odyssey, or *Rath Yatra*, was intended ostensibly to awaken Hindus from their apathy, and mobilize their support for the building of a temple at the very spot where a fifteenth-century mosque stood, while also reminding them of the trauma their ancestors had supposedly suffered at the hands of Muslim invaders. A ragtag procession of cars, trucks, buses and a Toyota van dressed up as chariot with the politician himself at the helm had covered some 6,000 miles of countryside, sparking off Hindu–Muslim riots in towns and villages along its path, a deadly swathe of hundreds, thousands of people torched, maimed and killed. The ritual vermilion with which the politician had daubed his forehead was the colour of innocent blood.

His party, which essentially held that India was a Hindu nation which should be ruled by Hindus, claimed that a Ram temple had been demolished by the Mughal aggressor, Babur, to make way for the mosque 470 years ago, and now the Muslims had to make reparation, whether they liked it or not. Other parties espousing the cause of 'Hindutva' were getting ready to reap the rich harvest of votes they expected this emotional issue to supply.

The Ghorpad Fauj in Bombay was one such party. Started rather a long time ago by Dada Ghorpadey, this political group claimed to represent the interests of 'sons-of-the-soil'. Its main demands were of a nativistic nature: job reservations for Maharashtrians, and a ban on the influx of migrants to Bombay from other parts of the country. It had always remained a small, regional party noted primarily for its violently agitational style of politics.

The party symbol was a ghorpad – an alligator-like giant iguana, its tail lashing through the air. During public speeches and press interviews, at every opportunity, Ghorpadey never failed to clarify the significance of his party's mascot.

'Every Maharashtrian schoolboy knows the stirring tale of Tanaji Malusure, the great hero who strapped himself to the back of a ghorpad to climb the unscaleable cliff of Kondana from the rear. Once at the top, he threw down a rope to his brave band of fighters, who quickly joined him. The fortress of Kondana was liberated from the Mughals and given to Emperor Shivaji as a gift. Never mind that many, including Tanaji, had to lay down their lives in the process – they were proud to.

'Now Shivaji's days have gone with the wind, and once again the proud Marathi *manoos* has become an underdog. I am convinced we will have to wage another war of liberation before we can be free . . . Some people ask me, Why have you named your party Ghorpad Shakti Fauj? Ghorpad brings bad luck, no? Well, I tell them: Look, my name is Dada Ghorpadey, and I know only one thing – once the ghorpad has gripped something, he never lets go. He's a climber. He will claw his way to the top, come what may. We will take inspiration from the ghorpad. And ghorpad will bring bad luck only to the ruling party . . .'

Ghorpadey, a self-confessed admirer of Adolf Hitler,

was accused by his critics of megalomania. But his answer to them was simple: 'We do not believe in democracy – that is why my party never holds internal party elections.' Dadasaheb was supreme Commander-in-Chief of the Ghorpad Shakti Fauj, and after him, his sons would take over. In moments of candour and self-indulgence, he spoke of ruling India with an iron fist, as it should be, once his policies had captured the popular imagination and mandate. And then he would teach Pakistan, India's malignant neighbour, a befitting lesson.

Now, in the wake of the *Rath Yatra* to Ayodhya, his party, too, had jumped on the bandwagon of 'Hinduness', hoping to widen its appeal and rope in more support from 'loyal' Hindus all over the country.

Jingo found it depressing that while neither of them had the slightest notion of politics, Shiv and Gopal had connected with this pernicious political formation. But then, the Fauj had always enlisted its cadres from among the underprivileged and the lumpen. Essentially, the boys were only being provided 'protection' in return for a small fee. Nevertheless, they seemed to savour the idea of belonging to a local outfit like the Ghorpad Fauj. They had an identity now, which was larger than that of waiter, cook and streetside snack-stall owners; they had become proud Hindus as well, having learned the subtle, first lessons of their indoctrination well.

Perhaps Ayodhya was just too far away, and the machinations of the GSF too vulgar to hold Jingo's attention for long. Anyway, one of the news snippets at the bottom of page one caught his interest instead.

It spoke of an SDM in Bihar, an assistant district magistrate, who had kidnapped a young, married tribal woman and imprisoned her in a shed behind his house for one and a half years, regularly using her as a sex slave, as did his friend, a landlord's son. She was given a diet of gruel, just enough to subsist on, and frequent beatings. She was forced to undergo two abortions during this period, which were privately conducted by a doctor from the district hospital at the selfsame SDM's shed. Somehow, the woman managed to escape and was given shelter, first by a social worker, and then an institution. There was a public outcry, following which the DM, in tandem with the police department, was looking into her case.

The world is full of sad stories, perhaps my country especially so, thought Jingo. What happened to the woman was simply dreadful and disgusting. Even though she was free now, this savage episode had probably twisted her life forever. Those men, even if they were convicted, would probably get away with a sentence of no more than five or seven years.

It was eight now. Work at the construction site was beginning in earnest. The foreman was shouting to make himself heard above the noise of the cement mixer. It had begun to grunt and growl and roar, occasionally purring, as one after the other the women fed it headloads of sand, cement and stones: offerings to appease a hungry, atavistic deity.

They were getting ready to lay the slab for the first storey. A whole team of workers, moving in perfect coordination, passed up the mixture as it was regurgitated by the machine. The mason, towering above them all, seemed quite relaxed, casually emptying each consignment as it reached him into the wooden cavity, urging the women to keep the flow going.

At least from a distance, the women all looked power-fully sexy.

Given the power and opportunity which the SDM must have felt he had in that remote district in Bihar, would he, Jingo Moos, have behaved differently? (If so, then why was it titillating to read about the incident? Did even this report seem distant and unreal, an abstract pornographic event?) Why, as he watched from a distance those poor women toiling in the dust and sun, was he aroused? So long as he was ensconced in his cool, airy flat, at a safe distance from the storm clouds of fantasy, it was all right. But when brought up close to his objects of desire, what went wrong? Why did the unreality of his fantasies become so overwhelming only when within reach? He had to work this out for himself once and for all. It was crucial.

He still had that little piece Chandu had given him as a parting gift. He had decided not to touch it until the assignment was complete. Now that it was over, today he planned to reward his abstinence. But there was a caveat: it was to be his very last smoke, his final bow to Chandu and the substance he purveyed that had swamped Jingo's life with euphoric nothingness. At the same time, if he was going to smoke it, he'd better not feel guilty about it.

On the pavement outside the park, an aphrodisiac seller was advertising the potency of his compounds to a small audience. Occasionally, he pointed with his stick to sections of a crude hand-drawn chart depicting the human reproductive organs, while speaking continuously in a persuasive, soft voice.

'Within one month you'll feel the difference,' he was saying, a soothingly hypnotic and pauseless spiel. 'Not just in the welling up of desire, but – hard. At the drop of a hat it'll become stiff as an iron rod. This is a scientific product which works on nerves, glands, increases production of sperm. You'll stay like that for hours. More you use it, harder it'll get. Of course, after a few hours this may become painful to your partner. But don't worry, I've got something for her too. Both *miya-biwi* can enjoy like anything. This is a scientific product which works on nerves, glands and . . . No, no, not for you.' He waved his stick at a couple of small boys who had joined the crowd. 'Go on, now. Go home like good children.'

A small flea market gathered every morning on the broad pavement outside the Victoria Gardens. There were palmists who read your hand for a fee, astrologers who utilized the services of oracular parrots, innumerable food vendors and sellers of ice-cold sherbets, chirpodists, ear-cleaners, tattoo-artists, *hakim*s with neatly labelled jars filled with arcane herbs who swore they could correctly diagnose and cure the unlikeliest of ailments. The gardens would close at six, but the market continued till later, even after the street lights came on.

Jingo purchased his 25-paise ticket at the booking window and entered the zoological and botanical gardens. Calm and silence presided over these acres of greenery. Paved pathways criss-crossed the wooded expanse, punctuated by wooden benches, leaf-screened arbours, open animal enclosures and cages. Outside, the city continued to splutter and fume. But somehow, once inside this generous sanctuary, the city's lesions and sores – or at least his unrelenting awareness of them – seemed magically to heal.

He had a special relationship with this park, which began in childhood. Whenever he was here, Jingo felt very much at ease. So did most others it would seem – the negligibly small entrance fee attracted all kinds of unemployed layabouts who passed the day dozing on the lawns. But the gardens were large enough never to feel crowded, except perhaps on Sundays. Jingo walked a bit, then found himself a nice shady bower under the prickly ferns of a small casuarina. Seated on a bench, he began to discreetly unroll a cigarette.

In the early days when he was staying at Gurdeep's, he'd had many good times at the zoo with Cris. She would cook a meal for them (Gurdeep was hardly ever home), or sometimes carry a packed lunch with her from home. They would take it to the park and make a picnic of it. Before leaving for Baroda, she had told him she would rather he didn't try to contact her. Instead, she would write herself when she settled down. But she hadn't. Not once. He phoned her place and spoke to her sister. She's fine, said Jocelyn, but very busy with her studies. The good news, she said, is that Daddy is better now, and able to move about the house. Come over some time . . .

Well, was it finished, then, with Crissy? Probably. Was he glad? In a way, yes, relieved.

Thinking back on all the times she'd threatened to end her life if he decided to leave her, he felt dismay and disbelief. Such threats came only at the end of days of desperate probing, manipulation and hysterical violence whose purpose, ostensibly, was to ensure his continued faithfulness – but which invariably had quite the opposite effect. He wanted to run away from her obsessive fears, her clinging, her desire to possess.

'There's no point, really,' he had consoled her. 'We'll only end up destroying each other. We can still be good friends, you know. That's better than stooping to such beastliness.'

'It'll never happen again, I swear to you. Please forgive me, I beg of you, Jehan. Let's forget this ever happened and start all over again . . .'

But it happened again. And again. Entirely enmeshed in the other's being, even their thoughts seemed no longer private. A fleeting glance, a private smile, an animated response to some stranger at a party was all it took for Cristina to sense trouble. Always, it was other women which sparked off these wretched quarrels, women who were often completely unaware that they had been the cause of such terrible pain.

Sometimes Jingo too would be drawn into the frenzy of retaliation, punching and slapping, grabbing her by the shoulders and shaking her till her delirium had subsided in tears. And after every such fight, a voice inside him murmured, 'Cry now, break into uncontrollable sobs.' That was what he wanted to do, horrified by the animality he hadn't known he was capable of. 'Observe the abject poverty of your spirit and be ashamed.' But the voice seemed to speak from very far away, and perhaps wasn't even addressing him.

He would have liked to stand outside himself, assume total control of his judgement. But that was never easy. Even thinking back on all their nasty rows, he could never quite figure out how they led up to that point and got so out of hand. It had always seemed to him that Cristina's fears of infidelity and betrayal had something to do with a context larger than himself – her childhood, her past. But thinking about it now, he wondered if perhaps what Cris sensed as his secret desires in fact had a real and independent existence which he had never admitted even to himself. Perhaps that's why he was never able to convince her of his honesty.

Now *she* had decided to leave him. Before she went away, she made a confession that shook him. Not because he took a moralistic view of it; he was hurt, of course, but it only served to confirm a niggling feeling he'd always had. That even after all their years together, he didn't quite know her; that her private erotic impulses would always remain for him an area of darkness. Perhaps the impression the snake-girl had made on her was more powerfully rooted than he knew . . .

'In those early days, our childhood wasn't so entirely unhappy.' She had told him the story over a plate of bhejamasala and roti, at a cafe close to their college. 'Daddy had still not thrown in his job, and maybe driving trains to Churchgate and back kept him sane. Sometimes, on his weekly holiday, he would bundle us three children into the back seat of his DeSoto and drive out into the wilderness. Mummy sat in front next to him. He drove us all the way to Kashi-mira in Vasai every year, for the feast of St Bartholomew.

'A mela congregated on the church grounds. There were all kind of stalls with games for kids. Aunties from villages around had baked cakes and coconut cookies and put them up for sale. Vindaloo, sorpotel, pickles, all sorts of treats. But I was fascinated by only one stall – a freak show I couldn't tear myself away from. I must have been only seven or eight. I had paid my 10 paise to enter the tent. What I saw there was something I never forgot . . .

'There was this little girl on the floor, my age, maybe a year or two older. She was penned up inside some sort of bamboo fencing. The upper part of her body was naked.

She had no arms, I think, but otherwise seemed normal. But the lower part of her body was encased in a sort of tube-like casing made of snakeskin. I couldn't believe my eyes . . .

'The barker outside was busy yelling into his megaphone, calling to all God-fearing folk to witness for a mere 10 paise one of God's weirdest freaks – half girl, half snake! He'd probably not noticed that I hadn't re-emerged from the tent. Or didn't care. I was so tiny myself, and I kept walking round and round the snake-girl, back and forth, to observe the strange sight from every angle.

'Now I think about it, she must have been drugged with opium or something. Her eyes were dazed and far-away, her face was bluish. In a moment when there were no other spectators around, I spoke to her. I asked her if she had always been like that. I had to repeat my question a second time. Then she looked at me and shook her head, very slightly. With the impatience of a pesky kid, I persisted.

'"No, tell me really, were you always like that? Were you born a snake-girl?"' What she replied couldn't have made much sense to me then, but I remember it clearly. She spoke in a faint voice, as though she didn't care if I heard her or not: "They picked me up from the road and carried me off. Then they broke my bones. They did this to me. They take me everywhere and put me on show."

'Do you understand, Jingo? That child had been kidnapped, and maimed. Then turned into a freak of nature to be exhibited to ignorant, superstitious people at village fairs all over the place! To earn off her! What a fate . . . for a child who was hardly eleven . . .'

Even as she finished telling him the story, Jingo realized

Cristina had a catch in her throat and her eyes were glistening. He was moved himself. They had this one thing in common. They were both terribly emotional people. In fact, Jingo was moved not just by the story itself, but also by the courage a seven-year-old Crissy had displayed in wanting to get to the bottom of that riddle of the snake-girl . . .

But there was also that difference between Cristina and him: he liked to work things out in his head. She liked to – no, felt compelled to – act them out in real life and find her answers that way. Maybe that was why he loved her. They shared great affinities, but in certain fundamental ways they were completely at odds. And, sadly, they had never really been able to trust each other. Jingo had always felt there was something shadowy and mysterious about Cristina, a great deal she had never revealed to him. And Cristina had always believed Jingo desired some woman other than her.

That whole matter of Tina, for instance. Cristina had told him once about a school friend she had run into, who was working as a call girl. During the day, she was employed at a 'dancing school'. Jingo knew this euphemism for the seedy joints where men visit, ostensibly to learn ballroom dancing but really to get into a clinch with their female partners while feeling them up in small shuttered cubicles for a prearranged price.

Now, he didn't care that Cristina had a friend who did this kind of work. A lot of his own acquaintances did all kinds of things for money, which he didn't necessarily consider more honourable. He didn't even mind that Cris visited her at the 'dancing school' once in a while. But could he be sure that while she was there with Tina she had never herself 'danced' with a stranger just to find out what it felt like? Could he be sure that on certain lazy mornings when she lingered on in bed, refusing to relinquish the chimerical world of her dreams, that she wasn't reliving the exquisite caresses of a stranger she had taught how to foxtrot?

His own jealousy knew no bounds at times, though he never put it on display like Cristina did. While he was at Nehrunagar, during his most febrile hours of aloneness, it struck with the force of a blow that Tina was in fact a segment of Cris's own name. Did this girl really exist? Or was she just an alter ego invented by Cristina, a mask she wore while conducting her experiments in love? It was a terrifying thought.

She had a strong internal life. He knew that, and respected it. She treasured her dreams, loved to linger on in bed for hours after she had awakened, as though trying to reclaim that twilight world. Running her fingers through the sands of her subconscious, like a child playing on a beach, she would want to prolong that state of half-sleep as though hoping that while sifting through the silken grains of her dream-life she would suddenly alight upon a wondrous pink shell, whose intricate whorls would unravel for her the meaning of everything . . .

Sometimes he felt frightened by the quality of desperation she brought to her love for him. She saw him as an enlightened soul, a 'true writer', who would be able to understand, absorb and absolve all the sadness and sin and terror she had known in her life.

'It's because you have the mind of a novelist that you understood my pain,' she told him once as they sat gazing at the white durgah in the sea at Haji Ali during the monsoon. The waves were lashing against the parapet they sat on. There was a slight drizzle, too. 'None of my other boyfriends lasted out even a month. They used me. To pay their bills, for sex . . . Only a writer could have lasted out so long . . . The question you have to ask yourself is, is this worth it for you? Can you really love a creature who might one day destroy you?'

Even as a grown woman, she continued to blame her parents for everything that had gone wrong in her life.

'We never knew what love was,' she told me. 'Right through childhood, we never saw my father and mother behaving as though they loved each other, never even pretending to be in love. As we grew up, it got worse. Not a day passed without abuse and curses, violence and bloodshed. I guess I never learnt what love was, how to recognize it, or trust it . . . At least, my dear friend, you had a normal childhood . . .'

Her idealization of him was not something Jingo could easily go along with and it made him uncomfortable, even angry, that they had to deal with the barbs and entanglements of a complicated past instead of enjoying what could have been a perfectly normal and healthy relationship. Or was that being idealistic, too? Perhaps there was no such thing as 'normal'. Everyone had to contend with their own demons. All relationships were blighted from the start, until they were worked at, and painfully sorted out.

His normal childhood? Could his days of growing up at Khareghat Colony be deemed normal? Jingo smiled sardonically, as he roasted and mixed his last bit of hashish into the curly strands of tobacco he had saved to refill the cigarette's paper shell.

His own parents, it was true, had behaved in a much more civilized fashion. There was none of the drama, the murderous violence which Cristina talked about as a daily occurrence. But normal?

He thought of one Sunday morning very long ago, when the three of them had visited the zoo. Sunday mornings were for elephant rides. Only children below ten were allowed. It was a memorable event for him to be seated atop the huge animal as it set off on a graceful trundle across the park. But he could see that it made his mother extremely edgy. She followed behind the elephant, gesticulating to him to hold on tight. When the ride was over, the elephant returned to its starting point and stood beside the concrete steps of the staircase that stopped in mid-air. The mahout carried Jingo and put him on the topmost step, from where he descended into his mother's waiting arms, as much relieved as she that it was over.

Afterwards, as they walked through the park, Khorshed reminded him frequently to keep a safe distance from the cages. Animal fleas could result in incurable allergies which would be difficult to shake off once they set in, she stated with an air of quasi-medical authority. His father, irritated by her fussiness, refused to say anything that might spoil the child's fun.

While she sat sipping a Gold Spot, his father had taken him for a rowing-boat ride in the pond. Now the same pond was overgrown with weeds and the boat rides had been stopped. The tin shack on which 'Canteen' was inscribed in white paint still stood exactly where it had so many years ago. Then, however, a boatman had allowed them to row, and Jingo had clumsily lost his oar in the water. The boat rocked wildly as his father reached out to grab the oar but luckily didn't overturn. Mother watched breathlessly as they made slow progress round the pond, exhaling another loud sigh of deliverance when her son clasped her outstretched hand and climbed back onto solid ground.

Come to think of it, he *had* developed some kind of rash on his thigh and shin, just a few days after their visit to the zoo. Several tubes of a sulfa ointment had to be rubbed on his skin before it went away. His mother had been quietly triumphant, not saying a word to his father – just as he had disdainfully debunked her fears with his silence when they were walking past those filthy cages – but while examining those mildly red patches, and applying the ointment twice daily, her demeanour became positively sorrowful, as though deeply anguished by the suffering an innocent child had to bear thanks to one parent's obtuseness.

One evening when Khorshed was in the kitchen, Boman had said to Jingo, between clenched teeth, in the quietly bitter manner he had developed: 'When you fear something so terribly, it comes to pass. You see? This is the proof of it,' he muttered. 'I didn't pick up any rash, nor did your mother. Though it was she who instilled the fear in you. You must make your mind stronger, Jaungoo. Be fearless.' That was all he said, and Jingo had merely nodded dumbly.

What Boman himself had been most apprehensive about in his own life had, in all probability, come to pass: the fear of his wife becoming romantically involved with another man. The bitterness must have been festering at the time, Jingo imagined, the wound gradually growing deeper and more grievous. And the irony that the man his wife was involved with had crossed their path during a foolish and desperate attempt to reclaim Rumi's lost soul must have been positively galling.

By the time they made that last visit to the zoo – or was

Victoria Gardens

it even later? – the matter of his brother's restoration to the family had been completely laid to rest. Even the lamp-in-a-glass had been extinguished. Yet secretly, his mother's affair with Hansotia was probably raging. Presumably it was again for his sake, Jingo's, that the charade of his parents' marriage was never aborted, or openly denounced.

Short and dark, probably unattractive at first sight, with a snubbed nose and small eyes that sparkled. He found it almost impossible to describe Cristina's intrinsic beauty, or even to imagine those earthy features when she wasn't in front of him. But he knew her smile. He could remember its warmth, which was tangible and electric: when she smiled, her skin, the colour of sun-bronzed sienna, glowed.

He had never seen her in action on the sports field, but there was a whole row of silver cups lining the family's glass showcase which she had won at her school annual athletics meet. For a year she had even been captain of her school's basketball team. Despite her short stature, she was incredibly agile. He could imagine her dribbling the ball away from her opponents with the grace and agility of an animal, the same fierce mastery she displayed while making love to him. And yet in most other situations the same body made her feel awkwardly clumsy. She always felt she was much too ugly and dark to be his partner. She was certain it was only a matter of time before he fell for someone as beautiful and fair-skinned as he.

Well, skin colour had always been an important issue in her own life, and her parents'. She had taken pains to explain the background to him.

/ 345

It was late, and the deserted office blocks of Ballard Estate looked elegantly gloomy in the dark. They had been walking around for hours, talking. In the side lanes and back lots of some of these buildings, Jingo glimpsed desolate-looking groups of men huddled together under a lamp-post, or squatting on the pavement. These were brown-sugar addicts, he knew, waiting with unwavering anticipation for their turn to inhale a substance that held them in thrall.

Her father was very dark-skinned. Her mother was wheatish-fair and beautiful in the more traditional sense of the word. Domasso was proud of his beautiful young wife, but terribly jealous that she attracted so much attention from all the dandies and beaux of Orlem. He was rich, but dark. She was poor, but had stunning looks. Like many other landlords of his community, Domasso had inherited a large amount of land in and around Orlem from his father, most of it leased out for agricultural cultivation.

He could have lived off the income of that land, like his father had before him. But from childhood, Domasso had been obsessed with trains.

After marrying Celina, at a rather late age, he joined the Western Railway as a trainee motorman. Well past the required age limit for applicants, some influential string-pulling ensured his selection. After training, he became a fully fledged motorman himself. At that time, there was only Clyde and Cristina. Jocelyn, the youngest child, was born later. For seven or eight years, Domasso worked shifts, driving the suburban trains of Bombay.

Once, he'd taken Crissy and Clyde for a joyride. 'There was an unusually long and unscheduled halt at Bandra, where my father got off and bought us ice creams. He left us alone in the driver's cabin for a while, which was a dangerous thing to do, because I could see Clyde was itching to get his hands on the controls, and might easily have caused a disaster . . . But that was the only one time he took us along and broke the rules for us. While he was still working, he was happy. He should have kept his job. From some inexplicable reason, he threw it in even before we had finished school. He didn't need it for the income, anyway.'

Otherwise, Domasso was known to be a strict disciplinarian. Whether to make his children work for better marks at school, or as a penalty for some childish misdemeanour, he could be decidedly sadistic in his punishments. He owned a selection of canes he'd carved himself from the branches of a drumstick tree in their backyard; drumstick canes were supposed to yield the most stinging slashes.

An active member of the church parish, he never missed Sunday mass except if he was ill, which was hardly ever. His discipline extended even to his own habits. Never overindulging in alcohol like his neighbours and other members of the village community, he had exactly two drinks of whisky and soda with ice every evening, and then sat down to dinner. Never more, never less. On days when he had to attend a night shift on the railways, he would forfeit his two drinks before leaving for work, but come back at dawn, down them with his breakfast, and sleep until late afternoon.

Celina was not only beautiful, she was vivacious, friendly and fun-loving. Domasso, obsessively particular about everything, found fault with her cooking, her housekeeping, or any form of self-indulgence, including laughing loudly at a joke in company, or sleeping too late in the morning. Sometimes he would beat her as well. According to Cris, when he became angry he was a terror to behold. His body trembled uncontrollably as though he were suffering from some nervous disorder. His voice grew thunderous and the victims of his wrath could only cower before him. His most frequently used term of abuse for Celina was whore. Later, his elder daughter was included in his circle of disparagement: she became a she-devil and a slut.

Celina began to drink a lot more than her husband, but secretly, while he was out at work. By now he had already left his job with the railways but still went out every day, inspecting his properties, collecting arrears of rent, chatting over a black coffee with some tenant. He suspected his wife of having an affair with her cousin, Bertie, who was quite a charmer and had good looks. To the horror of the young children, there were frequent and terrible fights between the parents, screaming and shouting, solemn oaths sworn over the Bible in the name of the Virgin Mary and the Baby Jesus; but he never believed her.

One night, Domasso's strangely obsessive behaviour took a turn for the worse. While the children slept in their room, and Celina in the double bed, he attacked her with a broken whisky bottle. It was a fit of madness, but even while in its throes, he remained particular.

'We were fast asleep,' said Cristina, describing the scene to him years later. 'Clyde and me were the first to rush into her bedroom. Mummy was screaming like a stuck pig. There was blood on her pillow, in her eyes. He had climbed over her and was jabbing her face with the broken glass. She thought he had blinded her. But even in his fury he had been careful not to damage any part of her except her face. He was not trying to kill her, only disfiguring that beauty which never seemed to age . . . He scarred her terribly.'

Bertie made a police complaint and, for a day, their father was detained at the local cop station, but Celina wouldn't press charges. Though he didn't want to kill her, within a year she had wilted and died. Did she drink herself to death, or was it the grief of her disfiguring that killed her? The children were too small to know. Christina herself was only twelve. One of the last images she retained in her mind from that terrifying time was of her mother sitting on the low stool of the dressing table in her nightgown, her swollen wounds still not fully healed, gazing into the mirror at her lost beauty, her eyes streaming with tears.

'How those tears must have stung her,' said Cristina, shaken by the memory that was resurrected in its telling. Jingo had never met her, of course, but he had seen her framed photograph in their living room. She *was* beautiful.

After she died, Domasso stopped going out and sat at home, in a state of shock. The punishment his mind wreaked on itself took some time to become completely manifest. He hired servants to cook and wash and look after the children. Clyde left home soon after – he was only sixteen – and went to Dubai to earn his fortune; Cristina helped to raise her younger sister.

Now Jocelyn was at college herself, but much of her time was spent in looking after Domasso, who had become too helpless even to manage his own needs. He had become almost catatonic in his silences. Terrified of insanity, he felt he must be mad to have done what he did to his wife. He sat silently all day on the stone bench outside his cottage, communicating with no one, not even his friend of many years, Father Cecil, the parish priest, who dropped by from time to time just to be with him. They sat together in silence, until the priest got up and informed Jocelyn, if she was at home, or the servant, that he was leaving.

This ghastly childhood had taken its toll on Cristina, as no doubt it would have on her brother and sister as well. But while Clyde had physically removed himself from the scene of their psychological depredation, and Jocelyn had perhaps been too young to feel the full brunt of it, Cristina seemed to have internalized its perverse horror completely.

She really loved Jingo. That was one thing he was reasonably certain about. She saw him as a great soul. How else would he able to love a fallen creature like herself? She would never be able to find a better husband even if she searched for aeons, through countless rebirths, she had once said. Yet a part of her believed it was impossible that he could really care for her. She wanted to test his love, perversely pushing it to the brink of hatred to see if he would still love her.

Finally, one day, she told him she was pregnant and wanted an abortion. There was no question of their keeping the baby. It was her decision and they hardly even debated it. It would the best thing to do, under the circumstances. He wasn't earning very much, certainly not enough to support a family. And she had always spoken of wanting to pursue a career. She wanted to get herself a diploma in graphic design or fine arts before she had a baby.

He was with her through every minute of those traumatic two days when they went to see a gynaecologist.

A buffalo of a man with a toothbrush moustache, who seemed to sneer at their unmarried status. Jingo couldn't help disliking the doctor. But they had heard excellent things about his surgical skills. He insisted on carrying out the procedure the very next day.

It was a cloudy morning. Not quite monsoon weather, but looking very much as if there could be some rain. When Cristina resurfaced from the anaesthesia, the doctor gave her a cup of tea and two Gluco biscuits. Then he told Jingo to take her home, and Cristina to come back after a week for a check-up.

They were both silent in the taxi on the way back. At one point, he tried to put his arm around her but she shrugged it off. He, too, was feeling depressed, wondering at his cowardice in not wanting to keep the baby.

When he phoned her the next morning, she didn't want to meet. She told him to leave her alone for a few days. Four days later, Jingo called again and went over to meet her. On the way, he bought a dozen oranges for Cristina from the Malad market. But as coldly indifferent to his oranges as to his company, Jingo saw that she was not herself yet.

'Hell, Cris,' he said, not unsympathetically. 'You can't go on brooding like this. Have to put it behind you, somehow. Anyway, it was your decision, too. And I think a very correct one. But I do understand how you must feel. Believe me, it's only a matter of time before—'

Suddenly she turned the full force of her anger on him.

'You understand nothing, you wimp!' she snapped at him. 'Just be quiet. Or go away!'

Jingo was hurt. He looked away. All that week he had been as supportive as anyone could have, under the circumstances. Now why was she directing her anger at him? 'Okay,' he said, bitterly. 'If that's how you feel I'll go . . .' But, at the front door, before walking out, he said: 'Just because you're going through something right now doesn't put you at the centre of the world. Even a stranger would have deserved a little more kindness . . .'

He had no idea why those words should have had the effect on her that they did, but before he could leave Cristina broke down.

'Please . . . don't go,' she stuttered, her small body racked with sobs. 'I'm sorry . . .'

Jingo turned back and slowly sat down again in his chair in the spacious hall. Nearby in a corner of the room brooded the large oval table with all the clutter of her father's train set, stagnant and dusty. He sat quietly, without speaking.

'I feel nothing,' Cristina said at last. 'Just drained . . . empty . . .'

Jingo nodded, but she wasn't looking at him.

'It's as if that doctor's scalpel scraped out not just my foetus, but every organ of my body – my heart, my brain, my liver . . .'

'What you're feeling is natural,' said Jingo. 'It's completely natural, believe me. I've read about this. In just a few days' time you'll be feeling normal again . . . You need to go out, do things. You'll soon find your mind is filling up again. You have to . . . experience things . . . taste the joy of living once again . . .'

He wasn't sure if Cristina was listening, but he felt he had to go on talking. He was feeling foolish now for having reacted resentfully to her rudeness a little while ago. Clearly, she was going through a bad time.

'And I also have to say, sweetheart, I'm sorry.' He moved his chair closer to hers. 'In a way I'm responsible for all this. If I had been more serious about working, earning a regular salary, we might even have wanted to get married and keep the baby . . . I'm willing to do it now. We can plan for the next one . . . You know, all those guys working as systems analysts in the office – Pankaj, Piyush – they're making four and a half, five grand a month . . . I guess I've been footloose for too long. I'm willing to get serious . . . I'll speak to Hingorani right away. It means two months of training on a stipend of about fifteen hundred, and then they'll start me off . . . She offered me the position once before, a couple of years ago. I think I'd told you . . . I turned it down myself in favour of freelancing. What do you say? Then we can think about our next baby, whenever you're ready . . .'

All the while he had been speaking he had no way of knowing what Cristina felt, or if she was even listening. No word, no sound, no eye contact. Now, unexpectedly, she buried her head in her hands and started sobbing again. It went on like that for a few minutes, but Jingo was quiet. He let her cry for as long as she wanted to. For some reason he felt lighter himself, as if a great load had been lifted off his chest. At last, he felt, she was coming to grips with her sorrow.

'I'm sorry,' he murmured, 'I'm sorry, Crissy . . .'

She wiped her tears and shook her head; waited until she was composed. When she spoke, he was surprised to hear the hardness in her voice.

'There's something I have to tell you, Jingo,' she said. 'It's better I tell you now . . . You don't need to feel so bad about this whole abortion. That baby probably wasn't even yours.'

He was stunned. He wasn't sure he had heard right.

She went on, 'Two months ago, one evening, a man

gave me a ride in his car. This was during that time you were so busy with that workshop on marketing techniques or whatever – we hadn't met for nearly a month . . . It was I who thumbed a lift. We got talking . . .

'He was very suave and cultured. Middle-aged, at least ten to fifteen years older than me. We talked about literature, about books. He invited me to have a drink with him in a restaurant before dropping me home. I agreed . . . Then he asked me to come up to his flat and have a few more. He said he had some art books to show me . . . I agreed. When I went up, he made love to me, and I didn't resist . . . Before I left, he offered me money. I still don't know why, but I took it. I'm a whore, Jehan. You deserve better than me. I'm setting you free. Run away, while you still have the chance. I'll destroy you. Please never try to contact me again.'

What bewitchment drew men and women to the unknown? What was that compelling promise buried in strangeness that was the root cause of broken promises, of so much pain? For a week after, Jingo didn't try to call Cristina. He was filled with conflicting feelings of rage, self-pity and disgust. Then he couldn't control his desire to talk to her again.

She answered the phone herself.

'I'm glad you called, Jehan. I want to say goodbye. A few days ago I got a letter from Baroda. They've given me admission to the Institute of Fine Arts.'

He was thunderstruck. He hadn't even known that she had applied for admission to this institute. Despite their intimacy, there was always so much that she never told him. So what was all that desperation about, all those threats of suicide if he left her? Was it only manipulation to bind him to her even as she explored her own sexuality as much as she liked?

But even if it were so, he had to admit that the quality of her dependence on him must have suited him well. After a whole year of being separated from her, he was able to see his own part in the relationship more clearly. He must have derived much satisfaction from feeling morally superior to her. Was that why he had stuck with her all these years? Did he see himself as a Christ among lepers? His own motives had never been so clean as her idealized version of him would have it. For years, he had enjoyed talking down to her, correcting her, pointing out to her all that was unhealthy and neurotic in her behaviour. And simultaneously, for years, he had fuelled her insecurities with his own frivolous attractions to other women, attractions which never progressed beyond fantasy. Now he was free. So why wasn't he looking for someone else?

In their final months together, Cristina did a self-portrait in oils. It was a gloomy picture in which the most striking thing was the skin tone she had achieved, which was at least two or three shades darker than her own. And the eyes, which glinted with a manic, diabolical fervour. She had drawn her features without giving them the softness that he knew, making them foreshortened and angular. She looked almost negroid in the portrait.

'That's not you,' he said as soon as he saw it. He looked at it longer, in silence, and repeated: 'It may be powerful and all that, but it's not you.'

'There are so many areas of me you know nothing about,' she said. 'Maybe some years later, if we are still together, this is how you will see me . . . I'm quite mad, you know. And very dark.'

Here, she literally meant skin colour. Her paintings on canvas were relatively few. She didn't feel comfortable with oils. But even the ones she'd done on paper, even her pencil sketches and doodlings were informed with an unerring sense of proportion and beauty. Yet, when it came to being able to perceive her own self, her artist's sense was completely betrayed. Among the contradictions that tore them apart, this was one: she could not see even an iota of beauty in herself. She felt that way, ugly.

Part 4

Night

Long ago, Jillamai had stopped taking the papers. It was an expense she could do without. For some time now she'd had an arrangement with her downstairs neighbour, Nemoana Sheikh, who would lend her her old issues of the *Mumbai Samachar* to read. Nemoana usually allowed two or three days' papers to collect before passing them on to Jilla when she remembered.

Jilla was grateful for these, and the other small ways in which her friend and neighbour helped out. Glancing through the headlines gave her something to do during the long, quiet afternoons. She would first turn to the DEATHS column, and read all the names printed in bold. It was an unchanging routine.

Hardly any member of her immediate family remained alive, so her morbid preoccupation with this page couldn't be attributed to scrupulousness about not wanting to neglect social obligations. Rather, in the slow relish with which she read aloud the names of the recently dead, it was as though she were only checking to confirm she was still ahead in the race. With a slight sense of foreboding, and even expectation, she was making sure that her own name had not appeared among those printed in bold, in the clusters of the dear departed. Even if it had, she wouldn't have minded terribly: Jilla was very tired.

She made it a point to return all the old editions to Nemoana every time her neighbour brought her more recent ones. Old newspapers could be sold for good money, she knew, and Nemoana, on top of providing this generous service, wouldn't have liked to lose out on that.

'*Maai!*' declared Nemoana, on hearing the familar squeak of Jilla's canvas shoes on the stairs.

The old woman was holding on tightly to the banister with both hands as she descended sideways, stopping after every few steps to catch her breath and find her balance.

'This is no time for going out!' Nemoana called from the landing below.

'And why not?' asked Jilla, a little surprised at her peremptoriness.

'Well, you haven't seen the papers,' said Nemoana matter-of-factly, raising a bunch of *Samachar*s in the air like a heraldic salute. 'I was just bringing these up for you. See, see! Read what they've done!'

Since Jilla was already halfway down the stairs, Nemoana waited for her to reach the landing. Today's edition was open in her hands, some back numbers bundled tightly under her fleshy arm.

'What? What have they done? Oh dear, oh dear,' muttered Jilla, squinting at the black banner headline briefly through her bifocals. Then folding the paper again, she quickly handed it back to her neighbour. Nemoana wasn't sure she'd actually read anything at all.

'I'm not through with this one yet,' said Nemoana. 'But I'll pass it on to you in a while. Now tell me, what new pot of madness are they trying to bring to a boil?'

'Don't know what to say, Nemoana,' said Jilla. 'Sometimes I just feel like telling you: I don't want to look at the papers any more, please don't bring them up to me. But then one can't live like that, can one, not knowing what's going on in the world?'

Wearily, she turned to climb up the stairs again.

'These old ones!' called Nemoana after her, remembering. Jilla stopped in her tracks. 'Never mind, later sometime, when you're going down . . . But don't, Jillamai. No point going out anywhere. Parties have all called for a *bandh*. Everything's closed.'

'You're right. I don't think I will. Not safe, is it?' Jillamai was already halfway up the stairs again, and evidently undecided.

'There's trouble in the streets, *maai*,' said Nemoana. 'Well, what do you expect? It wasn't just some old pile of stones they knocked down. It was an ancient house of God. Four hundred years old! Our boys are incensed, naturally! . . . If you need food, I've got plenty to eat in my fridge.'

'No, no, thanks,' replied Jilla. 'I think I'll just stay put. Anway I don't eat much in the evenings.'

'I'll bring something up later, if you like,' offered Nemoana.

'No, no, no,' said Jilla. 'I won't eat anything . . .'

Jilla opened her door and re-entered the flat. Nemoana had gone in, too, so good: she could sneak out quietly again after a minute or two, buy her eggs and bread and take a look-see for herself as to what the fuss was all about. Five minutes later, she did exactly that, this time creeping down as quietly as she could.

*

Even if Nemoana hadn't warned her, Jilla would still have realized something was not quite right as soon as she stepped out.

There was hardly any traffic on the road, and very few people about. These shutdowns which political parties called every so often were rather nice in a way, thought Jilla, looking around. The streets became quiet. Almost peaceful, like in the old days before Bombay became so very crowded. No tumult of cars and buses, taxis, cyclists . . . Of course, there would be trouble, Nemoana was right.

For a moment, Jilla rubbed her eyes, wondering if her cataracts had finally begun to ripen. No, there was a definite smokiness in the air, a faint but acrid smell of burning rubber. She heard something that sounded like distant gunfire. Oh well, maybe. She could have imagined it. Then she heard it again. She would pick up her dinner and quickly go back up again. Cafe Noor was only two buildings down the road . . . But what was this? Shutters pulled down? But the waiters lived inside, she knew; they'd sell her eggs and bread, surely.

Jillamai went up to the corrugated-tin shutter which was securely padlocked from outside and hammered on it with her fist.

'*Arrey, kholo!*' she demanded. For a moment there was no answer. Then a small side window beside the shutter opened two inches, and one of the boys peeped out.

'*Arrey*, who's that, Abdul?' she asked.

'Jameel,' the boy muttered, but Jilla wasn't listening.

'What's all this fuss, why aren't you opening? Ouch, my bones are hurting with all this banging.'

'*Maiji*, you shouldn't be out at this time.'

'Stop fussing, it's not even dark yet,' said Jilla.

'No, not dark—' poor Jameel tried to explain. But Jilla cut him short.

'So what should I do then if I'm hungry? Cook up my hands and legs and eat them?'

'No, no,' said Jameel, humouring her. 'Please don't do that. I'll give you your eggs and bread . . . But there's no pao today.'

'Why no pao?' asked Jilla angrily.

'You won't find it anywhere, *maiji*,' said Jameel. 'Slice bread only: Brittania. That too yesterday's. No deliveries today. And stock up, *maiji*, stock up for a few days please, things'll get worse tomorrow.'

'Okay, okay,' said Jilla, making light of the boy's earnest concern, 'I get all the news. Something happens in faraway UP and you-all pull down your shutters and hide like hens? Cough up my two eggs, please.'

'You don't understand. Cops have gone berserk,' said Jameel. 'A mob attacked the Umerkhadi police station and set it on fire. Now they're retaliating, shooting at Muslims everywhere. At random. Shooting to kill!'

Another voice from inside the restaurant called out to Jameel to shut up and give the lady what she wanted. That must be Ijaaz. They were probably all inside, listening behind the closed shutter.

'*Ja, ja*,' Jilla retorted, 'they're not going to start shooting for nothing. Now don't get mixed up in any nonsense yourself, you hear me?'

'Yes, *maiji*,' said Jameel obediently, wrapping two eggs in a sheet of lined paper. 'What about tomorrow? You should take at least six, or a dozen.'

'Have you gone mad or something?' said Jilla in astonishment. 'Do you want to kill me, making me eat a dozen eggs?'

'No, no, just saying, to keep,' said poor Jameel, flustered. 'Tomorrow, they may not be available . . .'

'Just give me what I asked for,' said Jilla decisively, and Jameel slipped the two eggs and the loaf of Brittania bread into a plastic carry-bag, passing it to her through the bars of the window.

'Such a big loaf!' she muttered to herself. 'What'll I do with this? Don't even like this sliced bread . . . Just two paos would have been right, but no pao today, he says.'

As she went back home slowly, rocking from side to side down the wide expanse of empty pavement, she didn't feel at all alarmed. This was all stuff and nonsense. Let the world pursue its madness if it wished, she was not involved. Holding on to her dinner protectively, she was feeling rather cheerful, in fact. So few people around, no fools nudging and pushing, no insolent idiots nearly knocking you down, eggs and all. Now that she had her bread and eggs, there was nothing to worry about. Whatever today's skirmish was about, she wasn't going to let it faze her. She had seen much worse. Oh yes, that was really something. Her mind wandered back in recollection of a horrific day she had lived through and survived almost fifty years ago.

Ha! These paltry wisps of smoke in the air? What comparison to the vast conflagration that had leapt up to the skies on that day when the big ship carrying ammunition and explosives caught fire in the Bombay docks? Two explosions, one after the other. Even miles away buildings felt the tremor; those nearer had every one of their windowpanes shattered. Shreds of burning cotton flew in all directions, starting dozens more fires. The ship's dangerously inflammable cargo included not just bales of cotton, but crude oil as well. Flaming drums of oil spun through the air. Some ten or twelve other ships docked alongside were reduced to scrap iron. The whole place became a hellish inferno which took days to be properly extinguished.

Before Jilla's eyes the white-hot blade of a ship's propellor struck a victoria, decapitating the horse and killing its driver in an instant. People later said that the headless horse ran the whole length of the street before collapsing, but that she hadn't seen. She was too dazed to notice much. Another flying piece of metal made a hole in the roof of Billimoria House, the building across the road from her. There were rumours that gold bricks were flung high by the two explosions, crashing down randomly at various places around the dock, and of men who had made their fortunes in a day. More likely, others said, the million pounds of gold bricks which the ship had been carrying along with ammunition and explosives had melted and gone down in the water along with the shattered ship . . .

So had Jilla's own life on that very day. For Keko never returned home.

Thank God his mother was already dead, or she would have certainly preferred to kill herself rather than live on alone with that vicious harridan. Even today, sometimes, when an unexpected shadow flickered in a corner of her vision or loomed up suddenly against the wall, she flinched, subconsciously preparing to defend herself against a rain of blows.

Only when she finished climbing two flights of stairs did Jilla remember she had no oil to fry the eggs. Now she was feeling too exhausted to go back down the stairs again, and which shop would be open to sell her oil? She decided to borrow some from Nemoana. She's a good woman, she won't mind . . .

For years, even after Keko went away, Jilla wasn't able to completely trust Nemoana.

A widow herself for many years now, Nemoana's two sons had grown up and left. One of them was well settled in London, a doctor or something; the other was in import–export somewhere in the Gulf. They kept in touch with her still, and sent food parcels every year. Sometimes, as a gesture of friendship, Nemoana even passed on to Jilla a tin of sardines or a packet of Jello.

Keko had once remarked on how beautiful Nemoana looked when her long black hair was set loose, cascading down her broad back like a mountain stream.

Maybe he said it only once, maybe it was just a poetic impulse that got the better of him. But that once was sufficient for Jilla to immediately suspect that he had a more-than-neighbourly interest in the young widow. She was not far wrong. Deep down she had never been able to trust Keko. Always searching for fresh stimulation, fresh conquests to confirm his superior intelligence, his stunning good looks. Always craving for more, never content to treasure what he already had . . .

She wished he could see Nemoana now. Wrinkled and obese, her long luxuriant hair had been cut short since it had thinned so much and was almost entirely grey. But, to be fair to her, she had to admit she couldn't remember Nemoana ever responding to Keko's unchaste interest in her. In fact, even after he had gone, Nemoana never failed to help in every way.

Wherever she could, she never stinted. And gradually Jilla had grown to regard her as a true friend. The mother and her sons had been like a foster family to Hoshi during her difficult days when she was working at the post office.

Now she knocked at her front door, which was on the second floor exactly below her own. Nemoana opened it and immediately asked her in.

'Just went out and bought some eggs and bread,' said Jilla. 'But my mind is really going. Completely forgot I have no oil.'

'Never mind, happens to me also,' said Nemoana, thinking to herself, what an obstinate woman. She pretends to go back into her flat and then, once I'm out of the way, stealthily sneaks out again. 'Please sit. I've plenty of oil. Anyway, you wouldn't have found a single shop open.'

She went in for a few minutes and came back with a steel cup half-filled with oil.

'I have some extra food, too. I could give you something—' she began saying, but Jilla interrupted her.

'Oh no. This is my dinner,' she said, indicating the packet in her hand. 'Can't take very much at night. I'd have gone out again for the oil, but . . .'

'Don't be silly, *mai*,' she said. 'You're very welcome to anything in my house. It's late now. And there's trouble outside, didn't you hear anything? You shouldn't have gone at all.'

'That Jameel was muttering something down at Cafe Noor,' said Jilla. 'About some masjid being broken down by hoodlums.'

'I showed you the headlines in the papers, *mai*!'

'Yes, yes, but have mercy, my eyes have grown feeble, Nemoana, takes me time to focus . . .'

'Not just any masjid. That one at Ayodhya where

they've been clamouring to build a temple for Ram for years! Build your temple, but why break our mosque? Is that the only spot you can find to build a temple? Court said we won't allow it, government said we'll protect it, who shall we trust any more?'

'God is one,' said Jilla. 'Hindu god, Muslim god, Parsi god. This is all politics, Nemoana.'

'But don't these hooligans fear the wrath of God? Now Muslims, too, are on the rampage. They've burnt some buses and a police station. Nafisa, my niece, just phoned: police opened fire at a mob on Mohammed Ali Road. Dozens are dead, many more injured. And all, almost all of them are Muslims!'

'I smelt smoke in the air,' said Jilla. 'No smoke without fire . . . It's a terrible time. Anyway, dear, don't worry, it'll pass . . . I'll return this oil first thing tomorrow.'

'Never you mind, Jillamai, what's a little cooking oil between neighbours?'

'No, no. Definitely. In the morning shops will be open again. Thank you, dear, thank you.'

'Shall I point a flashlight for you on the stairs?'

'I can see perfectly well . . . thank you.'

'Tomorrow we'll change the bulb. Only remind me.'

After she left, Nemoana smiled and shook her head. Jillamai never returned anything she borrowed, though she made it a point to insist on saying that she would. That was all right, she supposed. It was her way of keeping her dignity. She felt sorry for the poor woman who had long ago suffered a terrible tragedy in her youth. A double blow. First her husband disappeared, presumed dead in the great dock explosion. Then she lost the child she had been carrying – at first Nemoana hadn't known about that second loss, no one in the building had. For almost a month and a half after her husband went missing, no one even saw Jilla. She could have fallen dead in her flat for all they knew, except that sometimes her light would come on, and in the night Nemoana would occasionally hear a strange scraping and scrubbing sound from the flat above, a crazy soft keening of despair. Alone among the neighbours, she went up one evening to investigate.

When the door opened, Nemoana couldn't recognize her neighbour. Jilla had become thin as a scarecrow. She was filthy and smelling, hadn't washed in days. But she flew at Nemoana with a violent frenzy that belied her feeble appearance and made Nemoana tremble with fright.

'So? You've come to find out if he's back. Look, you slut, he's nowhere here . . . But he'll come.' Her gaunt face twisted spitefully. 'Don't you worry, he'll come. But you won't hear of it, I promise you. He'll come not for you, but to see his child.'

A wave of anguish swept through Nemoana as her eyes involuntarily turned to Jilla's dirty nightgown, which was caked with dark blotches of dried blood. Jilla was no longer carrying her child, that was obvious. But there were cloths tied around her midriff and many others stuffed into her gown to poorly simulate a swollen belly. Her arms and face had become pale and skinny, probably from days of not eating and the loss of so much blood. Scattered on the floor around the room she saw a whole brood of bloodstained rags, heaps of them lying around.

'What do you *want*?' screamed Jilla suddenly. Nemoana fled.

The next morning, when she had mustered enough courage and compassion, Nemoana took some food up to

Jilla, who ate it greedily, like a starving animal. Later, Nemoana called in her doctor. Even he was amazed that the woman had survived a miscarriage and so much loss of blood all alone by herself, locked up in her room. He prescribed chicken soup, a healthy diet and tranquillizers. For some weeks Nemoana plied the staircase between their homes carrying bowls of soup and other nourishing foods, although it took four months before Jilla seemed to have definitely regained her health. And perhaps even weathered the psychological turbulence.

Through all that time, however, she was never once pleasant to Nemoana, never once said a word to her in thanks. Her man must have hurt her badly, thought Nemoana. She had never liked him very much, for his insinuating ways, the manner in which he used his eyes to say what was left unspoken in words. But he was gone now, and slowly Jilla began to accept that he wouldn't return. Then a year later, a child entered Jilla's life.

Once again, for weeks she had remained secretively cloistered in her flat. If Nemoana took something to her door, she accepted it, opening the door only as little as necessary and then shutting it again quickly. Once or twice Nemoana thought she heard a child crying inside, but she preferred to believe she had imagined it rather than dare to ask.

At last, one day Jilla called her in and showed her a snotty infant lying on her bed. She picked him up and told her his name: Hoshidar. She had adopted him, she said. All the nappies and vests she had stitched for her own baby had not gone to waste, she told her, for they fitted Hoshi perfectly well. Now at last, thought Nemoana, Jilla will be happy again.

When Jilla started working – she had little choice in the

matter – Hoshidar would be left with Nemoana for the day. He grew up before her very eyes and, even after he started attending school, often spent his evenings at her place, till his mother returned home from the post office.

Nemoana's own husband had died long ago, but, unlike Jilla's, who had left her nothing, he had provided her with a substantial sum of money. Being a charitable-minded person who was essentially grateful to God for everything that came to pass, she thought nothing of looking after the little mite and giving him his afternoon meal and a glass of milk in the evening. Every month Jilla gave her 40 rupees to cover the expense incurred. It wasn't enough, of course, but Nemoana never complained. Besides, her own sons, who were more grown up than Jilla's child, helped to keep the boy busy once they got home from school. And she herself had a soft spot for little children. She could never tire of looking after them.

That boy, God bless his soul, wherever he was, had grown up to despise his mother. Maybe he despised her, too, his foster mother, but that didn't matter so much. For poor Jilla, it had been another blow. She loved her son to distraction, she was pining for him to return home. But Hoshi had simply walked out on her, on all of them.

Nemoana had a guilty conscience in this matter. It had nagged her for many years. She had made the mistake a very long time ago. A thoughtless act. Perhaps just plain stupidity. But she prayed to Allah to correct any harm she might have caused, even though she had never intended any. Jilla didn't know about it. She was the last person Nemoana dared confess her error to.

Can't make out a damn thing, thought Jilla, peering through her peephole, a little frightened.

If only the passage light had been on she'd have been able to see more clearly. The bulb had fused more than two weeks ago. She had mentioned to Nemoana that it needed replacing, but that woman could be quite spitefully forgetful when she chose to. It was already dark when the knock came at her door. A gently persuasive knock. She could make out the silhouette of a figure standing outside, but for the life of her couldn't guess who it might be.

'Who?' she called in a quavery voice. 'Who's it?'

'It's me, Aunty,' replied a voice she remembered hearing before. 'Hoshi's school friend, Jahangir.'

Ah, that market researcher. After months he's responded to my calls now!

'Are you alone?'

'Yes,' replied Jingo.

He heard the groan and rat-a-tat of several bolts being drawn. Finally, with a juddering, the door opened, and she let him in.

'I got your messages, Mrs Gorimar,' he said, apologetically. 'I'm sorry, I couldn't come earlier – I've had no luck at all in finding Hoshi.'

'Never mind,' said the old woman. She looked frightened, but spoke with authority. 'Sit down.'

The six chairs in a row were still there. The chest of drawers with its black slot where a drawer was missing. The cupboard with the broken leg. The four-poster. All of it was still there, though it looked different by the shadowy yellow glow of a dim bulb that hung from a naked wire. Jingo sat on one of the broken chairs, and Jilla sat beside him on another, rather close. She smelt musty, like a room that hadn't been aired in ages.

'At first I made those phone calls to remind you about

finding Hoshi,' she said in an expressionless voice. 'But it won't be necessary any more. He's already been to see me. Twice.'

'Why, that's wonderful!' Jingo declared. 'So Hoshi's been in touch with you! You must be very happy.'

'The last call I made to your office, though, was *after* he met me,' continued Jillamai in her hoarse undertone, grimly. 'I made that call out of desperation. I need your help.'

'Help?' repeated Jingo stupidly, and Jilla nodded.

'He was angry . . . Stormed out of here abusing me, like he used to when he was a schoolboy. Maybe you could talk to him, plead with him if necessary,' she said. There was a long pause, as she collected herself. 'Or maybe it's too late for talking now. When he wants something he usually gets his way. Even if he has to slit his own mother's throat for it.'

Jingo wondered if he was hearing right. For a moment it occurred to him that Jilla might have sent for him precisely so he could provide an audience for her delusionary fantasies. Could her sense of reality have grown more tentative since he last met her? Could the weight of loneliness and grief have finally snapped something in her mind? He noticed that she kept glancing towards the door nervously, as though expecting Hoshi to kick it open any moment, leap in with a razor and slit her throat . . .

'Jillamai! Mrs Gorimar . . . please calm down,' said Jingo. 'Please tell me exactly what has happened.'

She took a deep breath, and shook her head regretfully.

'He's discarded his family name. You'd never have found him, if you'd kept searching for ages. Goes by the

name of Hoshi Olundaz now. Does that name mean anything to you?'

He had in fact come across that unusual name in the
news, but hadn't given it a second thought. Olundaz?
When enunciated distinctly, the three syllables of his new
name might make sense to some of his schoolfriends,
reflected Jingo, for Hoshi had always claimed to possess
a dazzlingly impressive *lund*.

'He's a politician now, holds a high post in that party
of hooligans, what's it called, GSF . . .'

'You mean the Ghorpad Shakti Fauj?' Jingo asked.

'Yes, that's the one.' She nodded. 'It was about fifteen
days ago, after all that trouble over the mosque, with the
police firing at rioting Muslims and all, once things had
quietened down a bit, he came and knocked on my door
one night. It was at about this same time . . . He had two
lackeys with him. Such awful-looking fellows! Real ghor-
pads. You can imagine what I felt when I opened the door
and saw his face. And those two thugs behind him . . .'

'And then?'

'I made his friends wait outside. I insisted. He told
them to go downstairs and wait for him. Then he came in
and told me what he wants . . . he wants this flat! He
wants me to move out of here, lock stock and barrel. I
refused point blank. Over my dead body, I shouted at
him, never! I'll never move! And do you know what his
reply was?'

'What?'

'You shouldn't say things like that, he said to me with
an expressionless face. I was frightened when I saw him
looking at me like that. But he realized at once that he
had started off on the wrong foot. He began again. Called

me Mama for the first time since he had come, and told me his story . . .'

For a moment her eyes grew tearful.

'He's had a hard life, my Hoshi. He's done many bad things in his life, and so many people had done bad things to him, too, that's what he said. But now, at last, he says, he has a chance to become somebody . . .

'Once he got thrown out of school, he ran away from home. Began life at the bottom, in the street. A degenerate old Maharashtrian gaffer took him in, but used him badly. After some years, he ran away from him as well, after robbing his hoarded wealth. By then he knew many people and spoke Marathi fluently. There were people willing to help him. He began as an ordinary shakha-level member of the GSF, and worked his way up in the party. He was tough and ruthless. They used him to extort money for the party from shopkeepers and businessmen, to run gambling joints and whorehouses, smuggle drugs and sell them at street corners. He gave me a whole list of jobs he'd been doing. He's even taken beatings from the cops, and sat out a jail sentence, just to protect his leaders. At last they took notice of him. And afterwards, he became very friendly with that Ghorpadey's younger son, Ganesh. He took the boy under his wing, became his guru, taught him how to be tough, gave him ideas for making money.'

Jillamai's bass drone cracked several times in the course of relating Hoshi's story. There were moments of pain and falsetto, and tears brushed aside. But not once did Jingo feel she was lost in delusion. She was fully in control of herself. In fact, at times she sounded positively proud of her son's achievements.

'"At last," he said, "I'm quite well off,"' she continued

his story, '"and now I'm going to become respectable, too. That's why I need your help, Mama." And he repeats his offer again. He has a one-bedroom flat in Bhayander which he'll give me in exchange for this one. It's about the same area as this. And 60,000 rupees in cash.'

'But what does he want the flat for?'

'Two reasons: he wants to set up a campaign office for himself. He said his boss has promised him a ticket to contest the municipal elections next year from this very ward – Prarthana Samaj.'

'Imagine Hoshi as a city councillor!' said Jingo irrelevantly. 'Then again, why not?'

'And the other reason is because of its location, he said. He's entering into a business partnership with Ganesh Ghorpadey. He wants it to become the booking office for an amusement park they're setting up somewhere. The idea for this project, this flat, and the management of the whole enterprise are to be his contributions to the partnership.'

'Amusement park?'

'Some kind of resort-cum-amusement park, with an artificial lake and all. That's what he said.'

'But where in the city will he create all that?'

'Outside it. They've seen a big plot of municipal land somewhere far away, at a place called Ambavali. Some top dog in the municipality's offered it to them for a small rent if they can get rid of the slums occupying the land. Ganesh, Hoshi's friend, has already placed orders with agencies abroad to buy roller-coasters, giant wheels, merry-go-rounds, whatnot. And they're going to have an artificial lake specially constructed, with cottages around it, paddleboats and the like.'

'So that's what he needs a booking office for?'

'Yes. It's a gold mine, he says. It's going to make him very rich. This place is somewhere far away – outside Thana, he said, and they've figured that people might want to stay there on weekends or whatever, after they visit the park. The booking will be done here for the cottages.'

'That's amazing!' said Jingo.

'He's even got a name for it. What did he call it?' said Jillamai, trying to remember.

'But I've seen this place, Ambavali!'

'Yes . . . he's registered a company called Pasha Enterprises. He's calling it Pasha Amusement Park!'

'You don't understand. This is an immense slum, if he's talking about the same place,' Jingo said to her, still amazed. 'I guess it might be possible to prettify it, if they planted a lot of trees. There's a creek nearby. But the water's filthy! There are mangroves, too, further down, a lot of birds come there. But what are they going to do about all the people living in the slum?'

'Don't ask me,' said Jillamai. 'They've got their plans all worked out. He begged me not to throw a spanner in the works, now that he has come so close to becoming a decent citizen again. He needs this flat. Everything is coming to a head, he said. It all has to happen at the same time, or it may never. I don't know what he could have meant by that, but he frightened me. He said that everything was changing in Bombay. There's going to be a great conflagration. Far worse than the dock explosion of fifty years ago . . . A lot of people are going to die . . .

'He tried to convince me what a lovely, quiet place Bhayander is. "You'll love it," he said. "It'll be much safer for you to be out there than in the city. I'll get a tempo and move everything for you," he said, "don't worry about a thing." Then he took out a wad of hundred-rupee notes and gave it to me. "Please take this," he said. "You can treat it as an advance on the 60,000." But I refused outright. Then once more he started to try and frighten me . . .

'"There'll be rioting and arson, people will die like flies," he said. "And it'll be safer for you to be away from here, much safer in Bhayander than here." It's his party that's planning all this, so I suppose he knows . . . I haven't even told Nemoana downstairs, or she'll only panic. I watched him from the top of the stairs to see if he was stopping to meet her. I know he didn't . . . Anyway, he said they've decided to teach Muslims a lesson they'll never forget. They've worked out an action plan, he said, a blueprint for the massacre of the circumcised. That's the word he used.'

She shrugged. 'He could have asked more politely, more lovingly. Instead what did he say? A heap of dried-up old sticks just ripe for the bonfire . . . that's what he called my home. "It's in such bad condition, it has no value in the real-estate market," he said. "I've got the money to do it up, make a nice office here for Pasha Enterprises . . . Please don't throw a spanner in the works now, at this stage!"

'But I told him, "You should have asked me before making all these plans. I'm not moving nowhere. You hear me?" He left, cursing.'

The old woman stopped talking, and took a few deep breaths.

'If you go to his party office in Dadar, you can meet him. Olundaz, that's his name now. He didn't even give me his home address . . . Talk to him, son, if you think you can convince him. Tell him these are my last days, leave me alone. After I'm gone, anyway, it'll be his flat. But I'm not moving now.'

There was a long silence. Jingo decided he should be going home. Even now the streets were not entirely safe to move about in at night. He got up to leave. Jilla barely nodded to him as she saw him out, still engaged in a silently furious argument with her prodigal.

For days on end there had been no news from Gurdeep at all.

Generally speaking, Jingo liked having the flat to himself, but this time, there were days when he missed Gurdeep sorely. He wondered how he and Thiru were doing in Delhi, if they were still stalking the corridors of the Supreme Court, whether they had had any success with their writ petition. While he had been living in Nehrunagar, there was no phone in the CPSDR office. But he knew Thiru had applied for one. Could the line have been installed by now? Probably not, or Gurdeep would have given him the number before he left.

It had been a troubled time anyway. More than two hundred people had died in Bombay in the last fifteen days during riots that had been sparked off by protests against the demolition of the Ayodhya mosque. The casualties had been mainly Muslims, and most had fallen to police bullets. There had been some cases of arson, and attacks on police stations. Some Muslim-owned businesses had been set ablaze, too. Timber marts in Asalpha and DK Nagar were still smouldering. A few temples were stoned and a mosque in a Malad squatters' colony set on fire. Since the GSF was the self-proclaimed torchbearer of Hindutva in the city, it was an open secret that its men were behind some of these incidents. There were rumours that their leaders might be arrested.

But suddenly the tension in the city had seemed to dissipate. Things were relatively calm and people began to believe that normalcy had returned – which was when Jingo had decided to take the opportunity and visit Jillamai.

A whole week had now passed since Jingo's meeting with Jillamai, but he was in no mood to visit the GSF's headquarters at Dadar to meet Hoshi and plead on his mother's behalf. For one thing, he was a little scared of venturing into the Fauj's stronghold. He could not hope to do so discreetly. He would stand out in that locality as much as if he were an alien from Mars seeking an interview with a local politician, and besides, Jingo didn't speak enough Marathi to be able to talk his way out of any sticky situation that might arise.

Meanwhile, *Lalkaar*, the afternoon tabloid which Dada Ghorpadey had founded two years ago to serve as the official mouthpiece of the GSF, was frothing at the mouth in print, so to speak, making venomous attacks against the Muslims, paranoid allegations about their breeding prowess which would enable them to soon overtake the population of Hindus in the country, their dirty dealings in arms and opium, and other underworld activities that were empowering them while rendering Hindu Maharastrians in the city economically bereft. He had never read the Marathi tabloid, but a report in the *Indian Express* had summarized the kind of stuff they were carrying.

No, clearly this was no time to be going wandering into Dadar even if he could justifiably claim that Hoshi Olundaz-Gorimar had once been a schoolfriend of his.

He might easily be mistaken for a Kashmiri saboteur by a mob of Fauj loyalists, and lynched before he was able to even utter a single comprehensible word in his own defence.

And Jingo had begun not just to miss Gurdeep but also to worry about what might have happened to him. The easiest way to find out would be to ring up his parents' home in Malabar Hill and ask for news of him. The problem was Jingo didn't want to call them and draw attention to the fact that he had moved into the company flat once again, and that too while Gurdeep himself was away. They might put pressure on Gurdeep to end this arrangement of having a permanent guest in the flat who didn't even pay any rent. Then where would he go?

No, there was another way he could try first, even if it was just an off-chance. He remembered he had scribbled Menezes's phone number at Jogeshwari, where he was staying as a PG, in the notebook he had been using while staying at Nehrunagar. He found the notebook, then the number, and dialled.

The phone was engaged for nearly twenty minutes. Jingo was about to give up on it, thinking perhaps he had copied the number wrongly. Then, unexpectedly, it was answered by an elderly woman, possibly the landlady. She told him that Malcolm had gone out for a while, but his fiancée was in. Would he like to speak to her? He said he certainly would like to leave a message with her. Well, well! Quick work, brother Malcolm . . . There was a long wait before another voice spoke. This was a voice he knew. He couldn't be sure, but . . . what the hell, he was sure!

'Hello . . .'

'Hello, yes?'

'Is that Gloria?'

'Yes, it is. And isn't that Jingo?'

Both of them laughed with relief like long-lost friends who had made a serendipitous connection.

'What a surprise,' she said. 'I'm so glad you called.'

'So it's true? What the lady just told me on the phone?' asked Jingo. 'Are you and Malcolm really engaged?'

'Why, yes, it's true,' said Gloria. 'I've asked the land-lady not to, but she insists on telling everyone who rings up. She's very proud of her liberalism, for having agreed to let me stay here even before our nuptials are done.'

'Does Thiru know?'

'Just before he left for Delhi, Thiru and I decided it was better for us to break up,' said Gloria. 'It just wasn't working out . . . I used to be so scared of him, you know. Of his temper.'

'Well then, that's great news. I mean about you and Malcolm,' said Jingo. 'Congratulations!'

'Thanks, Jingo,' said Gloria. 'Well, I've not had a chance to tell Thiru about Malcolm. You see, he pro-posed to me only the day after Thirn and Gurdeep left for Delhi.'

'Well, so long as you're happy,' said Jingo.

'You know Malcolm, don't you? But of course you know Malcolm,' said Gloria. 'He's really such a sweeeet person.'

'And are they back from Delhi?' said Jingo. 'That's what I called to ask.'

There was a long silence.

'Hello?'

'Yes . . . By God,' said Gloria, wheezing into the phone asthmatically. She'd remembered something. 'By God,' she repeated, 'I must be sick to be chatting with you about my engagement, and I've forgotten everything else completely . . . The situation is bad, Jingo. I should have told you this at once.'

'What's happened? The petition . . .?'

'No, no . . . Early this morning we got a call from Girish,' said Gloria.

'Girish?'

'Ranade.'

'Ah.'

'Something terrible happened last night, just before dawn,' said Gloria. 'Luckily Girish himself got saved. He'd spent the night in the office with Thiru and Gurdeep, who got back only last evening.'

'What happened?'

'Somebody bolted the front and back entrances of Suryavansh Chawl from outside and set fire to the place. The chawl is too isolated, nobody heard a thing. They noticed the fire only after it was too late.'

'You mean there were people trapped inside . . .'

'All thirty families who lived there. The outer walls and doors of the old factory were quite solid, made of wood. I don't know if you saw it . . .'

'I did – once.'

'All of them burned to death. Ranade lost his old father, and his unmarried sister is in hospital with 90 per cent burns. He's devastated.'

'What a terrible way to die,' said Jingo. 'But who could have done such a thing?'

A horrible thought struck him, even as he asked that question. It might seem far-fetched, but it meshed with what he'd heard from Jilla. Was he privy to an awful knowledge that no one else had? Now certainly the Fauj would blame the Muslim residents of the slum, and target their huts as retribution. Those huts of tin and cardboard and plastic would need just one spark to ignite an all-consuming inferno. Hoshi would have cleared the ground for his Pasha Amusement Park in one shot.

'A few people told the police in the morning they were aware of some unusual activity,' Gloria said. 'Outsiders had come in during the night. But it was in the small hours. Nobody woke up and came out to challenge them.'

'There's something I urgently need to discuss with Gurdeep. I wish he'd ring.'

'Well, if he calls us, we'll certainly pass on the message. But I'm stuck here, too. I was able to spend the weekend here,' explained Gloria, 'because my aunt stayed over to look after Mum. I was supposed to go back today, but looks like I won't be able to for a while . . . Street fighting has already broken out here in Jogeshwari. The riots are starting again, Jingo. Malcolm was on the phone all morning trying to get through to a neighbour in Sion who could pass on a message to my aunt. But the line's down. The landlady had some calls of her own to make, so he's gone out to try again from a public phone.'

'Maybe I should just try and get on to a train to Ambavali.'

'No, no. I don't think you should.'

'It's very important,' said Jingo.

Gloria's curiosity was aroused. 'What can you do?' she said. 'You'll be putting your life at risk travelling so far at a time like this.'

'Well, let's see. I'm not sure what I can do, but it's important that I go. When we next meet I'll explain. Okay? Is there any message?'

'Promise me you'll turn back if there's any danger. And

do me a favour. If you do meet Gurdeep and Thiru, don't
tell them you spoke to me at Malcolm's. In fact, don't
mention that you spoke to me at all. Okay?'

'Okay.'

'Thanks a lot, Jingo. Take care.'

Ambavali Again

There was no queue at the ticket counter – only one open window, but no booking clerk.

'*Koi hai?*'

A man with greying hair and small beady eyes emerged and peered through the grille at Jingo, doubtfully. Yes, he said, trains are running. Jingo asked for a ticket to Ambavali.

Walking onto the concourse, he saw that there were hardly any people about. Utility stalls, newspaper kiosks, tea stalls, everything was shut. Only the automatic weighing machines remained operational, their red and yellow lights flashing, their tinny electronic jingles looping mindlessly. Well, a canteen on platform number 1 *was* kept half open. But there was no attendant inside, and no customers waiting to be served.

Across the tracks, where the down trains stopped, the platform was entirely deserted. The one he was standing on had a few people waiting, but just a very few. From here trains would go north, and east. A man squatted on a tin trunk, his head in his hands; a woman in a red sari beside him was suckling a drowsy infant. Nearby, another man and his family were huddled on the floor. The man's kurta-pyjama was mud-stained and dirty, his eyes red with sleeplessness.

The indicator for departures remained non-committal. Blinking rapidly a few times, it went dark again. A vegetable vendor with an empty wicker basket told Jingo he'd been waiting for more than forty-five minutes, but no train had passed in either direction. Just then the indicator lit up again, showing a train to Ghatkopar in five minutes. Twenty minutes later, one rumbled in.

Its compartments, normally packed to overflowing, were almost vacant. For a moment Jingo wondered if this could be a train heading for the yard to be washed and serviced. But after much crackle and flicking of switches, an announcement was heard over the PA: 'The 10.45 to Ghatkopar has been cancelled. The train on platform number 1 is the 10.55 to Mumbra. It will run fast between Byculla and Dadar, Dadar and Ghatkopar, Ghatkopar and Thane stations . . . From Thane to Mumbra it will stop at all stations.' The announcement was repeated in Hindi and Marathi.

That meant it would halt at Ambavali. For a moment, Jingo felt childishly elated. He'd get there faster then he had expected. But before he could board the train, doubts wormed into his optimistic resolve. An eerie business, wasn't it, catching an almost empty train at this time of day . . .? From an almost deserted station? Was he doing the right thing going up to Ambavali? Should he just sit at home and wait for Gurdeep's call? While debating this in his mind, he heard the announcement again. Just as the train began to pull out, Jingo grabbed a handlebar and jumped on.

A beggar woman in a filthy sari squatted in a corner by the doorway. A small baby was sprawled on the floor beside her sucking its thumb. The woman appeared to be indifferent to Jingo's presence in the otherwise empty compartment; nonchalant about everything else too, possibly even her own destination. He walked up and down the length of the carriage before choosing a seat. Fast trains tended to be more crowded than slow ones, but this was like riding a ghost train, he thought sourly, one that would jump not merely stations, but dimensions, landing its bewildered passengers straight into the twilight zone. Well, if it was carrying him to his doom, so be it.

He shouldn't have waited so long after his meeting with Jilla. But then, according to Gloria, Gurdeep and Thiru had only just returned from Delhi. Well, at least he should have caught the train to Ambavali as soon as he had heard the news of their return. But hoping that Gurdeep would phone him, he had allowed two more listless days to pass. By then the riots had broken out again all over Bombay, this time in deadly earnest.

Without admitting it to himself, could he be avoiding having to convince Gurdeep and Thiru about what he had heard from Jilla? They might ridicule his hypothesis. But now that the tragedy of Suryavansh Chawl had actually happened, at least one piece of the jigsaw had fallen into place, corroborating Hoshi's malevolent predictions.

In Bombay the identity of the rioters was openly vaunted. The cadres of the Ghorpad Shakti Fauj, commanded by their leaders, had assumed the mantle of 'defenders of the Hindu faith'. It was they who were doing all the killing, burning, inciting. In the forty-eight hours since he'd spoken to Gloria, the situation in Bombay had deteriorated completely.

There had been random stabbings at street corners. Gangs of thugs roamed the suburban trains tormenting women, at least all those dressed in salwaar-kameez, or otherwise identifiable as Muslim; men, on the other hand, were being forced to strip, circumcision taken as incontrovertible evidence of their faith. The sentence for belonging to this persuasion was variable, but immediate and awful.

For a whole month since the protests against the mosque's demolition, violence hadn't entirely subsided. Stray incidents continued to flare up in areas like Dharavi, Kurla and Sandhurst Road. But for a few days there was a lull, some semblance of order. The government appointed a retired official to inquire into the lapses and excesses of last month's police action.

Then, about a week ago, a spate of stabbings plunged Pydhonie, Dongri, Cheera Bazar and other Muslim areas of Bombay into panic. The killers seemed to be randomly picking on non-Muslim passers-by. But was it all that random? Were some individuals taking advantage of the deteriorating social climate to settle personal scores? Or was a vicious political party drumming up support to justify its cadres running amok in the name of vengeance?

Two Hindu truck-loaders asleep in a godown at Mandvi were knifed. Then the Suryavansh incident followed, and Ghorpadey's editorial in *Lalkaar*, almost exactly in Hoshi's language, minced no words : 'The third eye of Shiva has opened. Enough is enough. The Muslims must be taught a lesson they will never forget!' The editorial ended with the line saying: 'The next few days will be ours.' That was all it took to spark off a fresh burst of violence.

The Faujis were on the rampage. Lootings, killings, rape,

arson, all systematically planned and executed. An entire community was being targeted in a most bloody manner, and this was continuing unchecked. The civil adminstration was paralysed. The papers were comprehensive in their reporting of daily events, but the thickskinned government only made embarrassed noises. The city police, accused of partisan behaviour when they opened fire on Muslim mobs in December, now preferred to stand by and watch, cheering the Faujis on as they did their bit for Hindu pride. Curfew had been declared in many areas of the city and the army called in to control rioters. But the soldiers' lumbering trucks were easily dodged by the arsonists. Ransack-and-loot became the preferred mode of revenge.

Yesterday's paper told of a newly married Muslim couple who had arrived in the city from Nanded only the previous day. The taxi they were travelling in from Bombay Central station to Antop Hill was doused with kerosene and torched by a mob. All three of them, including the cabbie, who also happened to be a Muslim, were burnt to death in the taxi. Incidents like these had become disturbingly frequent.

At night, terraces of Hindu buildings in poor areas crackled with violence, both planned and spontaneous. Neighbouring Muslim *mohalla*s were rained down upon with sodawater bottles, tubelights, petrol bombs and burning tyres. Residents of middle-class Hindu colonies had organized themselves in shifts, staying awake through the night to guard against possible attacks by Muslims mobs. The rumour mills had begun to grind and no one knew for sure what to believe. Hindu *bhaiyya*s of Arrey Milk Colony, it was claimed, were supplying poisoned milk to the city. Muslim bakers were lacing the city's supply of pao with cyanide. Pakistani terrorists were poised to land on Bombay's beaches armed with AK47 machineguns . . .

Was this the Bombay he believed he knew so well? The resiliently cosmopolitan city he had thought would never change?

As the train for Mumbra passed Parel, he got up and leaned out of the doorway. There were very few people out in the streets, and even fewer vehicles. The main roads, too, were deserted. He saw a couple of police vans pass by. The railway tracks were glistening in the sun as the fast train sped past stations it was not scheduled to stop at. Far in the distance several thick black columns of smoke were rising slowly, merging into a tall, grey sky. He went back to his window seat.

The train entered Dadar station. Large groups of people on the platform were agitating, he couldn't make out what they were shouting. They were getting ready to invade the train. It was slowing down; then, surprisingly, instead of coming to a halt, the train picked up speed again. In that one instant, Jingo saw something from the corner of his eye: a passenger in a white crocheted cap with a long, waggish beard, clearly Muslim, jumped out of the carriage just ahead of his. The waiting mob, thwarted by the motorman who clearly didn't intend to stop, gave a hungry cry of triumph. Here was an impulsive goat who, wanting to disboard at Dadar, had actually jumped off the moving train right into their arms. Turning back to look, Jingo saw the long glint of steel flash in the hands of some of the predators on the platform. He could no longer see the middle-aged Muslim – on whom awareness must have dawned too late of the mob's deadly intent – though Jingo couldn't but imagine

the terror in his eyes as they fell upon him. The grating of
steel wheels on rails rose to a shriek as the tableau was
lost to sight.

The despair that had overwhelmed Jingo when he
walked out of his father's home some months ago had
had to do with an internal disorientation, a feeling of
having lost his way in the thicket of life's complexities.
Now this feeling was finding translation in an objective
reality. This was his city he was watching through the
window of a speeding train: the city he loved so much,
which he had believed would remain unchanged, eternal;
where he could always live the life of unhurried ease he
had grown so used to. The city that had supported him
and nurtured his dreams, the city for which he had denied
the world. That city had died on him today.

Nothing would ever change so drastically here, he had
believed. Maybe the price of a cup of coffee or a dosa
would go up, as it had in the Udipi fast-food restaurants.
But some enterprising young man would roll up a cart in
the street outside, offering the same fare to customers at
the old price, or even lower. The city had a million faces
that waned and waxed like the phases of the moon but
remained unchanged, no matter what. Or so he had
believed.

Jingo's confidence in the inviolable nature of his own
future was based on this complacent belief. There were
just too many by-lanes here, too many houses and
tenements, too many people staying in them, too much
life, for anyone to be able to impose uniformity on its
multifaceted shimmering chaos. But clearly he had been
wrong. Somewhere down the line a great betrayal had
taken place. This country, supposed to be home to people
of all beliefs and persuasions, was being pinched, shrunk

and squeezed into a straitjacket. Religion was never meant to be the basis of its social framework. And yet, people were now saying, well, why not? Unless we assert ourselves as the majority, how will the world respect us?

There *had* been a betrayal, and no one was exempt from the responsibility for it. These were horrific times. As a writer, or at least someone who had once wanted to write, he should be recording them, raising his voice in protest, along with others who felt the same as he did. But it might be too late now. There was nothing he could do except watch helplessly as events took their course. There had been signs in public life, of course, that should have made him anticipate this. But, too preoccupied with his own navel-gazing, he hadn't noticed the lengthening shadows.

Now the train didn't stop at Ghatkopar, either. It just sliced through the crowds gathered on either side of the platform. These were violent crowds, waiting to attack. When it was clear the train wouldn't stop, they pelted it with stones. At a few other stations, however, where no crowds had gathered, the train did halt briefly. A few people got off, a few others got in. The motorman was making his own decisions, it appeared – jumping signals, stopping in the middle of nowhere, or at small, obscure stations where he felt it was safe to do so. Anyway, there wasn't much traffic on the tracks, only a skeletal service was being run.

The train was no longer so empty as when he boarded it. It was difficult to tell for sure which community passengers belonged to, or what their religion was, but most seemed to be ordinary working people. More importantly, they were not travelling in groups. All of them eyed their co-travellers surreptitiously, trying not to show their tenseness.

A middle-aged man who had been standing in the gangway finally decided to sit on the same bench as Jingo, but leaving one seat vacant between them. Jingo ignored him, and continued to stare out of the window. Earlier in his ride he had seen slum pockets flash past which were ablaze or still smoking. Now he saw more of them: at Deonar, Baiganwadi, Vikhroli. Would he make it to Nehrunagar before it was too late? Then somebody tapped him lightly on the knee, and kept tapping.

It was a little waif of a girl, probably no more than two or three. Naked, except for a pair of multicoloured patch-work knickers. Wagging the palm of her hand in front of her face mechanically, she kept nudging Jingo's knee with annoying frequency, even after he'd taken notice of her. A few feet away near the doorway stood an older woman, presumably her mother. It was the same pair he had seen sprawled in the doorway when he boarded the train. Now the woman had decided there were enough people on board for her daughter to start begging. *Was* it her daughter? He had read in the papers about a flourishing racket in which women in slums rented out their infants and babies to beggars at ten rupees a day. Presumably the investment was worth it, if it brought in better returns.

Maybe this woman hadn't realized before she got on the train that today was not a good day for begging. Maybe the fact that people were being slaughtered in the city didn't affect her, if she was aware of it at all – she would be, Jingo supposed – because her rounds with the child were an inflexible drill without which she might not be able to provide the bread for their supper. He found a small coin in his shirt pocket and gave it to the child, who took it and moved on briskly, without acknowledgement. He didn't do this sort of thing often – giving alms to beggars – but then one's response to such appeals depended on the emotion of the moment, surely. One could hardly maintain a routine or principled stand about such things.

The middle-aged man sitting beside him waved the child beggar on. Somehow, unlike she had with Jingo, she didn't persist in her appeals, as though she had prior knowledge of his inflexibility.

Taking his cue from the beggar's exit, the man said to Jingo in English: 'Always the poor who suffer, in these situations.'

Jingo nodded, but didn't speak himself. The man continued in Hindi, with which he was obviously more comfortable:

'I'm a Hindu myself, but at my workshop in Mumbadevi, I employ only Muslim weavers. They do the best *zari-kaam,* embroidery. Now for one week, nobody's reported to work.' The man was not looking at Jingo's face as he spoke. His eyes were fixed on the cityscape flashing past, outside. 'Most of them were from UP. I suspect they've fled to their villages. But even when they come back after some months, they'll prefer to work for Muslim bosses. Mind you, I was paying them one rupee more per day than they'll get at any of the Muslim sweatshops in Nagpada. Now who's losing in all this, you tell me?'

Yes, Bombay was about money. People came here from all over the country to make a living and, if luck was with them, more than a living, even a fortune. Nothing, he had believed, would be allowed to disrupt this passion. But something strange was going on. Ghosts of fifty years ago, from the time of the country's Partition, were being resurrected and shrieking in louder, more vehement voices. These zombies of the past were stirring up communal feelings he'd never have suspected still slumbered within people.

Himself, he was neither Hindu nor Muslim, so perhaps in a deep sense he failed to understand the intensity of emotion these identities aroused in people. But everyone knew, and everyone claimed they knew, that hatred could never be resolved by more hatred. The workers – people Jingo thought should know better than anyone that they were all in the same boat, that caste and creed didn't matter so much as bread, or a roof over one's head – were being manipulated back into those deadly emotions of hatred so easily by the politicians. People who had lived in amity for years were now looking on their neighbours with distrust, searching for signs of treachery.

Was this some predetermined sequel that people were collectively living out, a suspended flowering of their own actions? Did places, lands, entire countries have their karmic destiny lurking in the soil like an ancient curse, impossible to evade, or reorient, until fully expiated?

They couldn't be more than twenty minutes away from Ambavali station. The train, which had stopped in the middle of nowhere, started off again, then halted briefly at a deserted platform which seemed not to have any board stating the station's name; or Jingo could have missed it, for he had been staring at the face of a lame man who climbed into their carriage with great effort.

Elderly and feeble, he needed to hold on to the steel grips mounted on the corners of benches as he moved between them. His clothes were unkempt, his beard straggly and grey. But what had absorbed Jingo's attention was the stream of tears endlessly pouring from the man's bulbous eyes. Weeping silently, while his beard soaked up the tears that had smudged his face. If he had had a satchel round his shoulder one might have mistaken him for one of those itinerant vendors who travel on the suburban trains selling joss-sticks, haircombs or railway-pass covers. But this man was carrying nothing. He was merely limping from one passenger to the next in the uncrowded compartment, palms briefly joined and raised high in front of his nose, pathetically. He was stopping before every passenger and bowing low, his face streaming with tears, as if begging for forgiveness. What crime did he believe he was guilty of?

The businessman sitting near Jingo was feeling more generous now for some reason, and offered a coin to the man. But the old man didn't even see it. He wasn't begging. Just bowing low, his hands raised in a formal *pranam*, still weeping, begging for absolution.

Others in the compartment had begun to notice him, too. There were embarrassed smiles and comments. One youngster nudged his companion and tapped his own forehead to say, there goes a screw-loose. Well, perhaps he was one. But what could have so disturbed him that he found it necessary to personally approach every individual, limping cautiously through the sparsely populated compartment, apologizing, craving forgiveness for some awful deed while profusely weeping out his sorrow? What act of violence had he witnessed that drove him to this demented condition? Had he seen his daughters being raped while he stood by helpless, or had he been terrified out of his wits by the crude edge of an axe splintering his front door in half? By the baying mob that dragged away his young sons into the unknown never to be seen again, despite his hysterical screams for assistance which his neighbours didn't dare not to ignore?

Or was he just a spokesperson for the smothered humanity of a city gone mad, where men were behaving like savage puppets, stomping out a bestial dance of hatred against their fellow creatures? Perhaps it was his way of saying that this is all wrong, insane. Perhaps he was only reminding us of a truth that had been drowned out by the din of murder and politics. That we were all human, and being human, there was nothing he felt but the utmost respect for each of us. That life was precious and worthy of adoration. That everything else was a lie, a perverse travesty of the natural law of right and wrong. Maybe he was also expressing a collective shame. For among the passengers in the train there must have been at least a few who had joined the crowds to indulge in the horror, as well as many others who only stood by and watched. For in truth Jingo thought, we were all guilty.

The train stopped. They were at Ambavali. Jingo rushed to the door and stepped on to the platform.

As the train rolled out of the station again, he saw there was much activity on the platform opposite the one he stood on. It was packed with adults, squatting on their haunches or sitting on the ground, children running about among trunks, suitcases and holdalls. A woman had lit her Primus and was cooking something in the midst of all this bustle. What was going on, Jingo wondered. Then it sank in. They were waiting for a train to take them away. These people were abandoning their homes and fleeing to VT to catch another train that would take them back to their villages.

He noticed someone he thought he knew. Wasn't that

Kishen in the crowd with his wife and child, the young man who had stopped Gurdeep to ask his advice on the morning of his first day in Nehrunagar? Maybe he should cross the tracks and find out where he was going and why. But it was pretty obvious, wasn't it? Besides, the youth might not even remember him. Among the crowd he also recognized Salim 'Chemist', the old man Shanti had told him about who sold packets of rat poison outside the station. Was he leaving too? And a couple of other faces he knew, including one of those rat-catchers whom Shanti had refused to talk to.

But Jingo decided he should move on, get to the CPSDR office as soon as he could. When he stepped out of the station it was already late afternoon. The sky was the colour of slops, its edges flecked with the pale mauve of a dying sun.

Outside, stood a cluster of auto-rickshaws. Half a dozen drivers were hanging around in a group, talking. When they saw Jingo emerge from the station they all turned to him expectantly. One of them called out, 'Where to, saab? Come 'long . . .'

Jingo shook his head. But another rickshaw-walla, already seated in his vehicle with the engine running, followed after Jingo at a walking pace, soliciting a fare.

'Nehrunagar? I'll take you for twenty rupees.'

'Twenty rupees!' Jingo exclaimed. He noticed then that all the rickshaws had flagged their meters to the side. By the meter the distance to the slum should cost no more than the minimum fare.

'I'll walk,' he said.

'To go walking at a time like this can be dangerous.' The rickshaw-man shrugged. 'And to *Nehrunagar* . . .'

The name of the slum colony was uttered with a doubtful leer. 'Come. I'll take you for fifteen. I'm going that way.'

In an hour it would be dark. Jingo couldn't waste any more time. He climbed into the auto and the man revved up his engine.

'Well,' Jingo asked him, 'has there been any more trouble here?'

'Trouble's all over Bombay, saab,' the driver replied, for a moment looking searchingly at Jingo in the rear-view mirror.

'I mean after that chawl was burnt, have there been any more incidents?'

'Everyone's scared. Something ugly is bound to happen . . . You a reporter, saab?'

'No.'

'Then why come to this godforsaken place?'

'I have friends here.'

'Ah.'

That might have been the wrong thing to say. The man stopped talking after that and drove in silence. Occasionally, he sneaked a glance at Jingo in his rear-view mirror. There was something pathetic about him, hunched over the steering with his back to Jingo, something curiously vulnerable about the folds of fat on his thick neck. He could well be a member of the GSF, or a sympathizer, thought Jingo. Was this the kind of person then, ordinary and vulnerable, who earned his living by day to provide for his family, but at night went out to join the marauding mobs to burn and loot and rape?

For a minute they waited at the level-crossing while a goods train passed through very slowly. Abruptly, the man shot a question at him, as if he had been turning it over in his head for a while before he could bring himself to speak it.

'See, in these times it's better to know for sure exactly what kind of fare one picks up. Are you Hindu or Muslim?' He, too, had been trying to figure out Jingo, it would seem.

'Neither.'

'Bombay's not safe place for outsiders any more,' he said. Jingo remained silent. 'So why do you come here? For holiday?' There was a little sarcasm intended in that, perhaps.

'But I *am* from Bombay. I'm not on holiday,' Jingo replied, slightly annoyed. In his mind, though, he heard a chuckle: his father ribbing him about being on perpetual holiday!

'Ah,' said the man, still unconvinced, and dropped him off on the outskirts of the settlement. Jingo paid up, and the rickshaw-man repeated, 'Be careful where you roam. This is not good time for holiday.'

As Jingo entered the slum, a family of four hired the same vehicle to take them to the station. Somehow they all squeezed in, placing their one suitcase beneath their feet. A very old woman was cradled by the man, probably her son, in his lap. He was taking his wife and child and mother away. The walking stick, made of gnarled wood, was too long, and jutted out on one side of the rickshaw.

The door of the CPSDR's office was wide open. Gurdeep saw him first and gave a yell, then a hug. 'Jingo!' he exclaimed. 'Hey, man, how *are* you? This is a really freaked-out surprise! I was thinking just a while ago I should go out and phone you.'

Thiru was seated at his desk talking to a man in Tamil. He, too, smiled and waved to Jingo from where he sat. Presently, the other man handed over a key to him, joined his hands gratefully, and left. Thiru came round the table and shook Jingo's hand warmly.

'Well, well. What brings you all the way here?' he asked. Jingo said he'd tell them, but he needed a moment to catch his breath; upon which Thiru remembered his duties as host and pulled up a chair for him. He excused himself for a minute to go order some tea.

'How did you come? Any trouble on the way?' Gurdeep asked.

'By train, of course,' Jingo answered. 'Saw a lot of fires ablaze in the suburbs . . . Your work in Delhi kept you away longer than I thought it would . . .'

'We had to change our lawyer after we got there. The first guy, we realized, was just giving us the run around. Finally, we found the right guy to represent us. And you know what? The court gave us the order we wanted.'

'That's great.'

Just then Thiru returned and said to Gurdeep, 'Looks like Pandit's packed up and gone, too.'

'Can't be,' Gurdeep responded. 'Must have just gone out for a bit.'

'Well, I can't see him anywhere,' said Thiru. 'Even his shack is cleaned out. All his cups and glasses, *chai ka saamaan*, everything's cleared out.'

'He wouldn't have left without telling us,' said Gurdeep, puzzled. 'Unless he came to say goodbye while we were at the cop station.'

'That's possible, I suppose,' agreed Thiru.

'More trouble with the cops?' Jingo asked.

'No,' replied Thiru. 'This time it's us who went to them asking for protection.'

'You must have read about what happened at Suryavansh three nights ago,' Gurdeep said.

'That's part of the reason I came.' Jingo nodded.

'Anti-social elements need far less provocation than that to create trouble,' said Thiru. 'It's a dangerous situation.'

'The people here are terrified,' continued Gurdeep, 'expecting a backlash any night. The cops agree there might be. But they're too short-staffed, as it is.'

'They can only spare two men who'll be posted near the entrance to Nehrunagar every night until things cool down,' said Thiru.

'Hope one of them's not the chappie you bashed up in Byculla,' Gurdeep added, good-humouredly needling Jingo. 'That'd be ironic indeed.'

'The people have organized to defend themselves against any violence,' said Thiru, ignoring Gurdeep's remark. 'They've been collecting their own weapons – bottles, stones, iron rods, tubelights – they're prepared for the worst. What worries me is that if the police decide to raid their huts and find these stockpiles, they'll book them for conspiring to riot.'

'And the same cops plead helplessness about not being able to provide us with protection! Good to have you here, old chap,' said Gurdeep. 'One needs a few brave-hearts for company through the long, dark nights. Menezes is stuck in Jogeshwari, it seems. And Ranade – did you hear about his loss? Poor guy's taken it very badly – he's gone to his village in Sindhudurg to attend some ceremonies for his father and sister.'

'His sister? She didn't survive then?'

'With 90 per cent burns,' said Gurdeep, 'not much chance . . . She died the next day. Now tell us about yourself, why you came. You're not planning to go back tonight, are you? That'd be dicey . . .'

'No, I think I'd better stay here tonight,' said Jingo. 'I came to give you some news. I think it's pretty serious.'

'What is?'

Jingo took a deep breath before commencing his story. He rather relished his position as storyteller. Describing Jillamai's lodgings and the old woman herself in colourful detail, he kept Thiru and Gurdeep listening raptly to the curious tale of the mother and her missing son, although they couldn't help wonder where all this was leading to.

'Based on years of random market research, I have come to believe in one thing: infinite diversity of the sort one finds in Bombay implies a metaphysic of coincidence,' said Jingo. 'In Bombay, coincidences spring at you erratically, from the backstreets of reality, so to speak. And usually, when they occur, they seem imbued with great significance, but the question is, are they . . . or is it that life itself is just a string of brutal, funny and pointless coincidences?'

'Okay, okay,' said Gurdeep, showing signs of impatience. 'We accept that you're the unquestioned king of market-researching philosophers. But do you mind coming to the point?'

'I'm about to. Two weeks ago, I met Jillamai again. She told me that Hoshi had been to see her after twenty-odd years. He's become quite a big shot, it seems, in the Ghorpad Shakti Fauj. Hoshi Olundaz, that's the new name he's taken. He told his mother details of a plan to build an amusement park with attached residential cottages on the land that Nehrunagar now occupies. Once he sweeps the slums clear of it.'

'Amazing . . .' murmured Thiru, below his breath.

'He even predicted the communal disturbances in the city, which he must have known his party was planning to instigate. He implied that the moment to strike was now, while the riots are still on. To drive out the slum-dwellers and annex the land for his amusement park,' said Jingo. 'Ganesh Ghorpadey, apparently, is financing the project. When I heard what happened at Suryavansh Chawl, I became convinced that Hoshi is working to a plan. I've thought about it a lot. I'm afraid we are only at the second act of this drama. The finale is yet to be enacted.'

'It's very good of you, Jingo, to come all the way here just to warn us,' said Gurdeep. 'But don't you think your theory is just a little fanciful?'

'Look, you don't know this guy,' said Jingo. 'He was with me at school. He's – evil. He's capable of going to any lengths to get something he wants. He's even got someone in the BMC who's agreed to lease the land to them at a very low rent. Provided he gets rid of the slums first. He has plans to become some sort of tycoon-politician himself.'

'What you're suggesting is really very interesting,' said Thiru in his soft-spoken, but authoritative manner. 'And believe me, I, too, am quite touched that you cared enough to make this journey just to tell us all this. The thing is' – he frowned, lightly scratching his cheek through his thick growth of beard with a ballpoint – 'the conspiracy theory is very credible' – turning to Gurdeep for a moment – 'it's really not that unbelievable, if you think about it – but now the situation has changed. BMC is one thing and the Supreme Court is another. The order we have secured from Delhi states in black and white that until arrangements are made for rehabilitation of all legitimate residents of Nehrunagar, it is the duty of the state to protect the slum. They've already sent a copy to the government and, at our suggestion, even asked it to prepare a feasibility report for moving the settlement to an alternative site.'

'The people here,' said Gurdeep, 'are jubilant about the court order. They are prepared to fight it out if there's any sort of attack. Won't be easy for anyone to sweep the land clean of slums just like that.'

'From one point of view, you're absolutely right, Jingo,' said Thiru. 'This is the perfect time for the land-sharks to get into action.'

'I don't know if you saw a small news item tucked away on page six of the *Times of India* yesterday,' said Gurdeep to both of them. 'It reported that the K-Ward municipal office in Andheri was burnt down in a fire, and all land records of the area destroyed. How convenient.'

'But you guys aren't worried?' asked Jingo. 'You think what I heard from Jillamai is far-fetched?'

'We are worried, of course,' said Thiru. 'But don't forget. The GSF is also a political party. All this violence is political – to become identified as protectors of the Hindu faith. First, they create insecurity among Hindus, polarize the voters, then storm their way into the legislature at the next elections. That's what they're aiming for. They can't afford to be seen as anti-people by dishousing slum-dwellers to start an amusement park. There are enough Hindus staying here, too.'

'But it's a blueprint for making money,' said Jingo, 'this idea of an amusement park with cottages, all this land!'

'Agreed,' said Gurdeep, 'but looting and extortion are what the GSF specialize in. For the first time maybe in the history of Bombay, the party has taken its extortion racket into upmarket areas. They have old voters' lists with them, mind you. So buildings with flats owned by rich Muslims are being approached for protection money. Some thugs even came to my uncle's building in Malabar Hill asking for five lakhs.'

'Did he pay up?'

'No chance,' said Gurdeep. 'The housing society decided to remove all the nameplates from the doors, and give protection to their Muslim members themselves.'

'All this happening in a place like Bombay,' said Jingo. 'The most cosmopolitan, supposedly most secular city in the country . . .'

'Only thing that should amaze anyone is that it didn't happen earlier,' said Thiru. 'Did you know, 60 per cent of Bombay's thirteen million people occupy 12 per cent of the land. We've been sitting on a timebomb all this while, without even knowing it.'

'And yet Hindus and Muslims have always lived together peacefully. Even here, in Nehrunagar,' said Gurdeep, 'there's never been a hint of communal rancour. Until the politicians stir up trouble – then the people don't know where to run, who to trust . . .'

The conversation would have probably continued in this vein for a while if Gurdeep hadn't noticed it was past seven and already quite dark.

'I'd better check if everything's in order,' he said, picking up a large flashlight on his way out, which Jingo hadn't seen before. 'I'll be back quite soon.'

'Just make sure the volunteers are absolutely clear about schedules,' Thiru called to Gurdeep as he stepped out. 'Hey, wait – what about some food? The dhaaba closes early these days.'

'Don't worry,' said Gurdeep. 'I'll make sure about the arrangements first, and pick up some biryani on my way back.'

There were a few minutes of silence in the cabin after Gurdeep left. During this time Thiru opened an office file and started flipping through it. Presently, he looked up and said to Jingo, 'Before leaving for Delhi, we had conducted a census in Nehrunagar. To be able to maintain a clear record of all legitimate residents. Some documentary proof might become necessary in the light of legal complications and all this talk of resettlement.'

'What arrangements was Gurdeep talking about just now?' Jingo asked.

'Oh. Security . . . for our defence. Able-bodied men in small groups of five will start patrolling soon after dark,' said Thiru. 'All entry points into Nehrunagar are being guarded by sentries. The stockpiles I mentioned earlier? They're hidden in select huts at strategic intervals; a few men have been put in charge of this arsenal and hold the keys to it. Lastly, the women: they've been instructed to create a din by striking steel thalis with a ladle if they smell any trouble. That's the best we've been able to do.'

'Pretty thorough, I should say,' said Jingo appreciatively. 'But then, I noticed, a lot of huts *are* empty, aren't they?'

'Well, about a third of the families have moved out,' Thiru said. 'Some left soon after the December riots, but many more after the Chawl's gutting. Some have even left their keys with me, asking me to look after their huts. As though I were the bellhop of Hotel Nehrunagar.'

Jingo laughed.

'The thing is, there are just too few of us,' Thiru continued. 'In the three weeks we were away in Delhi, even those guys who used to come by regularly have stopped. Chavan, Delna, even Malcolm . . . Of course, it's a bad time.'

'What about Gloria?' Jingo couldn't resist asking. 'How's she doing?'

Thiru frowned. 'Gloria's another one,' he said. 'So passionate about working for CPSDR when she started out. Now she's stopped coming altogether. She's been having her own problems, too, I guess, with her mother bedridden and all. Actually, I do find that women are too much trouble in general. What do you think?' he asked Jingo with a smile. 'Really, they take up so much time . . . Anyway, it's very nice of you to have come. And I just want to say' – he mumbled, embarrassedly – 'sorry about the last time. I'd asked Gurdeep to apologize . . .'

'He did. Please forget it,' said Jingo. 'But what news of the girl, Shanti?'

'Well, a couple of months ago I met a sub-inspector I happen to know. I asked him to find out for me . . . She's still in the remand home at Kalyan. But it's a progressive institution, apparently, where they teach the inmates a trade. She's learning tailoring or something.'

For a few minutes they sat quietly while Thiru pored over the file again. It was very quiet outside. Jingo noticed that even the voices of children playing, which he'd grown so used to during his previous sojourn at Nehrunagar, had ceased. Soon Gurdeep returned, carrying three greasy packets of biryani and a bottle of Joachim's jeera.

'Dogmeat biryani?' asked Jingo.

'Chah!' replied Gurdeep. 'That crazy girl used to make

up all these stories. I questioned the dhaaba owner. There's no truth in it at all.'

'The biryani's fine,' said Thiru, 'but you should have avoided the booze. We might not get much sleep again tonight.'

'The guys on sentry duty will alert us if there's any problem,' said Gurdeep. 'I just met them. I thought we could just relax a bit and chat. And then again – *Bambai se aya mera dost* . . .' He sang a line from the film song, slapping Jingo affectionately on the shoulder.

'Don't make me the pretext for the drink you're dying to have,' said Jingo.

'I'll admit it, pal,' said Gurdeep hoarsely, 'I need one badly. It's been so tense here, you can't imagine . . . Don't you want one?' he asked, turning to Thiru.

'I didn't refuse, did I?' said Thiru. 'Now get the glasses.'

It was already dark outside by the time they had folded the chairs and stacked them against the tin wall in a corner. Spreading out a woven coir mat which had been donated to the CPSDR by Gloria, they sat on the floor under the suspended light bulb with their glasses and the bottle of jeera.

Jingo found the silence slightly spooky. Clearly Thiru and Gurdeep had been more on edge than they had allowed themselves to show earlier. Their very first drink loosened them up and made them both rather giggly. They tried to keep their laughter down, but the mood was set for a pleasantly frivolous evening, even an oddly nostalgic one – for what they reminisced about was their schooldays and the eccentric teachers each of them had survived.

Jingo remained quiet through most of the early part of

the evening. He was feeling strangely disturbed by the lightness and inconsequentiality of the conversation. But given its subject, he did mention his own shenanigans at school in Ghanshyam's class, his association with the profligate Hoshi, and how it came to an abrupt end after he heard of Ghunto's personal tragedy.

'Once I'd heard that his wife was dying of cancer in hospital, I was so stricken by remorse, I stopped everything – I mean all the mischief,' he said. 'I became quiet again, and even studious. But in my last year at school – and this is a real puzzle – one of the senior teachers mentioned to me in passing that Ghanshyam-sir had remained a confirmed bachelor all his life! I guess I'll never figure out the truth about that one now.'

'I'll tell you,' said Gurdeep. 'It was a ruse on the part of the priest to awaken your conscience and buy some peace. Saw that?' He turned to Thiru. 'Even in his younger days this Jingo was a *pucca budmaash*!'

They managed to restrict their drinking to little more than half a bottle, and ate early. During dinner, Thiru brought the conversation back to a more serious plane.

'What's interesting about all this, it's not only Muslims who have fled Bombay,' said Thiru. 'Even Hindu migrants from other parts of the country have chosen to leave. The Shakti Fauj has always wanted them out anyway, and now they've created this situation, they're turning the screws on all outsiders.'

'Some 60,000 people, the papers estimate, have left the city. The underlying motive is economic, no doubt,' said Gurdeep. 'See what's happening in all the factories and workshops in the Ambavali–Thane belt. The labour force has become 100 per cent Hindu after the trouble started. No Muslim dares to report for work. You should see the noticeboards at all the GSF shakhas near the station – calling for a boycott of Muslim businesses, restaurants, even social intercourse. They just want to make normal life impossible for them.'

'I still find it difficult to believe that all this bloodshed and horror can just be a political ploy,' said Jingo, 'a means to get votes during some future election.'

'Well,' said Thiru, 'politics is a strange game. And all kinds of things are possible in this country. Besides, it would be incorrect to believe that all this is just about vote-bank politics.'

'I mean, yes, there's all this talk of Hindu self-assertion,' said Jingo, 'cultural nationalism and all that.'

'Well,' said Thiru, 'you guys have always stayed outside the mainstream . . . I mean, Parsis. Don't think you could possibly understand what a deep emotional significance Ram has for the Hindu psyche. Centuries of Muslim invasion have subdued the Hindu, you must understand. A backlash was inevitable . . .'

Jingo could hardly believe what he was hearing. And from Thiru! He felt like retorting, 'Scratch a Tamil Brahmin, and sure enough you'll find a communalist!' But he decided that might not be entirely fair, and anyway an argument on this subject was the last thing he wanted. He was feeling too depressed to argue.

But Thiru didn't mean to be unfriendly. Presently he changed the subject himself, and asked, 'Gurdeep told me you were writing a novel,' he said. 'That's fantastic! What's it about?'

'Not true,' said Jingo. 'I'm not writing anything, in fact.'

'You know,' Thiru said. 'There's something I've always felt about India. I don't know if you'll agree with me, but

I think in this country documentation should take precedence over fiction. The truth here is much stranger than anything the best fiction writer can imagine. What do you say?'

Jingo didn't fully agree, but he had had the same thought himself at times. 'Well,' he said, 'you're right in a sense. But it'll be a sad day when people stop fantasizing, imagining, exaggerating . . . or writing and reading fiction.'

Thiru didn't say anything. Instead, he reached for his packet of Charminars. Conversation became desultory. Gurdeep and Thiru lit up, but Jingo declined when the pack was passed to him.

'You've stopped completely?' asked Gurdeep.

'Well, yes,' Jingo replied. 'I'm tempted to, sometimes, but I've stopped liking the taste of tobacco.'

'I think giving up the hash was the best thing you could have done for yourself,' said Gurdeep. 'It's very creditable, after all these years of smoking.'

'Well, I don't know,' said Jingo, 'Life seems dull without it sometimes.'

'I think I'll stay up and read for a while,' said Thiru. 'You guys can catch forty winks, if you like.'

'More like a hundred and forty,' said Gurdeep, rolling out the spare mattress on the floor. Thiru slid the bolt on the door into place from inside, leaving the light on. Jingo had the spare charpoy, Thiru lay in bed reading, and Gurdeep began to snore almost as soon as his head touched the mattress.

He hadn't slept enough. He was still groggy when he opened his eyes. The light in the room was on. Thiru had fallen asleep with a book open on his chest. Gurdeep was fast asleep, too. He looked at the time on his wristwatch. Oh God! It was a still only a half past two.

He was about to turn over and go back to sleep when he became aware of the sound that was probably what had woken him up. It seemed to be coming from very far away, like a distant howling of wind. But it was growing steadily louder. He listened more intently for a moment and, as he realized what it could be, what it was, it chilled him.

Now he was wide awake. He listened. The noise grew louder. He knew what it was. People. A huge aggregation of people, perhaps five hundred or a thousand or more, he couldn't guess how many, marching towards the slum. What he was listening to was the collective frenzy of yelping, shouting, catcalls, hysterical laughter, the murderous bravado of a mob, muffled by considerable distance.

He got out of bed and quickly shook both Gurdeep and Thiru awake.

'Listen!' he said, and gave them time to hear the distant hum for themselves. 'Something's happening . . .'

'Fucking bastards,' said Gurdeep and jumped out of bed. Thiru was up in a flash and at the door.

'Ya,' he said, grimly. 'This is it.'

What happened that night was so nightmarish and bizarre, Jingo's experience of it was fogged by a film of unreality. The brief sleep he had snatched before being awakened by the ritual ululations of the marauders left him feeling as though he had not entirely emerged from some dream level of consciousness, and throughout that night on several occasions he found himself wondering if the events were actually happening. And why, if it was real, was he not awake and alert, why was he almost paralysed by a kind of sleepy-eyed, impotent terror, as one feels when something awful is happening in a dream to which one is merely a passive witness?

Perhaps Gurdeep and Thiru had rehearsed this eventuality in their minds several times in the past few days. Even if they didn't believe it would really happen, it must have lurked somewhere in their subconscious: in a way, wasn't this just a replay of the demolition raids they had grown used to expecting over the years? Both of them bounded out and ran in the direction of the clamour, the shouting and screaming, the desperate clanging of steel plates that sounded the alarm. Jingo followed, but he got only a few steps beyond the door. His legs were like jelly, and by the time he stepped on to the pathway, he couldn't see his friends any more.

It was very dark outside. Nehrunagar, never properly electrified, had been strung up with light bulbs at certain bends and dark stretches by the residents themselves, powered with electricity tapped from high-tension cables that radiated from a sub-station on the highway. Now, even these scattered bulbs were snuffed out. The attacking mob had probably cut the line, preferring the advantage of darkness to commence the onslaught in.

Jingo's eyes took some time adjusting to the dark. Just as he was wondering if he should shut the cabin door and follow in the direction Gurdeep and Thiru had gone, he became aware that the turbulence was growing in intensity and closer than he thought. Underneath the screams and wailing, the pandemonium of war-cries, he heard the crackle of tinder, smelt the burning of plastic, jute and thatch. Suddenly it was no longer so dark. The sky had turned a dismal crimson, mirroring the flames on the ground below. In the crepuscular, unnatural half-night, everything was hazy. His eyes had begun to smart from the smoke in the air.

Suddenly he saw them. Not Gurdeep or Thiru, but people in the distance, rushing towards him. They were still too far away for him to see their faces, and there were too many of them, but he could see their live torches reflected in the stagnant waters of the murky green pond.

Bare-chested and in shorts, muscular and burly, or thin and wiry, they were, he supposed, the cream of the lumpen, the pride of the Shakti Fauj. Some carried curved swords, ceremonial tridents, lathis. One carried a pitchfork. A few others brought up the rear carrying large jerrycans filled with kerosene, or possibly diesel.

It was a massive operation, well planned and coordinated. First, the men with the weapons frightened the slum-dwellers, roughed them up, shouting at them all the while to get out. Before they had barely time to react, the men with the jerrycans splashed their huts with the inflammable liquid. Then the torch was applied and, in a matter of seconds, a whole row of huts became a raging inferno.

Even the attackers were organized in teams, it would seem. Such resistance as had been planned by the local people seemed nowhere in evidence. One of the leaders of the attacking teams, barrel-chested and short, was bloodthirstily cheering on a gang of young boys hardly out of their teens, not very far from the CPSDR office. Kicking open hut doors, he was yelling at the top of his voice: 'Come on out, everyone! Out! Out! Your time is up! Go back to Bangladesh while you still have the chance! You hear me?'

People were frightened. Scuttling out of their huts,

overwhelmed, only a few of the women, more outspoken, begged the assailants for a few minutes to pack their belongings, but such requests were contemptuously ignored. A man with a short beard emerged from one of the huts. He was white-haired but strong and broad-shouldered, very agitated. Jingo had seen him many times before, but never spoken to him. Now rage had made him fearless. He was trying to initiate a dialogue, refusing to give up without attempting at least a discussion.

'There are no Bangladeshis staying here,' he shouted back. 'Our families, our children, only we stay here. We've been living here for seven, eight years. Why are you trying to throw us out?'

'Eh, *bhhonsdi-ke*, Sayyed Mia!' screamed one of the other leaders of the attacking mob. 'You want me to show you what we are capable of? Out, while you still have the time!'

'No, no. Listen to me. We have to talk. We've been living here for donkey's years. Hindus, Muslims. Good neighbours. We've never made trouble.'

'*Chal bey*, *buddhe*, don't try my patience,' said the goon. 'Get out!'

'And if we refuse? What will you do?' spluttered the elder, choking on his rage.

'You asking what I'll do?'

'I'm telling you let's just take things peacefully,' the old man said. 'Let's sit down for a minute and talk . . . Whatever problem can be solved . . .'

But the thugs were not in a mood for this kind of pacific resistance. The white-haired patriarch was given a hard slap that sent him sprawling on the ground.

'Your time for giving *bhaashan*s is over, old man,' said the barrel-chested, short hooligan who was carrying one of the heavy jerrycans with both hands. For one inexplicable moment, he reminded Jingo of the uncouth obstetrician who had performed the abortion on Cristina. This man, too, filled him with loathing.

'You should have thought of all that before burning those poor Hindus of Suryavansh Chawl,' the hooligan shouted.

'That wasn't any of us,' said the old man. 'I swear to you we had nothing to do with it. Wait. No . . . ! No!'

With a semi-circular movement of his hands, the thug splashed the hut with the inflammable liquid; then laughing, he continued the sweep of the can and spilled some more of it onto the old man, who was still on the ground, trying to get up.

'Ohhey! For Allah's sake, what are you doing?' the old man shrieked, scrambling finally to his feet, still angry, but now his voice was shrill with fear. He shouted out to members of his family who must have been cowering inside, 'Come on out, come on out, Fatima, Shernaz . . . Out, everyone. These *shaitaan* are setting fire to our home.'

'At least we're not locking the doors from outside,' said one of the leader's henchmen, laughing hysterically.

'Now he's remembering his Allah,' said another, and the hate-drunk boys and young men laughed. In the ghastly, smoky night, Jingo saw the tear-stained faces of two women and a young child who emerged from the hut. There may have been more. So many people were milling around in the dark, he missed the exact sequence of events, but suddenly the torch was applied. Not just to the hut – even the old man was up in flames. He was screaming, trying to run. The women were screaming, too.

'Abba, abba . . . Oh help him, someone . . . Water!'

But within seconds he had collapsed on the ground, a charred and probably hideous sight, shrouded by the dark, but still twitching.

Paralysed by horror, Jingo stood there watching, once again wondering if all this was really happening or if it was only a bad dream. He didn't see Gurdeep approach, didn't notice him until his friend took hold of his arm. 'Gurdeep!' he exclaimed. But even his vocal cords seemed to have jellified, and Jingo could barely hear himself.

'Quick,' Gurdeep said, rushing into the office. 'Thiru wants me to rescue some files.'

'They're killing people,' Jingo said, finding his voice again. 'Isn't there anything we can do?'

'Cops never turned up,' Gurdeep said. 'Thiru's gone to phone the fire brigade. In any case, even if they were here, the cops would have been badly outnumbered. There are at least eight hundred of these ruffians.' He opened the drawers of the table in the shack and pulled out everything. 'They're giving people a chance to get out while they can.'

'I saw them set fire to an old man in front of my eyes!' said Jingo. As Gurdeep handled the files and papers, Jingo saw that his hands were trembling.

'They're not hurting people, by and large,' he said, 'unless they resist. People are scared. There are too many of those guys. Here are the files . . . Come on! Let's get out of here.'

But in that instant there was a sharp slap of steel on tin, and they saw that sword-wielding men were already at their door. Now he could see their faces clearly. They were short ugly men, muscular, hirsute, inebriated.

'Hey, this place is not bad at all,' said one of them.

'Ya,' said another. 'Fancy palace they've built on slush!'

'These are those same guys, *yaar*,' said yet another, who seemed better informed, 'who've been encouraging these *lowndey*. Filing cases, getting court injunctions, what not. Come on, now, all of you out. Your time for social-*giri* is up, too.'

'Ya, we're going,' said Gurdeep, 'we're going.'

But Jingo wasn't, for just then the short, barrel-chested man with the jerrycan staggered into the room.

'This is that bastard,' screamed Jingo in a strange falsetto that sounded unreal even to his own ears. He was pointing at a man who was so drunk he could barely manage the weight of the can. 'This guy burnt the old man alive!'

'Come on,' said Gurdeep. 'This is no time for heroics.'

But the man had heard Jingo.

'*Saala!*' he said to his compatriots in Marathi. '*Mala gaali deto!* He's calling me names? Who the hell's this son of a sow?'

'We're going,' said Gurdeep, moving towards the door, which was blocked by the thugs. 'Come on,' he said to Jingo.

But the drunk was not willing to let them pass, nor the insult Jingo had uttered with a finger pointed at him. 'You motherfucker, you're giving me *gaalis*?' he said. 'Sure, I burned that old goat, sent him to his *kabar*. So then what're you going to do about it, eh?'

'I don't need to do anything,' said Jingo.

'Come on,' said Gurdeep. 'We're going, let's go.'

'– but the police will.' Jingo completed his sentence.

'Police?' exclaimed the drunkard in surprise and burst out laughing. 'He's threatening me with the police? Ha, ha, you sisterfucker, the police is with us! Yes,' he repeated, 'I burnt the old goat, and I'll do the same thing for you.'

In the same instant, almost before he spat out those words, he swung the can he was carrying and doused Jingo in kerosene.

Jingo turned cold. The night had turned cold. He saw stars. The fires blazing outside couldn't stop him from shivering. He was wet and trembling uncontrollably. He was so shocked, he was about to burst into tears. Is this really happening, he thought. Oh God, I'm not ready to die yet. Not like this, please . . . Then he thought of his parents, who didn't even know he was here. For a moment he thought of the picture in a brown wooden frame of his dead brother, Rumi.

'*Arrey, arrey,*' said Gurdeep, aghast, '*yeh kya kiya?* He's an outsider. Leave him alone.'

'You can go,' the man said to Gurdeep, making way for him. 'This guy I won't leave. He gave me *gaalis*, called me bastard! You motherfucking bastard, let's see now who's the bastard. Hey, where's the boss gone with the *mashaal*? Go call him. Otherwise, wait, I have a box of matches somewhere.' He put down the can and began to search his pockets.

Jingo couldn't stop trembling. He was crying. It's all absurd. More of the hoods were blocking the door, there was no way out. I've not even begun to live yet, please God . . . In a few minutes the man with the torch would appear. How long did the body suffer the agony of flames before losing consciousness? Soon nothing would be left of him but a heap of ashes. A little mound of ash that might perhaps remain faintly luminous for a while, flushed by the dull fever of unsated desire, the brief radiance of unfulfilled hopes and dreams . . . before it is

forever extinguished and turned to ice . . . No! He wasn't
going to die yet!

With dream-like precision, the people at the door
moved aside and made way. A lit torch appeared at the
door first. Only then did the enormous figure holding it
bend his head and press in through the doorway.

The giant's small eyes were focused on Jingo's face.
Jingo, too, stared back. A faint smile of recognition
seemed to flicker in those otherwise expressionless eyes.

'Hey, come on, men,' the big man rumbled. 'What are
you guys wasting time here for?'

'Boss,' said the goon who'd been insulted by Jingo,
holding out his hand out for the torch. 'This one I want
to finish off right here before we go. It'll just take a
minute . . . Acting too smart with all of us, he has,
deserves to die! Looks to me definitely a Kashmiri, or
something. An Afghani terrorist, I think.'

'Nonsense!' said the hulk, dismissively. 'This is no
Mussalman. Let him go. You can come along with me.'
The big man turned to go, and the blustering *chela*
followed obediently, but not before a threatening glance
at Jingo. Almost as an afterthought, the boss said to the
other hangers-on, 'And this is all first-class *puttra*, won't
burn easily. Just knock it down. You can sell it to your
local *bhangaarwalla* by the kilo.' He was half serious,
half joking; the others laughed tentatively.

'Hoshi!' called Jingo after the receding man mountain,
at last finding his voice. 'It's me. Jingo.' The man turned
and looked at him strangely, but did not respond. Then
he walked away, followed by the short, stocky man who
had threatened to end Jingo's life.

Despite the stench of kerosene, Gurdeep hugged him.
'That was close, man,' he said. 'Let's get out.'

'But that *was* him,' he said. 'Hoshi, my schoolmate. He recognized me, I know it, but pretended not to.'

Though Jingo hated him for the destruction of Nehrunagar, though he was repelled by the monstrous criminality of the mind that could have planned and executed this attack, he felt a wave of gratitude for Hoshi, his saviour, whose providential entry had saved his life. For a moment his mind wandered irrelevantly back to their schooldays. All those times when he could have squealed on Hoshi and didn't – maybe he was just being paid back in kind.

'He can't afford to have witnesses identifying him later on,' said Gurdeep. 'Wait, I've got a spare shirt somewhere. You'd better change.'

By the time they left from there, most of the land that Nehrunagar had occupied was smouldering. Behind them some boys had finished dismantling what had once been the office of the CPSDR. Thiru had been back for some time. He was cursing, but beneath his breath. There were tears in his eyes. Gurdeep managed to restrain him from doing anything foolish by telling him of Jingo's own close shave with death.

Even if the fire engines had come in time, they would not have found it easy to enter the slum since no approach road was wide enough. Two engines that had arrived were spraying jets of water on the embers of burnt-out huts but from too great a distance. A few policemen had also arrived. Thiru and Gurdeep were planning to go back with them to the station and file a detailed FIR. Meanwhile, of course, the Faujis themselves had disappeared from the scene of their crimes.

A stream of tormented and bruised humanity was slowly wending its way towards the station, stragglers from a battle in which they had no chance of victory. They would camp at the station, for the time being. The morning's first train was due in one hour. Some of them would catch it in the hope that it would take them to some shelter, some camp where they would feel safer. This mass of people, in the space of a few hours, had become refugees.

That night, many fires blazed in the city. Far away from Ambavali, in south Bombay, another mob was making its way to a dilapidated building in Grant Road.

Years and years ago, this building had been in rather better condition. Owned by a Parsi philanthropist, it was sold quite cheaply to a Muslim charitable trust, and had steadily fallen into disrepair. One by one, Muslim families moved in; Parsis gradually shifted away. The men who were leading the mob knew from the electoral lists they had surveyed that though the building was badly in need of repairs and many flats were vacant, a number of Muslim tenants still lived there, along with a handful of Parsis. One of their leaders had specifically drawn their attention to this building as 'worthy of inspection'.

Five or six days of rioting had engulfed the city, exactly as Jilla's son had warned her. If anything, it had been more cataclysmic than he had predicted. She had stayed indoors, living off eggs and slices of stale sandwich bread, reading the *Samachar* whenever an edition came out. Usually Nemoana brought it to her within hours of reading it herself or else, if there was some news item that caught Nemoana's attention, she read it out to Jilla in the upstairs flat. The two women had grown closer. The very old woman, and the woman who was just beginning to feel old. They depended on each other, for company, for

news, for mutual assistance in warding off panic, false
alarms and fear. Sometimes, quite often, the younger
woman took up a plate of some rice and daal. If she had
cooked a vegetable, she added a spoonful of that, too. But
Jilla didn't feel very hungry these days. If she ate, she ate
no more than one small meal a day. Mostly she fasted,
and lived on water.

She had a premonition that her end was near. She had
lived much too long, as it is. No doubt, this feeling had
something to do with the threats her son had hurled at
her during his visit. Her Hoshi had indeed become a most
powerful man. In a strange way, she felt proud of his
achievements. In the past few days, whenever she read
about rioting and arson, murder and mayhem in the city,
though her son was not mentioned by name in the
Samachar, she knew he was one of the main moving
forces behind these events. She felt a great deal of shame
about it, too. And guilt. But then, power has its own
prerogatives. He had moved outside the ambit of her
influence now.

For years she had decided not to think about the past.
She had not even discussed it with anyone. Not
Nemoana, nor anyone else. There was a chasm within her
life, a discontinuity she had never tried to breach. When
she had got better after her illness, she decided to get on
with life. She was too busy making ends meet, sending
her son to school, trying to keep up with doing her job,
too busy even to cope with her own grief. The deed was
done – she *had* done it, there was no doubt about that,
though her mind sometimes played tricks with her even
on that score – but for a while she had almost erased it
from memory. Thirty-seven years ago, in a moment of
madness, she had done it. But the chain of events that was

born in that moment was now almost fully unravelled, its terrible denouement was drawing close. The guilt begotten of such unremembered deeds grows on you, slowly, unawares, bit by bit . . .

Now it had grown monstrously huge, like the boy himself. Jilla was unable to ignore it. There was no way she could retrace her steps, undo the harm she had done. Anyway, now the time had come to stop fretting about all that had gone so wrong in her life, It was time to close the chapter, the very last one in her book. She had lived too long.

An urgent but restrained knocking was rapped out on the door. She had been expecting it. She looked through the peephole and quickly opened the door. Once Nemoana was in, Jilla triple-bolted it again.

'They've come,' said Nemoana, breathlessly. 'I saw them from my balcony. A *lashkar* of at least five hundred people, carrying swords and staves and fire.'

'Well,' said Jilla, remarkably composed. 'I heard the noise they were making. I guessed they would come tonight.'

'I've left my door slightly ajar. Let them go in and take whatever they want, instead of breaking it down. Let them see there's no one in the flat. I would have unscrewed the nameplate if I'd thought of it earlier. I just hope none of the neighbours tell them where to look.'

'Calm down, Nemoana,' said Jillamai. 'Come and sit here, close to me. They'll never suspect you're hiding here.'

For some time they sat close to each other on Jillamai's bed. They were quiet, trying to listen to sounds that might tell them what was happening downstairs.

'Do you think that our Hoshi's here himself?' Nemoana asked Jilla.

Jillamai shook her head.

'If he is, I could talk to him,' said Nemoana. 'After all, I am his foster mother. I helped to bring him up. He can't have forgotten.'

Jilla said nothing at first, then only shook her head again.

'Why do they hate us so? What is our sin that we are Muslim?' said Nemoana. 'Let him look into my eyes and give me an answer. What have I done?'

'He's not here,' Jillamai repeated solemnly. 'I know.'

'But he's behind all this, you say?' Nemoana asked. 'How awful . . . our Hoshi turned out like that?'

Again they listened for sounds on the stairs. Again it was Nemoana who broke the silence. 'When he came to ask for your flat,' she said, 'you should have given it to him. I would have come and stayed with you in Bhayandar. We would have escaped all this madness.'

'Never mind, Nemoana,' said Jilla. 'Try and be quiet.'

'When he came to see you,' she said, 'he could at least have stopped at my door for a minute and said hello. I still feel bad about that. After all, I raised him, too. Perhaps he's angry with both of us?'

'Be quiet, Nemoana!' said Jilla more sternly.

But Nemoana continued in an urgent whisper: 'There's something I have to tell you . . . I've never had the courage till now,' she said. 'One day, just before Hoshi left home, I told him you had adopted him from an orphanage. I meant no malice. I wanted him to love and appreciate you. But from that moment I think he began to hate us both.'

Just then, they heard the thunder of scores of feet

charging up the stairs towards her flat. Nemoana started, and turned pale with fear. She was very quiet. Jilla felt a little frightened too, but also curiously expectant. The knocking came on her door. It was loud and insistent.

A male voice she didn't know was shouting something. Such was the uproar outside, they could barely hear what was being said. The man repeated his words, speaking louder this time: 'We know you have a Mussalman hiding in there,' he said. 'Send her out, and we will not harm you.'

Jillamai raised her bony index finger to her lips and sternly gestured to Nemoana to be quiet.

'Believe me, no harm will come to you,' the man called. 'Open the door and hand her over to us.'

'They may break down the door,' whispered Nemoana to Jilla.

'They won't find it easy,' said Jilla, with a grin, almost as if she was beginning to enjoy the war of nerves. 'It's made of solid Burma teak.'

'We will give you thirty seconds to open the door. We know you are hiding someone in there. Open it and you will come to no harm. If you don't open in thirty seconds, we'll bolt the door from outside and set fire to this flat!'

'Never mind,' said Jilla to Nemoana, whispering excitedly in her ear. 'Let them do what they can. I've got plenty of water filled up in the bathroom. When they go, we'll open the door and put out the fire.' The front door, made of good, solid wood, would not burn easily, Jilla had calculated. The seconds ticked away; the women sat very still on the four-poster. But they had not bargained for the swiftness with which the end was to come.

Suddenly they smelt petrol. It was being poured in generous streams through the crack under the front door.

Within seconds there was a large puddle in Jilla's living room. As soon as the match was applied from outside, flames leapt up inside the room, quickly moving towards the old broken chairs placed in a row by the door.

Nemoana screamed and scrambled off the bed, but already she was unable to get to the front door where the flames had shot high – nor could the men outside have heard her scream, for they were already charging down the stairs.

'The back door,' Nemoana's eyes lit up for a moment. 'Maybe they've forgotten to latch that one from outside.' She rushed past the *mori*, and Jilla, who had remained motionless so far, heard her rattle and shake and slam her large body into the back door. But they had remembered, and that door, too, like the one in front, was made of old wood and would not budge.

By the time Nemoana gave up on the back door, the flames had spread to the window area, so she could not even fling those open to be able to scream, or jump. It would have been too high a fall anyway. She dragged out a vessel of water and flung it at the flames. It made no difference.

'Come, Nemoana,' said Jilla feebly. 'Come sit on the bed close to me.'

Nemoana burst into tears. And then fear and heat engulfed Jilla.

'Why . . .' cried Nemoana embracing the old woman. 'Why does it have to end like this?'

A faint smile had appeared on Jilla's lips.

'It goes back even further.' She shook her head. 'Don't feel bad, Nemoana, you had nothing to do with it. When Keko disappeared, I kept hoping . . . But I knew that if he came back, it would only be for his child . . . After my miscarriage, one afternoon I walked into the Parsi Lying-in Hospital. The nurses there were all at lunch. There was no one around. I picked up a baby that was unattended, and walked out. The watchman of the place stopped me. I said I wanted to give the baby some fresh air while his mother finished her bath. I turned a corner and got into a taxi . . . A year later, even after my madness had left me, I never tried to trace the real parents, never tried to make amends for my evil deed. You see, I did not have the courage to do the right thing . . . Perhaps, though I did not know this then,' said Jilla in conclusion, 'somewhere in his mind even a just-born infant remembers a grievous wrong that was done to him.'

The two women were embracing now, choking with fear and regret and smoke. Their eyes were smarting, their bodies were bathed in sweat. When the flames caught the mattress, Nemoana shrieked in horror and clung to Jilla, who it would seem had lost consciousness. The four-poster, made of good, old, solid wood, would become their funeral pyre.

When Jingo got back to the flat, he spent a good hour in the bathroom washing himself. But steaming water and plenty of soap couldn't cleanse his nostrils of the smell of kerosene, which seemed to have soaked into his skin. Gurdeep wouldn't be back for a while. He and Thiru were at the Ambavali police station, filing a detailed complaint about the night's incidents. Later, Gurdeep was to bring Thiru to the flat.

When he finally stepped out of the bath, Jingo heard that the phone was ringing. Naked, he ran and picked it up. It was his mother.

'O Jaungoo, where have you been?' she wailed. 'For

three days I have been trying to phone you!' Then she started weeping uncontrollably.

'Mummy! What's happened?'

'Daddy! . . . Your Papa,' she said, through sobs. 'Boman is no more . . . The funeral is in the morning. If I hadn't got you now, we couldn't have delayed it any more.

'No, his death had nothing to do with the riots . . . He had stepped out for just five minutes to fetch his pills from Vesawe Medicals. The pavements are all dug up along the whole stretch of Hughes Road . . . He fell into a three-foot trench and snapped his thigh . . . Surgeon decided to insert a steel support for the broken bone . . . Managed to get Antia, the very best. But during the operation, while still under anaesthesia, he suffered a massive attack . . . My poor Boman never came out of the theatre alive . . .'

Jingo wasn't listening. His mind had wandered off to a Sunday morning long ago when his father had beseeched him not to cry. His mother had not been in favour of the outing, but his father had insisted that he would take his son to Chowpatty and teach him how to ride a bicycle. They had hired a bicycle for an hour from the shop in the lane off Babulnath and taken it to the broad pavement that runs along Chowpatty beach.

No one learns how to cycle without having a good tumble or two, his father had warned Jingo. Holding on to his bicycle seat, Boman ran along with him as he pedalled furiously. But Jingo had fallen and scraped his shin badly and hurt his knee. He was bleeding.

When they limped back home after returning the bike, outside the front door of their flat his father stooped down and whispered into his ear, 'Please don't cry,

Jaungoo. Be a brave boy, okay? You won't cry?' He was barely three feet tall. He had nodded briefly, but resolutely. 'Or your mother'll really let me have it.'

Poor Dad was worried. Then, as quietly as possible, he inserted the key into the latch and turned it. His mother was standing in the front room, waiting for them behind the door. One look at the expression of horror on her face, and Jingo started bawling all over again.

'I knew it, I knew something like this would happen,' she muttered through clenched teeth, and promptly took her son into her fawning care. He had failed his father even then. He hadn't been able to control his tears and protect his father.

'Jaungoo! Hello! Are you there?' Khorshed asked.

'Yes, Mama . . . I'm sorry . . .'

She told him he'd have to be at Doongerwadi by seven in the morning, not to be late. Jingo replaced the receiver quietly. For a long time after that, Jingo sat beside the phone, naked, shivering, silent. Then he broke down and cried.

Postscript

Two years later, my mother fell. Not in the street, but in her own bathroom. She sat heavily on the hard tiled floor.

In my panic, I accused her of playing up the pain. To prove to me that she wasn't seeking sympathy, somehow she dragged herself out of the bathroom and on to the sofa in the hall, all this movement punctuated by groans and short, stifled screams. But in the end she had to be carried away on a stretcher. The X-ray showed a hairline fracture in her pelvis. Now she's in the female ward of the PGH, her leg suspended by a pulley on a 10-kilo traction.

For the first five days after Mum's accident, I took leave from work to be able to stay by her side. Subsequently, I stayed at the hospital only during the nights. The obese Irani who occupied the other half of the room, screened off by an olive-green curtain, had no one staying with her. She had a thigh fracture complicated by age and diabetes. Already there

for two months, her daughters visited her only
in the evenings.

More expensive than the general ward, these
rooms provided a small extra cot for the
patient's companion. The nurses are quite
competent, so it wasn't really necessary for
someone to be there all the time. The problem,
though, was with the ayahs, or maitranis, as
they are called. Given the nature of their
work, these women responded most
reluctantly to the bedside buzzer.

I would pass Mum the bedpan myself while
I was there. The maitrani came in her own
time, for the clean-up job. But poor Mrs Irani
had to buzz several times to elicit a response.
She sometimes got a dressing down too.

'Can't control a little?' the maitrani would
scold her if her ringing had been too
persistent. 'I've got other patients too, see?
You're not the only one.'

Mrs Irani's own response to this rebuff
depended on her level of desperation: frantic,
stentorian or pleading . . .

'Chaal ni, give fast, give fast.'

Sometimes, the maitrani showed up with
reasonable speed, but there could be other
complications instead.

'The pan is not properly in place, mai . . .'
Mrs Irani would cajole her abjectly, attempting
to squirm into position. 'Please adjust it, good
woman, it's not in place I can feel it.' But her
requests were not always heeded.

'It's fine,' the maitrani insisted, 'now just
relax and do it.'

The old woman's obesity must have tried
the maitrani's capacity for estimation.
Sometimes from behind the curtain, I would
hear despairing sobs.

'I told you it's not in place! Now my whole
bed is wet . . .'

There was another way in which I could
sometimes help Mother. Night nurses came on
their rounds to turn the fracture patients.
Apparently the turning and airing is done to
prevent bedsores, and should probably be
done more frequently. But the day nurses were
too busy with other chores and, for some
reason, only the night nurses remembered to
attend to this, and that only after patients
were already fast asleep. Being a light sleeper
myself, if I knew my mum had taken a
sedative and only just fallen asleep I'd jump
out of bed as soon as the nurses entered the
room and plead with them in whispers to let
her sleep. Sometimes they obliged and moved
on to the other half of the room, behind the
olive-green curtain.

When Mum was sedated, not even Mrs
Irani's screams of agony would wake her. It
must have been painful for the old woman, I
guess, what with her fracture and her kilos of
flesh, but the mere sight of the night nurses
terrified her, as though she had been roused
from her slumber by the Prince of Darkness
himself.

'Aaiee! They've come to turn me!'
All around me, there was suffering:
sometimes so outrageous, and unnecessary,
that it seemed funny. Humour became the
lifejacket that kept me afloat through my days
in hospital. Clearly, there's a tremendous
potential here for a black comedy. I doubt,
though, if I'll be the one to write it.

Only two years after Dad's death, and
everything's changed so much . . .
I could have refused to move back, but the
fact was I had nowhere to go. A senior
executive of the company had been transferred
to Bombay, and Gurdeep's father needed the
flat for him. Initially, his son was allowed to
keep his own room in the flat. But Gurdeep
actually asked if I could stay on, too, and
share his room with him. His father put his
foot down then and said, enough is enough.
The only other option for me was to rent a
room in a distant suburb. Even that I could
barely have afforded. Mum, on the other hand,
was welcoming and gracious.
As most people anticipated, the GSF has
formed the new government in Maharashtra.
Murderers who led mobs have become
ministers. If Dad were alive, he would have
been ranting with rage, bombarding
newspaper editors with his letters.
Victims of the riots – dishoused, widowed
or orphaned – are still to receive the monetary
compensation they were promised by the

*previous government. There's no proper
investigation underway, no desire to identify or
punish the guilty. A High Court judge has been
appointed to record testimonies of witnesses
and submit a report. That'll take a few years,
I guess.*

*The city I knew as Bombay is now called
Mumbai by the collective dispensation of the
new government. Not that it matters. It was
always Mumbai in Marathi and in Gujarati.
But now it's official, in all languages . . .*

*After the orgy of violence, the city's
character has changed. Ethnic Maharashtrians,
many of them migrant to the city themselves
from the interior of the state, feel empowered
by the GSF's show of strength. For months
after the riots, the city had no night life to
speak of, except in the luxury hotels. Even
now, shops close early, people hurry home, no
one loiters in the streets after 8.30. Only the
passion for making money flourishes unabated.*

*The GSF has also taken control of the rich
municipal corporation once more, and Hoshi
Olundaz is a high-profile councillor. The Pasha
Amusement Park is now a reality, raking in
profits. It advertises on TV and has become a
popular picnic destination for young people.
The residents of erstwhile Nehrunagar,
meanwhile, have been scattered, some on
government land in Mulund, others in
Goregaon. They've been given no assistance,
apart from permission to rebuild their huts on
no-man's land.*

*Mum is much better now, though they'll
keep her in the hospital for another two weeks
for physiotherapy. So now I spend my nights
at the Khareghat Colony flat. Neighbours
smile at me warmly, inviting conversation.
I speak to them when they ask for news of
Mum's condition, but my answers are
monosyllabic. I visit the hospital most
evenings, like the Irani sisters, to see if there's
anything Mum needs. She is very anxious
that I don't neglect my office work on her
account.*

*'If your father were here to see this,' she
often laments, 'how proud he would have
been.'*

*Given his completely justifiable scorn for
market research, I doubt it.*

*Despite all my resolutions to the contrary,
when Mira Shivdasani offered me a full-time
job as data tabulator and analyst, I thought I
should take it on. Perhaps I was afraid it
might be the last offer of a regular job I would
ever get. The work is light, but utterly drab.
Not a day passes without my being tempted to
throw it in. At least when I was freelancing
door to door, I was meeting interesting people
all the time. Mum is very satisfied with this
turn of events. At last, she believes, under her
own edifying influence, I've come 'on line'.
Something good, she believes, came out of the
trauma of a fractured hip.*

Today, after work, I couldn't bear the

thought of spending my evening once again at the PGH, so I phoned and asked the nurse at the desk to pass on a message to Mum that I had an appointment to keep and wouldn't be there this evening. It was Sister Philipose at the other end. Please don't worry about anything at all, she reassured me, I'll help her with her dinner tray. So I caught a very crowded train from Churchgate, got off at Grant Road station and started walking. I didn't really know where I was going or why, but perhaps I had some idea.

I'd never been to Jillamai's flat again after that night when she told me about her meetings with Hoshi. Then, at the fag-end of the riots, I read a newspaper report about an old woman who had been burnt to her death along with her Muslim neighbour. The reporter had used his imagination to give the story a heroic twist. Jillamai was portrayed as the kindly but brave old Parsi spinster who had dared a mob to do its worst and refused to hand over her Muslim friend, even at the cost of her own life. When the fire brigade broke down the door and doused the dying embers, the bodies of the two asphyxiated women were found in bed, in a tight embrace.

The stairway at the main entrance of the building had now been permanently closed. I had to go round the structure to its other staircase. There must have been people inside their rooms, but I didn't see anyone and I wasn't looking. I didn't even know why I had come there.

It was very quiet. When I was already past the second floor, someone made a loud smooching sound with his lips from the landing below. I ignored it and kept climbing.

'Oi, hero!' a voice called, and a pair of hands clapped until I stopped and turned. 'Kidhar jaata hai?'

Though he wasn't uniformed, I presumed the man was some kind of watchman. I answered him, 'Third floor.' But he was not about to let me proceed and kept beckoning to me to climb down again to the second-floor landing where he stood.

'There's nothing there,' he called, still waving his hand at me. 'No one lives up there.'

'I know.' I said. 'Just want to see . . .' And I took a few more steps up.

'But there's nothing there. Do you understand?' the man said rather aggressively. 'Just come down, I tell you.'

I didn't like this guy and the way he was talking to me from the landing below. I was annoyed, but at the same time I was scared. Intuitively, I knew that if I ignored him the whole thing could take an ugly turn. Luckily, another man, obviously a companion of his, came out to see what the matter was.

'What is it, what is it?'

The first guy explained to him.

'Well, let him go see for himself, if he

doesn't believe you,' said the other man more
reasonably. 'I'll go up with him.'

Of the two, this guy was obviously in
charge, and therefore more polite. He climbed
up behind me.

'The old lady who died in the fire . . .' I
explained to him. He nodded. He seemed to be
aware of the incident. 'I knew her. Just wanted
to see her flat.'

'Come with me,' he said. 'But there's
nothing to see. It's all finished . . .'

There were no lights in the third-floor
passage. In fact, once we had climbed the
stairs, I couldn't see a thing.

'Wait,' the man said. 'I have a torch.'

Then these two were some kind of security
guys. But who had appointed them to guard
this dilapidated building? The man switched
on a little pocket torch which had quite a
powerful beam.

Jillamai's front door was entirely missing.
The passage led straight into what was once
her living room. The watchman obligingly
swung the beam of the torch all over the room
to show me that what his partner had been
saying all along was true – there was nothing
here except a heap of rubbish. The walls were
blackened. There was not a single piece of
furniture left in the room that I could
recognize; though, in the debris, I saw some
articles that looked vaguely familiar. I
borrowed the torch for a moment from the
watchman's hand and directed the beam of

*light more slowly along the heaps of cinder,
soot, dust and burnt wood.*

*'No one's allowed to come up here,' said the
watchman, by way of conversation. 'It's just
because you were so keen, I let you.'*

*Of the six chairs, there was nothing left.
That thing there could be the mahagony chest
of drawers. Yes, it was, with its empty slot
where a drawer used to be missing. The bed
had probably crumbled altogether. There was
a peculiarly unhealthy smell to the room. And
that little table-like stand . . . her ornate
chamber-pot?*

*'Whole place is going to be cleaned up and
painted. Workers are supposed to start
tomorrow, in fact,' said the watchman. 'Proper
office is going to be made here. That's why
saab said not to allow anyone to come up till
the work is finished.'*

*'Olundaz saab?' I asked. It was a shot in
the dark. The man's face brightened.*

*'You know Olundaz saab?' he asked,
wondering why I hadn't mentioned him earlier.
'Well, he's not here now, of course, but if you
want to meet him—'*

'No, no,' I said. 'I don't want to meet him.'

*The beam of the torch in my hand had been
idly traversing the floor. I was about to hand it
back and leave, when its beam caught
something that glimmered briefly in the
rubbish.*

*'What's that?' I asked and bent down to
pick it up. It was a little bauble, like a*

miniature mace. Though completely soot-
coated, you could see it was made of brass or
silver. That was why it had caught the light.
A child's rattle.

'It's nothing,' said the watchman, examining
it himself. 'A child's plaything . . .' Then, as an
afterthought, 'Since you knew the lady who
stayed here, if you want, keep it. Tomorrow
it'll all be swept out.'

The rattle had melted down a bit and
become misshapen. The beads in it had
probably melted, too, and stuck to the sides,
for they didn't rattle any more. It was
generous of him. But I shrugged and tossed it
back on the rubbish heap. I thanked him and
left.

Back in the street, I breathed more easily.
Every time I remember Hoshi or think of that
dark January night in Nehrunagar, I break out
in a cold sweat. The smell of kerosene fills my
nostrils, real and suffocating. I know I should
loathe the man, despise him, and perhaps I do,
but more than anything else I feel grateful to
him for saving my life. For that one minute
in the CPSDR shack I really thought it was
curtains for me. But that one minute, which
seemed to last an eternity, changed me forever,
decisively.

In some recess of my mind I must have hoped
that I would get back with Cristina once her
studies were done. Our oneness seemed
irrevocable, even after all this time. But it was

three years since she went to Baroda, and she hadn't written to me at all. I knew that she didn't write letters, not even to her closest friends, so I wasn't surprised. Now this bulky letter, out of the blue – postmarked not Baroda, but Orlem.

As I raced through the first paragraphs, profusely apologetic about her silence, for a moment I did believe that a proposed reconciliation was what they were leading up to. But I was quite wrong. By way of preamble she had written a rambling and self-indulgent summary of all she had been through in the three years since we parted.

Only a few months after she joined the Institute of Fine Arts, she fell for a guy called Mahesh. For two and a half years they were very happy, she wrote, until just a day before her diploma presentation, when she discovered he had been cheating on her all along. She was devastated. She took an overdose of sleeping pills. It was a major scandal, because she nearly died on the way to hospital. When she came out of it, the director of the institute prevailed upon the police not to charge her, and persuaded her to go back home to her father. So even after three years, she hadn't yet got her diploma. He'd promised, though, that some other time he would let her come back and finish the course, if she really wanted to.

Her dad was much better now, incidentally,

*she wrote. The real news she had to give was
that with some help from Father Cecil, the
parish priest, he had arranged a marriage for
her. She had accepted. The marriage was fixed
for next month.*

*His name was Owen Fernandes, captain of
a merchant navy ship. He was a good fourteen
years older than her, but that didn't matter
since she found she liked him very much when
they met. Till he retires he'll be away from
home on board ship for six months in a year,
she wrote. 'I could travel with him, if I want
to, he says, but you know how seasick I tend
to get.' She wanted to settle down, have
children, before it was too late. Of course, the
cards were not yet ready, but she would send
one for me and my parents as soon as they
were printed. She was really looking forward
to meeting me again at the reception, and she
wanted me to get to know Owen as well, who
was a really nice guy. A lot of the letter went
on about how grateful she was to me.*

*'Can't tell you how much. You stood by me
in everything. I learnt so much from you about
life. You shouldn't have any cause for regrets,
Jehan. If ever you feel bad, or miss me, just
remember what a destructive person I've been
for you. Finally, you'll see, it's all for the best
that everything turned out this way. I'm sure
you'll come across a really nice girl soon,
who'll be really good for you.'*

*Everything turns out for the best in the end.
An old and meaningless consolation I had*

*heard repeated a hundred times by my mother,
even in moments when she was dreading the
worst possible outcome. How could everything
turn out for the best when just about
everything had gone wrong? It was only a silly
trick of words for subtly altering one's own
perception of events.*

*My immediate reaction was to want to pick
up the phone and yell at Cristina. But my
fingers felt numb. I couldn't even recall all the
digits of her phone number. I was feeling hurt,
even betrayed, perhaps unreasonably so. Now
she wanted babies with this Owen guy whom
she hardly knew at all! And when she went in
for the abortion, she was so sure she didn't
want a baby . . . so sure that that baby wasn't
even mine . . . though I did share in the guilt
of destroying it.*

*Maybe I should remind her of all the things
we did together during our college days, those
amorous escapades in deserted classrooms, hot
bhejamasala and roti at Mayrose, drowsy
afternoons at Hanging Gardens amid sculpted
hedges and chirping sparrows, the gorgeous
fountain at Kamala Nehru Park which began
to gush precisely at 5 p.m. . . .*

*How we drank in the breathtaking view of
the bay over a beer, sipping it slowly at dusk
on the terrace of the hilltop Naaz; the aimless
bus rides, the long walks . . . The city was our
love affair, we were unafraid and free. Those
gourmet street meals on Mohammad Ali Road
during Ramzaan; of course, I didn't need to*

remind her of our favourite park, the Queen's Gardens, with its smelly cages and stoical beasts, the white Haji Ali mosque shimmering in the moonlit sea at night . . .

Those classic German films subtitled in English at the Max Mueller; and after a fish-and-chip dinner at Wayside Inn, the lonely walks through the sodium-lit squares of Ballard Estate, past the gates to the docks which were guarded by sentries in naval uniform. She had thought it was called 'Ballad' Estate, and once asked me what the ballad was, and who it was for . . .

Yes, all that we did together, our conversations, all that we understood together, about each other, and the world. Perhaps there was still a chance, if I could talk to her, and get her to listen. I could warn her of the unhappiness she might be unwittingly perpetuating for herself and the unsuspecting Owen. Was there any meaning I should attach to the information she had passed on to me so casually, that he would be away for six months in the year? That he was fourteen years older than her?

It wasn't easy, but finally I decided I wouldn't phone.

Both of us had changed too much, I suspected. Quite as much as our city, which had been the backdrop for all those things we did together. All that was past, those crazy romps without a care in the world, intoxicated by the confidence of youth, those casual

*rambles through the unfamiliar and seedy,
where we felt, or imagined we felt, a raw
throb of life – those thrills and delights could
never be reclaimed again. For some other
young couple, perhaps, yes, but for Cris and
me it was all over. We were not so young any
more, for one thing, and the city which had
been the setting of our romance was itself
transformed. When her wedding invitation
came, I wrote to Cristina about my father's
death, my mother's hospitalization, and
regretted that I would not be able to attend.*

*A psychic healer by the name of Dubash visits
Parsi General every evening. He's gaunt, old,
rather short and unsmiling. He goes on his
rounds through both male and female wards
every evening during visiting hours. The
'healing' he performs is entirely without
remuneration or expectation of any personal
gain. The nurses have grown accustomed to
his ritual, priest-like presence.*

*Patients who have experienced the power of
his touch, I'm told, look forward to his visits.
They say his hands are able to generate a great
warmth that melts away their pain. He spends
only four or five minutes with each patient,
placing his right hand on the affected limb or
ailing organ with a frowning concentration,
and then moves on to the next bed. He rarely
speaks to anyone, hardly acknowledging the
gratitude that patients feel for him. Only on
very special occasions, he smiles. According to*

my mother, the relief from pain and discomfort those five minutes with him gave her lasted through the entire night and the next day. Is this, too, a subtle alteration of perception that makes for a feeling of well-being? Or is the world really like that, a changing, shifting reality, a flux that moulds itself around the shape of our most fervent desires? So that even pain melts away if we really believe it will?

One evening after he had passed through and she was glowing with the radiance and peace that Dubash's touch induces in people, I asked Mum what had become of the other faith healer, our family friend, Uncle Rusi. She shook her head and answered rather sorrowfully.

'Well,' she said, 'no one really knows for sure. He has a British passport you see, and he's always travelling. But the group in Bombay has split up. There was some sort of scandal. Some members accused him of embezzling donated monies. After Papa's death, he sent me a card from England inviting me to come for a holiday and see the big Centre for Fali Baba Studies he's started there, the following Baba has among the English . . .'

'Why don't you go?' I asked her. 'It'll be a nice holiday for you.'

'I think I would find the journey too strenuous. And anyway, what would I go there alone and do?'

Mother could move about the ward now with the aid of a specially designed three-toed walking stick. She had prevailed on the surgeon not to discharge her for another week. 'There'll be no one to look after me at home,' she pleaded. 'I'm a widow, and my son has to go to work.' Actually, she wanted to stay on because she had begun to enjoy herself here, doing what she called 'social work'. At breakfast, tea and meal times, she would wipe up her own tray rather briskly and wander out looking for some some very old patient in the general wards who had no one to help them. If his or her tea had gone cold, she took it to the pantry and reheated it. If it was evening, she would pull up a chair and bring cheer into their lonely lives, or so she believed, chatting sympathetically about their families who did not visit them any more, the better days they'd seen, the improvement or deterioration in their condition.

She had always wanted to do this sort of work even when she was younger, but Dad used to mock her 'Florence Nightingale' instincts. Maybe deep down he was just afraid she would stray too far from him, and finally she did. Come to think of it, since Boman's death, Khorshed has really blossomed. It shows in the glow on her face. Was it his personality, which she found oppressive, that always worked to muffle her own instincts? Had I been doing the same thing to Cristina without even being aware of it?

Gurdeep had urged me to testify before the

one-man commission investigating the riots.
He called my office the other day, suggesting
that I should name Olundaz as leader of the
Ambavali carnage. After all, I was an eyewitness.

'I don't think much will come of the
inquiry, anyway,' I told him.

'You may be right,' replied Gurdeep, 'but
how apathetic can one get about these things?
You saw that old man being set on fire . . .
Those poor people who lost everything . . .'

'I'll think about it. But you were there, too,'
I said as an afterthought. 'Why don't you?'

'I would, too,' he said, a little sheepishly,
'but you see I've applied for admission to Yale'
– this was the first I'd heard of it, but I wasn't
surprised – 'and as it is my passport has gone
for renewal. If I'm involved in something like
this, the government can hold up my
immigration clearance indefinitely, you never
know.'

His father was a successful industrialist. It
was only a matter of time, I knew, before his
family reclaimed him.

'Well,' I told him, 'don't be so apologetic
about it. That's great news.'

'I wanted to study international law,' he
complained. 'But my father won't hear of it. If
I'm paying for it, he says, it has to be business
management.'

Thiru, the other eyewitness to the
destruction of Nehrunagar, had moved south
again. He was in Bangalore working with

another NGO that recycled organic garbage to create experimental quantities of bio-gas.

Yesterday, Dubby phoned. Apparently, during the riots, she and George Paul had set up a telephone helpline to assist affected persons. They would network on phone with the police, fire brigade and the ambulance getting help to victims speedily. After the riots, her father, who's chairman of a company manufacturing consumer goods, provided space and money to set up a relief camp. I was very impressed that she had been able to do so much during that tense period, and I told her so.

'It was a crazy time,' she said. 'Working day and night, sometimes going without sleep altogether. But I'll tell you something, I've never felt so happy in my life. To actually be able to help people in distress . . .'

My mother's back at home. She's offered to send me home-cooked food to the office with the dabbawalla, but I prefer to pick up a snack whenever I want to.

I spend most of the day in the office reading the newspapers. Mrs Hingorani has warned that they're watching me. I still have two months to go before my probation period ends.

A terrible thing has happened at the zoo. According to the papers, an aging tigress (whom I've probably seen prowling about her cage several times in the past), died yesterday.

Somebody got into the cage at night, skinned the tigress while she was still alive and left her to die. Obviously, she must have been heavily sedated before he put the knife to her. Was it a gang of poachers who wanted her skin for the two lakhs it fetches in the black market? Not likely, for then they would have taken her claws, too, which also fetch a hefty price. The police say they must have had an accomplice among the zoo staff. A journalist has speculated that flaying a live tiger was part of some arcane tantric rite, performed to bring success to a knee-replacement operation which was carried out that very day in the city, on a prominent politician . . . In this city, this country, the bizarre and the surreal are constantly with us.

No, politicians aren't the only superstitious ones. There's another report from rural Bihar. Less than 70 kilometres away from the ruins of the famed Nalanda University, a husband and wife who had been childless for seven years, kidnapped and beheaded a seven-year-old boy, their nephew, offering his head to the goddess Kali. They had been assured that such a sacrifice would ensure the woman's fertility, and her first offspring would certainly be male . . .

Further east, in rural Orissa, there have been more starvation deaths. A family of ten, who hadn't eaten in days, dug up a rich farmer's dead cow that had been buried the previous day, and ate its meat. All ten of them

The Radiance of Ashes

died. The minister in charge of food supplies denies any shortage. The peasants died of food poisoning, not starvation, he says, which, in a sense, is probably true.

The pavements of Mumbai are increasingly war-ravaged. That is, ravaged by the wars of corruption and sleaze that the councillors of the Municipal Corporation excel in waging. They're supposed to look after the roads, but every few days a road or footpath is dug up for some official work, then poorly refilled, then a few days later, it is dug up again. The contractors who are allotted the work give large cuts to the councillors who sanction it. Everywhere, disrepair and oodles of dust. Everywhere, a sense of incompletion. Work is commenced and left unfinished, or poorly done. Does the environment reflect the spiritual condition of a people who inhabit it? Or is it vice versa?

And now the crowning glory. A grotesquely straight-faced report in today's Times *about a man who was accidentally electrocuted while urinating. He was peeing behind a lamp-post, and didn't see the live cable that was exposed in the broken pavement.*

I know these pavements. They claimed my father, too, albeit in a less ridiculous fashion. Even sitting here in the office, my eyes fill with tears sometimes. If he had only lived a little longer, perhaps I would have had a chance to show him that I did in fact respect him; to admit that I was wrong about so many things

454 /

*I'd argued with him about so brashly ... I
miss him very much, but to be truthful, these
are tears of self-pity. I realize now that many
things he said made a lot of sense. Maybe I
should have gone abroad after all. At least for
a few years, to get myself an education. It
would have been such a relief. Maybe I would
have found a more civilized haven in which to
lead a creative life, become a writer in the real
sense of the word. But then, what would I
have written about in a foreign land?*

*Sometimes it seems to me that Time is the
villain who played a dirty trick on me. As it
does to all who remain inattentive to its
slippery, meretricious guile ... Why, only
yesterday I believed I had plenty of years
before me to prove myself as a writer. Only
yesterday I'd never have believed it if someone
told me my father would die so soon. But
Time outpaced me, even before I became
aware it was a contender in the race.*

*Now, of course, it's too late. I'm thirty-
eight, and I have nowhere to go.*

*Gurdeep phoned again. There were some
books I'd left behind at his flat which he
wanted me to collect. Incidentally, he said, his
admission to Yale Business School had come
through and he'd be leaving next month. He
was having a farewell party on Saturday for all
his friends, which I absolutely had to attend –
he would be expecting me. That would be at
the Malabar Hill residence, of course. But*

*before that, if I could come and pick up my
things, and leave the key on the table, in case
he was not in . . . I said I would. Privately, I
decided that I wouldn't be going to the party,
even if he felt hurt by my absence. I'd find
some excuse once the party was over. Anyway,
he'd be too excited about his impending
departure to miss me.*

*That evening, after work, I caught a bus
and went to Byculla. When I got to Winifred
House, the compound was full of people. I
asked the watchman what had happened. He
told me that Poonjwani had passed away. I
went up to the flat and packed all my books in
a bag I'd brought along. Gurdeep wasn't in, of
course. Then I took one walk around the flat
to check if I'd left anything behind. From the
balcony, I looked up to the second floor of the
next wing. Poonjwani's balcony was crowded
with people. The belligerent old man never
had any visitors in all the months I stayed
there; now his flat was brimming with noisy
relations.*

*I left the key on the living-room table, as
Gurdeep had suggested, picked up my bag and
shut the door. Just as I stepped out into the
compound, I saw that the procession had
started from the next block. Poonjwani was
being carried out on a bier. The group of
relations or friends carrying him, or following
behind, were all shouting, rather lustily:* Ram
Nam Sat Hai . . .

Before I got on a bus, I thought maybe I

*should just look up the boys at Kanara. The
restaurant was there all right, only I wouldn't
have recognized it. Small as it was, it had been
pretty smartly done up, and there was a neon
sign outside which hadn't been switched on
yet: LAGOON, the fish place. But the man at
the counter was someone I'd never seen
before. I asked about Shivappa and Gopal, but
he had never heard of them, and no one by
those names worked there any more. He said I
could come back after ten and speak to the
boss, Janardhan, if I wanted to. Sahab might
know something about them, but he had
himself joined the restaurant as head waiter
only a few months ago.*

*The bus I took was not crowded. The
conductor insisted I buy a ticket for my
'luggage' as well. The bag of books wasn't
really so big as to merit the purchase of
another ticket, but I didn't argue. Just a stop
before the bus reached Babulnath, an old
Muslim got on.*

*'Next stop, last stop! Only up to next stop!'
the conductor yelled, and rang the bell, but the
next stop was where the old man wanted to
go. He grabbed the handrail and jumped on
just as the bus sped away. Bearded, and
wearing a sort of long muddy-red kaftan and a
string of amber beads around his neck, he
seemed to be a down-and-out fakir of sorts.
He had a short feather duster in his hand. He
took out a ten-rupee note from the folds of his*

robe and gave it to the conductor to pay for
his ticket.

The conductor was a clean-shaven, ruddy
young Maratha.

'What do you think this is?' he said rather
rudely. 'A bank or something? Please give two
rupees. Exact change.'

'But I don't have any change,' said the old
man.

'Then do me a favour and get off the bus,'
said the conductor.

He was being deliberately unhelpful. The
old man heaved a sigh of tiredness and turned
towards the exit. The conductor had already
pulled the bell-rope as a signal to the driver to
stop. But before the bus could come to a halt,
I said aloud, 'Wait, I have the change.'

I bought the old man's ticket. The
conductor yanked the rope twice again, and
with a sigh of relief the old fakir sank into a
seat beside me in the empty bus. The
conductor muttered something unpleasant,
possibly about the Muslim community in
general or their lackeys, and scowled. Both the
fakir and I pretended not to have heard
anything, as he cut a ticket and thrust it into
my hand.

A few minutes later, everyone got off at the
terminus, including the driver and the
conductor.

'Wait,' the old man said to me. 'We'll get
change here, and I'll return your two rupees.'

'Conductor could have easily done that

himself. Instead of wanting to make you get off and walk all this way,' I said to him.

We stopped at a canteen, already quite full with staff of the transport company, to get change.

'Will you have a cup of tea with me?' he asked. I accepted, but on the condition that he wouldn't return the two rupees I'd spent on his ticket. He smiled a toothy grin, and agreed.

'Difficult times are on us, son,' the fakir said to me, as we sipped hot tea, standing by a side table in the canteen. 'People have become so bloated with pride, so full of themselves. They don't want to tolerate anyone who's even a little different.' We drank our tea, and he paid for it. As he collected his change at the counter, the fakir looked me straight in the eye and said, 'You're a good man, son. Be brave, never lose courage. You must learn to believe in yourself.'

Then he muttered some benediction in another tongue, dusted me with his feather duster, as though sweeping off cobwebs from about my head and shoulders, thumped me on the back with its thick end and went his way.

But his words remained with me. Learn to believe . . .

The next day, Mrs Hingorani handed me my confirmation letter, signed by Madam Mira herself.

I had decided not to accept the job and asked her if she could put me back on field *research instead. It'd mean less money, no security or employee benefits, but what the hell, I had a flat to stay in now, and I could eat at home whenever I was broke.*

At least half my life is over. I have to admit I've always been a loser, yet curiously, always satisfied with being one. I had no educational qualifications worth the name, no steady job. I could have had one now, but I just threw it in. Confused and on the wrong track about most things I'd staked my life and career on, now I'd lost my one friend, Cristina, as well.

I'd always blamed other people and circumstances for the things that had gone wrong with me. I blamed my parents for the unhappiness of my childhood, I blamed my dead brother for the guilt I believed I had imbibed at his death, though it took place even before I was born, I blamed Cristina for not knowing how to love, for never allowing us to be truly happy, I blamed her parents for maiming her psychologically. I even blamed the misfortunes of others, the whole of society and history for what had happened to me. I still didn't know who I was, but one thing I had begun to realize . . . surely at some point I would have to start taking responsibility for my own life?

I've never had much faith in myself. I constructed elaborate hypotheses to sustain my credo, my lifestyle. One such belief was that the surge of empathy I felt for the millions around me, embattled by indignity and

*ignorance, misfortunes, mishaps and
deprivation, was my one tenuous link with
reality. This ability to empathize was precious
to me because it made me feel more real.
Without creating space within myself to
contain those mountains of misery I saw all
around, there was no way I could remain
within this infernal social order, or so I
believed, and not become stone. Everywhere
around me I saw faces that were tired,
dejected, hope-worn. To read the morning's
newspapers was to find relentless confirmation
of this hypothesis. What an enormous dead
weight it had grown to be – and here I was
carrying it around with me all the time. I felt I
deserved to be admired for the sincerity of my
compassion, for my outright rejection of any
form of privilege in this hideously unequal
society.*

*How odd that it never struck me that
beneath this unctuous ghee of compassion
might lurk a supreme arrogance: for quietly I
had believed I was superior, just for being able
to feel all these things, just for being able to
ask all those questions. It occurred to me that
the kind of cushioning life had provided me –
which gave me the freedom to think the way I
did and live the way I'd lived – was itself a
grand privilege very few could avail themselves
of. At the same time, I had never wanted to
put my superior cognizance to the test by
actually doing something, either for myself, or
for the poor souls who excited my*

compassion. Real work was for others, the
poor toiling masses. I was the spiritual
aristocrat, by virtue of my superior sensibility.
With hindsight, I found it laughable that I
prided myself on my sense of empathy,
claiming to abjure privilege of any sort, when
in actual fact I was just being bone lazy. And
most likely, afraid as well. Afraid to test the
mettle of my alleged superiority.

The miseries and misfortunes of other
people can be overwhelming. They can make
one feel like giving up, like lying down and
letting things drift unto death. But suddenly a
terrible fear has gripped me. All my theories
have turned to dung. I don't want to be
submerged in the common mire. I want to be
different. I'll say it now. I want to be special.
I want to be happy . . .

When I reached home, Mother was reclining
on the sofa with the newspaper. I didn't tell
her immediately that I'd thrown in my job.
Instead I told her I would be working late,
that I was going back to my unfinished novel;
to put the food away in the fridge once she
had had her dinner. Then I went into my dad's
study and opened his portable. It needed some
dusting, but it was still working fine. I slipped
in a sheet of white paper and began typing . . .

A muddy golden sun slunk out from a chink in the overcast sky. Heaps of great grey clouds parted momentously,
momentarily, flashing bright beams of yellow light . . .

Maybe tomorrow I should pay a visit to Chandu's? A little piece of good hash might add some colour to my writing. No, no, that's absurd. It's out of the question! What on earth is wrong with me?

Acknowledgements

The prologue to this novel appeared as a short story in a slightly different form in *Debonair* magazine in 1983. Subsequently it was also published in *London* magazine, and in Hebrew translation in an anthology.

The next two chapters were written at the University of Kent, UK, where I was resident writer in 1998. I am grateful to Lyn Innes, then Head of the English School, for giving me time to work, and to the Charles Wallace Fellowship Trust and the British Council for making the fellowship possible. I am grateful to Rebecca Wilson of Weidenfeld and Nicolson for advice and encouragement during this period. To Pankaj Mishra for showing the first two chapters to Mary Mount of Picador, and to Mary for commissioning the novel. And also to Sam Humphreys for all the work she put in towards editing the manuscript.

I am also grateful to Valencia, Avian and Trevor for making it possible for me to live and work comfortably in Mumbai during the two and a half years it took to write the novel. To Firuza, who always believed I could do it, despite my illness. To Adil and Veronik for reading the first draft. Most of all, I'm grateful to Jill and Rushad for the love and patience they gave me during what must have been for them a very trying period.